DEB ON ARRIVAL — LIVE AT FIVE

This Large Print Book carries the
Seal of Approval of N.A.V.H.

A DEBUTANTE DETECTIVE MYSTERY

DEB ON ARRIVAL —
LIVE AT FIVE

LAURIE MOORE

THORNDIKE PRESS
A part of Gale, Cengage Learning

GALE
CENGAGE Learning

Detroit • New York • San Francisco • New Haven, Conn • Waterville, Maine • London

GALE
CENGAGE Learning™

LIBRARY OF CONGRESS CATALOGING-IN-PUBLICATION DATA

Moore, Laurie.
  Deb on arrival—live at five : a debutante detective mystery /
by Laurie Moore.
    p. cm. — (Thorndike Press large print core)
    ISBN-13: 978-1-4104-3150-9
    ISBN-10: 1-4104-3150-9
    1. Debutantes—Fiction. 2. Texas—Fiction. 3. Chick lit.
4. Large type books. I. Title.
PS3613.O564D43 2010b
813'.6—dc22   2010027949

Published in 2010 by arrangement with Tekno Books and Ed Gorman.

Printed in the United States of America
1 2 3 4 5 6 7 14 13 12 11 10

To my daughter Laura

ACKNOWLEDGMENTS

Many thanks to editors Mary Smith and Tiffany Schofield at Five Star, to Roz Greenberg at Tekno Books, and to Tracey Matthews and Alja Collar at Cengage. But especially to the beautiful little debutante who motivates me to write.

CHAPTER ONE

Goals for the day:

1. Pick up the most debu-licious ball gown <u>ever</u>!!!
2. Avoid Mr. Pfeiffer like the plague
3. Arrange bail

Ever since the cities of Dallas and Fort Worth installed photo enforcement traffic cameras to catch speeders and red light violators, people with busy lives can't catch a break. After picking up the mail from my grandmother's sprawling two-story plantation home in Preston Hollow, one of Dallas's ritziest neighborhoods, I sat behind the wheel of my car at the traffic light waiting for the signal to turn green. Since this particular intersection takes forever for the control device to cycle, it gave me time to sift through the letters.

Mail goes to Gran's house because that's my permanent address. At the moment, I'm between residences. This is my last semester at Texas Christian University in Fort Worth and I still need to successfully complete one class for my Radio–Television–Film degree — an unpaid internship at WBFD-TV. When the sorority house closed for the summer for maintenance and repairs, my two best friends, Venice Hanover and Salem Quincy, found the most amazing townhome for the three of us to move into.

Only we hit a stumbling block.

The previous renter refused to move out when his lease ended and the landlady had to evict him. Believe me, getting rid of a squatter isn't as simple as it sounds. Eventually, the constables were called in to bodily remove the man. The process took almost two months including thirty days' notice and a court hearing.

Once the law took over, he went all *Pacific Heights* on them.

The maniac changed the locks, barricaded himself inside, and turned the place into a battle zone by destroying what was available to him: sheetrock, plumbing, kitchen appliances . . . you name it.

When the landlady and her sister showed

up to find that their key didn't work, the constable used a master key — a battering ram — to break down the door. While deputies stood by watching the movers haul out all of his stuff and dump it onto the curb, the raving lunatic holed up in a bedroom. For entertainment, he stopped up the toilets and overflowed the bathtubs onto the hardwood. Buckled flooring creates an obscene DMZ look, a sort of de-militarized zone-meets-ghetto kind of artistic statement when combined with graffiti spray-painted on the walls — things like *Die bitches, You suck, See you in hell* and worse.

Certainly shorting out the appliances by loading the dishwasher with dirty laundry contributed to the disaster effect. The guy even stored frozen meat in the stove long enough for it to rot. Putrefaction set in and the place took on the kind of stench you hear forensic pathologists speak of when they come upon the scene of a recently unearthed mass grave. Before the psycho tenant could be arrested for felony criminal mischief, he rappelled down an upstairs window and fled the scene, leaving a wake of chaos and destruction.

I heard by way of the neighbors that the cleanup crew wore level-four biohazard containment suits.

Suffice it to say that the damage was so extensive we couldn't move in on time. Now we're waiting for the new hardwood floor to be laid and for the walls to get a third coat of paint, which we're told will be in two weeks. Apparently the lunatic used one-coat black and red paint to write the obscenities and the words keep bleeding through. The landlady told us the guy lost his job and didn't want to move back home to California. But I actually think he's from Texas.

Texans do things bigger and better.

Especially when it comes to guerilla tactics.

I'm a seventh-generation Texan. One of my ancestors fought at the Alamo. I'm even a member of the Daughters of the Republic of Texas. So even though I was groomed to become a well-bred, refined young lady, I suspect there's a dormant streak built into my genetic bar code that would enable me to remove one of my Choos and drive the stiletto heel into somebody's skull, if the need arose.

Back to the mail.

The *Cosmo* subscription Gran paid for is about to expire. It's actually her magazine but I borrowed it because there's a quiz I want to take. Then there's the invitation to The Rubanbleu Ball next month addressed to me in an elegant hand. Two years ago, I made my debut at The Rubanbleu's annual debutante ball and now my younger sister Teensy, who attends college out of state, is about to make hers. Strayer Drexel Truett III — Drex, for short — is my date, which makes me cooler than cool. Like glacier cool. Drex is in law school at Washington and Lee and he's flying in for the event. He's been my boyfriend ever since we attended prep school together and his family's beyond wealthy. The Truetts make regular rich people look needy by comparison.

But I'd love Drex even if he happened to be poor. He's tall and lean with tawny skin and mesmerizing gray eyes that capture your attention, and thick dark hair that seems to hang perfectly no matter what length he wears it. Not to mention the wild streak running through him.

Oh, dear God.

What's this?

Not one, but two brown business envelopes.

The return address is in Arizona but I happen to know from experience that this fat one's from the city of Dallas and the other one's from the city of Fort Worth. My sinking stomach knotted. It's not necessary to open these but they have a kind of magnetic pull that compels me to see if they're what I think they are.

Sliding a lacquered fingernail carefully beneath the flap of the first one — don't want to chip my Beverly Hills manicure — I shook out the contents and groaned. Sure enough, a citation for running a red light dropped onto my lap along with three snapshots of a silver Porsche Carrera: one view from the back, a side view, and one from the front. At first glance, the window tint made it impossible for anyone connected to this lame attempt to extort money for such a bogus infraction to recognize the driver. After all, this could be anybody's Porsche, right?

Unfortunately, the personalized license plate, *DBUTNT,* which is easily read, is definitely mine.

Still, that doesn't make me the driver.

So . . . *ha.*

Not that anyone else has ever driven my car, but these extortionists don't know that now, do they?

Wait — what's this?

The side view snapped of my car shows a close-up of *moi,* Dainty Prescott, looking elegant of course, behind the wheel with the cell phone pressed to my ear.

Do I care? Not hardly.

14

Actually, I'm fighting back a sniffle. Truth is, there's not enough time to do everything I need to during the course of a day, and now I'm supposed to just drop everything and tend to these? Besides, Daddy's corporate lawyer says I can't be arrested if I don't pay the seventy-five-dollar fine because it's a brand-new law here — a criminal violation with a civil penalty imposed — and it's just a matter of time before the Supreme Court strikes it down for Constitutional reasons.

Fine by me.

The traffic signal cycled to green. I tossed the brown envelopes into the floorboard with the other twelve notices that arrived over the past few weeks, and the Carrera's engine roared to life.

The doors to Harkman Beemis open in less than thirty minutes, the length of time it takes to drive from Gran's to Fort Worth.

I can't afford to be late.

Harkman Beemis is a high-end retail store with locations in Fort Worth and Dallas. This morning I'm headed for the Fort Worth store; otherwise, I'll be late for my internship. Harkman's annual "Once And For All" clearance sale falls on the first Monday in October, and those who're members of their "Round Table" receive

15

personal invitations to shop before the unwashed public.

I'm part of the Round Table.

Normally, I ignore these invitations because I've always been able to strut into Harkman Beemis and charge whatever I want to Daddy's account. But since he got remarried a few months ago he put me on a budget — all because his new wife called my sister Teensy and me spendthrifts and said we were frittering away his hard-earned money.

Ha.

She's the one spending him blind. They just had the interior of the Rivercrest estate in Fort Worth redone — the home Teensy and I grew up in — because his new bride didn't want to live there surrounded by my mother's decorative touches. Well, hey — my mother may be dead but she isn't dead to me. And the last person I intend to take marching orders from is a woman who happens to be my age — twenty-two.

Did I mention my sister and I hate Nerissa? Or as I like to call her: *Narscissa.*

My father's new bride is living proof that bad people happen to good children.

Since Nerissa came into our lives, I often lie in bed at night thinking I should be a mystery writer instead of someday having

16

my own talk show with a major television network, because it enables me to plot ways to kill Daddy's little gold digger without actually being prosecuted. So far, I've flirted with three ideas that might work and dreamed up two others that have great potential.

I cannot believe I got two more traffic camera tickets.

To drown out the screaming in my head, I turned on the sound system and upped the volume to the new mix-CD my sister made for me. Teensy wrote "Angry White Woman" on the face of the disc with permanent marker because it features songs performed by Alanis Morrisette, Michelle Branch, Avril Lavigne and even a few old recording artists like Deborah Harry singing "Rip Her to Shreds," back when she sang the lead vocals for Blondie. Whenever I think about Nerissa, or when my mind strays to the time I found out that Drex took a Connecticut girl to Cotillion behind my back three years ago, I play these songs. In other words, when I'm stressed.

Back to Harkman Beemis.

I need to select an evening gown for the upcoming debutante ball. I'm leaning toward this sweet mermaid gown I found in a luscious shade of cherry red that matches this incredible lipstick I bought last week. Besides, red looks positively electrifying with my blonde hair and blue eyes and not many people can pull off that particular shade. But I'm blessed with pink English skin so cherry is a fabulous color on me. I'm also open to turquoise.

I cruised into the parking lot of Harkman's and zoomed into a space. Can't risk getting a nick in the Carrera's paint job, so I've taken to parking at the end of the row, as far from the entrance as I can get. You wouldn't believe how many people have tried to open the doors of their big ugly trucks and rusted-out junkers into the side of my baby just for meanness. If I can't pull in next to a new Lexus, Mercedes or Jaguar, I'd just as soon walk.

Which is what I did — power-walked to the double glass doors and joined the throng of customers awaiting the opening of the throw bolts. As if to signal the beginning of the festivities, the locks snapped open with the crack of a starting pistol and a crush of socialites fought their way inside like jackals.

A peal of laughter, jarring enough to make me look around for the source, came out of nowhere. If I hadn't gotten sidetracked at the shoe section, ogling a pair of alligator

18

boots by Christian Louboutin, I would've never seen my boss's wife at the jewelry counter — kissing a man who's not her husband. My smile slipped away.

My boss, Gordon Pfeiffer, is the station manager of WBFD-TV Channel Eighteen where I'm doing my internship. I met his wife, Paislee, at the Labor Day office picnic. Even then, I wondered what a woman like Paislee Pfeiffer would want with a portly old geezer like Gordon. I mean, he must be fifty-ish. And she must be . . . pushing thirty? And this man she's with — ohmygod. Could he *be* any hunkier? For a second, I thought it was Drex. Seeing him from behind in a gorgeous suit, he was square-shouldered with dark brown hair that shined like little bronze filaments beneath the light of the fluorescents. And he had a laugh like Drex's, deep and resonating. I inclined my head around the display of high-heeled boots and studied the man's profile. Even that reminded me of Drex.

As I moved into the couture section, the sales lady recognized me and rushed over with a happy smile tipping up her face. I put my finger to my lips and spoke in a hushed voice.

"I'm here to try on the cherry red gown you have on hold for me. Mermaid cut with a little fishtail train?" I waved my hands in an hourglass motion so she'd remember the fitted strapless made of heavy silk with a hint of ruching near the hemline.

"You're Dainty Prescott?"

I nodded, again placing my finger to my lips in a shushing motion.

"I'll get it for you."

At the moment, I wished I hadn't primped to perfection. It would've been better to look like one of those dowdy, rumpled, run-of-the-mill bargain shoppers than to have worn high-heel designer footwear with purple silk capri pants and the multicolored silk shell with the matching purple silk jacket. But Gordon Pfeiffer insists that the interns wear bright colors because gem tones photograph better on television. And since my competition — three Southern Methodist University coeds — and I will eventually be called upon to substitute-in for one of the anchors in order to receive a passing grade from our respective alma maters, and since Mr. Pfeiffer's no-nonsense attitude occasionally seems more like a cruel streak when it comes to inflicting grief and panic on me and the SMU mafia, our moment in the spotlight will, no doubt, be sprung on us when we least expect it.

On that day, I, Dainty Prescott, will be ready.

But I digress.

Had I worn my cream tropical wool gabardine slacks, matching shirt and button-down cashmere sweater, as is Rubanbleu appropriate, at least I could've gone unnoticed as I watched Paislee Pfeiffer from behind the formalwear giggling like there was no tomorrow. I envied her laugh. She had a laugh like musical chimes. The man accompanying her pointed at the glass countertop and the sales lady pulled out a tray with a sparkly diamond necklace on it. She held it to her neck while he fastened it. Then she tilted the mirror up from its stand and admired her reflection. When she nodded, her companion pulled out his wallet and purchased it with a credit card. Then they kissed. Not one of those little pecks but a full, throaty tongue kiss.

My mouth gaped.

PDAs — public displays of affection — are totally déclassé and not the sort of behavior embraced by Rubanbleu society.

My stomach knotted. For a moment, my heart clenched in sympathy for Mr. Pfeiffer.

"Here you are." The sales lady had returned without me knowing. She held the dress up for inspection. "Your fitting room's ready."

"Yes, thank you." I took the gown from her, feeling strangely defensive for my boss. Oh sure, he had a paunch from eating too much barbeque and he probably guzzled way too much booze. But running an independent TV station that he'd managed to pull out of last place, all the way to third in the ratings, sucked a lot of energy out of him. He had to worry about programming and lawsuits. Now he had a cheating wife.

Still, it wasn't my business. If luck holds out, Mr. Pfeiffer will offer me an anchor position for the ten o'clock news and hire me full time this coming spring when I graduate with my RTF degree.

Lingering, I couldn't pull myself away from this train wreck bearing down in front of me. I could almost hear the screaming grind of metal-on-metal. When Paislee darted a furtive look in my direction, I whipped the mermaid dress up high enough to shield my face from view.

I peered slowly around it.

She kissed him again. I watched like a voyeur as his hand grazed her breast. My heart almost beat through my chest.

Poor Mr. Pfeiffer; roly-poly, balding Gordon Pfeiffer with the wire-rimmed glasses that made his gray-green eyes look like magnified nickels behind those thick lenses. In a way, it was like watching Daddy compete with other men for Nerissa's affections. Whatever made two middle-aged men think they could catch and keep such beautiful young wives?

The man's arm snaked around Paislee's waist. They turned in my direction. I whirled around, putting my back to them, and handed the mermaid dress to the sales lady.

"I'll be right in. I want to look around a bit more in case it doesn't work."

She nodded, scurrying off with my beautiful couture gown held high above her head to keep the fishtail train from dragging on the floor.

Then I saw the two lovebirds dead-on. My stomach went hollow. My heart thunked.

Reflected in the mirror was my boyfriend Drex with Paislee Pfeiffer.

Blood pounded in my ears. Flesh crawled. My chin corrugated.

Drex wasn't supposed to be home for three weeks.

I closed my eyes, tight, to shut them out, only to have the ghastly apparition reappear behind sealed eyelids. The shock of them popping back up in a reverse negative image made my eyes snap open like roller shades. Sure enough, my boyfriend and my boss's wife were still at Harkman's, oblivious to my presence, trying to devour each other's faces like a couple of starving cannibals.

I was about to have a PDE — public display of emotion — of my own.

Much as I longed to make my presence known, I saw the wisdom in not creating a scene. After all, The Rubanbleu's the closest thing to stability that I have in my life right now. That, and the trust fund I'll be able to access on my twenty-fifth birthday. And knowing I'll have to stay on The Rubanbleu's waiting list for five years once I do become Mrs. Strayer Drexel Truett III — or, rather, Mrs. *Somebody Rich;* and since several of The Rubanbleu's doyennes were gliding toward Harkman's day spa and I didn't want to be blackballed because they witnessed unladylike behavior from me (translation: snot-slinging mad); I stood, stricken, while the love of my life and my boss's wife continued to throw themselves at each other.

I saw fireworks again.

As they walked clumsily toward the doors with their arms slid around each other's backs, I felt a lightheaded rush. The energy seeped out of my body. The room temporarily blurred as I staggered to a nearby chair and crumpled into it.

I sank my head into my palms and wailed.

Chapter Two

What's wrong with me?

I mean — I'm a nice person, aren't I? Didn't I risk my life last week, stopping on the side of the road in a driving rain to pick up that box turtle trying to cross the highway? It would've been smashed if I hadn't carried it to the opposite shoulder. And when those little kids came to Gran's house selling chocolate for their school's fundraiser, didn't I get a fifty out of her wallet and sign us up for all sorts of treats? And they weren't even from our neighborhood, for God's sake. You could tell these kids were imported from a different part of town and turned loose by some guy in an old hippie van to peddle candy.

So wasn't that a nice thing, giving them money? And they didn't even have on good shoes.

I just don't understand.

Am I not pretty enough? Oh sure, Paislee

Pfeiffer's tall and willowy and drop-dead-gorgeous with her raven black hair and big green eyes and a breast augmentation two cup sizes too large. She has that going for her now, but just wait 'til those things turn to granite — then see how my boyfriend likes kneading rocks. Her porcelain skin is practically translucent and her teeth are even, white and perfect. And when she laughs, men turn in her direction and get that lustful look in their eyes.

By comparison, anyone seeing me at close range would notice a petite blonde with large ice-blue eyes, full provocative lips and a straight nose that turns up slightly at the tip. A weekly visit to the tanning salon keeps my fair skin from looking corpse-like and gives me a healthy glow. Daily visits to the gym have kept my weight proportionate to my height. I don't need to have work done to make my body shapelier the way Daddy's wife and Gordon's wife and lots of my sorority sisters have done.

Mine are real.

And they're perfect.

And while I don't have thick, luscious, bouncy hair falling down my back in waves like Paislee Pfeiffer, my major flaw — thin, fine hair — is under control now that my hairdresser, David, whipped up a secret product for me to make it look thicker and feel coarser. He also styled my hair with a trim that we keep as secret as a Masonic handshake: a lightly layered mid-length cut that barely touches my shoulders and tapers to fall into a slightly diagonal forward-moving line. With liberal applications of David's magic styling volumizer to fatten up the limpness caused by this oppressive Texas humidity, and tons of hair spray applied until it holds up like a coat of shellac, I have a quick fix of heirloom information for lame hair that could've been handed down to me by my grandmother.

I didn't stick around Harkman's long enough to try on the cherry mermaid dress. After the crying jag, which attracted ladies from other sales departments and eventually mall security, I left the store with the dress still on hold and everyone within earshot fixing me with unemotional stares.

How humiliating. I've never been shown the door by security guards before.

I admit it. Street theater is *très* déclassé, but *hello,* I'd just experienced the worst day of my life.

Well . . . maybe not the worst.

Second worst.

The *worst* day of my life occurred last year when I flounced, giddy with delight, through the front door of my family's Rivercrest home flaunting a transcript full of As — and, yes, it does *too* count even though one of them was for advanced ballet; it's still a class and my chosen elective. Calling out to my mother from the marble rotunda, "Mom, you were right . . . I *am* smart enough to make the Dean's List," I repeated the declaration as I made my way through the rest of the house, only to find her lying dead on the bedroom floor.

Considering my fragile underpinnings at the moment, I'd rather not pull at that thread.

Needless to say, I did *not* make the Dean's List the following semester.

For the record, crying at one's mother's funeral is the *only* Rubanbleu-acceptable example of a PDE.

But I can't afford to think about that now.

I have to pull myself together.

My internship awaits. And no telling what kind of treachery those SMU divas are up to, or what they might do to undermine my standing at the TV station.

I can't believe I'm still shaking like a lathered-up dog.

I checked my watch, an eighteen-carat, loose-fitting Piaget that hangs around my wrist like a bracelet. There's less than thirty minutes for me to arrive at WBFD-TV on time. The area's familiar enough that I've been able to isolate most of the intersections with red light cameras around Harkman Beemis. So I felt pretty certain I only soared through a couple of amber lights on my way to Interstate 30. Besides, like Daddy's corporate lawyer said, even if I did run the red light, a girl has the Constitutional right to confront her accuser. And how can one do that when the accuser's an inanimate object?

Inside the Porsche, I volumed up the "Angry White Woman" CD, zoomed out of the parking lot and cut across three lanes of traffic to get into the turn lane that would funnel me directly onto the freeway. Listening to Alanis sing "You Oughta Know" until the veins in my head were pleading for an aneurysm, I tried to force the image of Drex and my boss's wife from my thoughts. As I roared down the freeway, outraged, Alanis channeled raw feelings into words I could make sense of. For no reason other than instinct, I shifted my attention to the rear-view mirror.

My heart stalled, then jumpstarted itself. Blood whooshed between my ears.

Red and blue emergency lights from a Fort Worth police car flashed behind me.

For a brief instant insanity took over.

Thoughts of flight vibrated off the top of my head.

I can lose him, I thought with the same diabolical right-brain thinking that allowed me to plot the perfect murder of Nerissa. Then the left-brain engaged and logic set in. I flipped on my turn signal, exited the freeway from an off-ramp and pulled into a residential area called Ridglea. My eyes flickered to the rearview mirror, to the shadowy reflection behind the wheel of the black-and-white. The door to the patrol car swept open and a cop got out and strutted my way with a ticket book in hand.

Oh, goody. A gift from the self-esteem fairy.

Tears blistered behind my eyeballs. Just what I needed — another ticket.

Ticket? I sucked air.

My eyes flickered to the floorboard. Fourteen citations rested there, festering like throbbing pimples begging to be squeezed. I dove across the console to scoop them up and that's how the officer found me when he reached my car door with his gun drawn — butt in the air, capri pants stretched tight across what probably seemed like an epic eggplant derrier from his perspective, high-heeled Jimmy Choos anchoring me to the floor mat and the festive silk top crawling up my back.

His face hardened into immobility.

Despite his *GQ* good looks, the patrolman cut a menacing presence in his black uniform. He yanked the door handle. When it didn't pop open he banged the butt of that scary-looking black gun against the window so hard it could've cracked the glass. I looked up from my wild scramble and clutched the citations to my chest.

"Open the door." The growling voice struck fear in my heart. He wore one of those angry facial expressions like the ones you see on despots in old war newsreels.

I came fully upright with tickets cascading into my lap.

Dazed by the horror of clutching incriminating evidence in my hand, I knew he'd caught me red-handed. Like a smoking gun, only without the ability to turn it on myself. When I hit the electric gizmo, brought the window halfway down and gave him a doe-eyed expression, he reached through the opening with his left hand and unlocked the door.

"Hi officer, is there a problem?" Said weakly.

With my eyes close enough to make out the orangey-red longhorn steer on the Fort

Worth police patch emblazoned on his shirtsleeve, I watched with dread as he yanked it open.

"Out of the car."

"I don't understand. Is something wrong?" I asked with practiced innocence.

Instead of answering, he holstered his gun, grabbed my arm and pulled me from the Porsche. Unsteady from the rude way he jerked me to my feet, I stumbled against him.

He spun me around, pushed me against the car and held me there with his hand flattened against the middle of my back as if he'd seen my photo posted on the bulletin board alongside the "Ten Most Wanted."

My voice corkscrewed upward. "What're you doing?"

"Pat-down for weapons," he growled, and then proceeded to manhandle me.

I caught myself whimpering and spoke in the whiney voice of a preschooler. "I don't have any weapons. I have pepper spray on my key ring, that's all." Like that would impress him. My keys are still in the ignition.

He ran his hands down my sides, kicked my feet apart until my legs formed an inverted "V" and briskly ran the backs of his hands up my capris as if he were smoothing out the wrinkles. Cars drove past braking enough to catch his act. He shoved an arm beneath mine and with the back of his hand at my neck, drew it down my torso in one swift move. Then he spun me around to face him.

"Do not *ever* dive out of sight when a police officer stops you. Do you understand? I could've shot you."

By this time, I was hyperventilating. A bizarre mixture of fear and humiliation electrified the hairs on my neck.

"I didn't do anything," I sputtered.

"You went through the red light back there."

"It was green. The arrow was green."

"The arrow was *not* green. The arrow was *yellow* when the car in front of you went through the light and by the time you entered the intersection the light had been *red* for three seconds. Didn't you hear the oncoming traffic honking?"

"I was listening to music." Said defensively, as if that mitigated the circumstances. To make matters worse, Alanis was belting out lyrics through the speakers, demanding to know if her ex-lover's new woman shared her perversions and performed sex acts on him in public places. I cringed. Bad timing.

"Want me to turn it off?"

He ignored me. My eyes dipped to his gold metal nameplate. I read J. BUCKMAN and assumed this was Officer Buckman. My mind made the leap and I started to think of him as Officer Butt Man in my head, turning him into a kind of superhero: Spider-Man, Batman, Butt Man — only without all the really cool superpowers.

"Look, officer, I'm already late for work."

"Where do you work?"

"WBFD-TV, Channel Eighteen."

The contours of his face went as hard as granite. His jaw torqued. Spooky blue eyes narrowed into the squint of an assassin. "WBFD, huh?"

Wide-eyed, I wanted to thunk my head with the heel of my palm. Didn't we just do that horrible exposé on the Fort Worth Police Department called "Asleep at the Wheel" last November during sweeps month? And wasn't it about five cops who were caught sleeping in their patrol cars while downtown businesses were being burglarized?

Stupid Dainty, stupid Dainty.

I inwardly groaned, acknowledging Butt Man's ability to coerce a confession out of me. Reminding myself to keep the conversation with this man to a minimum, I credited him with this scary new superpower and vowed not to be gulled into saying anything else incriminating.

"I'm an intern. I don't actually get paid. It's for my Radio–TV–Film degree. I'm a student at Texas Christian University." Like that would take the heat off.

Way to disenfranchise yourself from WBFD, Dainty.

Unimpressed, he leveled a double-barrel glare at me.

"So anyway, could I just go now?" As an afterthought, I added, "Please?"

"No you may not. I need to see your driver's license and insurance. And what're all those citations for?"

I swallowed hard. "Traffic camera stuff."

"Did you pay them?"

I went blank. *Yeah,* I wanted to say, *I just keep them around as mementos.* I inwardly took the Fifth.

He snorted in disgust.

I was starting to grow tired of his ability to read my mind and grudgingly granted Butt Man another superpower.

"Driver's license and insurance," he repeated, quickly adding, "let's step out of the road." He gripped the pressure points in my elbow and steered me to the other side of my car. I opened the door and reached into the passenger seat for my purse. After fishing out my wallet and handing over the license, I leaned in to open the glove compartment.

He grabbed me around the wrist. "Not so fast." He cut his eyes to the curb and I stepped away from the Porsche. Then he reached inside, opened the glove box and pulled out my proof of insurance.

"Couldn't you just give me a warning?" I asked in a lame attempt to wheedle my way out of this unpleasant situation.

He eyed me with a drill-bit stare. "So you can let it sit on the floorboard to keep the rest of them company? I don't think so."

He swaggered to the back of the Porsche and took a long look at my personalized plate.

"Debutante." His mouth angled up to one side in an evil grin. "Isn't that nice? I don't believe I've ever ticketed a debutante."

My blood pressure spiked into the danger zone.

He said, "Be right back," and left me standing in an ant bed.

With the sun beating down on my head, I became vaguely aware of stinging feet — *ow, ow, ow.* While I did a little jig and swatted red ants off my ankles, he sat in his air-conditioned car talking into the police two-way mounted on the dash. My hair went limp, welts popped up on my ankles from the bites and I relived the humiliation of seeing my boyfriend kissing the boss's wife.

Then Butt Man swaggered over with his aluminum clipboard and launched into a speech he'd probably delivered a thousand times over the past six months.

"This is a citation for running the red light at Green Oaks and West Freeway. Sign here." He poised his pen above a blank space.

My breaths went shallow.

Maybe I couldn't do anything about Drex playing grab-ass with another woman just like I couldn't do anything about the ant bites and the hair falling flat. But what I could do is refuse to sign Butt Man's citation. I squared my shoulders, held my head high and took a serene, almost Buddhist approach to the ticket.

"I'm not signing. I didn't run the red light."

"This isn't an admission of guilt." He spoke in the deadpan voice of a TV cop reading a suspect his *Miranda* rights. "It's merely a promise to take care of this violation within the next eleven days." He tapped the point of his pen near the signature line.

This evoked the kind of reaction I

would've had if my doctor had diagnosed me with an STD: "Oh goody — Chlamydia — the *best* of the sexually transmitted diseases!"

"I'm not signing." I braced my arms across my chest and literally dug in my heels, which had sunk so far into the dirt by this time that I'd probably need a backhoe to dig me out.

His mouth tipped at the corners. "You don't want to do that." Upturned lips creased into a broad grin.

He would've had a nice smile if I hadn't sensed all the cosmic bad vibes he was sending my way. If I could read auras, his would've been black, judging from the glint in his thinning blue eyes.

"Like I said . . ." I stood there, calm as a Hindu cow.

He took a deep breath, towering over me even though I was still up on the curb in my high heels and he was flat-footed on the street.

What transpired up until now had been a veritable merry-go-round of pleasure compared to what happened next.

He let go of the metal clipboard.

It clattered to the asphalt.

Without taking his eyes off me, he reached behind his back. An ominous snap pricked my ears. When his arm came back around, he was dangling a pair of handcuffs.

"Turn around. Hands behind your back."

"What?" I spoke on a whoosh of expelled air. "You can't do that." But inside, I was screaming, *Can he?* Then I remembered what Daddy's corporate lawyer said and I delivered this newsflash with the confidence of a runway model. "You can't arrest me for running a red light."

My brain echoed a victorious *Ha.*

In one stride he was up on the curb, spinning me around with my back to him. He ratcheted the first handcuff on. Fear lanced my heart. My vision blurred. Surroundings went out of focus as he clamped on the second one and tightened it around my other wrist. I saw fireworks — and not the good kind.

"My daddy's lawyer says you can't be arrested for a red light ticket. Isn't that true?"

Gripping me by the arm, he half marched, half dragged me to the patrol car. I plodded the dirt with my hands secured behind my back, through air noxious with the smell of exhaust fumes. With a finger looped through the handcuff chain, he opened the door to the caged area with his free hand.

"Watch your head, debutante."

"You can't do this to me."

"No?" He stared at me with a blank, scary expression on his face; my protests lost effect. Then he urged me into the back seat with a steel-handed grip and a sarcastic, "Oh, look. I just did."

My designer-shod feet were still teetering against the pavement when I decided to play chicken with him — a move that lasted all of two seconds once I realized my shins were about to become door stops. I pulled my Jimmy Choos inside seconds before the door slammed shut with an authoritative clunk. As he walked back to the curb to retrieve his clipboard, I twisted in my seat to open the door.

Police cars must have child locks.

I couldn't get out and I needed my mobile phone. Daddy and Nerissa might be out of the country but I had his lawyer's number programmed in on speed dial.

When I was little, I used to take gymnastics. It didn't take long for me to contort my cuffed hands beneath my derrière and wriggle them out in front of me.

Butt Man returned to the patrol car and slid behind the wheel. Slitty eyes flickered to the rearview mirror. He grabbed the two-way mounted on the dash and radioed the dispatcher. After a brief exchange, he returned the mike to its hook, wrenched the gearshift into drive and pulled away from the curb.

My voice trembled with the effort of speech. "What's going to happen to me?"

"You'll appear before the judge to answer for failing to sign the ticket. The judge will decide what to do with you."

"You can't just let me go?" I whimpered. Before I knew it, my thoughts pulled the hair trigger to my tongue. "What do you need — a quota?"

His eyes met mine in the rearview mirror, locking me in his invisible force field. His face relaxed into an expression as somber as if he were contemplating the reunification of Iraq. "Umm, let me think a minute. Uh . . . no."

I raised my hand to blot out the judgment and recrimination swimming in his spooky blue gaze. "You're mean."

"No, I'm not," he smarted off. "I'm protecting the public from menaces like you."

CHAPTER THREE

We drove in a scary silence for the next five minutes with Butt Man threading the patrol car in and out of traffic and me in the caged section suffering the angst and indignity of arrest. I entertained cruel fantasies that grew more violent the longer the tires droned along the highway. I'd finally sunk to a new low. Embarrassment got the better of me and I cracked under the pressure.

"This is a horrible, no good, rotten day," I blubbered, punctured and deflated.

"Not for me." Said cheerily. "I already got my first citation toward the daily quota and it isn't even noon yet."

Horrible tales of green baloney and moldy bread came rushing back, stories told by drunken sorority sisters and frat brothers who'd spent the night in jail. A shudder rippled up my back and raised the baby-fine hairs at the nape of my neck. I burst into tears.

"I just can't go to jail," I wailed.

"Betcha can." Butt Man regarded me intently through the rearview mirror.

I curled up like a cocktail shrimp and sank against the door with my drippy nose and hot breath fogging the window. The back seat smelled of other people's puke and urine and made my stomach roil. I caught part of my faint reflection in the glass — of the tear streaming down one side of my face — and tuned up for real.

"I'm sorry. I didn't mean to be a bitch. It's just . . ."

We made eye contact in the mirror. An arched brow prompted me to continue.

"This morning while I was in Harkman Beemis —"

"Let me guess. Daddy's little debutante can't find a dress to wear to the Cinderella ball."

"It's not like that," I sniffled. "I found this really pretty cherry red silk mermaid gown with a sweet pleated fishtail train . . ." He did a heavy eye roll and I hauled up short. "Never mind. You don't care about the dress."

Several seconds passed. "No, really, tell me about it."

"No."

"No, really. I want to hear."

"You just want to make fun of me," I said in a raw voice.

"You're right. Poor little rich girl having a bad day."

I squirmed closer to his ear, vaguely aware that if he slammed on the brakes I'd have waffle marks on the right side of my face for a week. "It's not like that."

"No, Miss Debutante, driving a Porsche, dripping in jewelry that would take me the better part of a year to pay for." He smirked. "Tell me what makes this a — how'd you phrase it — a sorry, rotten, no good day?"

"A horrible, no good, rotten day."

"You've got my attention." He flipped on his turn signal, changed lanes and returned his attention to the mirror.

Did I mention I get carsick if I ride in the back seat? This switching lanes business was starting to feel like Six Flags Over Hell.

A high-pitched bleep came from what appeared to be a computer anchored to the patrol car's dashboard. He diverted his attention from the road long enough to type in a few keystrokes.

While he messaged the dispatcher on his mobile data transmitter, I told him about my mom being dead and Daddy marrying Nerissa not even a year later. And them gallivanting across Europe with Nerissa ram-

45

pantly going through his money like a marauding Goth while I got put on a budget. My chest hitched. I recounted the townhouse problem that left me and Venice and Salem practically homeless — which got me nothing but a heavy eye roll — and finally reached the cringe-worthy part of the story where I saw Drex, who isn't even supposed to be in town for another three weeks, kissing my boss's wife. I didn't think Butt Man was listening but recounting the details served as a kind of therapeutic purge. Like eating an entire coconut layer cake with lemon filling and making yourself throw up.

Felt good.

Then I immediately wanted to instruct him to disregard, like in a courtroom.

"Men are assholes," Butt Man volunteered.

"You don't understand." I was sobbing now, with him watching me with the intensity of a brain surgeon. "If I confront him about it, I won't have a date to the ball. If I let it go it'll be the second time he's cheated on me and I don't deserve that. What makes matters worse is that I'll probably lose my job for being late to work. And even if I don't get canned today, once my boss finds out my boyfriend's porking his wife, he'll blame me for bringing Drex to the company picnic and fire me anyway. Now that Daddy's cut me off and everybody treats me like I'm the black sheep strayed from the flock, I won't have any money and I'll be ho . . . ho . . . homeless."

A vision of Drex eating Paislee's face flashed into mind, smashing my fragile underpinnings. Moderate hysteria disintegrated into a snot-slinging crying jag. I collapsed onto my side with my head pressed against the window and tried to suck in air from the A/C vent.

"I don't want to end up eating garbage soup from the soup kitchen."

The concept was about as uninviting as peroxide pudding.

By this time, I'd started to hiccup. Even as I tuned up caterwauling, I realized how much I sounded like the figure skater Nancy Kerrigan after that goon smashed her knee-cap with a club — *"Why? Why?"* But the next time I made eye contact with Butt Man through the mirror, I thought I saw a flicker of compassion radiating through his gaze.

"Bummer." The police radio let out a distracting squawk. He leaned in enough to lower the volume. "Can you call a friend?"

"I'd be mortified for any of my friends to see me locked up in jail." I sniffled. "Nerissa convinced Daddy I'm irresponsible and he told our corporate lawyer not to bail me out if I got into trouble so I'm screwed. I realize this doesn't mean squat to you but I really don't look good in orange."

"You're right. Jimmy crack corn and — you guessed it — I don't care."

I sensed him smiling through my pain.

"Besides, they only issue orange jumpsuits to Trustys — low-risk inmates who are trustworthy. That rules you out. And Trustys have to work pushing brooms and stuff. You probably never picked up a broom in your life." Long pause while I fumed in the back seat. "No, I expect they'll probably issue you the standard khakis and you can just kick back on your louse-infested mattress and relax. Try to think of it as a B-and-B."

Oh dear God. It's like I'm living in an alternate universe.

I swallowed. "They have bugs in jail?"

"More than you'd think." He added helpfully, "Ask your boss."

"Are you demented?" The words tumbled out before I could rein them back in. "He's not going to help me."

Gordon's philosophy hinged on several tenets: One, reporters were not to become part of their story; two, employees were not to do anything that might end up in a body cavity search; and, three, employees were not to cause the station to become involved in a lawsuit. I was pretty sure the first and third rules didn't apply but I was definitely nervous about the body cavity search.

I sat up rigid, sucked in my last sniffle, squared my shoulders as best as I could with my hands cuffed and said with complete sincerity, "If I sign the ticket will you take me back to my car?"

Municipal Court, an architecturally unimpressive multistory building, loomed up ahead so I was surprised when he drove past it and circled the block. He pulled into a sun-dappled area between two buildings and wrenched the car into park beneath the shade of an overhanging oak. Then he twisted in his seat to face me.

"Just so you know, I don't feel sorry for you."

Two fat teardrops teetering along the rims of my eyes spilled over onto my cheeks. They tracked the length of my face and splattered onto my capris, where they expanded into penny-sized watermarks.

"I know." My voice had that stuffy nose quality from having pitched a hissy fit. Arguing with Butt Man had siphoned off the last of my energy. I flopped against the seat back and eyed the pink stains on the liner of his roof. Disgusting. Like a wino had projectile vomited on the ceiling. I felt my shirt tacking itself to my back. "Can you vent some cold air back here? I think I'm going to be sick."

Instead of adjusting the air vents, he yanked up the emergency brake, bailed out of the car, hurled open the back door and pulled me out.

"Thank you," I said and threw up on his lace-up SWAT boots.

Which made me cry even more. Butt Man was going to hate me. And as soon as we went before the judge, I'd see the full range of his superpowers — starting with him making an ass out of me.

A muted click sounded inside his shirt pocket.

I alerted like a drug dog. "What was that?"

"Micro-cassette recorder."

"You're taping me?" My voice corkscrewed upward. A flock of birds broke from the trees.

He shrugged. "Not anymore."

I stood speechless and horrified, then let out an angry yelp that caused passersby to turn my way and peg me for a lunatic.

As I sucked in gauzy air so thick and unbreathable that each breath made my stomach flip, he pulled a handkerchief from his pocket and shook it out. Positioning it near my nose, he said, "Blow."

I did.

"Again," he said in an authoritative baritone and wiped my upper lip.

"Thanks."

He gave an almost imperceptible nod. "Let's get something straight. You're not the only one in the world with problems."

My gaze dipped to the strip of black electrician's tape over a badge that should've had a resting panther visible near the top of the shield.

"My best friend and police partner was killed by a drunk driver two days ago so you don't hold a monopoly on grief. But since I'm not real happy with the way the PD's treating his widow right now, I've decided to do you a huge favor and take you back to your vehicle — after you sign the red light ticket."

My body wilted under the weight of such news. It was as if a little release valve had been opened to drain out all the tension. "Really? You'd do that for me?"

"In spite of you. The stars and planets are aligned, Cinderella, so I'm taking off the cuffs and handing you a pen. All right?"

He got a huge head bob. And I do mean huge. My head shook like a bobble-head

Chihuahua in the back dash of a *barrio* low rider.

Fingers trembled as I wrote my name.

After I'd signed and he handed me a copy of the ticket, he seated me in the passenger compartment of the front seat with the A/C vented on high. I quizzed him about the computer, which he referred to as an MDT — mobile data terminal — and asked questions about the siren buttons: wail, yelp and phaser — a warbling, high-pitched, space age sound that had me imagining flying saucers landing with tiny wrinkled aliens on board. But when I tried to strike up a conversation about his deceased partner, Butt Man shut me down with a crisp, "We're not talking about him."

I detected a catch in his voice and tried to make small talk — a regrettable act that came creeping back to me each time he dead-ended the conversation. By the time we returned to the Ridglea neighborhood and rolled up behind my car, he wasted no time thumbing open the door lock mechanism. Audible clicks sounded in stereo, letting me know I'd worn out my welcome.

"I'm sorry for the trouble I caused." For the record, I've never been able to pull off sorry.

"Have a nice day."

But I couldn't let it go. "Look, what you did was a nice thing. I know I acted bratty and I'm really, really sorry. You have enough to worry about without having to deal with idiots like me. Want to know something?"

He leveled his gaze, searing me with those spectacular cornflower blue eyes.

"I think your wife's a lucky woman to be married to somebody like you."

At first, he didn't react. As I climbed out of the patrol car he said, "I'm not married."

I turned at the sound of his voice but the door slammed shut. He hit the electric button and the glass on the passenger side slid down.

I amended the comment. "Your girlfriend then."

He shook his head. "No girlfriend."

"Really?" For no good reason I felt an enormous temperature spike.

I don't know what I was thinking, exactly, but on some level, it dawned on me how good-looking he was now that he wasn't scaring the hell out of me. Actually, Butt Man was drop-dead gorgeous in a boyish but deadly sort of way. Until now, I hadn't realized that his hair was the color of wheat or that he had laugh lines at the corners of his eyes.

I poked my head through the window.

"Do you by any chance have a card?"

He opened the aluminum clipboard, pulled out a business card, flipped it over and printed something on the back. He presented it to me right side up and I scanned it. I must've been hallucinating when I glanced at the nametag on his shirt earlier because I made a startling discovery. The name printed in black ink on police department card stock read: JIM BRUCK-MAN.

When I asked him to pronounce it, it sounded like, "Brookman."

I blinked. His rank and place of assignment was written beneath his name: Detective, Major Crimes. So why wasn't he in plainclothes, seated behind a desk with a phone growing out of one ear and his booted feet propped up on the blotter?

I lifted my gaze. "I don't understand. If you're a detective, why're you in uniform working the street?"

"Everybody's at the funeral. Somebody has to patrol."

My jaw went slack. "Shouldn't you be at the funeral?"

He jutted his chin at the citation. "Eleven days. You can pay by mail, pay in person or set it for court. Read the blue sheet."

I glanced at the information insert.

"Just so we're clear, I didn't run the red light." I gave him the best advertisement my orthodontist could've hoped for and flashed a winning beauty pageant smile. "I'm setting it for court."

"Suit yourself." He shifted the patrol car into gear.

Fighting the urge to look over my shoulder, I prissed over to my car and climbed in.

As he waited for me to drive off, I figured he thought I was white trash for challenging him.

But how else was I supposed to run into him again? Commit a major crime by mowing Drex down with my car?

I stuck Detective Bruckman's card into the citation, folded the envelope and tucked it inside my purse. I checked my watch; a groan slipped out.

I'd be lucky if I didn't see steam coiling up from the top of Gordon's balding head.

CHAPTER FOUR

"Here's the thing, Dainty," said Rochelle LeDuc as she plunked a couple of coins down the chute to the soda machine in WBFD's break room, "you have to tell him. He's already livid because you were late. You know Gordon's policy about coming to work and being on time."

We chimed in unison, " *'If Hell freezes over then Hell is closed but you're still coming to work.' "*

With her dark hair strained back from her face in a French twist and a designer suit clinging to her body in all the right places, Gordon's drop-dead gorgeous assistant looked out from under penciled-on eyebrows. Early menopause had given her a mercurial personality. Instead of cracking the tab on the Dr Pepper can that rolled down the dispenser and banged against the stop, she pressed it against one side of her face. After a few long seconds, she shifted it to cool the other cheek.

"I can't tell him. He'd fire me." I looked up expectantly as Rochelle, dressed to the nines, slid into the bistro chair across the table.

"Gordon prizes loyalty above all else. The last thing he'll do is fire you — unless, of course, you keep this to yourself and he finds out that you knew. Besides, you're the one who brought the guy to the Labor Day party. Your boyfriend probably would've never met Paislee in a million years if you hadn't invited him to the barbeque." Scary pale gray eyes turned as hard and translucent as ice cubes. Pupils narrowed like BBs. She rolled the cold can down her neck and pressed it against her cleavage. "At least this way you might be able to salvage your job."

"I don't want to tell Gordon."

"Fine. Have fun finding work. You can probably get hired on by one of the independent stations. I hear there's a new Latino station trying to break into the market. If you dyed your hair black and changed your name to Lupita Gonzalez they'd probably hire you. How's your Spanish?" She measured an inch between her thumb and forefinger. *"¿Habla un poquito español?"*

I wanted to ask her advice on how to deal with Drex but distraction moved at the limits of my vision. Chopper Deke, the station's helicopter pilot, sauntered in from aerial patrol with a feral grin and bulging eyes that looked like Saturn — spectral blue irises ringed totally white. His white-blonde hair stuck straight up and his deeply tanned skin bore the leathery creases of an old saddle.

I knew Chopper Deke by reputation. He had a broken foot that he'd set himself and a missing back molar he pulled out with a pair of pliers after anesthetizing himself with cheap tequila. His *modus operandi* was to hit on women and then bring their panties to work to show the guys. In short, the females at the station found him icky.

Rochelle experienced a polar shift. Suddenly prickly, she darted a look at me and excused herself.

Deke called out after her, "Hey toots, want to go out tonight?" He whipped a couple of passes from his shirt pocket and flashed them. "I've got tickets to NASCAR."

"If you ever come near me, I'll drop you with my shotgun," she said in a casual but lethal voice.

Cock-of-the-walk, he spread out his arms with his hands palms-up. "Hey, baby, don't knock it if you haven't tried it."

She gave him a patrician snort. "You

forget. I've heard the rumors." Then she turned my way and thumbed at him over her shoulder. "Believe me when I say I've had flu shots that took longer."

With her nose inclined at a disdainful tilt and her backside swaying, she walked out with the Dr Pepper can stuffed down the front of her knit shell, looking like the carnival freak with three breasts.

I heard the familiar clunk of a soda can plummeting down the chute and glanced over.

Leering, he turned his attention to me. "Hey, baby, what's your name?"

"I'm underage." Snatching my Italian handbag off the chair, I bolted in Rochelle's wake while simultaneously playing the name game. Deke — rhymes with *eek*.

I barely had time for a momentary glimpse at the studio. Ten minutes later, the Paislee Pfeiffer sighting was out of my hands. Rochelle blabbed to Gordon and I found myself sitting behind closed doors trying to blend into the boss's new cowhide sofa with the black and white spots.

I stood out like a peacock.

"What'd he look like?" Pfeiffer asked, rheumy-eyed from too much booze and not enough sleep. The portly manager, with thinning brown hair silvering on the sides and ball-bearing eyes that functioned as an ocular lie detector, sat behind the oversized desk with his elbows resting on the blotter and his fingers tented.

I squirmed under his intent regard. "Please, Mr. Pfeiffer, I don't want to cause trouble."

"You're not." He leaned in conspiratorially and smacked his hand on top of the desk as if it were a fly swatter. "I knew she was fooling around on me — I just didn't know who she was fooling around with."

Numbly, I reverted to the image in my head of Drex and Paislee trying to perform tonsillectomies on each other using only their tongues.

Maybe Drex wanted to buy me diamonds and he asked her to help him pick something out. And he had to perform mouth-to-mouth on her because the jewels he picked out were so breathtakingly beautiful that just looking at them siphoned all the oxygen out of her lungs.

Or maybe they'd turned into cannibals and were taste-testing each other's faces. I looked around miserably, searching for a way to kill myself, and noticed the open door on Gordon's liquor cabinet.

Acute alcohol poisoning. Yeah, that's the ticket. Too bad I'm the designated driver for the world.

"Maybe there's a reasonable explanation," I volunteered. At least that's how I had it worked out in my head; but the scenario was fragile so I didn't want to mess with it.

Gordon arched an eyebrow. "Bull — loney. I discovered one of those birth control ring thingies in her cosmetic case. I had a vasectomy."

"Maybe you should hire a private investi-gator."

Why not? Let him pick up the tab. Gordon had plenty of money and I didn't. We could get to the bottom of this on his dime.

"Already did. Couple of weeks ago. She gave him the slip. Now she's more cautious than ever." Pfeiffer's eyes thinned into slits. "Let me ask you something, Prescott." I caught myself wringing my hands and stuffed them under my thighs. "You like to shop, don't you?"

Magic word.

The question energized the air between us. My eyes grew wide. Let's see: I'm an unpaid intern. My daddy pretty much put me in a chokehold, money-wise. Do I like to shop? Does a porcupine have a prickly disposition?

"I love to shop."

"Great." He pushed back from the desk

and stood, dug into his back pocket and slid out a wallet. Thumbing through the currency flap, he pulled out two hundred dollars. "I want you to do me a favor."

Okay, I draw the line at blowing the boss, end of story.

He pitched the bills onto the blotter, returned the wallet to his pocket and leaned far enough across the desktop to grab a pad of yellow stickys and scrawl out a number.

"Here's my address. Tomorrow's Paislee's hair appointment at the Cut Off. You know the place? It's near TCU."

My head bobbed on its own accord.

"Fine. Paislee drives a metallic blue Jag with vanity plates — *INVU*."

"Why? You shouldn't. My whole life sucks."

The boss shook his head. "INVU. That's her personalized plate. And, no, Prescott, I don't envy you."

"You want me to take her the money? Buy her something? Flowers maybe? Want me to take them to the salon for you?"

He picked up the bills and handed them over. "I want to hire you. Consider this a retainer."

"A retainer? For what?" Then it hit me. I waved my hands in a *no* motion. "Earlier, when this cop pulled me over, I was thinking about walking into court and slapping the prosecutor. And you know . . . I don't think I should do either of these things."

"Paislee recognized the private detective I hired. Now she's skittish. I need somebody who can go undercover and pull surveillance. Follow her around and take pictures of her and —" he waggled his hand "— get this Romeo on film."

"Why me?"

"Because you don't look like a private detective."

"That's because I'm not one. I'm in college. I'm trying to learn the TV business so I can become an anchor someday."

Gordon didn't pull any punches. "Here's the thing, Prescott. I'm opening up an externship position in a couple of months and I only have enough money in the budget to hire one person. Now ask yourself: 'Do I want to give my boss the old *"Buck you, fuddy"* routine or do I want to beat those SMU interns out of that extern slot?' "

I folded the cash and stuck it in my handbag. "Got a camera I can use?"

"See Rochelle."

"But what about my job here at the station?"

"Prescott, until we get to the bottom of this crap, spying on my wife *is* your job."

CHAPTER FIVE

Like I said, I'm the designated driver for the world. But later that night, when I met Venice and Salem at the new sushi bar near our townhouse, I ordered a couple of piña coladas and had the waiter bring both of them to me at once. I wasn't interested in eating as much as I wanted to dull the repeating image of my boyfriend and my boss's wife that kept looping through my brain like a computer glitch.

After recounting the day to my recovering sorority sisters, Venice, a beautiful jasper-eyed brunette with billowy waves cascading down past her shoulders, said, "Maybe there's a logical explanation. Maybe the necklace was for you."

Salem, a fiery redhead with eyes so aquamarine and electric they practically leap out at you as she becomes more animated, said, "Sure there's a logical explanation. Drex is playing hide-the-salami with Dainty's boss's wife." She turned to me and took my hand, sandwiching it between hers to convey solidarity. "We should torture him."

Venice said, "There has to be a better way."

Salem sipped her margarita. "There is, but Dainty would get caught. Then she'd plea bargain and sell us out for a lighter sentence." She turned to me, glassy-eyed. "You should kill him."

"Not right away, though," I said with the petulance of a five-year-old. "I want to hurt him first."

"First we hurt him, then we kill him." Salem, totally on board, clinked glasses with me. "You should get a gun."

"I don't know the first thing about getting a gun."

"You should find out. Then you should get one."

I clinked my glass against theirs.

"If you kill him, he won't suffer. You should make him suffer," Venice said cheerfully, as if we were discussing a movie we'd enjoyed. She spun out several scenarios that included Superglue and a nail gun until it got so grisly I jabbed my fingers into my ears like a couple of rubber stoppers. "Don't be such a lightweight, Dainty —" she raised her finger to signal a passing waiter "—

another round for my friends."

Then Tandy Westlake, another recovering sorority sister, walked in.

Venice slid out of the booth and gave her a seal hug — not the full bear hug embrace where you slide into each other's arms and affect a suffocating bond, but rather, where you move into just enough of an embrace to be able to use your hands like flippers and complete a rapid back pat. On me, it looks stupid. When Venice does it, it's endearing.

Tandy slid onto the bench where Venice had been sitting and Venice scooted in behind her.

Our friend Tandy is the most amazing person. She has the brains of a physicist, the lean, toned body of a swimmer, curly strawberry blonde hair that hangs in ringlets and compelling brown eyes the shade of melted milk chocolate. We hadn't expected to see her on this particular night — her father had gotten engaged the previous weekend and Tandy and her sisters were invited to a party to honor them.

Now that Tandy had settled in, I noticed her red-rimmed eyes beneath the harsh glow of the knockoff Tiffany lamp overhanging the table. I washed down the bite of spicy fried tofu I'd been chewing and daubed at my mouth with the cloth napkin that I'd had resting in my lap.

Venice and I chimed, "What's wrong?"

Salem did a conspiratorial lean-in and cupped a hand to her mouth. "Whatever's wrong, we'll take care of it. Dainty's getting a gun and we're all going to learn how to use it. Is that cool, or what?"

I silenced her with a glare.

"Umm-umm —" Venice came up a couple of inches out of her seat, flapping her hands to achieve lift-off "— hot wax. Hat pin and jalapeño juice. I thought of some more ways. Picture this — his nuts in a salad shooter."

Salem scowled. "Give it a rest."

Tandy poured out her heart. Her father was getting married again to a woman who could've been a clone of her mother. The way Tandy had it figured, if he wanted someone who looked like her mother, why'd he have to go and divorce her? To make matters worse, her mother went out and snagged the first man who came along. None of the kids liked the new boyfriend. Three days after Tandy's father announced his impending wedding, her mother did the same.

This had all the earmarks of one-upmanship.

"Everyone can see he's bad for her." Tandy's mouth trembled. "But my mom's blind to his bad qualities. Mom got this big cash settlement in the divorce — my dad bought her out of the company so he could run it without interference and now we think her boyfriend's trying to scam her out of her life savings."

I exchanged awkward glances with Venice and Salem. We'd gotten the blow-by-blow account of Tandy's parents' divorce while it was happening and knew the property division had been hefty.

Venice said, "You don't know that, Tandy. He might be a perfectly nice guy."

While Tandy flagged down a waiter and ordered a drink, the rest of us exchanged eye-encrypted messages, *The heck you say.*

Truth was, none of us liked him. There was something about Alex Garrett that I found off-putting. He had a smooth way about him, what my grandmother would call silver tongued, and he looked like he'd stepped off a soap opera set — perfectly groomed and not a hair out of place. But he wore shirts made of shiny fabric *à la* Las Vegas glitz and I found that to be a big turn-off.

And there was something else about him that I couldn't quite put my finger on. The word "oily" popped into mind.

I mumbled, "I'm sorry," and heads bobbed all around.

Then Tandy dropped the bomb that ruined our evening.

"I have to be her maid of honor. Since my mom set her wedding the same day as my dad's, my sisters are in his and she made me be in hers."

We grimaced on cue.

"Yeah," she said mournfully, "well don't look so sad. Y'all are in the wedding, too."

A collective gasp from Salem and me filled our shared space.

"I'm not going to be in the wedding," I said emphatically. I looked around for a steak knife to impale myself on and found only iced teaspoons.

Tandy slid Venice a sideways glance. "You didn't tell them?" For the benefit of Salem and me, she said, "We're all in the wedding and Venice offered to make the bridesmaid dresses. It's my mother's gift to you for helping out and being good sports."

"It'll be fabulous," Venice chimed in.

Now that was a stretch. We'd be ahead of the game if it just turned out to be plain dreadful.

I pitched forward and buried my head in my arm. No way was I going to be in Mrs.

Westlake's wedding. No damned way.

Tuning out my friends, my mind relived the passionate kiss between Drex and Paislee. Had he ever kissed me that way? Tears scalded my eyeballs. For no good reason, an insidiously infectious song got stuck in my head like a brain itch. It came from another CD-mix that my sister presented me shortly after we lost our mother. Using Mom's collection of 45s, vinyl albums and CDs, Teensy compiled a maudlin selection of tunes for the ultimate pity party and titled it "Swollen Eyes and Snot Rags." Sinead O'Connor's painful tearjerker played over and over in my mind, a harsh reminder that nothing compared to Drex.

The more I tried to concentrate on the conversation swirling around me, the harder it became to shake that melody. Like an earworm you can't get out, that clear Irish warble stuck in my head. Eventually, I surrendered, altering the lyrics to fit my sad, sorry situation.

It's been eleven hours, forty-three minutes and fifteen . . . sixteen, seventeen, eighteen seconds since you took your love away . . .

A teardrop spilled onto the table.

I sniffled. Not only had I crossed over into the state of Despair, I'd run out of gas in

70

Wallow City and was about to be elected mayor.

Wait — what?

My ears pricked up like those of a guard dog.

Tandy had said something and I didn't quite catch it — something about paying a thousand dollars to anybody who'd check Alex out for her. That yanked me out of my stupor and back into the present. I didn't see what she'd ordered to drink but when I lifted my head, she set the shot glass down, wincing at the burn.

I could use a thousand dollars.

Salem said, "You should hire a private investigator with that money."

I could use a thousand dollars.

"My mother would plotz if she thought I went out and hired a private eye."

I could use a thousand dollars.

"It'd be better if I could get a cop to check him out but I don't know any. Or one of my friends."

"I could use a thousand dollars." I stuck out my hand, palm up. "Hire me."

Tandy's eyes got big. Tears cut a track down her carefully made-up face. "Would you really?" She dried her eyes with the back of her hand.

"Sure. I can do it. Daddy knows everybody. I'll get to the bottom of it for you." My hand was doing the rapid-open, rapid-close, *gimme, gimme* motion while my head was trying to talk sense into me.

Tandy pulled out her checkbook and wrote me a check for five hundred dollars.

"You said a thousand." Petulant.

"This is business, Dainty. Here's enough to get you started. Seed money. You'll need to pay for gasoline to follow him around. And maybe a little push money to get people talking."

By this I figured she meant push it into their hands and they'll sing like a canary. Tandy loved old private eye movies.

"A thousand plus expenses."

Hey, I've watched a few reruns of *The Rockford Files* myself.

"I'll give you the other five hundred when you've got the goods on him." She closed her checkbook and stuffed it back into her purse, then rummaged around and pulled out a traffic citation and a yellow Post-It with a license plate number on it. "You'll need these to start with."

The ticket was issued to Robert John Taylor.

"What's this?"

"I found it in his car. The Lexus he's driving is a rental car out of Florida, where he's from, so it's possible that the previous renter left it there. But Alex was pawing through the car the other night when I went outside to roll the trash bins to the curb — which, you ask me, should be his job now that he's moved into our house — and when I asked him what he was doing, he said he'd forgotten to pay a ticket and now he couldn't find it."

Speaking of tickets . . .

By the time we finished our meal, I'd recounted the sad sorry story about the traffic tickets from the red light cameras and topped off the evening by mentioning that I'd been arrested, then un-arrested, then returned to my car and unceremoniously dumped there.

Salem snapped her fingers to signal a lightbulb idea. She pounded the flat of her hands on the table for silence. "If you don't know how to get a gun, why don't you call Butt Man?"

"I'm not calling him Butt Man anymore," I said regally, halfway to pig drunk. "He was actually pretty nice to me toward the end, considering I acted like a spoiled brat." The idea sounded good, though. Then I talked myself out of it. "His best friend got killed by a DWI a couple of days ago. I don't want to pester him. He seemed really bummed out."

"He told you that?" Venice asked, interested.

Tandy, who'd drunk shots until her eyes were sparkling, looked flustered.

Venice has tons of connections, most of them important. If she knew anybody on the police department they were probably working in the administrative detail, not your average flatfoot on the beat. I should've figured she could help.

"Want me to find out about Butt Man?"

"Don't call him that. His name's Jim. Jim Bruckman."

"Fine. Want me to find out about Mr. Bruckman?"

A shiver ran up my spine. Part of me wanted to leave bad enough alone. After all, I still had to do battle with him in court. A different part wanted to find out how to get a gun so I could kill Drex for cheating on me. Or myself, for being cheated on. At this point it really didn't matter. Either way, one of us should die and I thought it should be Drex since I'm the aggrieved party.

I heaved a sigh. *Okay, I don't really want to kill him. I just want to shoot his tires.*

Before leaving the table, Venice culled me from the rest of the herd, pulling me from my seat and steering me out of earshot. She reached for my hand and gave it a sisterly squeeze.

"Don't worry, Dainty. These things happen. Maybe Drex is just the guy you're with before you're with the guy you're supposed to be with."

It took a second to soak in. I even found myself diagramming that sentence in my head for it to make sense.

By the time I finished the shrimp-avocado sushi I'd ordered, Venice rejoined the group.

"Well, that settles it." She snapped the clamshell down on her cell phone and slid into the booth across from Salem and me. "Don't have anything to do with him, Dainty. He's a loose cannon."

"What do you mean? What'd you find out?"

"I know this guy who knows this guy and he says your superhero's one scary dude. That friend he told you about who got killed by the drunk driver a few days ago? The dead guy's wife was your hero's girlfriend. The dead guy was his partner until a few years ago." Winded, she took a deep breath. "The girlfriend ran off and married the partner. My source says your hero and his friend nearly killed each other over her. You want my advice? Stay away from him." She punctuated the thought with a nod.

"He's probably over her," Salem said.

"I know you crave excitement," Venice snapped, "but Dainty doesn't need the hassle right now." She swiveled her head and locked me in her amber gaze. "Do you, Dainty?"

But I was thinking otherwise.

I needed excitement. And I needed to be in the company of someone who'd been through what I'd just been through.

Jilted.

CHAPTER SIX

Venice, Salem and I were pretty tipsy by the time we finished dinner. Tandy was goat drunk. Our Asian waiter brought four vinyl check presenters and started to pass them out. With a buzz on, I grabbed all four tabs in the grandiose gesture of a Texas high roller.

"It's on me." I whipped out my credit card and slapped it on top of the pile.

The waiter sauntered off with pep in his step. He returned, ashen-faced, addressing me in broken English. "There is phone call. Please come."

I did a little face scrunch. Other than the friends surrounding me, nobody knew I was here.

After hip-checking Salem out of the way, I followed as he led me behind a six-panel Oriental screen that shielded the dining room from the hallway leading to the restrooms.

My eyes darted around in search of the phone.

"Credit card, snip-snip." He formed scissors with his fingers and cut the air between us.

"What?" I stared in the dumbfounded manner of a car crash survivor.

"Card no good."

"Wait." It took a few beats to soak in. "You cut up my credit card?"

"No more magic plastic. Snip-snip. You pay cash. No more credit for you." He wagged his scissor-fingers in a no motion.

Back at the table, I slid into the booth embarrassed and horrified. "He turned my credit card into confetti."

The girls were good sports, sorting through the tabs to pay their own freight. As I dug in my handbag for a twenty, my friends paid with their own credit cards. Turned out I'm a cliché — a day late and a dollar short.

Salem must've noticed the despair in my face because she snatched my tab. "This one's on me."

Since none of us were in any shape to drive, Venice called her brother to pick us up. While my entourage waited in the parking lot, breathing in restaurant smells that were suspended in the crisp night air, some drunk in a dark car nearly plowed into our little group. It's like he didn't even see us. As we scrambled out of the way, his side mirror clipped Venice's handbag and strewed the contents across the parking lot. We spent the next ten minutes picking up the flotsam and jetsam.

None of us got the license plate number.

At Salem's invitation to stay over, Venice's brother deposited us in the circular driveway of Salem's parents' house. While my friends stayed up late to watch movies and play card games, I crashed in one of the guest bedrooms. For the first time in weeks, I slept so late it's a wonder I didn't wake up with bedsores.

The next morning, Mr. Quincy hurried us out to his Suburban and drove us over to the sushi place to pick up our cars. I took the freeway to my grandmother's, where I showered, changed clothes and did a quick turnaround back to Fort Worth.

I wasted no time cashing Tandy's five-hundred-dollar check at the bank's drive-through window.

I didn't have to be at the TV studio until early afternoon so I went back to Harkman Beemis and tried on my mermaid dress. Since Daddy had apparently cancelled my credit cards before he and Nerissa left on vacation, I charged it to his store account. The saleslady bagged it in plastic and I draped it over the passenger seat of my car with care. Then I drove to the Cut Off, parked in front of the boutique four doors down and waited for Paislee Pfeiffer's metallic blue Jaguar to round the corner. From my vantage point, sandwiched between two SUVs, I could watch traffic.

When the boss's wife didn't show up on time, I went inside and got a pedicure.

I was feeling elegant in my hot pink silk capris and matching Manolos so I decided to drive over to the A. D. Marshall Public Safety and Courts Building down on Throckmorton Street to set my red light ticket for court. Daddy's lawyer said if I ever got a speeding ticket I should set it for a jury trial. The thought of having a jury trial scares the heck out of me but Daddy's lawyer says if you ask for one and win, you're home free. And if you ask for a jury trial and lose, you can always appeal the case to county court. They're more backed up than a sewer when it comes to crap from the city — his words, not mine — and so the ticket will die a natural death.

Sounded good to me.

The building looked like the inventors of Lego had designed it, only without the interesting colors. It was a typical government-issue shade of boring, faced with black marble slabs that gave the front exterior an art deco look. Husks of people, downtrodden and depressed, filed in and out of the entrance.

I parked at a meter on a side street and walked the distance to the huge wooden doors. Entire families of Mexican nationals traveling in generational hoards loitered near the entrance, cluttering the vestibule as they waited for their male pack leaders to run the show. I had to stand in line at the security checkpoint, monitored by city marshals, while the illegal aliens in front of me deposited a diaper bag, purse, billfold, key ring and pocket change into a plastic bin. I could tell this particular marshal really liked his job and had reached the pinnacle of his career. He wore a perpetual smile that looked more like a grimace. And he kept it that way the whole time, bobbing his head, talking through gritted teeth in a ventrilo-quist's voice, muttering stuff like, "I know just what you can do with that green card you son-of-a-bitch . . ."

As the marshal sent the tub down a con-veyor belt to be scanned for weapons by an X-ray machine, the illegals ran their five little kids and an infant in a stroller through the security arch. The buzzer went off. A second marshal motioned them through the metal detector one at a time and the buzzer sounded again. I huffed out my irritation as he passed a wand over each of them, made the man remove his belt and go back through. Finally, it was my turn.

I set my purse into one of the plastic buckets. The contents popped up on the monitor as I prissed through the metal detector and set the buzzer off.

The disgruntled marshal said, "Go back through. Take off your jewelry."

I did, but still couldn't clear security.

Oh, for the love of God, now what?

"Take off your shoes and go back through."

"There's no way I'm walking on this filthy floor."

He plucked a pair of paper surgical booties from a box and thrust them at me.

Wait — did he just call me a high-maintenance blueblood?

I must've misheard. "Beg your pardon, were you talking to me?"

"Lotta crud," he said through a tight grin. He pointed to the granite tiles. "Blends right in."

I took off my hot pink Manolos one at a time, and slid each foot into the disposable footwear as my third tub rolled through the X-ray machine. This time I cleared the metal detector.

The marshal gave me a dismissive wave.

Okay, now I'm sure. He just called me Lady Astor.

Cupping a hand to my ear, I called him out on it. "Excuse me — did you just refer to me as Lady Astor?"

The teeth were still bared in a forced grin, but his eyes weren't smiling. "Faster." He enunciated each word. "Move faster, young lady. You're backing up the line."

Since I'd leaned against the machine for balance as I shucked my shoes, I wanted a wet disinfectant towelette to clean my hands. The last thing I needed was to pick up a disease in this germ-infested place.

"Got any germicide wipes?"

"Restroom's down the hall." His jaw flexed and he refused to look at me.

This time, I swear I heard him say, "Well, aren't you the little hothouse orchid?"

I exchanged the paper throwaways for my designer shoes, tossed the used booties into the trashcan and grabbed my stuff. My options consisted of heading for the public restroom to wash my hands or scrubbing up later in order to join the parade of people filing into a cordoned-off area that formed a three-deep rat maze. This wasn't just any line, either. It reminded me of the endless crush of miserable people waiting for toilet paper in Soviet Russia. Only these pathetic folks were waiting to straighten out their business with one of the clerks seated behind the glass protector of a long wooden counter that stretched half of the length of the room.

In the time it took to put my jewelry back on, five people cleared the security checkpoint and filed into the cordoned-off area.

As for my run-in with the marshal, well, two could play that game.

"Later, you crusty old burnout."

The marshal jerked his head in my direction. Glowering, he rocketed from his chair. "What was that?"

"Nice turnout." Flashing a smile, I motioned to the rows of people standing orderly within the stanchions and ropes.

Before anyone else edged me out, I made a beeline for the rat maze.

For no good reason, the system bogged down at the counter. Apparently the language barrier between one of the clerks and the Mexican she tried to assist had ground to a halt. Now they resorted to exchanges consisting of blank-faced stares and shoulder shrugs.

Oh, for the love of God, if you're going to sneak across the border, learn the effing language.

A group of men who filed in behind me started up a game of driver's license poker to pass the time. Without warning, we were enveloped in a deathlike stench of a loaded diaper. Between the stink of decay and cheap perfume wafting over from a couple of streetwalker types, the rat maze reeked badly enough to melt eyebrows. If I didn't know better, I'd have guessed one of the rodents had died and the others sent carnations.

I stood for what seemed like a good half hour studying the kind of people who end up in Municipal Court. They all looked like lowlifes except for *moi*, Dainty Prescott, and that made me stew. Why should I be inconvenienced when Butt Man's probably sitting at home in a recliner with his feet propped up, watching sports on a big screen TV, eating a cheeseburger and washing it down with a cold Coors?

I was about to run screaming from the building and head for the post office to mail in the citation when three clerks suddenly freed up and I was first in line. There must've been thirty people behind me.

The devil on my shoulder goaded me. I

said, "Hey, I'll sell my spot for a hundred bucks," but I didn't get any takers.

A middle-aged woman with a couple of chins motioned me over to the protective glass window. I showed her the citation, denied running the red light and explained that I wanted to set it for a jury trial.

"Court Two," she said through a sigh.

"You don't understand." I enunciated my words as if she'd failed every grade twice. Then I slid the ticket past the glass and tapped the edge with my fingernail. "I need a jury trial."

"Talk to the prosecutor." Her eyelids drooped at half-mast. She pointed me to the elevator and looked past my shoulder. "Next."

I raced to the elevator with the illegal aliens and their crying infant and screaming children gaining on me. Alone inside, I selected the second floor and began pushing the Close Door button like I was tapping out Morse code. Just as the doors closed off the last sliver of light from the foyer, a dark-skinned hand shot through the opening. With sheepish smiles, the foreigners joined me, pulling the piping screams of their children in behind them. For several seconds, I thought I'd pass out. This was the source of the dirty diaper. I rode the elevator to the second floor with one hand clamped over my nose in self-defense and a fingertip jammed in one ear.

It didn't take long to realize I'd boarded the slowest elevator in town. Images of me killing Bruckman grew more violent with each passing second. As soon as the door slid back I flung myself out and race-walked down the hall to put some distance between this family and me.

After finding the proper courtroom, I went inside, paused near the door and took stock of the room as the place filled up with a small but decidedly creepy group of people.

The air in the gallery had plenty of body. Between personal odors wafting through the room, combined with liberal applications of cheap perfume and aftershave, I held my breath and walked toward a balding man standing beside a table stacked with files. He wore a medium gray suit and had wire-rimmed glasses and looked as if he carried the weight of the world on his shoulders.

"May I help you?" He flicked me a knife-like look meant to cut me dead.

"Yes, hi." I stuck out my hand to shake but he ignored it. Well, no matter. He's probably germ-o-phobic. I pulled the ticket out of my purse and handed it to him. "My name's Dainty Prescott and I've been wrongfully accused. I demand a jury trial."

He scanned the citation, then cut his gaze back to me and gave me a slow but dedicated eye blink. "You what?"

"Demand a jury trial."

"Just a minute." He motioned me onto a wooden pew. As I walked toward the row where he wanted me to sit, I was wondering where he was going as he disappeared through a side door. A half hour went by before I rose from my seat, walked to the back of the courtroom and began to pace.

Without warning, he burst back into the courtroom with his eyes darting about and my ticket held aloft. With a quick hand wave, I caught his attention from the back of the courtroom and he beckoned me over. I had a feeling I was about to get shellacked.

"No jury trial." He returned the citation.

My mouth went slack. "You can't do that. My daddy's corporate lawyer says I have a right to have a trial by a jury of my peers."

"Ordinarily you do. You're just not having one this time."

This raised my hackles. "You can't deny me. It's my Constitutional right."

Paying no attention to my objections, he spoke slowly, enunciating each word in a loud voice as if he were talking to someone with a low IQ or to the hearing-impaired or to someone who spoke English as a second language — like the illegal aliens I rode up with on the elevator.

"It *would* be your Constitutional right *if* we had this ticket on file but we *don't*. So you may *go* now and *hey* — you have a *nice* day, now, you hear?"

Soaking up every word, now it was my turn to blink.

"Wait a minute," I said, fist on hip. "You're trying to get me to leave so I don't show up for court and they issue a warrant for my arrest."

He stuck out his hand and wiggled his fingers. "May I see your citation?"

I handed it over.

He tore it to bits, grabbed my hand and deposited the pieces into my palm. "Have a lovely day," he said but his expression said *Hit the road.*

I had the overwhelming urge to taunt him until the bailiff shot one of us.

Just as I was about to protest, the judge swept into the room in a black flowing robe and the bailiff called the room to order with a throaty, "All rise." Everyone gave me blank stares as I slunk out of the courtroom, wincing as the door creaked behind me.

There went an hour of my life that I'll never get back.

Dazzled and uncomprehending and needing to find a photocopy machine to document what the State's slasher did to my ticket, I rounded the corridor on my way back to the elevator.

A husky voice called out.

"Debutante."

The utterance came from behind and to my right.

I whipped around.

Butt Man gave me a bland smile. "The great philosopher Henley said just leave well enough alone." Then he gave me one of those *lost cause* headshakes. "So why didn't you?"

"I'm familiar with Henley's works and you're right, he did say just leave well enough alone. But he also said kick 'em when they're up, kick 'em when they're down."

He's thinking bubble-headed bleached blonde.

I tried to incinerate him with my death ray glare but my only superpower seemed to be on the fritz so he just got a villainous look for mocking me.

He'd propped himself against the wall with his forearms braced across his chest and a sexy, smoldering look on his face. I almost didn't recognize him out of uniform with Italian sun shades perched on top of his head, a polo-type shirt with the Fort Worth PD logo stitched over his heart where a pocket should've been, wearing straight-legged, boot-cut blue jeans so tight they seemed to be embedded in his skin. I did, however, recognize the lethal-looking semi-automatic holstered against his side . . . and those piercing irises of an unexpected shade of blue. Those, I'd recognize from clear across the street.

"So, what's your point?" I said with put-on sweetness. If he wanted a legal sideshow, saddle up. "Did you show up to make sure I'd be convicted? To — let's see — how'd the great philosopher Henley put it?" I touched my finger to my chin, as if meditating on the notion. "Cut me down to size?"

"Moi?" He pointed to himself, teasing me with his eyes.

"Just so you know, I came to set this for a jury trial." I opened my hand and stuck the ticket giblets under his nose.

"And did you?"

"No. Because the *persecutor* ripped it up. He said it doesn't exist. Now I need to find a photocopier and some tape so I can put it back together."

I started to walk away but he spun me

around and brought his hands down on my shoulders to still me. "Are you really this dumb or is this just an act?"

I blinked back tears. Is it fair that every time I'm around this arrogant jerk he humiliates me? My chin corrugated. With emotions flaring, I bit down hard to stabilize the quiver in my lip.

"The ticket doesn't exist because it's not in the system. I didn't file it."

I could feel my mouth opening and closing like a catfish. "I don't understand."

"Papers get lost. The wind blows things away." Cornflower blue eyes sparkled throughout the ho-hum explanation.

I blinked again. "What are you doing here?"

"After I dropped you off at your car yesterday, I called the prosecutor and told him to contact me if you showed up. He did."

"So — wait — I don't have to pay this?"

He grinned. "Pay what? It doesn't exist."

"Then I'm off the hook?" I asked, slow on the uptake.

"Reckon so."

"Sweet."

I can't tell you what physical reflex it was that made me toss the citation confetti into the air and watch it drift down around us like paper snowflakes. I only knew that every now and then the roulette wheel falls on my day.

"Buy you a cup of coffee?" he said easily.

"You're not here to testify on a case?"

He stared at the ceiling as if it was a cue card. "Well, there's this ditzy blonde who's racking up traffic camera tickets, and if she doesn't take care of them she probably won't be able to register her car or renew her driver's license . . ." His voice trailed. "Seriously. You need to handle that ASAP."

Big head bob.

"About that coffee . . ." He pressed me for an answer.

I followed his unmarked patrol car as he led me through the east side of town to a place I normally wouldn't be caught dead in. When we entered the café, he chose a corner booth and claimed the bench seat up against the wall in order to keep an eye on the door. The diner had little jukeboxes at the tables. The records in this one hadn't been changed since Charlie Pride recorded "In the Jailhouse." While we talked, Bruckman's attention strayed past my shoulders to the goings-on behind me, flickering to the door each time the little bell jingled overhead.

I took in our surroundings in a sweeping

glance: Formica tables from the fifties with aqua cotton tablecloths and starched napkins that had random scorch marks left from a hot iron; a mural of cattle, cowboys and the camp cook dishing out chow painted across one wall; frayed gray carpet and white acoustical tile ceilings. The family business had been an east side landmark for over thirty years, African-American owned and operated. All of the help, including the cooks, were black.

As Bruckman listened to stories about the battered townhouse, my horrible stepmother and the friends I cherish, his eyes worked their hypnotic effect on me, unlayering the protective shell to my tender soul.

A caramel-skinned waitress sauntered up. She flipped open an order pad, then pulled out a pen that she'd tucked behind one ear. "What'll you have, baby?"

I made up my mind. "I'd like a cup of hot chocolate with three marshmallows. Not the big ones. The little ones." By way of illustration, I used my thumb and forefinger to measure the proper size. "And make sure they're melted, so you might want to zap it in the microwave after you toss in the marshmallow minis. And if you could shave bittersweet chocolate on top, that'd be great — but only after you heat the marshmallows. Don't melt the chocolate shavings." Her eyebrow arched. "No, wait — never mind. Do you have whipped cream? I'd rather have whipped cream, but only if it's fresh. I don't want the stuff in a can. If it comes in a can, or if it's the fake stuff from a plastic tub, just put the marshmallows on top."

"I'll get a team of specialists on it right away." She pointed her pen at Butt Man.

He asked for black coffee.

"Wait, I'll have the same," I called out as she headed off toward the swinging saloon door to the kitchen. She turned. Dark brows slammed together. The scary frown deepened. I flashed a high-wattage smile. "Only make mine with extra cream. Real cream. Not the fake stuff. If you don't have real cream, just bring whole milk." She scribbled my order and wandered off to get it. She returned with our coffee and a stainless steel creamer.

A heavyset man with a gleaming shaved head and skin so dark it looked almost purple showed up at our table wearing a chef's jacket. He balanced two pieces of homemade blueberry pie in his catcher's mitt hands. Steam coiled out of the sides of each slice. A dollop of vanilla ice cream melted over the flaky crust. He set the dessert plates down in front of us, backed away a few steps and eyed me up.

"Who's your sidekick?" he said to the air between us.

"I'm not psychic. But people have often remarked that I'm intuitive." Okay, so I misheard. Heat crept into my cheeks.

Butt Man grinned. "John-Q, this is Dainty. Dainty —" he made a swashbuckling hand motion "— this is John-Q, proprietor and world-class homestyle cook and pie baker."

I offered my hand and he gave me a finger-crippling shake. The waitress breezed past, pausing long enough to splash coffee into our cups.

He turned his attention to Butt Man but thumbed at me. "Is this the crazy one?"

"Can't tell for sure. Just met her."

John-Q cut his eyes in my direction. " 'Cause the last one pulled a knife."

"He probably deserved it," I announced merrily.

"Let me know how you like the pie," he said, turning to amble off, "on account of I'm entering it in the church bake-off come Sunday afternoon. There's a two-hundred-dollar prize ridin' on it."

Butt Man waved him off and picked up his fork. He cut into the pie wedge, balanced the piece on his fork and lifted it halfway to his mouth. "So, have you talked to Poindexter?" When I shot him a wicked glare, he said, "Your buddy, Dex."

"Drex. Short for Drexel."

"Yeah. You back together with him?" Blueberries disappeared into his mouth.

"No." I toyed with my food, raking out the fruit with the tines. I don't eat crust. Too fattening and no flavor. Besides, who needs a butt built like a switch engine? But the filling . . . I barely restrained a sigh at the first scrumptious bite. "It's not the first time he's done this, just the first time I actually saw for myself."

As our waitress bustled by to give us a warm-up, Butt Man reached past a glass sugar container, pushed it aside and snatched a cheap napkin from the metal dispenser. He wiped his mouth. "Yeah, that's always a bitch."

"Sounds like it's happened to you," I ventured.

He lifted one shoulder in a noncommittal shrug. "So what do you like to do in your spare time?"

I'd hoped to draw him out about his dead partner's wife but he didn't take the bait.

"Who has spare time? That's why I got so mad when you pulled me over. I'm spread too thin as it is. That ticket was the straw that broke the pack mule's back."

"You're not too busy to go to the Cinderella ball," he challenged.

"The Rubanbleu ball."

"Right. Not too busy for that, are you?"

The reminder scalded me. A visual of Drex and Paislee rose up before me like an apparition. I gave an involuntary shiver and went back to digging out blueberries and forking them into my mouth.

When I glanced up from my plate he was staring.

"So how old are you?" I asked.

"Thirty."

I didn't realize I was bobbing my head until I'd been doing it a few seconds. "That's pretty old."

"Not if you're fifty." He winked.

Touché. "So do you date middle-aged women?"

"I date smart women. Doesn't matter how old they are." He raised his cup to me in a kind of toast.

My face cracked into a smile. "You think I'm smart?"

"I don't know," he replied innocently, "is this a date?"

Other than a subtle chin duck and that "Shy Di" expression of coyness made famous by the late Princess of Wales, he got no answer from me. The left side of my brain was analyzing whether he might have serious boyfriend potential. The right side still thought of him as Butt Man.

We finished our coffee and I waited outside by the Porsche, watching Bruckman through the plate-glass window as he stood in front of the cash register and talked to John-Q. The topic *du jour* seemed to include me because they kept casting sideways glances in my direction.

He squared our tab and sauntered out the door, then walked to the unmarked car and opened it with the keyless remote. "So . . . do I get your number?"

"I've got *your* number," I said, brimming with playfulness.

"I've got yours, too." He got the joke. "What I'd like is your phone number. You have mine. I wrote it on the back of my card. Never know when you'll need a cop to come . . ."

I held my breath.

". . . to your rescue."

I pulled out my wallet and removed his card, flipping it over to verify he'd really given me his phone number. I recognized the exchange. He'd not only given me the number to his cell phone but he'd written down his home phone as well.

"You thought I'd call you?"

He must've been hallucinating when he gave this to me.

Guess he wasn't Butt Man anymore. This posed a problem: if I ever got it in for him again, what would I call him?

Douche bag had a musical ring to it. I filed that away for future reference.

"So . . . want to catch a movie some time?" His eyes searched the sidewalk before drifting up to meet mine. I felt that invisible first-date punch in the gut that I hadn't experienced since junior high.

"Not really."

I wanted to thunk my head with the heel of my palm. I don't go to movies on first or second or even third dates. It's a waste of time. Why spend two hours sitting next to someone you don't know when you could be ferreting out important details such as: Why'd you and your last girlfriend break up? or Have you ever been arrested? or Are you familiar with Harkman Beemis?

I covered my tracks. "It's not that I don't like movies — I love them. I watch them all the time with my recovering sorority sisters." Then I told him about my little quirk.

"Smart lady." A gust of wind blew a tendril of hair across my face and he grasped it between his thumb and forefinger to brush it away. "What *do* you like to do on a first date?"

It'd been so long since I'd gone on one that I had to think. "I like dinner."

Boring.

"You want to go out to eat?"

I couldn't tell from the way he asked whether he was asking for clarification or if I was being invited out on a date. As we stood between our cars with him leaning against his and me propped against mine, I had the sudden urge to take his hand. It was warm and swallowed mine up and it felt good to the touch.

"You really want to know what I like?" I expected a nod and got it. "I like surprises. Surprise me."

CHAPTER SEVEN

If luck means winning the lotto, then I just hit the crackpot.

I dropped by the TV station and couldn't even get inside the building without being accosted by Chopper Deke in the parking lot.

"Unbelievable," I said when he asked me if I'd like to lick something big and hard. "You look just like the guy topping the sex offender list down at the police department. Do the cops know where to find you?"

I skirted him with the precision of a cutting horse.

"Aw, come on, don't be cruel." He whipped out a big candy sucker formed and flattened into a blue and yellow pinwheel design.

I scoffed at this attempt to dazzle me with his virility.

"How'd you like to go for a ride?" he called out behind me.

I gave him a backward glance meant to cut him dead. He thrust his hips at me in an obscene gyration. I shot back, "Sure thing — soon as I pick up a pair of tweezers."

"Oh, you'll be able to find it, no problem-o. I've got Viagra."

"I've got a Taser." I looked hard at him but he didn't get the message.

Inside WBFD, the morning guests had emptied out of the lobby. I found Rochelle at her desk — the clearinghouse for gossip — typing a letter. Gordon's voice leaked out of the ear buds to her tape recorder.

"Deke's creepy," I said.

She shut off the recorder and tugged out the ear buds. "He should treat me with more respect. Someday my tax dollars will be financing his prison term."

"No, I mean . . . *really* creepy."

Gray eyes coolly narrowed. "Did he hit on you?"

"Like a piñata."

Her face relaxed into a peaceful palette of pastel colors — gray eyes, heavily fringed with dark mascara, shadowed with the palest purple to match the Chanel suit she had on, signature mauve gloss over a darker plum lip liner and a hint of blush on the apples of her cheeks.

"I wouldn't worry about Deke," she said. "I just called the police and told them he threatened to kill the Mayor."

I sucked air. "You called in a false report? Aren't you afraid they'll file charges on you?"

She shook her head. "Not really. I used Paislee's name."

Sometimes I think Rochelle's twelve frames out of sync.

"Is Gordon in?"

Before she could answer, one of the SMU interns approached the desk with what Rochelle referred to uncharitably as "homework."

"So . . . like . . . is this what you wanted, Ms. LeDuc?" The intern, a busty girl with processed blonde hair and a haughty air, presented the document to Gordon's assistant. The only thing left for her to do was to vamp a pose and drill a finger into her dimple.

"Yes dear, and thank you. We're all challenged by your unique point of view." Rochelle flicked her wrist dismissively. To me, she said, "Gordon's on the telephone but he said to send you in."

The boss was sitting behind his desk looking like he'd been kidnapped by Al-Qaeda and was hoping for a good outcome. His eyes were rimmed red, his hair looked like he'd survived electrocution, and his skin appeared pasty under the harsh glow of the fluorescents. He motioned me onto the couch and cut the phone call short.

"What'd you get?"

"Nothing," I confessed. "She didn't show up to the Cut Off. When I went by your house, her car was gone."

He dug out his wallet, pulled out another two hundred dollars and tossed it across the desk. "Try again tomorrow. I head for work at five o'clock in the morning. If she's going to leave, you'll need to be there early so you can tail her."

I nodded and took the money. I still didn't want to tell him the man Paislee was fooling around with was Drex. After all, there could still be a reasonable explanation for what I saw . . . right?

CHAPTER EIGHT

Venice called on my mobile phone as I was leaving WBFD's parking lot. Salem's parents had invited us to spend the night again if we'd pick up dinner for five. I didn't want to tell her what I was up to so I told her about the telephone call I'd gotten from Gran earlier asking me to come home before she went to bed so we could talk.

That didn't sound good.

Then again, my birthday was coming up and Gran probably wanted to give me my gift.

In truth, I'd planned to spend the night in Dallas, pick up my mail and then head out early to pull surveillance at Gordon's house in the morning.

When I turned into my grandmother's Preston Hollow neighborhood, the big two-story red brick Georgian loomed in the distance. The house isn't just beautiful, it's architecturally and historically significant, with lots of fireplaces, high ceilings, beautiful plank floors, plenty of crown molding and staircases. It even has a mezzanine that overlooks the informal living room from three sides. The furnishings are mostly period pieces and the majority of the upholstered pieces are done in white silk damask. The idea of wallowing on a two-hundred-year-old camelback sofa with a provenance makes my stomach clench. This is a fabulous house but it's not a kid-friendly house.

The solenoids on the iron gate started clicking as I buzzed myself in. The gate yawned open like a big, hungry mouth, enabling me to travel the length of the brick driveway to the back of the house. There, I parked the sleek little sports car under the pavilion near the pool and let myself into the house through the sunroom.

The sunroom has a cheerful, airy feel with plenty of windowpanes and plants and lots of ambient light slanting in and bouncing off the terrazzo tile floor. On this particular afternoon, the sunshine made a latticework of light through the square glass panes.

Rattan furniture lends this area a kind of Hemingway-esque feel but because the cushions are upholstered in white linen, I moved on through to the breakfast room.

The breakfast room overlooks an outdoor

terrace on one side and from there one can see the pool. Gran had this room done in muted blues. There's a white wool Oriental rug on the floor beneath an American walnut gateleg table from the late 1700s, plain walnut chairs with seats upholstered in blue plaid and a Baccarat chandelier hanging from the ceiling. I kept walking.

I practically ran through the formal dining room to keep from touching anything. That one is all white with a mahogany Duncan Phyfe table with twelve Chippendale chairs — all "of the period" — which means only the Queen of England or heads of state can sit in this room on those chairs. I avoid this room like the plague.

I entered the formal living area, a fabulous room with a Baccarat chandelier dripping with prisms. When sunlight hits the crystals, tiny rainbows appear on the walls. This room has a curved staircase, black-and-white checkerboard floors made of marble, a huge red and blue Oriental hand-tied rug and a shiny black baby grand piano. I can play "Chopsticks" and "Heart and Soul" but that's about it.

The fireplace facing is gorgeous — all done in white — with Chinese vases on the mantle that are about a thousand years old, that camelback sofa Gran had reupholstered in white damask, and a library table abutting the sofa with an eighteenth-century chair pushed up against it. You can't sit in the chair — too valuable — because it's a Philadelphia hand-carved chair. If you read by either of the matched Staffordshire spaniel lamps, Gran hangs around like a hovercraft and frets until you leave the room. The spaniels are museum quality so if one of my friends broke one, I'd have to enter the witness protection program just to keep Gran from having me killed. If I broke it myself, I'd be expected to do the honorable thing and weight my ankles with cinder blocks before jumping into the deep end of the pool.

Real people can't live in this house.

Gran lives here because she's a blue hair, one of those cultured, refined Texas women who know exactly where multiple pieces of sterling silver should be placed at a state dinner. She's super clean and smells of a delicate mixture of freesia and face powder and I don't think I've ever seen her get dirty in my life except when she's fussing over the lush foliage of those persnickety tropical plants that have to be moved indoors every winter in order to keep them alive.

I came to the informal living area — the one with the mezzanine — and paused to take stock of the room. This is my favorite place in the whole house. Teensy and I used to play hide-and-seek upstairs because of the secret doors and fake walls. To me, it's the best room in the house with its wood walls painted aqua and lots of rich mahogany Queen Anne pieces upholstered in white, green and red floral print — emphasis on the white part. The fireplace is fabulous, faced with four-inch white tiles with little rosebuds fired onto each one. I love this room and find it uplifting. Too bad I'm not allowed to hang out in here.

I took the stairs up to Gran's room and that's where I found her, reading a book beneath the gauzy canopy of her four-poster bed. The walls to her bedroom are painted a bold shade of cranberry and she had on matching lipstick that made her pale, fragile skin appear even more like parchment paper. Although age has stooped her, Gran — the family crepe hanger, dream crusher, and mood killer — can be a formidable opponent. Dozens of wrinkles fishnetted her face. Blue eyes glittered as she folded the dust jacket over the page to mark her place. Her whole body seemed to sigh as I walked into the room.

"Have a seat, dear," she said in that high-pitched, warbling old lady voice.

She closed her book and motioned me into one of the overstuffed moss green chairs positioned next to a white fireplace with smooth wooden boards and lots of dental molding. When I was little and the gas logs were turned on, I liked to pretend I was a princess, inches from the yawning mouth of a big-toothed, fire-breathing dragon.

"How are you, Gran?"

Dracula style, she trapped a cough in her sleeve. Looking anxious and vaguely resentful, she ignored me the way she does when she has an agenda to run.

"Dainty, are you familiar with the story of Deng Xiaoping?" She pronounced it "Dung Chow Ping."

A headshake.

"He was to be the successor of Mao Tse Tung, the leader of the Chinese Communist Party from 1935 to 1976."

I gave a polite nod.

"Deng Xiaoping had a number of detractors, and of course, subversives who wanted to destroy him. In fact, Chairman Mao purged him in 1966 for his strong objections to the excesses of the 'Great Leap Forward'."

Lost me there.

I had no idea what she was talking about.

111

She must've read the confusion in my face because she said, "He kept getting sent to the re-education camps when the Chinese felt he was being a diversionist."

"Is that a euphemism for prison?"

"Pay attention, Dainty." She took in a deep breath.

I checked my watch and inwardly congratulated myself for making it an entire two minutes before pissing her off.

"In fact, it wasn't until after Chairman Mao's death that Deng Xiaoping became the *de facto* leader of China until his own death in 1997."

My eyes flickered to the moss green ottoman positioned between the fireside chairs that Gran used as a coffee table, topped with large books of Gran's favorite painters. I read the spines, expecting to see a book about Oriental artifacts so I could understand why she felt the compulsion to regale me with the history of some Chinaman I'd never heard of and couldn't care less about, but no such luck. I started to say something innocuous but wasn't all that certain I even wanted to participate in the conversation.

"Deng Xiaoping had a little boy, Deng Pufang, who was crippled in an attack during the Cultural Revolution. Chairman Mao's Red Guard — a cruel and torturous lot — burst in and dropped poor little Deng Pufang out a three-story window."

I held my breath, wondering where this was all headed. Had Gran acquired some of Deng Xiaoping's treasures and added them to her collection of Famille Rose vases?

Did she need help getting out of bed?

"The boy survived but his back was broken and he became a paraplegic. Deng Xiaoping had to carry that crippled boy around on his back even though Deng Pufang was nothing but dead weight, dragging him down with every step, wearing him out physically and mentally because of the extra care he required."

"Seems like he could've gotten him a wheelchair."

Glittery blue eyes thinned into slits. "Deng Pufang became a grave burden to his father, Deng Xiaoping." She let out a wistful sigh. "Imagine that poor old man having to carry that kid everywhere even though the father wasn't in good health himself. Would bathe him, feed him . . . tend to him to make sure his invalid son didn't lack for a thing . . ."

I sensed we'd come to the part where I was supposed to comment. I kept my trap shut. When Gran starts one of these stories, it bears all the hallmarks of sticking your finger into one of those Chinese finger traps

— the harder you try to get out of it, the tighter it constricts your finger.

"Well, of course, Deng Xiaoping didn't want to put his son down — this poor, pitiful cripple who was only alive because the father did practically everything for him long after they both grew into old age . . ."

Lacking patience, I looked at her slitty-eyed. "Seems to me Deng Xiaoping was just being a good daddy."

The half-smile slipped away. She withered me with a look. A conspicuous silence grew between us. The harder I tried to avoid making eye contact, the more I could feel the weight of her judgment boring a hole in me.

"What?" I demanded, unexpectedly broken by her unnerving stare.

She held me in her sapphire gaze. Crimson lips thinned.

"What's your point?" I said with a huff.

"Your father doesn't intend to be Deng Xiaoping."

I stared through the hurtling confusion and wondered if she was senile.

"Accounts receivable at Harkman Beemis called. They want their dress back. Your father cut you off."

Chapter Nine

I swear when Daddy said, "I do," he checked his nuts at the door.

The credit card slasher suddenly made sense. I fell against the chair back, pole axed, staring at my grandmother's sharp facial features, blue coiffed hair, and a glare that could slice cold butter.

"Are you kidding me?" I shrieked, glancing around for something to impale myself on. "This is Nerissa's fault."

"No, Dainty, dear. It's your fault. And don't slouch. It'll make you hunchbacked." Gran gave me another one of those eternal Sphinx-like smiles. Actually it was less of a smile and more of a baring of teeth. "You need to take responsibility."

"You're taking up for her?" I sat up rigid. "You can't take her side over mine — I'm family." The tears I wanted to cry spilled over onto my cheeks.

"Watch the upholstery, dear. That's silk,

you know. It'll water spot."

My voice went ultrasonic. I half-expected neighborhood dogs to tune up howling. "How can you do that, Gran — take her side against family? Aren't you always the one who says family means everything?" I thumbed at the lapels on my pink silk jacket. My chest hitched. "I'm your flesh and blood . . . and . . . you're . . . taking . . . her . . . side?" My shoulders wracked with sobs.

"Really, Dainty, don't ruin the upholstery," she repeated with a trace of danger in her voice.

This was like walking into a bank heist and, instead of being told to get on the floor, you were instructed to find a chair where every seat was occupied — like a sadistic game of musical chairs — last one standing takes a bullet to the brain. "Where do you want me to sit then?"

She gave a little shoulder shrug and lifted a gnarled finger. "You could go into the bathroom."

I rocketed from the cushion. "You don't understand. I absolutely have to have a dress to wear to Rubanbleu. If I take back the mermaid gown, I'll have nothing to wear."

"Oh, piffle. Wear what you wore last year."

Some people believe it's okay to wear clothing you've been seen in before. These are obvious lies spread by communists and terrorists.

"Are you kidding me?" Her expression telegraphed she wasn't. "Please, Gran —" I moved to the bed with my arms out-stretched and pleading "— you could buy it for me for my birthday."

"I already bought your gift."

I clasped my hands together in prayer. "Take it back. Let me keep the dress."

Without so much as a dismissive wave, she opened her book and traced a finger midway down the page until she found her place. "Go wash up for dinner, Dainty."

"I'm not hungry."

"Very well. Close the door on your way out."

The room I stay in when I visit Gran is actually attic space that's been transformed into a bedroom. It's furnished with all the boxed-up Madame Alexander dolls that I wasn't allowed to play with as a child as well as cast-off antiques that make their way up here when the antique dealers Gran patronizes find suitable upgrades to replace pieces downstairs. It's better than sleeping in the basement because that's actually a billiard room-slash-pub and back when I was in junior high, nobody trusted me and my rowdy friends anywhere around the liquor cabinet without adult supervision. Which is stupid, in retrospect, because I never became a big drinker despite the allure of the forbidden wine collection. Had I ever opened a bottle of the good stuff, I'm certain I would've been marched out to the diving board at the point of a decorative Samurai sword and summarily run through over the pool for easy cleanup.

Since this is my room, I painted the walls in the same restful aqua as the informal living room. If there's anything white in here, it doesn't stay that way for long. There are a couple of fireside chairs next to a *trompe l'oeil* fireplace that Venice painted on one wall one summer after we went off to college. It's amazingly realistic and when the moonlight slants in through the little windowpanes at night, I like to pretend I'm a beer wench in the overlord's manor, waiting for my prince to ride up on a silver stallion and rescue me from a life of indentured servitude. Sort of a "Rapunzel" meets "Braveheart" meets Heineken. And if the place catches fire, I'm to flee through the trap door to the widow's walk and wait for the fire department to arrive with a safety net. God help me if I couldn't get out and

118

had to break out one of three windows.

I swear Gran's instructions to the household help would be to dust the furniture while flames licked the walls.

I brought the mermaid dress up from one of the second-floor guest bedrooms and hung it over the doorframe so I could lust after it while I called Venice and poured out my misery. Flopped on the bed, a Jenny Lind frame with a lumpy twin mattress dressed with Waterford linens, I pounded her number into the keypad with my finger. My promise to remain stoic tanked as soon as I heard her voice. I couldn't even finish recounting the worst part of my day before my composure disintegrated into a crying jag.

"I know you're upset. I'm not trying to minimize your misfortune but this isn't the end of the world, Dainty."

"What am I going to do?"

"Let's be rational. You could buy off the rack . . ."

I sucked air. As far as I know, I've never in my life worn a formal gown that came off the rack. Off-the-rack means a flame-retardant party dress with a traditional butt bow and a silk flower securing the cleavage or a sleazy gown that showcases every body flaw.

"Or you could see if Harkman's will let you open your own line of credit."

Great idea if I had a paying job.

"Or you could put it on layaway. Wait —" she paused to consider this "— they do have a layaway plan, don't they? I wouldn't know. I've never bought anything that way."

"Even if I could find a job, I'd never be able to pay for the dress in time for the ball." My upwardly corkscrewing cry filled the small space until misery reverberated off the walls.

"Listen up, Dainty — three words guaranteed to change your life — lower your standards."

Wracked with sobs, I had to put the phone down. There's no bathroom in the attic so I padded down to the second floor for tissue. When I returned Venice was still at the other end of the line, her voice vibrating with excitement. Lying flat on my back, cocooned in covers like a human pocket protector, I propped the cell phone up to my ear and listened.

"I just thought of the answer to your problem, Dainty, and you're going to love the idea."

"What?" I said dully.

"What if I came over and inventoried all of your old ball gowns, prom dresses and anything else you have where we might reclaim the fabric?"

"Huh?"

"What if I took your cast-off formals and made you a new dress?"

"Made me a dress? Like handmade? With a needle and thread? You?"

"Look, Dainty, it's not all that bizarre. I'm a fashion minor. You said yourself you like my designs. I could make you a dress and we wouldn't even need to buy the fabric for it."

I only told Venice I thought her sketches were dazzling because I'm her friend and I didn't want to hurt her feelings. In truth, her ideas were too bizarre for my tastes.

"What if it turns out to be ugly?" I sniffled.

"It won't."

"I dunno . . ."

"But you'd actually be doing me a favor, Dainty. Don't you want to help me?"

"I don't see how this could help you."

She concocted a scenario built around me showing up at the ball in the most ravishing dress, and all of the rich ladies there com-missioning her to make designer clothes for them under her own label. I've actually seen some of Venice's class projects and they're stunning. But I had an idea she was using reverse psychology to get me to come

121

around to her way of thinking. Desperation made me rethink my options.

One, I could let her do the dress and wear it to the debutante ball.

Two, I could let her do the dress and if it turned out horrible, wear last year's dress to the ball, which wasn't going to happen because I'm not about to be seen in last year's gown. I'm not kidding.

Three, I could let her do the dress and if it turned out horrible, I could sit home.

"Okay, fine. You can have my old dresses. Or wait — maybe I should sell my dresses. Then I'd have money to put it in layaway, like you said."

"You still wouldn't have enough to get it out before the ball," she reminded me.

And there it was, the acknowledgment that I'm poor.

Then she suggested I call Timmy Armbruster to see if he'd be my escort to the debutante ball. Last time I saw Timmy he was setting fire to his house.

"What about Sterling Rockwell?"

I drew in a sharp intake of air. "What's wrong with you? He made a foil hat so the extra-terrestrials could find him when the spaceship landed. He claimed the CIA embedded a computer chip in one of his testicles so it'd be easier to track him."

"Now, Dainty . . . we discussed that way back when it happened and we agreed it was a medication issue."

I looked up at the little diode on the security system burning red.

The lights in my room were switched off. I lay enveloped in the gloom with pillows propping me up in my lumpy bed, waiting for one of the Madame Alexander dolls to turn into "Bride of Chucky." Eventually, I resorted to dialing the phone numbers of guys I'd been matched with at past sorority functions to see if any of them wanted to escort me to The Rubanbleu. When I came up empty, I tried calling boys I'd gone to prep school with. Then I phoned guys I barely knew from summer camp back in junior high.

I came across Arnie Dundovic's name and wondered how he'd turned out. Arnie was a neighbor boy who lived down the street from my parents, a geeky guy everybody thought would end up being a mad scientist or working at NASA. He was always blowing things up in chemistry lab so my parents always kept the garden hose at the ready.

Last time I saw Arnie he was on TV.

It was breaking news about a hostage situation. Film footage of him trading bullets with the Dallas police as SWAT officers fired tear gas cartridges into his apartment eventually ended with Arnie being hauled out wearing nothing but his Fruit of the Looms and a pair of handcuffs. I think his girlfriend had broken up with him. Or maybe it was his boyfriend.

Scratch Arnie. Too needy.

By the time I'd exhausted all the names in my address book, the list of men I'd called to take me to the ball was starting to look like the voter registration rolls for the state of Rhode Island.

I hung up the telephone, set the alarm clock for three in the morning and decided to put the day out of its misery. Crushing the pillow against my head, I drifted off with one prevailing thought. What I needed was money. Lots of it.

CHAPTER TEN

> Goals for the day:
>
> 1. Spy on Mr. Pfeiffer's wife
> 2. Drop off film at 1-hour photo
> 3. Figure out way to make extra money

When I arrived at WBFD at four o'clock the next morning dressed in the camouflage fatigues I'd bought to wear to Salem's annual Halloween party, still a few weeks away, Gordon had already arranged for me to trade cars with Aspen Wicklow, one of the anchors. You'd have thought he'd asked her to donate a cornea. But once he explained that she could drive my ferocious little supercar in exchange for her ten-year-old Honda Accord, she agreed.

Aspen can be so naive. It didn't even occur to her to ask why we were switching vehicles. I know she didn't go along with this out of the goodness of her heart. The people at WBFD aren't the kind of employees who flit around brimming with goodwill or helping others out. This is one of the most cutthroat places I've ever seen, with the on-air talent being so competitive and all. Gordon asked if I wanted to use a Hummer belonging to Tig Welder, one of the investigative reporters, but that seemed like overkill. Even I know that in order to successfully pull off surveillance, you need to be discreet and low key.

So there I was, parked a half block down from the Pfeiffer's house an hour later, sitting behind the wheel of the Accord with the motor running like the getaway driver in a bank heist. With a long lens camera on the front seat and a digital camera as a backup, I watched Gordon's car bounce out of the driveway and waited for Paislee to leave in her own car if that was her plan.

Around five-thirty, while I had the key notched at the Accessory option and was listening to random songs playing on the no-commercial radio station and reading the *Cosmo* quiz under the dome light on how to make my boyfriend scream in bed, a car rounded the corner at the far end of the block. Headlight beacons made a broad sweep over the road. I quickly extinguished the dome light, grabbed my binoculars and sharpened the focus.

Anybody can drive a black BMW, right? Only the tags were vanity plates that spelled out GLTYSN. I watched in horror as my guilty-as-sin boyfriend slowed to a crawl. Flopping over into the passenger compartment, I pulled *The Dallas Morning News* off the floorboard and covered myself with it like a homeless person. Close by, he killed the engine. In my advanced state of panic, my ears pricked up. Every noise, clear down to a cricket chirp, became as enhanced as if it were occurring in the front seat next to me.

Drex's door clicked audibly and then softly snapped shut. My heart raced as I wondered whether he'd cross the street and see a body proned out in the front seat with a newspaper over it and call the police.

I counted, one-one thousand, two-one thousand, all the way up to ten before rising from the seat like a Phoenix. With his back to me, I could barely make out the looming silhouette all dressed in black and headed for my boss's house.

He disappeared through a wooden privacy gate.

About ten seconds later, a light came on upstairs. A minute went by and the light went out again.

My heart sank. My lower lip reflexively curled into a pout.

It wasn't a mistake.

He really did ditch me for an older woman.

For the next few minutes, I sat, paralyzed, an emotional cripple with my feelings mortally wounded, and my body as inert as a gas as I listened to blood whooshing between my ears.

As I waited inside the borrowed Accord half expecting to stroke out, I rolled down the window and snapped a few photos of GLTYSN's car.

My work here is done, I thought —

— or is it?

While the angel on my shoulder told me to pack it in, the devil on my other shoulder goaded me. The angel part of my conscience warned that I'd done what I'd been paid to do. But the devil part replayed Gordon's voice in my ear.

"There's an extra five hundred in it if you can catch them doing something."

At the same time, I heard Gran's voice telling me the sales lady from Harkman Beemis called to say their accounts receivable department phoned with bad news. Apparently Daddy had flagged his account before he and Nerissa left for Europe and I could no longer charge anything on his dime. Meaning I had to return the cherry red mermaid gown with the fishtail train or face possible criminal charges. Or worse — banishment from the Round Table, forever unable to shop at the most exclusive store in the Metroplex.

A harsh choice but look on the bright side . . .

Now that I'm hearing multiple voices in my head, I suppose that makes me schizophrenic. At least that's what I plan to tell the county psychiatrists when they evaluate me if I'm arrested for criminal trespass. Maybe I'll get off with an insanity plea. It's a cinch Gordon already warned me if I'm caught, he'll disavow any knowledge of me. Kind of like *Mission Impossible,* only without the sweet cars and the latest spyware.

The shoulder devil was speaking again and this time I listened.

A real detective would get closer.

Maybe catch Drex coming out of the house zipping up his fly.

I imagined him breaking it off with Paislee, telling her he was in love with me and that he was going to escort me to The Rubanbleu ball after all. Then I imagined she'd take the news badly and I'd get a shot of him leaving her house dripping blood and carrying his penis in his hand.

Well, hey — don't act so surprised. I told you I'm a seventh-generation Texan.

Doing things bigger and better extends to the gory and grisly. Like the Gulf Coast doctor who caught her philandering husband having an affair with a Jezebel home wrecker and ran him down in the hotel parking lot multiple times. She even parked her Mercedes on top of him. Venice and Salem and I talked about it at the time and we all agreed we'd acquit her if her attorneys got a change of venue and moved her jury trial to Fort Worth and we got picked to serve as jurors.

The only thing I would've done differently would've been to swallow the key to make it harder to get the sleek German-engineered car off him.

Shaking off the reverie, I returned my attention to the job I'd come here to finish.

I needed to get that million-dollar shot like the paparazzi who photographed a member of the Royal Family frolicking bare-breasted on the beach with a financial advisor. I know him, by the way. We're distant cousins five times removed.

Only I'm not paparazzi.

I'm no detective, either, just a heartsick debutante with no money, no real job and no date to the Cinderella ball.

And today's my birthday.

Blinking back the tears I wanted to cry, I refolded the newspaper and stuffed it into its plastic sleeve, deciding to tote it along with me in the event Paislee Pfeiffer or one of the neighbors came out the front door before I could sneak through the back gate. I'd toss the morning edition onto the sidewalk as if this was my paper route and my boss was getting a complimentary copy. If discovered, I'd make a quick U-turn and scamper back to the car.

As I alighted the Honda, the temporary blindness that resulted when the dome light came on quickly abated. After a few seconds, my eyes adjusted to the dark. I skulked down the sidewalk toward the Pfeiffer's backyard. When I arrived at the gate, still undiscovered, I punched in the key code Gordon had given me and let myself inside.

Wow.

Sweet digs.

Since Paislee and Gordon didn't have children, I assumed the treehouse and swing set had conveyed with the property sale. According to Gordon, they hadn't lived in their two-story sandstone French château long, and I assumed they hadn't gotten around to dismantling the kid stuff and donating it to their charity of choice.

Nice pool, though.

I imagined Gordon routinely barbecuing meat on his state-of-the-art grill in the backyard and wondered if any of the regular employees like Rochelle or the on-air talent ever got invited over to spend lazy Sunday afternoons at backyard cookouts.

I tiptoed around the pool, to the back of the property where the privacy fence blocked the alley from view.

Stupid Dainty, stupid Dainty.

If I'd been smart, I would've gotten on the computer and done a street view search of the area. The alley would've been a great place to park the Honda, get out and climb onto the hood and photograph Drex coming out the back door, sated.

Since I was already trespassing and since I was pretty sure Gordon would disavow any knowledge of me if I got caught on the property, red-handed, I opted to climb the ladder to the treehouse. The treehouse would provide an excellent vantage to the upstairs bedroom since there weren't any curtains on the windows. From that altitude, I might just be able to get a good photo op to document the goings-on in my boss's bedroom.

The words *Don't try this at home* ricocheted off the nonstick lining of my brain like the disclaimers that precede those TV programs featuring home videos.

I'd almost made it to the top of the ladder and was breathing a sigh of relief when the last rung snapped under the weight of my camera gear and me. An involuntary yip popped out before I could stifle it. With the camera slung over my back, I clung to the side of the opening, kicking wildly until my foot touched an unbroken rung below my hovering point. I shrugged out from the camera strap and hoisted it into the tree-house.

I froze in place as Drex appeared, buck-naked, in the window, and peered out to make sense of the commotion. Willing myself into invisibility, I tried to blend in with the tree. He turned halfway — enough for me to see his flagpole at half-staff — and I pulled myself up the rest of the way. I crouched, perfectly still and unblinking, as if by doing so, the human shape framed in the glass could be voided.

Then Paislee joined him at the window, also nude. I raised the huge lens to the tree-house window opening and rested it against the wall support. I would've been happy enough just photographing the two of them together *sans vêtements* but I captured the full Monty and then some.

For no good reason other than lust and animal instinct, Paislee bent over. Her augmented boobs hung down like a couple of feedbags.

I felt myself slipping into shock as I watched Drex's, *ahem,* "Beemer" collide with Paislee's "Jag."

Blood sloshed between my ears.

An eerie sense of calm overtook me. I watched this rear-ender in stricken silence. They might've come up with a good reason for being naked in Paislee's bedroom — perhaps the A/C went out and the windows were painted shut; or they were taking an art class together and were painting nude self-portraits on canvas; or Paislee was having trouble ramming a suppository up her ass and Drex offered to drop by and help. Suffice it to say no amount of lame excuses could explain away this lurid debacle.

I rued the day that I took Drex to the company picnic.

By remaining stoic and professional, I got the goods on them. A half hour later, dawn broke and I snapped a great picture of Drex tucking his shirt into his jeans as he exited the back door.

I wanted to kill him.

Actually, what I really wanted was to take a close-up of his withered pecker and start a revenge website where jilted lovers could forewarn others by posting it on the Internet. And I wanted to collect my five hundred dollars from the boss.

About a half hour after Drex left, I tracked Paislee's movements through binoculars. There's something slightly off kilter about watching the woman who just naffed your almost-fiancé open the nightstand drawer, remove the battery-operated boyfriend, and use it on herself. I told myself several times to skip this part and stop being such a voyeur but this woman had stolen the man I thought I'd be spending the rest of my life with. If he thought she was better than me, I owed it to myself to find out, first-hand, how she got that way.

When she finally finished relieving her tension — or maybe the D-cells went dead — she shrugged into a robe and disappeared from view. Angry and fidgety and bothered by carpenter ants crawling over me, I took a calculated risk and decided to climb down the ladder.

Before I could get on all fours and shove my hindquarters out the opening *à la* Winnie the Pooh, the back door flung open. My breath caught. A huge black Beauceron with tan jaws the size of construction scoops strutted out of the house.

Paislee followed him. She set a huge bowl down onto a wooden deck that extended past the porch overhang and ducked back inside. The screen door sucked shut behind her and the bug light went off.

Good news. If the dog filled up on chow he probably wouldn't eat me.

Maim me, yes. Devour, no.

I had no idea how to escape this death trap. Why Gordon didn't warn me about a guard dog on the premises, I'll never know. Maybe he figured if the gigantic beast ate me alive, he wouldn't have to pay me the five hundred bucks he owed me.

A few minutes before seven o'clock, a brilliant pulsing sunrise topped the trees. The garage door groaned open and, within the minute, Paislee fired up the Jag's engine, backed out onto the street and roared off.

The dog lay down with his jaws between his front paws. His lids grew heavy. He appeared to be napping.

I fished out my mobile and dialed the TV station.

Rochelle answered with a chipper, "WBFD, may I help you?" and promptly disconnected me.

I'd seen her do this a hundred times mostly when the pace picked up and all the lines were glowing yellow. She'd answer with put-on sweetness, then disconnect the caller and put the same line on hold. When I quizzed her about this sketchy practice she said it was the only way she could get any work done.

I tried phoning again. This time when she answered, I hissed, "For the love of God, don't hang up."

She disconnected me anyway.

The third time I tried to call in, I muffled her name as soon as she picked up. "Rochelle, help. It's me — Dainty."

"Dainty who?"

"Rochelle, please." I drawled out the word until it sounded like a squeaky door. "It's Dainty Prescott. You know me. I'm the TCU intern. For the love of God don't hang up on me. I'm in trouble."

"I see," she answered in a bored monotone. "Haven't you heard of the pill?"

"Not that kind of trouble. I'm in real trouble."

"Lawsuit trouble? Because Gordon doesn't like lawsuits."

"Let me talk to him. It's an emergency."

"I'm sorry." She used her lilting public

relations voice. "But Mr. Pfeiffer isn't available to take your call at the moment. May I give him a message?"

"No message. I have to speak to him personally. Give me the number to his cell phone."

"I'm sorry, who'd you say this is?"

"Don't fuck with me," I snarled beyond the point of good manners.

My voice must've gotten loud because the dog's eyes snapped open like roller shades. For no good reason I thought of the scene in *Omen III: The Final Conflict* when Damien Thorn, the Antichrist, awakens on the floor after a night of sex and debauchery.

"I beg your pardon," Rochelle said, unassailably indifferent.

"I'm in trouble. If I live through this and you don't help me, I'll personally chop off your head and stick it on a post as a warning to others."

Dead silence.

I lingered over my mistake expecting her to go all *Mommie Dearest* on me.

Dead silence.

"Rochelle? Rochelle? I didn't mean it."

"Of course you didn't mean it, dear. If you did, I'd have to kill you. Now what seems to be the problem — and make it good, I don't have all day."

I was crying now, blubbering to a fare-Thee-well. As the sobs got louder in inverse proportion to my tanking confidence, the Beauceron came up off the deck. Huge paws hit the ground running. As he skidded to a stop at the foot of the ladder, dust shimmered up and landed on his back. A low rumble vibrated in his throat. He demonstrated a vertical leap.

With eyes closed, I took in the sensations of what might be my last moments alive: the fresh cut grass of the adjacent lawn, the scent of chlorine coming from the pool, the rustle of leaves on the breeze.

"Please give me Gordon's cell phone number."

"Sorry, kid, no can do. Is there anything else I can help you with?"

"I need that phone number." My eyes popped open.

"Yeah. Like I said . . ."

"Fine — take down my number and you call him. Tell him to call me back right away. Say it's an emergency."

"Is there blood?"

"What? No . . ."

"Don't call back unless there's blood."

She disconnected me. I redialed and got a busy signal.

The thought of spending the day in Gordon's treehouse got the better of me. I decided to climb down and make friends with the dog, but before doing so, I redialed Rochelle. From that contact I learned the dog's name.

Czar.

Instead of cutting me off, she proceeded to grill me. "Why do you want to know?"

I pulled the phone from my ear and stared in disbelief. It's not like I was asking for the PIN number to the boss's bank account. I struggled to keep my voice calm.

"I'm doing a paper on dogs — dog names. Yeah, that's it. I'm doing a paper on dog names."

"I have a cat named Attila at my house. Attila The Hun. 'The' is his middle name. He's in charge of Homeland Security."

Lovely. Now she wanted to chat . . . when I had a dog in charge of Border Patrol trying to seize a chunk of my ass.

"Did Gordon ever come back?"

"I don't see him."

"Could you ring his office for me?"

"He's busy."

"How would you know if he isn't there?"

"I didn't say he wasn't here. I said I didn't see him."

I wanted to instruct her to swivel her chair around and look into his damned office since her desk was less than thirty feet away and Gordon's office had glass walls. But before I could say anything else, she told me to have a nice day and left me pleading with thin air.

From my place in the treehouse, I poked my head through the window frame and spoke to the dog.

"Here, Czar. Hello, puppy. Good boy. Doggie wants a treat?" I dug into my pocket and produced a stick of gum.

Without unwrapping it, I tossed it over the side and watched him pounce. It disappeared, foil wrapper and all. With Czar standing guard near the foot of the treehouse, I began my descent.

"Good, doggie. Yeah, you're just a big ol' scary puppy, aren't you? Where's your slut of a mommy? I'll tell you where she is — waxing my boyfriend's carrot." I delivered this information, singsong, as though praising a child.

The closer I got, the bigger he looked.

His brow wrinkled, confused.

"What a good puppy you are. What a magnifi—"

The rest of the word died in my throat. I sensed him lunging approximately one-tenth of a second before he projectile launched himself into the air. As I scrambled back up the ladder, he clamped his jaws around the hem of my fatigues and hung on. I forged ahead, bringing him with me a foot or more off the ground. As he shook me like prey, he propelled himself into a pendulum swing.

For no good reason he let go, dropping back onto the ground with a throaty growl. While I hiked my cargo pants back up, he did a little doggie dick dance at the base of the tree. That convinced me to stay put until I could either get Gordon to come home and lock him up or think of another way to clear out without becoming dog food.

Safe in the treehouse, I scooted as far from the opening as I could get and pressed my back against the wall. Then I pulled out my cell phone again. This time I called Salem.

CHAPTER ELEVEN

"You're where?"

"Treed."

Long pause. "Are you telling me you're stuck in a tree?"

"That's exactly what I'm telling you." An ominous scraping sound came from below. It seemed to be getting closer. "Wait."

I set down the phone and crept on all fours toward the opening.

Czar was climbing the ladder.

I let out a piercing scream, then grabbed the long lens camera and used it as a bayonet. He lost his balance and toppled to the ground. Momentarily stunned, he picked himself up and started back up.

"Oh, no you don't." Fear moved me to action. I grabbed a low-hanging branch and broke it off, beating him back as he made a second attempt to flush me out. Once he retreated, I grabbed the cell phone and proceeded to tell Salem about the dog and how I came to be in this predicament.

"You actually caught Drex in the act?" she said. "He's such a douche."

"Look, we can talk about how to deal with him later. The phone battery's about to give out and I need help."

"Say the word."

I gave her the address. "I need you to create a diversion. Just something to get Czar to come after you instead of me."

"How thoughtful of you."

Frustrated, I said, "I'm not asking you to sacrifice your life for me. I just need a head start."

I laid out the plan as best I could considering I was dressed all in various shades of drab green and brown camouflage — like Charles Whitman when he went up to the UT Tower and killed all those people. It was fully daylight and neighbors had come out of their houses to do yard work or merely enjoy their decks. I'd be less conspicuous if I just stripped naked and streaked down the street.

A half hour later, the crunch of gravel came from the alley behind Gordon's house. I stabbed out Salem's phone number.

When she answered, I said, "Ease up on the throttle. Go slow until I can see you." When I got her in sight, I told her to stop.

Then the engine shut off. The door of Mr. Quincy's Suburban opened with a prolonged squeak. Next thing I knew, my red-haired friend was standing on the running board peering up at me from the top of the privacy fence.

"Maybe I can distract him, and you can make a run for it," she offered.

I shot her a glare of the *Are you kidding me?* variety. "Have you seen his teeth? You could make keys with them."

As soon as Czar saw her, he bounded over and stood on his hind legs with fangs bared and jowls pealed back.

"What'd you bring?" I shouted.

"A ham bone."

"Ham bone?"

"Well, technically it's the whole ham. But you said he was huge so I thought a picnic ham might work. And what the hell? You didn't tell me he was as big as a rhino."

She wanted to talk over the plan before surrendering the meat.

"Do you have any string?" I asked.

"What for?"

"So I can hang myself." Said sarcastically. "What the hell do you think it's for? Tie it around the damned ham and dangle it over the fence."

She wanted to argue.

"Look, if you just toss it over, he may eat it right there and I'm screwed. If you dangle it like a fishing line, you can probably keep him busy while I at least have a fighting chance to run for my life."

"It doesn't sound like a very good idea. Surely there's a better way. We just need to think of one."

"Look, if you do it my way and it doesn't work, blame me. If you do it your way and it doesn't work, murder-suicide."

"Do you really think it'll work?"

"Of course not."

She disappeared from view. Rat-like scratching came from inside the big truck. After a few minutes of digging, Salem resurfaced.

"No string."

"I'm going to die in a treehouse," I announced to the clouds.

"No string," she said, brimming with cheer, "but I found a couple of bungee cords."

"Perf," I answered with abbreviated speech. "Now listen carefully. I want you to wrap it around the ham and hook it to the other end of the cord."

"Check."

"Then do the same with the second bungee cord like you're wrapping a present.

That way the ham won't slip out."

"Check." As an afterthought, she added, "What do I use to dangle it?"

"You don't have another bungee cord?"

"No."

I wanted to tell her if she was really a friend, she'd poke three holes in it, grip it like a bowling ball and dangle her hand over the fence. Instead, I asked if she had on a belt. She did but she refused to use it.

"It's Chanel."

"Bummer." A drop of sweat rolled down my back and into my underwear. "Take off your bra."

She huffed out her disgust. "It's lace. And it cost a fortune. I won't."

"Why not? I'd do it for you."

"I've got news for you: Isaac Newton called. Gravity's set in."

"I'll buy you a new one."

"You're broke."

"If it gets torn, I'll fix it."

"Ha. You couldn't fix a sandwich."

The ante just went up on this poker game. Then, because every-blessed-thing about this situation had to turn into a bloody freaking problem, I conjured up my scary voice. "Don't make me come over that fence." Of course she just laughed. My problem is that I have no street creds.

Then she relented. "That ought to give it some bounce."

It never occurred to me that Paislee might come home and catch us. It never occurred to me because when you're staring death in the face and you have a choice, you pick the lesser of the evils. Like asking would you rather burn to death or drown?

I'm for whatever causes the least amount of pain.

Death by shrimp tempura would work. Or death by devil's food cake.

I sighed.

Better to end up in leg irons and a belly chain, with an ugly mug shot and a criminal identification number, than on a marble slab with a wad of cotton up your butt and a tag on your toe.

I gave her the ready sign.

As she held the ham over the top of the fence, I made my descent.

The plan worked well for about ten seconds. Czar made so much noise jumping up and down, clawing at the fence for traction as he tried to get to the ham that I was able to reach the ground. But as Salem yanked the snack beyond snapping jaws, the bra broke loose and the ham ricocheted back over onto her side of the fence.

Then everything moved in slow motion.

"Run, Dainty, run."

Instinct told me to haul my ass back up the tree but I'd passed the point of no return.

I sprinted for the gate with Czar closing in on me. Knowing I'd never reach the exit before he dragged me to the ground like a lion on a gazelle, I chose the pool over mauling.

When I came up for air, the Beauceron was standing at the water's edge with his lips peeled back, fangs bared and a lethal growl vibrating in his throat. The camera strap had slipped off my shoulders and sunk to the bottom of the deep end. As I dove underwater to retrieve it, Salem's muffled voice came from the surface.

"Here, doggie-doggie-doggie — vicious little fucker."

I broke through the surface, sputtering, and saw the dog trotting back toward the dangling ham. Wading to the shallow end dragging the camera behind me like a tail, with the binoculars still hanging around my neck weighing me down, I gave Gordon's dog a sideways glance and plodded up the steps.

After a couple of tentative steps in the direction of the gate, Czar sank his fangs into the ham and hung on. As Salem tried to wrangle it from him, I yelled at her to give it to him and ran like hell. I didn't feel safe until the lock snapped shut behind me.

CHAPTER TWELVE

Immune to indignity and dripping water onto the marble tile in the foyer of WBFD, I stalked up to Rochelle's desk slinging the camera behind me with the door of the film compartment popped open, the frames exposed and dog snot streaking the camera lens.

She didn't utter a single protest. She did offer an unsolicited fashion tip. "You should've worn a Tupperware hat with that outfit, kid, and plastic wrap, because you look like leftovers."

"I want to see Gordon and don't tell me he's not here." Pumped into fearlessness after listening to the "Angry White Woman" CD, I summoned my best *Don't make me hurt you* look and bypassed her in favor of the boss's office.

My shoes squished as I stepped over to his door. I gave it a sharp knuckle rap before walking in. Gordon looked up from his desk and grimaced. He was talking on the tele-phone; without breaking stride he pitched me the newspaper and made a whirling gesture with his hand. Assuming he meant I should put it on the floor and drip-dry on it instead of leaking on his new carpet, I opened the paper and spread it out to soak up the water.

He got off the phone and eyed me up. "Get the door." Without stepping off the paper, I shoved the door closed. When it snapped shut, I glanced back over to find him pouring whiskey into two shot glasses. He said, "What the hell?"

My mind was telepathically warning *Do not start with me* but I wanted the five hundred bucks and needed the paid extern-ship.

"Here's the deal: It's exactly what you think it is. I took tons of pictures but the film got exposed when I went into your pool."

"You don't have proof?"

Actually, what I had was 80-proof. I regarded my drink before pushing it away.

His face flamed beet red. "You ruined the camera?"

I kept my voice even and metered. "You didn't tell me you had a dog."

"I don't. Czar belongs to Paislee's sister.

She's in Madrid for two weeks on a fashion shoot so we're keeping him."

"Well, see, that's the kind of thing that'd be handy to know ahead of time, don't you think? And by the way, just so you know, Fort Worth has a vicious dog ordinance."

"Did he bite you?"

I shook my head but lifted my foot and pointed to the missing mouthful of fabric where the hem of my cargo pants should've been. The lines in Gordon's forehead tensed. This was the first scintilla of concern I'd gotten out of him.

"Anyway, I'm here to collect my money."

The chair groaned as he stretched back in it. "Where's the evidence?"

"Like I said, the camera popped open when it hit the bottom of the pool. The film's exposed. No pics."

"No evidence, no money."

I stood in stricken silence and gnawed my bottom lip. "Is that your final answer?"

"What'd you see?"

I pretended to search my memory. "Pictures would've painted a thousand words."

"Did someone come to the house after I left?"

Head bob.

"Did they have sex?"

I closed my eyes against the vision rising

before me. Another head bob.

"You saw this with your own eyes?"

Huge, slow head bob.

"What'd he look like?"

"Dark hair, tall, good build."

"Young?"

Another head bob. "I'm sorry about the camera."

"Let it dry and then drop it off at the repair shop." He flipped through a rotating card file, stopped on a particular card and jotted down the address. Then he handed me the yellow sticky note. "Are you still game?"

"I need more money."

"How much?" He opened his wallet and waited.

"I want half of the five hundred dollars I already earned and I want a thousand dollars to buy spy stuff."

He blinked.

"I've been researching the topic and I think we should have a couple of pin cameras — one for your bedroom, one for the living room and one to go by the back door. You'll pay for them but when we're through, I want to keep them for my efforts. Deal?"

We shook hands and he gave me what he had in his wallet — three hundred dollars. He told me to come back for the nine hundred fifty dollars mid-afternoon. Then he handed over a bright blue envelope with my name on it.

"Happy birthday, Prescott."

I almost cried. It looked like the standard birthday card, but when I opened it, out fell a plastic Harkman Beemis gift card for a hundred dollars.

"Live it up," he deadpanned. "There'll be no gift cards in Hell."

As I was going out the door, he gave me a piece of advice. "I'm going out of town tomorrow and I'll be out of the loop for two or three days. If you'll get those cameras I'll set them up before I leave. Remind me to give you the alarm code to the garage. From there, you can enter the backyard without being seen from the street. And I rented you a car while I'm gone. You can pick it up this evening. It's at Junkers-R-Us."

But I'd had my fill of key codes to gates and big, ugly dogs. I figured any surveillance I pulled at this point would best be done from the alley using super-duper equipment just like the professionals.

CHAPTER THIRTEEN

> Revised goals for the day:
>
> 1. Buy spy stuff
> 2. Birthday dinner/dancing
> 3. Find suitable man to take to Rubanbleu

I hadn't intended to call Jim Bruckman, but when I stopped off at the spy shop the inventory confused me.

He answered on the third ring in a voice so gruff that, for a second, I inwardly questioned whether I'd pressed the right number into the keypad.

"Is this Detective Bruckman?" My heart picked up its pace.

"Hello, heartburn."

Wait — who does he think he's talking to?

I swallowed hard. "This is Dainty Prescott.

I hope I'm not bothering you."

He chuckled. "Are you locked up?" I sensed him smiling at the other end of the line.

"No."

"Under arrest?"

"No." Muscles tense along my back.

"Detained on a traffic stop?"

"No."

"Then what can I do for you?"

Throw me down. Tear off my clothes with your teeth. Savage me with your perfect lips and dangerous body.

Okay, I may not have said it out loud, but I'm not ashamed that I thought it. I liked that he'd teased me with his tone.

I told him I was at the spy shop and needed to purchase surveillance equipment. He burst into laughter. I didn't find this the least bit funny but when he volunteered to drop by and assist, I wasn't so offended I didn't take him up on the offer.

The spy store displayed an array of briefcase cameras, pin cameras, DVR surveillance kits, voice-activated pen recorders, spy software for Gordon's PC, PI cam sticks and micro-cassette recorders. They even had a back room with wigs and other simple disguises — I particularly got a kick out of the foam hump for that hunchback look —

157

and camouflage clothing like T-shirts, cargo pants, work shirts, socks and lace-up boots.

I was in the back room trying on a long brown wig, primping like a starlet before a mirror surrounded by marquis lights when Bruckman walked through the curtained-off area with a somber expression on his tanned, impenetrable face. He framed himself in the doorway and gave me a blank look. Then he considered me for a second and recognition kicked in.

He coiled his fingers, shaped his hand into a telephone receiver, and raised it to his ear. "Hello, Natasha, this is Boris."

"Raskolnikov!" I used my best Pottsylvania accent — spy code to show familiarity with these cartoon characters.

But this was serious business and I told him so.

"What're you doing — going *in cognito* to confuse the traffic cameras? Because you should know cops have image enhancing software that can compare the bone structure in your face . . ."

"I'm starting my own detective agency."

Howls of laughter doubled him over. I waited for him to knock it off but he was having a rollicking good time at my expense. After wiping tears from those spooky blue eyes, he let go another round of guffaws before he finally ran out of steam. Much as I hated to admit it, Bruckman had an infectious laugh. My mouth cracked into a smile despite the fact that inside my head I was cowing him into submission with a stun gun.

"That's great — The Debutante Detective Agency." He fell into a fresh fit of laughter.

My smile slipped away. "That's not the name of my company."

"No? What is the name of your company? I might want to hire you."

I set my jaw. Truth was, I didn't have a name picked out yet. I had no idea how to run a business — heck I didn't even know what it took to be a detective. I only knew that I was living from hand to mouth and something had better change quickly or I'd be in the soup line over at the Union Gospel Mission. I got right to the point.

I pushed back from the vanity and walked over to him. Inviting him into my secret world had turned out to be a self-inflicted wound.

My fingers involuntarily curled into his shirt. "Are you going to help me or not?"

"I'm game. I love lost causes."

I hip checked him out of the way. He followed me back through the curtained-off area to the showroom where we spent the next forty-five minutes talking about the pros and cons of different equipment. By the time we were done, I'd selected a PI cam stick, two voice-activated pen recorders, a micro-cassette recorder, several pin cameras, the spy software, a tracking device for Paislee's car, the dark brown wig and a pair of non-prescription eyeglasses that made me look smart. After paying the bill with Gordon's money, I turned to Bruckman.

"I want a stun gun."

Blue eyes coolly narrowed.

"Seriously, I have to be able to protect myself. And mace. And a gun. A big one. Big and scary. The kind of gun that's so intimidating people take one look at it and hand over their money without me even asking."

"Whoa-whoa-whoa." His hands came up in surrender mode. It was the sort of response a man confronted by a masked gunman might have. "What's going on?"

"Like I said, I'm going into business for myself."

"You'll need a permit to carry a concealed weapon, which you have to apply for. Mentally unstable people can't get one — just so you know."

"I'm not mentally unstable. For the first

time in my life I know exactly what I'm do-ing."

He looked down at me from behind a fringe of thick brown lashes. "You're talking about things that should be purchased through a police supply store. And applications to fill out for the concealed handgun permit. You don't strike me as the kind of person who'll follow the law. You're the kind who colors outside the lines. I have a bad feeling that all you're going to do is talk yourself into three hots and a cot."

"You don't have to get smart with me. I need help."

"I know. But it's a full moon and the psychiatric unit's full."

"Go ahead, have your fun. You should be flattered I asked you."

"Flattered? I'll probably end up getting filed on for racketeering and conspiracy under the RICCO statute."

"So you'll help me?"

He folded his arms across his chest. Cocked his head and eyed me up. "Give me one good reason why I should."

"Because I need direction from somebody in law enforcement who knows what they're doing so I don't get myself killed. And you're the only one I know well enough to ask. So, tag, you're it."

"Tell you what. I'll arrange for you to ride-in under the police buddy system."

He described how the PD allowed people without criminal histories who had an interest in police work to ride along. A police buddy could ride-in once every six months, although Bruckman admitted officers had been known to fudge if they liked the rider.

"We don't let felons ride-in, though. You don't have any felony convictions, do you? And you do understand when I ask you this that I'm making the distinction between committing felonies and actual convictions, don't you?"

"Have you always been a jerk?"

He pretended to search his memory. "Uh, no . . . I used to be a Republican."

Lacking patience, I said, "So is this your way of asking me to ride-in with you?"

"Want to go tonight?"

In less than an hour, I was supposed to meet my friends for dinner.

"Can't. It's my birthday."

I gave him another hip-check and left the store with the sack of spy toys slung over my shoulder.

Gordon was keeping late hours at the TV station when I stopped by with the gadgets. After I explained what they were and how to use them, I left for Gran's house to change clothes for my big night, certain that my happiness was circling the drain.

But what saddened me more was that, because of me, my boss had been forced to confront the idea that his wife's cheating would now take his life down an entirely different path.

And what path was that?

The psychopath, of course.

Thoughts turned to Drex. I wondered how many other times he'd done this to me and gotten away with it. Would it have been better to suffer in silence? If I had, it might've taken years for Gordon to realize he'd married a cheater. Heck, he might've grown into old age and died never knowing.

Or she might've contracted an STD — one that could kill — and passed it on to him.

With counseling, I might've eventually come to terms with Drex's fling with Paislee and stayed in the relationship with a man who I knew, deep down, loved me.

With my thoughts free-associating, I made the drive to Dallas secure in the knowledge of only one thing.

You get what you settle for.

CHAPTER FOURTEEN

The birthday plan was to meet my friends for dinner at the new Japanese fusion restaurant on West Freeway. Then we were supposed to go *honky-tonkin'* at a dance hall in the Fort Worth Stockyards. I don't listen to country music, hence the "Angry White Woman" CD. But I have cool western wear. A few years ago Daddy commissioned Justin Boots to custom-make me a pair of sweet pink lizard wingtip western boots with pearlized pink shafts. I wore them up to New York City with ice cream pink jeans and a silk shirt. Plus, I carried a pearlized pink hand-tooled purse and a hand-tooled belt with DAINTY centered on the back that Daddy had the King Ranch custom-make to go with my boots. Topped off with the *pièce de résistance,* my pink Lady Texas High Roller, ten-X beaver hat that came from Texas Hatters — hat makers to the stars — also custom-made for *moi.*

I looked uber-hot on that trip.

Wall Street types kept stopping me on Broadway wanting to know where I got my cowgirl costume.

If I said it once, I said it a thousand times, "It isn't a costume — it's a way of life."

They liked the way I talked and found my Texas accent charming, which translated into a lot of dinner offers. As for those guys who looked sketchy, I discouraged them by pretending I didn't speak English.

"Je ne parle pas anglais" can discourage a player when accompanied by a dumb-as-dirt look and a shoulder shrug.

Actually, I'm surprised it worked as often as it did. "I don't speak English" is the only thing I know how to say in French. That, and *"Voulez-vous coucher avec moi ce soir?"* like the song.

Playing dumb worked most of the time. But in a few instances it backfired when the person I was speaking to actually spoke French. Then my fake country of origin was about as convincing as my accent.

Back to tonight's dinner plans.

When I pulled into the parking lot, I didn't see Salem's hot pink Smart Car or Venice's blue Lexus SC. Tandy's car, a red VW Beetle, wasn't there either.

Except for the bug, the problem with the

cars we drive is that they're all two-seaters so if the four of us want to do something together, we have to take a minimum of two cars.

I was parked in a space with my foot on the brake, about to go inside the restaurant and get us a table. Then the cell phone rang and when I thumbed it on, Venice was at the other end of the line telling me Tandy's car wouldn't start and she needed a ride.

Resentful — party of one, your table's ready.

I headed off for Tandy's house dressed to thrill even though my heart hurt that Drex hadn't even bothered to call to wish me a happy birthday.

Nothing left to do but volume up the sound on the "Angry White Woman" CD.

Tandy's mother lives in a huge Tuscany-looking stucco house with a speckled red tile roof in a ritzy, gated community in southwest Fort Worth where you have to stop at the guard's kiosk and give your name before you're admitted. They check to see if you're on the list, and if you are, they press a button and the little mechanical arm that looks like the ones you find at railroad crossings lifts to allow entry. It's all very James Bond only without the dashing gentleman and hot cars. The guy in the kiosk rides a racing bicycle.

He found my name on the permanent list and waved me inside. I drove along the road that ran to the country club, with the golf course to my right and houses rolling by like huge squares of fabric in a giant quilt on the left. After a couple of turns, I saw the two grand oak trees spreading their limbs like kindly old grandparents wanting to be hugged, and pulled into the circular driveway in front of Mrs. Westlake's house. I tooted the horn and waited for Tandy to come out, using the wait time to apply a fresh coat of lip gloss.

Whoa. Who died?

I'd just noticed all the cars parked up and down the street. There are only two reasons to have that many cars lining both sides of the street in a residential neighborhood as upscale as Mira Vista: death or festivities. And I ruled out the latter because anybody living over here has the money to hire TCU guys to do valet parking for their guests.

As I finished touching up my makeup, a white pickup truck slowed just enough to pique my interest. Mostly you see high-end autos around this place but the fellow driving could've been allowed in to pick up a high schooler for Homecoming.

When Tandy didn't appear right away, I killed the engine, got out of the Carrera and walked up to the tiled porch. Two heavy wrought iron door panels obscured a second set of massive wooden doors. The ironwork was handmade, not cast from a mold. Intricate cutwork on the lockable entrance grilles was so ornate that, from a distance, it looked like black lace.

I hate this house.

You need a GPS to find your way around inside it.

I've been here maybe a total of five times since Tandy's mom invested part of the money from her divorce settlement in this behemoth mansion, and I've gotten lost every time. The decorator from hell *faux finished* the interior in paint shades designed to keep the evil spirits away. Every room had a different color scheme. If houses were flags, this one would represent gay pride.

Even the layout made no sense. There are thirteen staircases in this multilevel hellhouse. Once, when I thought I'd figured out where I was after excusing myself to the powder room, I found myself in some weird half-story with bedrooms I'd never seen before. I had to call Tandy on my cell phone to launch a search party. I'd told myself then that the next time I came here for any length of time, I'd bring a handful of peppermints to drop like breadcrumbs.

I rang the doorbell and waited for someone to answer. Music and laughter filled the air. The back of this house overlooks the golf course so I figured maybe there was some sort of tournament going on. Then I heard Alanis Morrisette belting out what was fast becoming my theme song, a cruel reminder of the mess my boyfriend made when he went away:

"*. . . you, you oughta know.*"

Alanis is the consummate angry white woman. I love her. At least if I had to stand on the porch of Hell House I'd be entertained.

I closed my eyes and imagined myself on stage singing a remake of this song for millions of fans as TV cameras shot my latest hit video. The crowd loved me. And just when I got to the part where a huge floodlight singled out Drex in the crowd, exposing him for the lying, cheating douche bag that he is, a sliding bolt retracted with a violent crack and the huge doors to Tandy's house unlocked. Propelled into the present, my eyelids snapped open.

What hellish sight is this?

Tandy's mother stood in the entry with the latest model Internet phone scrunched between her ear and shoulder. Parting the ornate grille panels enough for me to slip inside, she mouthed *Hold on a second* without sound. Then she air kissed my cheeks with a *mwah, mwah.*

Her appearance hit me full force. I pretty much just stared.

Bette Davis eyes flashed. So did her Edward Scissorhands.

Wait — are those fingernails real?

And are those chigger-eye diamonds lacquered onto the tips of each one — is this a joke?

I could eat for a week on what that manicure must've set her back.

Not to mention the tailored white shirt made of lace, and black leather slacks that looked like they were spray-painted on. With a smile on her face and a network of wrinkles around her eyes from years of lounging by the pool without sunscreen, she steadied the wireless phone and shifted a champagne flute into the hand that cradled her crossbred miniature Xoloitzcuintli — Mexican hairless Chihuahua.

I didn't know there was any such thing as a toy Xolo-Chihuahua cross. I thought they were called rats.

While Mrs. Westlake continued the phone conversation, Satan's sidekick challenged me to a staring match. This speckled gray-bodied dog looked more like a gargoyle with a skin pigmentation disorder — like vitiligo — and had fangs that jutted out almost perpendicular to the rest of its crooked teeth. The ugliest dog in the world wore a pink sweater stitched with a "K" in silver sequins on it.

Imagine. A pet dressed like a disco ball. *Très gauche.*

Seriously. To rich people, tiny dogs are just jewelry with a heartbeat.

The idea behind this particular companion pet must've been to breed an intelligent (loosely translated: "barks out a two-second warning before the home invasion"), hairless (loosely translated: "looks like chapped, withered penis foreskin"), people-friendly (loosely translated: "won't tear the fingers off your houseguest's newborn") companion pet.

I have little or no use for yappy pets of this size. The dogs we had, growing up, were considered hunters, not pets — pointing bird dogs and performing retrievers who didn't spook at the blast of a twelve-gauge shotgun. And as such, they weren't allowed indoors except during ice storms. The last time Daddy brought home another Brittany spaniel that Mom said he couldn't keep, he offered to let Teensy and me name it. We named him Barbie even though it was a male. Mom said it served Daddy right for ignoring her.

Mrs. Westlake's dog, Kiki, hates me. It's good at hiding — like the Viet Cong. When you least expect it, Kiki will jump out and try to bite. The operative word is "try" since it can't open its snaggletooth jaws wide enough to do damage. Still, it's a scary little dog if you're not expecting an ambush, and if Kiki catches you just so, those crooked little fangs hurt.

I think the only reason Tandy's mother makes a big to-do over this animal is because her new boyfriend gave it to her. Unfortunately, none of the other family members bonded with Kiki so it's a Velcro dog for Mrs. Westlake. I'm told Xolos live a long time — fifteen to twenty years and up. That's a long time to put up with dog neurosis, if you ask me.

"Come on in, Dainty." She thumbed off the phone and stepped aside to let me pass. "Make yourself at home."

When I headed for the little settee near the door she said, "Not there. Try out my new chair in the living room. It's more comfortable."

More comfortable than what? Being stabbed?

Besides, I already tried it out the last time

172

I was here and decided if the heat ever went out in this place it'd make good firewood. My opinion hasn't changed.

Mrs. Westlake guided me through the marble foyer. She has the same strawberry-blonde ringlets and standard-issue brown eyes as her daughter. If she didn't have little crow's feet and stress wrinkles around her eyes and mouth, she could pass for Tandy's sister. In other words, Tandy's a clone of her mother when it comes to looks.

As for brains, my friend takes after . . . well, somebody else. A throwback. She got the recessive gene for intelligence that nobody else in the family inherited. Which proves a point I've long held — that God protects dogs and stupid people.

A shudder ran through me. The house was giving me the creeps. I asked Mrs. Westlake if Tandy was ready.

She looked at me Bambi-eyed. "I think so." Her head bobbed with such enthusiasm that her strawberry ringlets bounced like little Slinkys. "Would you rather wait for her on the back deck?"

Oh, dear God.

I've only been on the back deck twice and I didn't plan to end up there either time. I wasn't sure I could find it again without following a set of stick-on footprints. She motioned me inside one of three arched entryways and pointed me through to the main living room; here's where the trouble starts.

There are eight openings that lead into and out of the main living room. One leads to the kitchen and a funky little breakfast room that's not big enough for four people to turn around in, but at least I know you can get to the back deck from there. One of the doors leads into the den and the others lead into bedrooms, bathrooms or corridors with staircases. Did I mention there are thirteen?

So, thanks but no thanks. Forget about me wandering the house. I'd sooner be caught wearing white shoes before Easter.

"Thank you just the same, Mrs. Westlake, but I'll stay put. That way I can admire your dreamy living room."

"Suit yourself." Then she was off, *Ta-ta for now,* scampering across the marble floor with her heels echoing like friendly fire.

Did I really use the word "dreamy" to describe this place? It's a wonder lightning didn't strike me dead for lying. What I meant to say was, "Just shoot me."

I wasn't about to take another step without a pocket full of M&Ms to mark my trail. Or my cell phone to call for help. I pulled out my mobile and scrolled to Tandy's number. Hit the talk button and *voilà*.

Tandy answered with a chipper lilt.

"Where the heck are you?"

"My house. Where are you?"

"Your house."

"Where in my house?"

"Living room. And I'm not moving until you come get me."

"Oh, Dainty, don't be so dramatic." She disconnected.

That or the call got dropped. Either way, I was waiting uncomfortably in the dead zone. But hey — look on the bright side. Mrs. Westlake had finally moved further into the millennium. She'd gotten rid of that creepy French canvas by Gustave Moreau hanging over the fireplace and replaced it with a surreal painting of a man in a bowler hat by René Magritte. *Très* whimsical. Huge improvement.

Music and laughter penetrated the walls. The noise had taken on the din of a block party. I wondered if it bothered Mrs. Westlake, not being invited, but she didn't stick around to make conversation.

Temporarily distracted by the Ranger baseball game on the big screen TV, I didn't hear Tandy enter the room until her voice came from behind and to the right. I spun around, relieved. Relief gave way to confusion.

What have we here? Well whaddaya know? It's Dances with Nobody.

She was wearing a sleeveless navy dress with matching evening sandals and a lightweight cashmere sweater, not boots and jeans like we'd talked about.

"You can't dance in that. Why aren't you dressed?"

"I'm not going."

I gave her a dedicated eye blink. "Then why'd Venice call to say you needed a ride to the restaurant?"

"I'm eating here."

Emotions flared. For a tenth of a second, I experienced a ghetto moment of unacceptable behavior bubbling up. "Are you freaking kidding me? It's my birthday, Tandy. Aren't you coming to celebrate my birthday?" Tears stung my eyes.

A sigh seeped out. "I suppose if you really want me to go, I will," she said in a voice tinged with dejection, "but first I have something to show you."

She took me by the hand and pulled me through the house, which is the only way anybody without a GPS or a compass should try to navigate this place — under the buddy system — like scuba divers who

176

go underwater in pairs.

Next thing I knew, we were in her bedroom.

She said, "Could you get my boots? They're on the back porch." She pointed to a door that I assumed led out to the deck. When I stepped outside, a crush of people screamed my name. Balloons floated up into the air and duck calls blown from little party favors filled our shared space. The scent of char-grilled hamburgers wafted on the breeze and snaked up my nostrils. Best of all, my eyes went wide at the number of gifts stacked atop a card table draped with a paper tiara-motif covering.

I whipped around to see Tandy beaming. "Is this . . . ?"

Big head bob.

"So we're not going to the Stockyards?"

She shrugged.

"Nobody's ever given me a surprise party before." I half screamed, half cried and flung my arms around her neck. The closest I'd ever come to a surprise birthday party was when my sister Teensy took matters into her own hands and invited her entire class over in direct violation of our mother's "no birthday parties, ever" edict. "I love you guys."

For the record, there are precious few

exceptions to the *No PDA* rule: loving on babies, kissing a child's boo-boo before applying the bandage, a soldier's "Welcome Home," and this.

Venice and Salem, taking advantage of this mild October night, waved at me as they dangled their feet in the heated pool.

As a brisk wind kicked leaves across my feet, I sat on the deck with my face tilted up to the blazing October sunset, visiting with friends and ogling my presents.

Hours passed beneath a silver platter moon with my drunken buddies stuffing their faces with delicious burgers and washing them down with Heinekens while I sipped Perrier or sweet tea. As I relaxed in a chaise lounge near one of six doors that led back into Hell House, I couldn't think of an evening when I'd had a better time surrounded by all the people who loved me.

While I enjoyed a conversation with Salem and a couple of the other recovering sorority sisters and their dates, Venice and Tandy strolled up. They fidgeted, politely waiting for a break in the conversation. When it didn't come soon enough, Venice touched my sleeve.

"Dainty, can you come with us for a minute?"

They shared one of those *Somebody died*

looks. For a few agonizing seconds, I thought this concerned news about Gran.

"Why? What's wrong?"

They each took an arm and culled me from the herd.

With the rest of the guests beyond earshot, Venice ruined my party more effectively than if she'd doused me with a bucket of ice water.

"Did you pay those traffic camera tickets?"

"What?" I drawled out the word as if delaying it would somehow change the outcome. "No."

I suspected in an instant that my Porsche had been towed.

Daddy's lawyer said that might happen. That I was risking getting my car "booted" with one of those clamp thingies the cops put on to keep you from moving your car. But wait — I'd parked in the Westlake's circular driveway. No way could the cops snatch it on private property. Could they?

Tandy took a deep breath. It hissed out like a slashed tire. "A couple of uniformed cops are here. They want to talk to you about those unpaid traffic citations."

I sucked air, then tuned up in protest. "They can't haul me in for those tickets. Daddy's corporate attorney says it's not an arrestable offense."

"You have to go with them, Dainty."

The words "Dainty Prescott" and "jail" should never be used in the same sentence.

"Are you on crack?" I might've shrieked. "I'm not going with them. Are you kidding? What's wrong with you? I can't be locked up in a cell. Besides, I haven't even opened my presents." Darting furtive looks, I formulated my exit strategy.

Surely this Godforsaken house has an attic . . .

Uh-oh. I might've said that out loud.

Well, hey — I snapped. Nothing like the trauma of impending scandal to clear my head.

Tandy's forehead tensed. "My mom wants them gone."

I wanted to tell her mom to go ahead and let the cops inside — if they could find me, they could have me. My turncoat friends exchanged message-encrypted looks and then led me away from my party as if by mutual agreement — like those prison guards in *The Green Mile* who escorted Death Row inmates to the electric chair.

I wasn't conscious of having left the deck but when I looked back over my shoulder hoping for a reprieve, the deck was no longer in sight and the living room lay behind me. My mind conjured up imagery of an inmate named "Big Martha" who wanted me for her "special friend," and a thin high-frequency tone broke from my throat. My stomach rolled over. This was turning into a birthday debacle from start to finish.

Time to face the music.

Two grim-faced uniforms — one with shoulders like a water buffalo — filled the front doorway. They assumed formidable stances with their arms braced across their chests.

It was a real *A-ha* moment.

"Dainty Prescott?"

Fire blazed behind my cheeks. I half-expected to black out.

"Are you Dainty Prescott?"

Marooned, I swallowed hard. "She isn't here." I tried to keep my voice light and convincing.

Two of my three best friends were looking at me as if I was the newest exhibit in the *Ripley's Believe it or Not!* Museum. The third was nowhere in sight. I re-thought my birthday wish and amended it to include Salem careening up the circular drive with the passenger door of her Smart Car popped open.

The last of my bravado evaporated. I'm pretty sure I curled my *Barely Pink* fingernails into the sleeves of one of the officers and hauled him closer.

"You can't take me in. It's my birthday." My voice made an upwardly corkscrewing sound. I turned to my traitorous friends. "Quick — take up a collection. It's seventy-five dollars per ticket, times fourteen tickets. That makes . . ."

Who am I kidding?

Let's face it. I could've been a lot of things if I hadn't been stumped by mathematics. Under stress, I couldn't even add using pen and paper much less cipher multiplication tables in my head.

With hands clasped together, I pleaded with my eyes.

"Ready to go?" said the cop.

What a ghetto birthday — like asking for Debutante Barbie and getting a Taiwanese knock-off with a paper tiara, cheap, tear-away gloves and no date.

"Please don't take me," I whimpered, "it's my birthday." Really, how was I supposed to be in two places at the same time? What'd I look like to them — an amoeba about to split off? "I promise to slow down. I'll even stop at green lights."

The other cop laid it out for me like a losing hand of poker. "Only way we can let you stay is if you have somebody to vouch for you."

Do what?

"Someone to vouch for you," he repeated, enunciating each word.

Venice and Tandy chimed in unison, "You mean like another policeman?"

The officers looked at each other and choreographed a couple of head bobs.

Venice said, "But we don't know any cops."

"Unless . . ." Tandy piped up.

Something moved at the limits of my vision. My eyes flickered past the cops' shoulders to Salem, coming up behind them with her arm linked through Jim Bruckman's.

"Guess what I found?" she said, beaming.

"What?" I drawled out the word.

"You remember Detective Bruckman, don't you, Dainty?"

"What're you doing here?" I sputtered. The cops were smiling now, high-fiving each other and chucking each other's arms like a couple of delinquents.

Strains of Michelle Branch filtered inside from the stereo on the deck, confronting her boyfriend as to whether she'd been replaced, and demanding to know if that made him happy now.

Bruckman's eyes sparkled in the flame of

the gas sconces. Laugh lines bracketed perfect lips.

"What're you doing here?"

"Followed you."

"You're stalking me?"

"Think of it this way, Dainty," Salem said, finally unhanding him, "you're not really a celebrity unless you have your own stalker."

CHAPTER FIFTEEN

Sitting next to Bruckman with the cuffs of our jeans rolled up and our feet skimming the water at the deep end of Tandy's pool, I watched the sunset with his arm lopped over my shoulder and decided that purple really does go with orange.

"Here's the thing," he said as the party went on behind us, "you'll never be able to make the Debutante Detective Agency work if you can't even spot a tail behind you."

"Stop calling it that. I haven't thought up a name for it but it's not going to be the Debutante Detective Agency, so stop calling it that."

"I think it's cute."

"And stop making fun of me. I need a job and there aren't any openings at WBFD until spring. I'll never last 'til then. I need rent money for when our townhouse's ready and even more important, I want my dress back."

"What dress?"

"Never mind."

The last thing I wanted was to get into a protracted conversation with Bruckman about the mermaid dress.

"The point I'm trying to make is that you don't have any detective skills. You're going out spying on people without a lick of training and that's a good way to get yourself killed."

"You're just worried the city of Fort Worth won't be able to collect all the revenue I owe from the traffic camera fines if I get bumped off."

"That, too."

"I hate you."

"I know. Want me to leave?"

"Yes." But when he pulled his feet out of the water and swung his legs back over the edge of the pool, my heart skidded sideways. I can't tell you what strange physical reflex made me grab him by the shirt and haul him close. Like I said, public displays of affection are high on the list of inappropriate behavior for debutantes of The Rubanbleu. Not as close to the top as Dainty Prescott plus jail. "No. Don't leave."

He gazed at me through sincere eyes. "Look, if you're really serious about the Debutante Detective Agency —"

"Stop calling it that." I chucked his arm for emphasis. Violence ranks just below PDAs on the list. Another Rubanbleu no-no.

"— then I'll help you."

Instantly suspicious, I reared back. "Why?"

"Because the world would be a lesser place without you."

My heart thudded. Our eyes met. I admit it. I felt the tiniest bit dizzy.

He looked like he meant it. For the next few minutes we sat in silence, lost in thought within the din of reverberating sound coming off the deck. I didn't even care that Drex hadn't called or come to my party. I was about to do something important with my life and I'd found somebody savvy enough to show me the ropes.

"Mind if I kiss the birthday girl?"

The question ruffled my perfect calm. There I was, snagged on the picket fence that separated raw animal lust from good manners, wondering which way to fall.

I weighed my choices . . . no, couldn't happen. It took all of my resolve to demur. "All these people . . . well, it's just not done."

"That wasn't the reaction I expected," he said in a controlled dispassionate voice; unnecessarily, I might add.

Unexpectedly, he took my hand and lifted it to his lips, holding me captive in his blue gaze. Then he turned my hand over and kissed my palm.

A warm shiver scurried up my back. I felt pretty sure no one witnessed this subtle show of affection, so . . . sue me, I liked it.

"Happy birthday, Dainty Prescott."

But I wasn't thinking about birthdays anymore. I was thinking if he could thrill me with this small show of affection, what could he do to my head if he threw me down on the bed and ripped off my clothes?

"Got you something." That broke the trance. He opened his wallet and pulled out two tickets to a concert at Bass Hall.

I sat speechless as he handed them over.

"Thought you might like to take a friend."

I dumbly stared at the tickets. "I have three best friends." The words rushed out before I could rein them back in.

"So you have." He stared out at the darkening horizon. The purple Texas sky glittered with stars. "It'd be hard having to choose between them. Maybe you should invite somebody who's not your best friend."

I watched him carefully, slow on the up-take.

"You really are that dumb, aren't you?" Relaxed humor showed in his face. He winked to show that he didn't mean it.

"You think I'm dumb?" I acted playfully annoyed.

"Like a fox. You may be so dumb you're smart, Dainty Prescott. You've got good instincts. Now we just need to temper them in a hotter furnace than you're used to."

I didn't for a moment believe I had good instincts. After all, I had to catch my boyfriend playing tonsil hockey with my boss's wife before I realized they'd probably been slipping around since the office picnic.

The night grew rapidly dark, and the lights around the pool hadn't yet flickered on. I felt Bruckman's warm breath against my ear and did a dangerous thing. I turned my head. When he kissed me, I didn't think twice about instinct. My lips felt all tingly as they met his and I only knew what was real.

Chills swarmed over my body. As far as I was concerned, the moment could've lasted forever.

"Want to leave?" If my words had come out any huskier, I'd have sounded like a drag queen.

"What about your friends?"

"They'll be fine."

He helped me to my feet and we walked up the incline to the deck, me with my pink custom-made boots in hand and him carrying his black ropers.

"What about all your presents?"

I tracked his pointed finger to the table with my unopened gifts. "They'll wait."

"We could load them in my pickup and take them to your house."

An ironic snort slipped out. "That's just it. I don't have a house."

By way of explanation, I told him I was staying at Gran's and recounted the townhouse disaster. He offered to drive my loot to Dallas — which I discouraged. The Preston Hollow estate might not be kid-friendly but my family's even less accommodating when it comes to bringing home strangers who haven't passed the social acid test.

But the guy did drive a pickup . . . and didn't I have a ton of previously worn party dresses I needed to get to Venice? I took him up on the offer. We'd haul my gifts to Gran's, load up the dresses and bring them back.

We arranged to return in a couple of hours and meet Venice with the clothes. I air-kissed everyone good-bye as Bruckman, Tandy and Salem ferried packages out to the truck.

We made the drive to Preston Hollow in forty-five minutes — a record considering we started from Hell House. He offered to take me dancing afterward but I declined. I didn't want to tell him I had to get up early to see if I could catch my boyfriend with my boss's wife again. Some things are better left unsaid.

At Gran's, I got us through the electronic gate with my key pass and pointed him around to the back of the house near the pavilion. Before we got out of the truck, I set the ground rules. He needed to be forewarned.

"My grandmother goes to bed around eight-thirty. She's asleep by nine." Gran was a deep sleeper but I didn't want to chance waking her up by trekking my gifts up two flights of stairs. "We can leave the presents in the sunroom and I'll take them up to my room tomorrow."

He eyed up the house. "Which one's your room?"

I pointed. "See the widow's walk? That's not it. But if you climbed through those windows you could get to it on the other side."

"Like Rapunzel," he said through a grin.

My eyes went wide, then immediately thinned into slits. "How do you know about

191

Rapunzel?" I demanded, wondering if we were telepathically connected and he'd somehow tapped into my fantasies.

"I have a four-year-old niece. I read to her."

Sweet.

"Let's get this stuff out of your truck. If you'll bring these boxes inside and stack them next to the door, I'll go upstairs and start hauling down the dresses we're taking to Venice."

"And why're we doing that?"

"Venice studies fashion and design. She's making a dress for me out of gently used garments," I said, ashamed to disclose the catch-and-release tale of the mermaid dress. "It's like a class project only I get to keep it. It's my birthday gift."

"Lucky you."

After I unlocked the door to the sunroom, turned on the lights and tapped in the code to silence the alarm's warning tone, I motioned Bruckman inside the house.

"Holy smoke," he said, scoping out the room with a broad sweep of his eyes. "No wonder you're the way you are."

We'd been mostly sitting in the dark this evening and I'd almost forgotten how fab he looked with his flaxen hair lying perfectly in place and those intense blue eyes holding my attention like those of a hypnotist.

I made several trips upstairs while Bruckman laid a blanket in the pickup bed to protect the formal wear. On my third visit, I stripped off the western wear, hiked up fresh undies, put on a button-down top in a tropical weight silk, and stepped into khaki shorts. Before I switched off the overhead light, I snatched a cashmere sweater off a hanger and tied it behind my back with the arms looped at the waist. Hurrying, I slid into a pair of neutral suede mules, transferred the contents of my hand-tooled bag to a lime-colored Italian leather purse that picked up the splashes of green in my shirt, and clopped unapologetically down to the second-floor landing with the grace of a buffalo in toe shoes.

I hauled myself up short.

Had I lost my mind? I barely knew Bruckman. Besides, the life I'd imagined for myself included lobster tails and drawn butter, not fast food and condiment packets. And yet, watching him with his back to me at the foot of the stairs made my heart gallop.

I paused at the top of the railing long enough to holster my libido, and behaved the way a proper lady should, descending the staircase, regally, with my fingertips barely touching the banister.

He turned toward me. The smile that rode up one side of his face took my breath away. Hungry eyes skewered me. A panic alarm went off in my head.

You. Dainty Prescott. Step away from the man.

The angel on my shoulder returned.

So did the shoulder devil.

You're a cop magnet, baby. Don't fight it. Embrace it.

Angel: *You're confused. You know deep down in your heart you want to win back the love of your life.*

Devil: *Screw Drex. No — wait — screw Bruckman. Bruckman's hot.*

Angel: *Revenge sex? Absolutely not. Gran's home.*

Devil: *Do it in her bed.*

Angel: *Gran'll stroke out and die and it'll be your fault and you'll go straight to Hell and everybody'll hate you and . . .*

That did it.

"All done," I said with an enthusiasm I didn't feel.

Once the last of the clothing had been loaded, Bruckman keyed open the toolbox mounted in the bed of the pickup and pulled out a snap-on cover.

"Wouldn't want to get a 'Failure to Secure Load' ticket," he said in that law-abiding way.

With the hatches securely battened down, I gave him a quick tour of the first floor without ever having to explain why I couldn't live here. As we stood in the formal living room, a small glow came from a wall sconce near the stairs. It cast a golden luminescence over the shellac, coated the banister and ricocheted off the glossy mahogany surface.

I could almost pinpoint the moment he became seduced by the location.

"Is this where you grew up?" he asked when we reached the library.

We stood on zebra skin rugs laid out before floor-to-ceiling bookcases. He fingered the books as he read the titles on their spines, his touch delicate, respectful . . . as is proper with books.

"I'm a Fort Worth girl. I grew up in Rivercrest, on an estate that faces the golf course. But I'm not welcome there anymore now that Daddy's remarried."

He cut his eyes in my direction. "Wicked stepmother?"

"Bimbo gold digger."

"She can't be that bad."

"She's like the wax you can't dig out of

your ear."

When we reached the basement, I sensed him slipping into the throes of a sensory overload as he took in the room in stages: billiards, Ping-Pong and poker tables, an area set up for backgammon and chess, big screen TV, comfy leather sofa, and the walk-in closet that my late grandfather had converted into an *ad hoc* wine cellar. A real man's place, complete with the scent of his pipe tobacco. I could almost hear Bruckman plotting with his friends about where to spend Super Bowl Sunday, not to mention visualize him and his rowdy cop-buddies wallowing on the furniture, stuffing burritos down their throats like shoving logs into a wood chipper.

That'd be a stretch.

Outdoors again, he seated himself at a wrought-iron bistro table on the terrace while I extinguished the inside lights, reset the security system and locked out the world. I joined him at the table beneath the starlit night.

"Ready?" I asked.

"In a minute." He studied the sky and finger pointed. "Big Dipper. Little Dipper. North Star." Then his gaze settled on me. Eyes sparkled like star sapphires beneath the reflected light of a full moon. "You like it here?"

My eyes involuntarily shut. A rush of breath blew out. When I opened my lids he was studying me with the intensity of a scientist on the brink of discovering a cure.

"Lord no." As proof, I stuck out my hands. "Look at them," I challenged. "Why do you think I bite my nails?"

Half-shrug. "Nervous habit?"

If the average lifespan of a human is seventy-five years, the unique perspective of my dysfunctional family had taken me almost one-third of a lifetime to understand. I certainly didn't expect him to grasp the concept in the course of a few minutes. Years of conditioning had worn down my resistance when trying to change them. These days, I just wanted to get along. That meant spending only short bursts of time around certain people, and living out of suitcases when it came to others. Whenever diplomacy and tact hit the skids, I made myself scarce.

"Look, I love these people but I can't be around them very long before the back-biting starts."

"What's wrong with them?"

I barked out a laugh. "You're asking me what's wrong? That's like asking how many grits come in a box."

"Can't be all bad," he said dismissively. "They brought you up in a privileged environment and paid for your education. Bought you a hot car . . ."

"That was just so I'd go away. You can't put much real estate between you and your tormentors without wheels in this town. Out of sight, out of mind."

"I like my family." He tilted his head skyward again.

"That's because they're normal."

He gave me the palms-up shoulder shrug. "Normal is what's normal for you." With a broad sweep of the hand he said, "This is what's normal to you. I think you turned out pretty good in spite of your privileged upbringing."

"You do?" This was a far cry from our first encounter.

He punctuated the declaration with a nod. "And now you're going to be a big entrepreneur running the Debutante Detective Agency —"

"That's it." I pushed back from the table, grating the feet of my chair against the concrete in a cringe-worthy scrape. "We're done here."

"Oh, come on, Dainty." He rocketed from his chair, following in a flash of exasperation. "Come back. I was just kidding."

"I told you not to call it that," I groused over my shoulder as I stomped toward the pickup.

Had I told him recently how much I hated him?

Note to self: make sure he knows.

He caught up to me in three long strides, grabbing my arm and whirling me around to face him. Before I could protest, his lips were on mine, parting and hungry and insistent as his tongue forged its way into my mouth. My eyes closed. I inhaled. It was as if I'd needed him to breathe life back into me.

That took the starch out.

I did not expect that.

"You're precious," he said softly, tracing a finger along the line of my pouty lower lip. "Downright irresistible, come to think of it. I'll bet that works on a lot of guys, especially the old geezers." He considered me for a second, then pressed his lips against my ear. "Worked on me," he whispered. "First time I saw you . . . scooping up all those tickets off the floor board . . . staring up at me, doe-eyed, with those baby blues . . ."

He could've been reading off a grocery list for all I cared. I'd gotten so caught up in the overpowering seduction that I quit listening.

". . . and then you opened your mouth."

What?

I heard that.

"I might've asked for your number right then and there if you hadn't challenged me."

Wait — I got dragged through seven circles of hell for a phone number?

I saw red — and not the good kind. What I wanted was to beat seven shades of blood out of him, secure in the knowledge that none of it would be blue.

I think I'm having a stroke.

Then he picked up where he left off with the sweet talk again, short-circuiting the trip switch to my common sense. Lulled by the sound of his voice, I closed my eyes and enjoyed more petal soft kisses. Chalk it up to attention-deficit disorder, I ignored the danger I'd seen lurking deep within him during our first encounter. Swept into an endless stream of pleasure, I flat disregarded what I shouldn't be doing.

He kissed me deeply.

Time froze. We stayed like that for a week — a day — a minute? In my defense, I shouldn't have to guess. I had to draw on my entire supply of reserve energy to keep my knees from buckling under the dizzying rush of raging hormones. When I finally went limp in his embrace, he backed me against the truck's door to steady us.

Bruckman continued to play psychic vampire with me, sucking out my thoughts and emotions, erasing the memory of more suitable candidates for my attention. Interrogation techniques included dazzling kisses paired with intoxicating questions whispered into my ears, my mouth, my neck — "Do you like this . . . does this feel good . . . has anyone ever done this to you before?"

Did he really expect to wring a full confession out of me? It's not like I could manage anything beyond a few whimpers. And this stimulating pillow talk . . . *très, très risqué*. Did he actually think he'd exhilarate a socially refined lady such as *moi,* Dainty Prescott, with utterances only streetwalkers would appreciate? He continued as if such talk was *de rigueur* with debutantes of The Rubanbleu.

Then a *très, très* bad thing happened.

The throbbing sensation that'd started in my head plunged to my feminine core. My perfectly contoured eyebrows slammed together. Could it be . . . no, not possible . . . that I *liked* it?

Bad, bad, *très* bad *moi.*

Then I felt the thrill of his velvet bite. A shudder of excitement rippled across my skin. Chills electrified my body.

You win — I confess — I did run the red light at Green Oaks and West Freeway.

Warm breath snaked down my ear canal.

I'm glad I ran it . . . so ha. And here's something else — I can't drive fifty-five — just like the song.

His hot tongue nearly drove me to the brink of revealing deep, dark secrets.

I haven't had sex in over two months.

Another high-voltage kiss eroded my resolve to stay strong.

I'm falling for you.

But the deepest, darkest secret lingered on the tip of my tongue.

My Porsche tops out at one eighty-five.

Caught in the grip of shared desire, I felt another velvety bite against the erratic pulse in my neck. At the moment our mouths slammed together again, I would've confessed to anything.

Signed, sealed, delivered.

Then it ended.

He let go. With my eyes still closed, the sensation of falling claimed me. But did I care? Not hardly. Isn't that the way it always is when you're hell bent on doing something that's probably bad for you?

Scooping me back into his embrace, he held me tightly. With minty breath, he blew the hair off my neck and applied his tongue to the back of my earlobe.

"Come home with me, Dainty."

The words carried a bit of hang time.

Well, I never! That would make me slutty.

My demeanor went suddenly frosty. My normally sweet Southern belle drawl became even more pronounced. "I barely know you. What in the world would make you think I'd go home with you?"

"You know me." His mouth curled up at one corner. Arresting blue eyes were level and unyielding. "I'm the guy your daddy warned you about."

I felt the oxygen being sucked out of my lungs. My heart beat so fast it echoed in my ears.

"I'm the guy who's going to teach you what it's really like to be in love."

In that instant, I believed him.

My world narrowed into a single focal point where girl-gets-guy and they both live happily ever after. On some level, I knew there were love-struck ladies out there sampling the Jim Bruckman Kool-Aid. A man couldn't be this gorgeous and not have women panting after him.

Women like Paislee Pfeiffer.

A sobering thought to say the least.

I took deep breaths to clear the dizzying head rush. He'd already melted my silk top off. Now his fingertips were tracing circles on my breasts. Call me decadent, I just couldn't stop him.

I spoke in an unstable voice. "We have to meet Venice."

Actually, she'll wait.

He took his mouth to me and I let him. Ball gown be damned, this felt almost other-worldly.

"Want me to stop?" he said between slurping sound effects.

"Please do," I said with polished reserve.

But my mind was screaming, *For the love of God . . . did you take a class?*

It was all I could do to keep from letting him have his way with me.

Hands off, he took a backward step. "We'll do it however you want, whenever you want."

"And if I don't want?" This was a completely inane response. On some level, we both knew if a transformer blew and the power grid for the entire neighborhood went out, we'd be in the swimming pool *sans* clothes, exploring every inch of each other's bodies.

"Oh, you'll want it all right." He stroked his knuckles along my jaw and held me in his azure gaze. "I'll give it a week tops."

I'm all for propriety when the need arises.

But then I did something that wasn't just *très, très* scandalous, we're talking *beaucoup* bad. I curled my perfectly manicured fingernails into his shirtsleeves and hauled him so close I could almost take a pulse through his jeans.

So, sue me. I liked that I brought out the beast in him.

Back on the road, Bruckman made small talk while I couldn't stop thinking about the smooth way he'd coaxed the buttons on my shirt undone, unhooked my bra and had my breasts out before I knew what hit me.

This had to stop. Even I knew that the only reason I'd behaved this way was because of the emotional battering I'd recently taken. Detective Jim Bruckman could teach me the ropes and serve as my mentor until I got my detective agency off the ground, but that's where it stopped.

And yet . . . I glanced over at him, silhouetted behind the wheel with his face intermittently blued by the glow of the street lamps we passed.

He looked over and considered me with a sexy, smoldering look, then lifted my hand to his lips and kissed the back of it like the perfect gentleman I knew he was not.

"You don't have to sit so far away." Dazzling me with his smile, he did a little chin jut to motion me closer.

I deliberated.

Uh, no . . . not gonna happen.

"I'm fine where I am." Where I come from, not even married couples sit that close.

An unwelcome visual of me flashed into mind, snuggled up against him like a suction-cup plush toy the way redneck girls do with their boyfriends in pickups. The only thing lacking to complete the trailer trashy picture was a rifle mounted against the back windshield, a couple of dead possums in the pickup bed and a Confederate flag to screen out the glare.

Again, not gonna happen.

"You sure?" He teased me with a look. "You don't seem fine."

"Eyes on the road, detective," I said with polite insistence. "You're carrying precious cargo."

"I'll say." A dangerous smile rode up one side of his mouth.

Okay, now I wanted to sit in his lap. Actually, that's not true. What I really wanted was for him to take the first dirt road off the highway, throw me over his shoulder, and carry me back to the pickup bed.

Bad girl.

Bad, bad, bad.

The uncensored thought of being with Bruckman, *au naturel,* didn't just lodge in my head like a pesky jingle from one of those television commercials you can't shake off; it actually grew in intensity. By the time we were ten miles down the road, I'd done so many naughty things in my mind that I could only thank my lucky stars my detective didn't have extra-sensory perception. Even streams of air sighing through the vents whispered, "Shame on you, shame on you, shame on you . . ."

In all fairness, I blame that certain *je ne sais quoi* dangerousness radiating from my detective, coupled with a kind of quiet strength, for making me take leave of my senses and do what I did next.

For no good reason I twisted in my seat. "Have you ever been to a debutante ball?"

"Can't say I have."

Lacking a trust fund, a man with a blue-collar job such as Bruckman was hardly Rubanbleu acceptable; Daddy'd hate him on sight, and Gran would be mortified . . . Teensy'd applaud me for finally rebelling, though she'd also suspect I'd invited him to upstage her . . . which made him perfect.

"Think you'd ever want to go to one?" I'd weighed my words carefully and held my arrested breath.

He scowled. "Would I have to wear a tux?"

I grimaced. " 'Fraid so."

"Sweet," he said and flashed the greatest smile ever.

"So *if* you were ever to attend one of these soirees, would you want to go with *me?*" I asked without making eye contact.

"Thank you for asking, Miss Prescott. I'd be honored to escort you to the debutante ball."

His hand closed around mine and we rode into Fort Worth that way. I thought about what I'd just done, and about the repercussions still to come. Chalk it up to bad judgment on my part, but what could I do? Uninviting him would've made for an even worse social *faux pas.* When we arrived at Tandy's house I trotted up to the door and rang the bell. The door flung open and Salem spilled out with Tandy and Venice in tow.

In the golden flicker of the sconces' gas flames, Salem surveyed my outfit with a critical eye, chopping her words at the very sight of me. "Oh. My. Goodness. Who did this to you?" Not only did these passion-rumpled clothes not work as an ensemble, in my haste to cover myself, I'd miscalculated and re-buttoned my shirt matching the wrong button to the wrong buttonhole.

If critical looks were the barometer by which I could measure my fashion *faux pas*, apparently the only thing lacking to complete my rumpled appearance was a street corner next to a hot-sheet motel, and a court-appointed attorney. "Friends don't let friends dress drunk."

My head snapped back. "I'm not drunk."

"Well, maybe you should've been." A sniff of scorn lingered in the air. "Have you seen yourself? Doesn't your grandmother own a full-length mirror? And what's this —" she twirled her fingers near her cheeks "— clown rouge? Have you been experimenting with Gran's blush?"

Bruckman's five o'clock shadow must've scuffed my face.

"Windburn." I may be blonde but I'm nothing if not able to think on my feet.

Hand to mouth, Venice blurted out what everyone else was thinking. "You didn't . . . did you?"

In an attempt to reclaim my patina of respectability, I shushed them. "Certainly not. Y'all know me better than that."

But I wanted to.

Oops. I might've said that out loud.

Bruckman loaded the dresses into the back seat and trunk of Venice's Lexus. When he was done, he met me by the Porsche.

My friends may have gone back inside the house but I sensed them peering out from behind the European shutters. Bruckman must've felt their eyes boring holes through us, too, because he didn't come any closer than three feet.

"Seven days," he said knowingly. "See you later."

It wasn't until I was on my way back to Gran's and stopped at a convenience store to pick up bottled water that I caught my reflection in the glass. I looked like I'd dressed from the rag bin. Pouty lips were smeared crimson.

The left side of my brain was asking *What the hell happened?* But the right side was saying *Why seven days, why not tonight?*

I stuck my mobile in the glove compartment to make it harder to call him. But that only made it more difficult when the phone rang and I had to lean over to retrieve it. I knew it was Bruckman before I answered. Still, the moment I saw his name displayed on the neon blue screen, my heart jumped. Three cleansing breaths later, I thumbed on the phone.

"Hello," I said coolly.

"Seven days." Bruckman spoke in a soft, hypnotic voice.

"You're pretty sure of yourself." *Très* hoity

toity of me, no? Considering I couldn't get those laser blue eyes and that infectious grin out of my mind.

"No, babe. I'm sure of you."

After I disconnected, dreamy feelings toward Bruckman soon sizzled. Lost in thought, with my reflexes on auto-pilot, I traveled through darkness as black as pitch, oblivious to the strip of roadway I'd driven hundreds of times over the years.

An explosion of light lit up the intersection like an Iraqi roadside bombing.

An audible yip broke from my throat.

My heart lurched in terror. I got a stranglehold on the steering wheel. Before I could comprehend what happened, a second blast of brilliance momentarily turned my surroundings into daylight — as though simultaneous bolts of lightning had struck in front and back. I knew, on instinct, that the traffic camera for this latest infraction had captured my face in a close-up, contorting into a grotesque mask of terror, my mouth frozen in an "O" and my eyes bulging like one of those fright-stricken actors straight out of a horror flick — or worse — like Chopper Deke's.

Later, once I was safely tucked in bed with my head resting in a fluff of down pillows, I relived Bruckman's kisses. With a wash of silver moonlight checker-boarding the covers, my subconscience kicked in. Two buried concerns popped up like coffins in a flood.

One, Bruckman didn't mention what time he planned to pick me up for the concert.

And, two — was I the only one who noticed when the cops arrived at Tandy's house that her mother's boyfriend fled out the back door and zoomed off in his Lexus?

CHAPTER SIXTEEN

Goals for the day:

1. Ride-in with police
2. Watch for dogs
3. Don't fall for Bruckman

Over the next few days, when I wasn't spying on Paislee Pfeiffer or researching Mrs. Westlake's boyfriend, I spent major chunks of time with Bruckman learning how to become a good private investigator without getting killed in the process. He even worked a shift for one of the uniforms so he could teach me the basics of police work.

Riding-in with Bruckman was sweet.

We made traffic stops, took calls the dispatcher assigned him, went on a couple of 10-7s — police code for coffee breaks — and stopped beneath a huge oak tree in a residential area and watched customers at a convenience come and go from several blocks away. Bruckman said a cashier about my age had been murdered there ten years before and it bothered him that the police never caught the guy who did it.

A week ago, I wouldn't have believed it if someone had told me Bruckman had a soft side. Now it's hard to remember how mean he was the first time we met.

Around four o'clock in the morning, I was sitting in his office at the Fort Worth Police Department, waiting for Bruckman to return from the Captain's office. The Pyramids were built in less time. Patience isn't my strong suit and I'd had my fill of boredom so I fished a stick of mint gum out of my purse and folded it into my mouth.

Chewing gum is *très* disgusting and makes you look like a cow. But I've been known to sneak an occasional piece in places where I don't expect to get caught, such as in the privacy of my bedroom or sunning by Gran's pool when it's just me and the maid who doesn't speak English. So when the door to the detectives' office unexpectedly swung open, I accepted my miscalculation and swallowed it.

A tall, good-looking guy walked in wearing blue jeans and a polo-type shirt with the

Fort Worth Police logo embroidered on the chest where a pocket should've been. He seemed startled to see someone . . . like me? . . . sitting at Bruckman's desk.

"So . . . you're riding with Jim tonight?"

I nodded.

"Don't believe everything he tells you." He strolled to a nearby desk and opened a drawer in search of something.

"What do you mean?"

"I wouldn't let my sister go out with him," he said knowingly.

After sifting through several documents, he huffed out a resigned sigh. I knew that expression. I'd worn it myself. Striking up a conversation with him seemed the polite thing to do.

"You look overwhelmed."

"I caught a pretty bad case." Intense brown eyes snared me in their grip. "Are you here to learn about police work or are you one of Jim's girls?"

One of Jim's girls?

Okay, why'd I feel a jealous pang when he said that?

I've got no vested interest in Jim Bruckman. This is strictly business.

Okay . . . maybe a little hanky-panky here and there. But only a little.

"I'm just here to ride-in. I want to learn

how to become a good detective."

"Good." He gave me a slow, deliberate nod. "I'll impart a bit of knowledge to you. Something all women should know — men, too."

"Feel free."

"Pay attention."

My eyes went wide.

"Never . . . never . . . never allow anyone to tie you up. If you're abducted at gunpoint, knifepoint, whatever . . . I don't care if the guy tells you he won't hurt you as long as you do what he says — and he wants to tie you up — do not *ever* let him do that. If you do, you're dead. FBI statistics bear that out."

I must not have shown the proper reaction because he demanded to know if I'd heard him. In fact, I'd been hanging on every word. This was good stuff. Who knew when I might need it?

"Only you're not just dead. You're tortured to death. I'm not kidding." He'd gotten loud and his words practically reverberated off the walls of the small office. "If you let somebody tie you up they'll take you wherever they want and do whatever they want to do to you and there's not one fu—" he caught himself "— 'scuse my French, not one flipping thing you can do about it." His

216

hand made a loud smack against the desk.

I flinched.

"Fight for your life right there. You'll stand a better chance of surviving." Compelling eyes glinted with knowledge and fury from having interviewed too many victims. "And I'll tell you something else. If you do make the mistake and let some sick motherfu— asshole — tie you up, the way God points the finger is through DNA. Understand?"

Huge head bob. I didn't even realize I'd been holding my breath until he finished talking.

"Very good, Miss . . ."

I introduced myself, extending my hand for a brief shake. His hand clasped mine in a powerful grip, pumped twice, and let go. It took a few seconds for the color to flood back into my fingertips.

"Pleased to meet you, Dainty Prescott. You get a gold star. Be careful out there, now, you hear?" He must've found what he'd come for because he scribbled a note on his desk calendar and was out the door.

A few minutes later, Bruckman returned.

"That guy who just left — is he working a big case?"

"Major case. And, yes, he is." He slid into a chair behind the desk.

"What's he working on?"

"String of rapes. Brutal. Perp leaves them for dead."

"Are y'all friends?" Call me nosey, but the answer would go a long way toward deciding how much emphasis to place on some of those comments I'd fielded.

"Who, Lance?" He considered the question. "We have a mutual respect for each other. He's just about the best there is. Not as good as me. But almost."

The license plate number Tandy had written on the yellow sticky had adhered itself to the gum pack. I peeled it off and asked if he'd run it through the dispatch office. Before he would agree to do it, he insisted on knowing why I wanted the information. I filled him in.

"Tandy thinks the guy's a con man."

"A con man?" Relaxed humor showed in his face.

"What's so funny about that?"

"Sounds funny coming from you."

"I don't find it the least bit amusing that Mrs. Westlake might be about to marry a man who wants to bilk her out of her divorce settlement."

"That's the mother of the girl who threw the birthday party for you?" When I nodded he said, "That's some house."

"It's an albatross. It should've come with

a GPS. And it's soundproof. So if Mrs. Westlake's fiancé turns out to be Mafia, we couldn't even hear her scream if she needed help."

"Mafia?" He seemed to be having a rollicking good time at my expense.

"Dixie Mafia," I said in my catty sarcastic voice. "And if you're not going to run the plate for me then teach me how to do it myself. I want to see whose name the car's registered in."

"It's a rental car," he said dismissively. "I can tell by the first letter in the LP."

"If you can't or won't get the information for me then give me back the paper. I'll figure it out on my own."

By way of an answer, he picked up the telephone, dialed an extension and said, "Hey, Annabelle, would you run a plate for me?" He winked at me from across the room. After a short wait, he grabbed a pen and jotted down the response. "Thanks. See you later." But instead of hanging up, he said, "Sure, we can do that. Name the date." And then, "Look, I'm with somebody right now so we'll have to catch up later." He hung up the phone and swiveled his chair in my direction.

It didn't take a voice stress analyzer to be able to discern guilt in his tone. What sounded like flirtation was a cruelty to the ear. Well, let me just say, I don't care. The last thing I need is to trade one Romeo for another. It's common knowledge within my social circle that I don't share — second place is just another way of saying first loser.

He must've picked up on the sheep-killing-dog expression settling onto my face, because he had the look of someone who's realized too late that the little rock tumbling down the path he's standing on is actually the boulder from *Indiana Jones.*

"It's not what you think."

"You don't know me well enough to know what I think." Said with cutting reserve.

"No, and you don't know me well enough to decide I'm a player."

"Are you?" From the moment Bruckman's colleague chatted me up, I'd worked hard to keep my "siege mentality" in check. But now, my stomach clenched.

"Why do you want to know?" he toyed with me.

"I don't care one way or the other. That's your business." But the little voice in my head was screaming, *For the love of God, how many times does it take before you learn the lesson?*

"I'm a one-woman man." And then, "Here." He handed me the LP number with the information on it. Sure enough, it came back to a rental car agency.

Discouraged, I crumpled it in my hand.

"If I were checking out this guy," Bruckman suggested, "I'd get one of the employees at the car place to check their system and see who rented the Lexus."

"Will they give me that information?"

"That's where a badge comes in handy. They probably won't want to give it to you —" he pinned me with his eyes "— but you're a manipulative little vixen. I'll bet you can figure out a way to weasel it out of them."

"Is that supposed to be a compliment?"

"Take it anyway you want. You want to run the Debutante Detective Agency —"

"Stop calling it that."

"— and you've asked me to train you. Get it through your head, Dainty — sitting in a henhouse doesn't make you a chicken and sitting behind a desk at the Debutante Detective Agency doesn't make you a private investigator."

My chin quivered. Despite the blonde hair, I'm a sharp cookie. So how was it that I continually managed to step on these verbal land mines?

"Being a cop gives me certain advantages that you don't have. But a good investigator

221

could find out what you need to know."

"I have an idea," I said with put-on excitement, "you could go ask them for me."

"I could but I won't."

I scowled. What was the point of having a buddy in law enforcement if you couldn't call on them to do clandestine stuff for you?

"There'll come a time when you'll call begging for information. Do you really want to use up a favor for something you can rustle up on your own?"

Made sense.

"What you really ought to do, if you're hell-bent on starting your own business, is to subscribe to a couple of these Internet companies that'll do your data research for you. There are good ones out there that you can get all kinds of information from: criminal convictions, lawsuit information, car wrecks, driving records, license tags. Then you have sex offender information that's free . . ."

He made so many suggestions that I had to pull out a pen and paper just to keep track.

"This isn't foolproof, you understand. You may still have to drive to the courthouse for collateral information, but you can sure streamline your research." He did a quick lean-in. "If you could get his Social Security number that'd open all kinds of doors for you."

Amazing how little I knew about checking people out.

I thanked him for the information and told him I had to get over to the TV station. I didn't exactly lie but he might've gotten the idea that I was expected to help out the on-air talent before the morning broadcast. Go figure.

What I really needed to do was drive over to Gordon's house in my undercover Junkers-R-Us rental.

Bruckman returned me to the police academy where I'd parked my Porsche.

While I waited in the passenger seat of the unmarked patrol car, wondering whether he'd kiss me good-bye, he sat behind the wheel with the engine idling, scoping out the parking lot with his internal cop radar humming. As his gaze danced over the cars, he told me about the building adjacent to the academy. According to Bruckman, it housed convicted felons who'd been paroled from the Texas prison system.

"It's full of sex offenders," he said.

I shot him an awkward glance. Was he scanning the area for parolees who hadn't returned to the halfway house by curfew?

"I won't kiss you in the patrol car," he

said in a matter-of-fact, roughly textured voice.

"I should hope not."

I wish. Wait — did he want to? Or, did he think I expected it? Making out in the patrol car would be so Rubanbleu unacceptable. And exciting! Wait — what if he thinks I'm flirting with him? What if I am?

I gave him an aristocratic sniff and flashed a smile so forced I felt my jaw go numb.

"Get out."

"What?" I'm not used to being harshly spoken to by people I haven't provoked.

He wrenched the car into park and cut the engine. "Get out. I want to show you something."

I trailed him to a pickup parked beneath the street lamp. Bruckman's truck is white but the one he stopped beside appeared blue beneath the glow of the mercury vapor lamp. I wasn't certain the vehicle was his until he fished for keys and beeped the remote. That's when I realized how different automobile colors look at night, depending on the lighting.

Note to self: file this away for future use.

Color me green as a gourd. I had so much to learn.

The truck barked, lights flashed on and the electric locks snapped open. He ducked behind the seat long enough to pull out a case of some sort, which, for all I knew, could've been a "Tommy gun" from an old gangster movie.

The evening had started out mild but the night air had turned nippy — the kind of crisp October night where you needed a jacket if you planned to be out in the elements longer than a few minutes.

I wished I'd brought a wrap or pashmina along.

Bruckman must've read my mind because he shrugged out of his jacket and whirled it over my shoulders. The faint outline of a bulletproof vest pressed against the fabric of his shirt. Then it hit me: What kind of man would lay his life on the line for people he didn't even know? A brave one? Seriously, ignorance is humorous. Stupidity is not. *If* — and I had to ask myself this in strictest hypothetical sense — if my relationship with Bruckman progressed beyond the research and development phase, would I stay up nights wondering if he'd return to me safely at the end of watch? He stepped back to his door, snapped open the case and pulled out a fiddle and bow.

My eyes fluttered in astonishment. "I didn't know you played."

"There's a lot you don't know about me."

"Are you any good?"

He let out an extended bray of a laugh and then rosined up the bow. For the next five minutes he played a private concert of Irish reels and waltzes just for me.

Me and the six hundred fifty sex offenders.

The fiddle cried out in an emotionally evocative wail. A series of lights flickered on next door, but not one word came from occupants of the halfway house as windows were lifted open to let the sweet, pure sound of Bruckman's music roll in. When he finished, he wordlessly packed away his fiddle and locked up as if nothing had happened, while I stood speechless in the clear night air wondering what the hell had just happened to my heart.

"Walk you to your car?" he said casually. Dumbstruck as a cow at a rendering plant, I shook off the trance and hurried to catch up.

"Where'd you learn to do that?"

"Where I learn to do everything." He tapped a finger to his head.

I blinked, unable to imagine keeping a talent like that to myself. If Bruckman got lonely he could always make music. But for someone whose greatest forte is shopping, well, I couldn't even enjoy that transient

226

pleasure now that Daddy's bleached-blonde tourniquet had stopped my money supply from hemorrhaging.

When we got to my car Bruckman eyed me up. Then he pulled me away from the street lamp behind a brother officer's van. Hidden from the watchful eyes of criminals and pedestrians, he swept me into his embrace and kissed me beneath the marble platter moon.

"Did you think about me last night after you drove back to Granny's?"

He was biting my neck as he said it and the roguish inflection resonating from his voice almost buckled my knees.

Not trusting myself to speak, I shook my head.

"Liar." His whisper turned my body to sand. He gently nipped my neck again and I half-expected to slide to the ground like a cartoon character.

"It's the truth."

Not true.

He bit my neck harder and with more passion. There was nothing left to do but wait to turn into a vampire and fly off with him.

"Admit it. You dreamed about me, didn't you?"

I felt his hot breath against my ear. "You don't need me dreaming about you —

you're so full of yourself you probably dream about yourself all on your own."

"Yes, you did." He teased me with his eyes. "I can read it in your face, Dainty Prescott. You're a terrible liar. You dreamed about what it'd be like to go to bed with me."

"Did not." Our mouths slammed together.

"Did, too," he said breathily, with his lips back on mine, harder and insistent this time.

I realized later on the drive to Gordon's in the crappy little dented tin can he'd rented that I couldn't be in love with Jim Bruckman. It was too soon and I didn't really know him. What I did know was that wherever this runaway mine train took me I wanted to stay buckled in for as long as the ride lasted.

Even if it crashed.

Especially if it crashed.

CHAPTER SEVENTEEN

A half hour after I left Bruckman, I returned to the scene of the crime — Gordon's house. Only this time I parked in front of the neighbor's place a few car lengths down from the Pfeiffer's driveway. I turned on the recording device at five-fifteen in the morning and, sure enough, found that my boss had planted the spyware. As I listened to Paislee stirring up a racket with her snoring, her phone trilled. Jarred awake, she answered on a sleepy hello.

"No, he's already gone," she said, drowsy and mumbling. "Sure. Come on over."

The disadvantage to this particular recording equipment was that I could only hear one side of the conversation. If Gordon wanted more, he'd need to bug the phone. The garage might be a good place to hide a recorder. Paislee probably only went there long enough to climb in and out of the Jag.

I listened to her singing in the shower to

the backup vocals of a band I didn't recognize. She was tone deaf, which further boosted my opinion that there's a huge difference between singing together and singing at the same time. Then I was treated to the sound of her brushing her teeth, gargling, and spitting in the sink. The phone rang again and she answered on the second ring.

"Hello. Oh, hi. Sure. I'll meet you at your house around nine. Me, too. *Ciao.*"

I wanted to thunk my head against the steering wheel. No way did I plan to sit here for hours while —

What's this?

I grabbed the binoculars off the seat, scrunched down behind the wheel enough to see over the top and focused the lenses.

A black BMW rolled brazenly by and parked a couple of houses down. I picked up the loaner camera from the repair shop and focused the lens on the license plate. GLTYSN.

Drex.

I snapped the first photo. I snapped another as he got out of the car and skulked up the sidewalk on the opposite side of the road. I got the third shot of him cutting through the Pfeiffer's yard and one of him pressing the keypad on the gate. I started the car and drove into the alley, stopping when I reached the back of Gordon's house. The upstairs light came on as I stealthily climbed onto the hood and crawled onto the roof of my old clunker.

I zoomed in for a closeup and focused the camera lens.

For a second, I only saw Drex standing by the window with his shirt off, and wondered how I'd lost sight of Paislee in the time it took to lift the camera to my eye. My attention dipped below the belt.

There she was, Paislee Pfeiffer.

The spike strip on the highway to my love life.

Paislee must've thought Drex had been snakebit because I'm pretty sure I got some great shots of her performing first aid on his —

Yikes.

Car.

Not just any car.

Cop car.

The closer it got the more defined the overhead emergency light bar became.

It rolled down the alley crunching gravel beneath its tires. I snapped the last picture, slung the camera over my back and jumped for the tree branch overhanging the junker.

Holy cow.

A spotlight came on, illuminating the area like a lighthouse beacon as its bright beam swept across the alley. My camera was dangling past the foliage so I did a one-handed lurch and pulled it onto my stomach.

The patrolmen took their sweet time. I clung to the tree limb for dear life while simultaneously running through the mental checklist of crimes I could be charged with if my prayer for invisibility went unanswered.

Squawk from the police radio sliced through the early morning air.

The marked unit stopped even with my rental car. The electric window slid halfway down. A male voice recited the license plate number while I tried to become part of the tree — like those drawings in *Highlights* where you pick out objects that are cleverly hidden within the picture.

A couple of neighborhood dogs tuned up barking. Then gravel crunched beneath the police car's tires as the officers rolled on down the alley.

Whew.

Home free.

An ominous fracture provided a two-second warning. It sounded like the sickening crack of a broken bone. The tree limb snapped under my weight.

I crashed to the ground, branch and all.

The car alarm went off.

The fall knocked the wind out of me. But hey — good news — the camera survived. So even if I died right here the cops would probably get the film developed and it would eventually make its way back to Gordon.

Oxygen deprivation's a scary thing. I patted my pocket for something sharp to perform my own tracheotomy and came up with car keys.

Torn between saving my life and shutting off the burglar alarm, I chose to stab myself in the throat. At least if it ricocheted off like it did the first time I tried it, maybe the neighbors would come out to see what the ruckus was. They'd find my cold, dead body before I bloated up and police had to use dental comparison charts to identify me.

Sometimes when I'm bored I watch the forensics channels. For no good reason I flashed back to a murder where the husband enticed his wife to go horseback riding, then injected her with succynilcholine and slammed her head against a rock to make it look like an accidental fall from the horse. Imagine being wide awake where you can hear and feel everything around you but cannot move a muscle.

And that's where I was, conscious of insect sounds and the occasional piece of paper kicked up by the breeze.

Then the tree went out of focus.

Everything around me turned a dull brown haze. A looming silhouette towered over me. In my weakened state, the camera was lifted from my grasp. My protests became insignificant grunts as someone grasped me beneath the arms and propped against a tire in a sitting position.

I sucked in air.

My vision came into sharp focus.

Bruckman was kneeling beside me. He had the look of someone who'd strolled into a convenience store with his mouth watering for a chilidog only to discover he'd walked in on a stick-up.

He keyed his hand-held police radio and spoke in a calm, detached voice. "It's Code-four over here. Code-four."

The radio squawked. "Whatcha got, Jim?"

"I thought it was a dement off her medication but it turns out she just had car trouble and needed to find a phone. She was just leaving," he said with a trace of mischief in his tone.

But when he directed his comments to me, his voice went suddenly stern, and his expression dark and forbidding. "Explain what you're doing here."

"That would be the answer to: *What is the stupidest thing I could possibly do at the moment?*"

"Just as I thought. You're not ready to start the Debutante Detective Agency. You didn't even notice you'd picked up a tail. Swear to God, Dainty, everything you touch is FUBAR."

I waved him off, exuding as much poise as I could muster. It was enough to know that the camera survived the fall.

"Fucked up beyond all recognition," he explained, looking every bit as dangerous as he had at our first meeting.

I gave a head bob of understanding for the cop terminology. I may be blonde, but I'm a quick study. And if I didn't go directly to jail, I'd find a way to use it in a sentence at least five times to commit to memory.

"Saying it louder isn't going to help, now, is it?" I shot him an equally cutting glare.

"What the hell are you doing here?" Bruckman again, giving my shoulders a hard shake.

"Working a case for a paying client." Now that I'd caught my breath, I tried to immobilize him with my death ray glare. "You?"

"Following you to make sure you didn't get yourself killed."

By way of illustration, I thumbed at the tree limb. My actions had been about as subtle as a drag queen at a monster truck rally. Oops, I might've said that aloud.

I took a stroll on the blunt side. "Am I under arrest?"

"No. You're lucky nobody called in a prowler."

"What about your partner?" My eyes cut to the patrol car idling at the end of the alley.

"He won't say anything if I tell him not to. But it's going to look bad when I introduce you at the police ball if you don't knock it off."

CHAPTER EIGHTEEN

After the tree disaster, I stopped by the Hanovers' residence so I could see how Venice was coming along with my ball gown. Venice's mother is Dr. Hanover, one of the city's leading pediatricians. Since she has her own practice on Hulen Street, it came as a surprise to find her home, mid-week, cooking breakfast. The air in the dining room was heavily scented with the sweet smell of cinnamon rolls. Bacon sizzled on the stove. As I walked into the house and followed the savory smells, I could see Dr. Hanover in the kitchen, alternately juicing fresh oranges and stirring scrambled eggs. Pats of butter danced across a skillet. Grits boiled in a pan.

She invited me to stay for breakfast. I accepted. My stomach loves Dr. Hanover's cooking.

"Make yourself useful." She jutted her chin at the cabinets and I knew, on instinct, that she expected me to get my own dishes and silverware and set my place at their table.

"Is Dr. Hanover here?" I was referring to her husband, a respected cardiologist.

Her dark ponytail switched from side to side. "He's at a conference in San Antonio." She pronounced it "San An-tóne-ya" like a native.

"You should be with him."

She had a robust laugh like heavy-duty wind chimes. It echoed into the dining room where I was trying to figure out how to craft my cloth napkin into a little swan like the ones that had already been folded at the other place settings.

"Are you kidding? If I went to San Antonio there'd be no one to run this house."

"You should hire some help."

"I have plenty of help." She glided into the room holding a tureen between potholders made to resemble lobster claws. "But every now and then I need a day just for me." She placed the tureen on the table, snatched the napkin from me and — *presto!* — a swan appeared.

"How'd you do that?" I marveled.

"Honestly, Dainty, haven't you ever heard of Origami? It's the same principle."

When I shook my head, she touched my

cheek. "Poor, deprived child. Origami's great for quiet time with children. You should learn the art because one of these days, you'll have screaming kids and Origami's a refreshing alternative to duct taping their mouths shut and locking them in the closet."

Made sense.

My daddy had a different way of handling disruptive behavior at the Prescott compound. Intimidation and threats to whisk Teensy or me directly to the Edna Gladney Home for immediate adoption usually put a cork in the bickering. One day I called his bluff. While Teensy, who'd started it, headed for the neighbors', I packed a train case full of Barbie dolls, put on my sparkly sunglasses, took Daddy the car keys and said, "Let's go." He upped the ante and drove me right up to the front door.

Before I got out of the car, I asked him to jot down where he wanted me to write him. He said my new parents might not appreciate that and sent me inside alone. When a reasonable amount of time passed and I didn't return remorseful, apologetic and in tears, he came looking for me. And that's how he found me, in the cafeteria, playing Barbies with my new best friend and scarfing down my third ice cream sandwich. Jig's up. So . . . *ha.*

Dr. Hanover pointed me to the sink to wash up. She has this obsession with multi-resistant staph — MRSA. It's a wonder her hands aren't as wrinkled as Gran's. After toweling off, I carried a plate of wheat toast and homemade strawberry jam to the table. Once Venice joined us, I told her about the ride-in with Bruckman and how much I'd been looking forward to our date tonight. Dr. Hanover listened with interest about the warning from Bruckman's colleague.

"What do you really know about him?" She unfurled the swan napkin and rested it in her lap.

"I know he passed a background check or he wouldn't be on the police department."

"I dated a policeman once." When Venice arched an eyebrow, she said, "Back when I was doing my residency." She buttered a piece of dry toast, pausing long enough to gaze at a distant spot on the wall and reflect. "He was exciting. He'd just gotten on the police department. A rookie. We met in the ER one night after he brought in a prisoner for stitches. We hit it off immediately. I liked his attitude. He said he'd joined the PD because he wanted to help people."

She put down her knife and lifted her glass to her lips, took a quick swallow and resumed buttering her toast.

Venice prompted her to finish the story.

"I noticed a change in him after the first year we dated. It was no longer about helping people. His state of mind turned into *Us against them* — *them* being anybody who wasn't a cop. After I finished my residency, I couldn't deal with the metamorphosis. He'd apparently warped on schedule because after a few years of *Us against them,* he had that *My shift against your shift* attitude where he no longer wanted to associate with any officers who didn't patrol directly with him."

There was a lull in the conversation.

"What happened?"

"Maybe we should drop it." Dr. Hanover made serious eye contact with her daughter.

"No," we chorused, gluttons for punishment.

"I ran into him at the ER a year after we broke up. He had that *Me against everybody else* mentality — very unattractive."

Rapt with wonder, Venice said, "Did you still like him?"

"I thought he was scary. There was something dark about him that I'd mistaken for a bad-boy type of dangerousness. An adventuresome, devil-may-care spirit. But by this time, he'd turned just plain scary." She fixed me with an unwavering stare. "You should be careful, Dainty. If this man's friend warned you about him, maybe you should heed the warning."

It's not like I didn't see this one coming. I haven't recently been inducted into Stonecutters. My friends' parents are all the time trying to scare their kids into submission with their caveman-like over-protectiveness. Now that my mom's gone and Daddy got caught up in his mid-life crisis, these people are hell bent on shepherding me, too.

Undaunted, I pressed for more information. "What happened to your cop-friend?"

"About five years after the last ER visit, I got a call from him out of the blue. He asked if I was happy." She shifted her gaze to Venice and back to me, like following a tennis volley. "I'd been married for about four years and was pregnant. Naturally, we were thrilled and I told him so."

"Why'd he call?" Venice asked.

"In retrospect, I think he needed a lifeline, although I didn't realize it at the time. I should've paid more attention."

"What happened?" I'm the one who asked but I could tell Venice wanted to know as much as I did.

"Your father and I were watching the news later that evening. The TV station flashed a picture of him on the screen and said he'd been found dead in his home by a relative who hadn't been able to get him to answer his phone. The medical examiner ruled the death a suicide. I think he'd been going through a divorce and his wife got custody of their child. It was very sad. I remember thinking that could've been me." She visibly shuddered.

Venice locked me in her amber gaze. "You should drop Bruckman before this even gets started, Dainty." She turned to her mother. "He had a girlfriend and she ditched him for another cop. That's the cop we saw on the news the other night — the one who was killed by the DWI when he stopped to help a stranded motorist."

Dr. Hanover reserved judgment. "I'm sure Dainty will make the right choice," she said, finishing the last of her orange juice. "She's got a good head on her shoulders." Then she shifted her *Poor little idiot* expression over to me. "Would you girls mind loading the dishwasher? I have to take the car in for an oil change." She pushed back from the table and excused herself.

After Dr. Hanover's story cast a pall over breakfast, my mood lightened when Venice took me back to her sewing room and showed me the sketch of my dress. She hadn't actually seen the mermaid dress before Gran had the housekeeper return it to Harkman's so I had to rely on memory when describing it. After a few minor changes to the drawing, Venice took my exact measurements.

Instead of a cherry red copy of the mermaid dress, I'm getting a rainbow-colored mermaid dress that'll be even more stunning than the one from Harkman Beemis since she's adding a little pleated stand-up ruffle to the strapless top. It looks sweet in the drawing — kind of like a fish fin to go with the fishtail train. Or gills.

Anyway, she'd already pulled out the dresses she's going to cut up and splice together to get the rainbow effect. She's taking the seven colors in the rainbow and pairing each one with similar fabrics a shade or two off. That way the rainbow effect will be gradual. I'm elated.

Venice showed me to the door. I thanked her for what I knew would turn out to be a beautiful ball gown. But instead of basking in glory, her smile slipped away.

"You're not supposed to fall in love with him, Dainty. It's perfectly fine if he can help you adjust to your break-up with Drex. But he's not the right guy for you."

Again, not Rubanbleu acceptable.

244

I absorbed her words.

She must've noticed a ghastly expression on my face because she grabbed my hand and held it tight. "Oh, Dainty, no. Don't do that. You know I wouldn't hurt you for the world. I only meant that he's not your type. You need somebody more like Drex — only without the wandering penis."

What a relief.

For a minute I thought she was about to say something stupid.

Brightening with *faux* cheer, I flicked my wrist in a dismissive hand wave. "Don't give it another thought. I know I won't."

We both knew that wasn't true.

After leaving the Hanovers', I dropped the film I took at Gordon's off at the one-hour photo lab and drove back to Gran's to get a little sleep so I wouldn't fall asleep tonight during our date to the Bass Hall. Around this time of day, Gran usually gets her driver to take her to the antique stores in search of treasures and then on to one of the upscale restaurants with one of her widowed friends.

I figured I'd have the house to myself. The last thing I expected was to enter the sunroom and find that I wasn't alone.

I stopped dead in my tracks.

Gran was sitting in the Philadelphia chair with her back to me, hunkered over the antique library table with an Italian Tole bouillotte lamp switched on and her Mont Blanc fountain pen resting on a half-written sheet of paper. The matching envelope had already been addressed in an elegant hand. Still doing things the old-fashioned way, she had her wax seal out as well as her personalized stationery and a roll of generic postage stamps — the kind you lick, not the peel-and-stick kind.

The trick was to back out slowly and hope she didn't notice. She must've had her hearing aids in and her bat radar turned on because she sat up rigid.

"Come in, Dainty."

As I slunk toward her with my eyes downcast, she rested her hands in her lap.

Without bothering to turn around, she said, "Are you familiar with the story of Evangeline Briscoe?"

The name grated on me like a rusty hinge, not because I knew who Evangeline Briscoe was, but because I'd stumbled into a trap and now I'd have to listen to another one of *those* stories. I'd started to think of these parables as tollways to hell, where the only way I could come and go was to pay the price by hearing her out.

I pretended to search my memory. "Come to think of it, I do believe I've heard this one before," I fibbed.

"No, you haven't," Gran said snippily, "because I've never told it. Sit down."

I did a heavy eye roll and flopped onto one of the rattan sofas.

"Evangeline's mother used to play bridge with my mother and a few other ladies. Evangeline was a year or two younger than me. Whenever the mothers would get together, the children would play outdoors so as not to disturb them. I played with Mary Margaret Engelking, Tilda Simonton and Ruth Grabel and her sisters — I believe I've mentioned them before because there were five girls in that family and they all had red hair and not a freckle among them."

I picked up a throw pillow and wondered how long it would take to suffocate myself. And whether that option was even possible given that Gran might remove the pillow from my face before brain death set in.

"Well, no matter about the red hair, which by the way, everybody wondered where that came from because Penny Grabel and her husband Eldon didn't have one red hair between them. But she was a McIntire so I suppose the color came from her side of the family."

I considered my options and decided smothering myself was out of the question.

In the back of my mind, I remembered from CPR class that it takes seven minutes of oxygen deprivation before brain death sets in and I didn't want to hear more than I had to while dying.

Electrocution might be the way to go, though. I looked around for a light socket with a cord I could bite down on. Sadly, the only one in the room seemed to be connected to the lamp Gran was working by.

"But, I digress. As I was saying, every Wednesday afternoon while the ladies' bridge club met, I'd play with their daughters. But Evangeline Briscoe would always run off in search of the boys. Now they were quite a bit older than she was — closer our age, I'd say — and every time the ladies would play bridge, there'd be Evangeline, tagging along."

I went rigid.

"Most always, she'd come back injured after roughhousing with these boys. Let's see, there was Jody Sutherland, Van Millstone, Edgar . . ."

Names fused together as I flopped over onto my side like a shot deer. I stared at some distant point in space, waiting to go glassy-eyed as the flowers in Gran's tropical garden turned into smears of color.

Gran was still talking but in my head, I

was playing the *I can't hear a word you say* game. It's a little diversion technique I use to distract me from the goings-on around me. It allows you to almost disassociate yourself from your surroundings by repeating these words in your head: "I can't hear a word you say; I can't hear a word you say; I can't hear a word you say," *ad infinitum.* Once the cadence of the chant gets going full bore, you start to believe it. After that, you can drown out just about anything and anyone, anytime and anywhere.

Except Gran.

The game doesn't work on Gran.

Gran is impervious to the game.

". . . and one time when Jody Sutherland's mother hosted the bridge club out at their lake house, the boys told Evangeline they were going to race down to the water's edge and back. Thing is, they'd always tell Evangeline that they'd already done whatever it was that they wanted her to do. She was what you might call their own personal human guinea pig. So the kid with the stopwatch said, 'On your mark, get set, go,' and Evangeline started running, petticoats flying, pinafore whipping behind her in the wind, her little black patent leather Mary Janes churning up dust . . .

"Did I mention Evangeline was near-sighted?"

I groaned.

"Pay attention, Dainty," she snapped as my eyes lost focus and banked off the walls and ceiling. *Hello,* could she not see this bored me to tears? "What's wrong with you? Maintain your concentration. You act like you've got ADOS."

"What's ADOS?"

"Attention deficit — *oh, shiny!*" she said, mocking me with a finger-slice through the air as if she'd just glimpsed a disco ball. Then she favored me with an eye roll that threatened to pop out of her head like champagne corks, spin across the floor and out onto the cobblestone driveway. I'm not making this up.

She picked up with Evangeline running the race, and the story droned on. "Well halfway down the path, there was this black rope coiled up. By the time Evangeline realized it was a water moccasin — what we called a cottonmouth — she couldn't stop the momentum and had to hurdle over it. She barely escaped being bitten."

I lay, cross-eyed, on my side, wondering if I could put on the brown wig I'd bought at the spy store and pass myself off as a stripper. How hard could it be? If I danced two nights a week, I could make enough money to move out of this Godforsaken place and hole up in a hotel until the townhouse was ready.

"I vividly recall the day those rascally boys came looking for Evangeline while we were playing Red Rover. You remember that game, don't you, Dainty? 'Red Rover, Red Rover, let Dainty come over.' "

A whimper of frustration escaped my lips.

"While the girls were playing Red Rover, the boys took poor little Evangeline off with them to the detached garage, where they'd removed a ladder and propped it against the roof. They told her they'd each climbed to the top and jumped off before she arrived and now it was her turn. That poor child climbed up the ladder with all those boys looking up her dress. I don't see how she kept from sliding off with those leather-soled shoes on but she made it to the apex and jumped. She wore a cast for six weeks after that. We all signed it."

This had to be it. I pulled myself upright, hopefully, to leave.

Hey, hey, good-bye, just like the golden oldie.

"But the worst thing I think happened . . ." Gran wasn't done. ". . . was when . . ."

"I just remembered I have a club meeting

251

to go to."

She peered at me through accusing sapphire beads. "What kind of club meeting?"

"Well, it's kind of a drinking club with a shopping problem."

"Don't get smart with me, young lady. Anyway, as I was saying . . ."

Flopping back over onto my side, I smashed my fingers into my eyes until blue comets arced across the backs of my lids.

". . . those boys took her out behind the garage. They convinced her they'd show her theirs if she'd show them hers."

Whoa.

My eyes popped open.

Now we're talking.

"They expected her to go first, of course. And she did. I wasn't there, mind you, but we all heard about it from our parents later. When Evangeline's mother went outside between games, looking for her, she found her spread-eagle with her bloomers off and her privates exposed. Those boys had formed a circle around her, gawking and yukking it up. Her mother like to have fainted."

I got a really ugly visual of this poor little waif, Evangeline, and wondered if she'd eventually gone on to have a successful career with a web camera and her own porn site. Several beats went by before I realized Gran had stopped talking.

Now that the story'd gotten interesting, my grandmother didn't seem to want to finish. Or maybe she really was finished. I should ask.

"Is that all there is?" I did a subtle lean-in to make out the address on the envelope. Sure enough, the correspondence was penned to one of the geriatric operatives in Gran's vast network of spies.

With her face serious and reproachful, she twisted in her chair. "That's it."

"What's your point, Gran?"

"Don't be gullible, Dainty."

CHAPTER NINETEEN

I spent the next hour lying saucer-eyed in my bed, listening to myself blink, paranoid that Gran might've peered out of her window the night Bruckman was here and had seen me with my button-down top askew.

In time, I dozed.

A call on the cell phone awakened me. It was Bruckman saying he'd pick me up around five-thirty. That'd give us time to get back to Fort Worth for an unhurried dinner before heading for the concert at Bass Hall. After hearing the story of Evangeline Briscoe, I decided to keep him as far away from Gran's digs as possible. No point killing a promising relationship before it even got started.

I had a better idea. "Why don't you give me your address and I'll meet you at your house?" There was a long pause that sounded a lot like dead air. "Bruckman? Are you there?"

"Yeah. Can't talk now. Something's up. Call you back."

Now I was listening to a dropped call for real.

My mind shifted into high gear. It wasn't like Bruckman worked Vice or Narcotics and a street person or confidential informant walked up to him. He'd warned me the first time I rode-in that if I ever met an officer who worked Vice or Narcotics, I should let the officer approach me first. That I should never-ever in a million years sashay up and greet them by name. He said he'd known guys who'd been killed because some police groupie or neighbor inadvertently outed them while they were deep undercover.

But Bruckman didn't work Vice or Narcotics. So why'd he cut me off without explanation?

By the time I put on fresh silk lingerie, hiked up my dark blue skinny skirt, slid into the dark blue and emerald green print silk blouse and slipped into matching blue strappy sandals, I'd decided on some level he wasn't being truthful with me. Either he was juggling women or — God forbid — he was married. Regardless, I needed to get to the bottom of it before I invested too much time in him.

I picked up the telephone to call him and it rang in my hand. It was Bruckman again, out of breath and panting.

"Armed robbery went down not fifty feet away from me. Had to stop it. Have to do a report now. Guy's in custody."

"Have you been running?"

"You could say that. On second thought, you should come here."

He gave me his address but when I asked for his home phone number, he denied having one.

"I cancelled my land line. No need for it. My cell goes everywhere I go."

After looking up his street on the computer, I decided to show up early. Since he lived in a suburb east of Fort Worth and west of Dallas, allowing for traffic and adhering to the speed limit, I could be at his residence in under an hour. If I left right now, I'd have plenty of time to check out the place before he returned home from the police station.

I managed to get out of the house without bothering Gran. As far as she knew I was going to the Bass Hall with the girls.

According to the computerized map, the shorter route to Bruckman's house would be via Airport Freeway instead of Interstate 30 so I left Gran's and headed north, then turned west toward Irving, the former home of the Dallas Cowboys. I passed DFW Airport and continued westbound through Euless, which is part of the mid-cities area. Around Bedford, I got caught in a traffic snarl in the middle lane of a three-lane highway.

Drivers routinely lose their loads because people don't think to tie down their cargo. I've dodged mattresses, sofas, chairs, bags of clothing, backpacks, lumber, car parts — you name it — and on this particular evening, traffic had ground to a screeching halt because a truckload of plush toys had fallen into the roadway.

I was thinking up new curse words when a dark metallic green blur shot past the on-ramp I'd just passed and forced its way into the slow lane. I probably wouldn't have noticed if the driver had been courteous, but he called attention to himself when he cut off the driver beside me and the guy leaned on his horn in protest.

My eyes bulged.

The Lexus had Florida plates. I felt inside my purse for a pen, chanting the number in my head. My plan to write it down dissolved when I saw the Post-It still stuck to my packet of chewing gum. I pulled out the yellow sticky note and held it up.

The car belonged to Alex Garrett. Or, rather, the rental agency that leased it to him.

I dropped back a car length to allow the driver beside me to pull in front. Then I picked up the cell phone and called Tandy.

When she answered, I cut to the chase. "I thought you said your stepfather went back to Florida on business."

"First of all," Tandy said with an edge in her voice, "he's not my stepfather yet. Second of all, he did go back to Florida for a few days to take care of business."

"When's the last time you saw him?"

"Couple of days ago. Why?"

A grin so big spread across my face that for a moment I feared Garrett's rearview mirror might catch the glint of my teeth in the setting sun and give away my position.

"You're not going to believe this, Tandy; he's not in Florida."

Tandy sucked air.

"I'm following him right now."

"I knew it," she growled. "Don't let him out of your sight, Dainty, not until you find out where he's going."

"That goes without saying."

Four exits after Alex Garrett whipped onto the freeway, he exited again. I followed him through Hurst, down several main drags, until he turned off on Highway 26 toward Colleyville. He turned off the highway and onto a residential street. I gave him a two-block lead and when I came to a four-way stop and actually yielded, a driver turned in front of me and served as a buffer. Down the block, Alex Garrett pulled into a driveway. As I crept up the street and watched the automatic garage door yawn open, I tracked his movements until he disappeared from view.

Since most houses in Tarrant County had been posted on a virtual street map, it was easy to get a visual on a house without actually driving by to see it. I jotted the house number down without getting a good look at it. Then I backtracked to Airport Freeway without a care in the world.

Tomorrow, I'd look on the county appraisal district website and find out who paid the taxes on the place. Once I perfected my spiel, I'd call the homeowner and ask if they'd be interested in renting the place. Considering Alex Garrett was supposed to marry Mrs. Westlake soon, I figured pretending to be a prospective tenant would provide a safe cover story. If he happened to be renting the place, I could tell the landlord I'd like to preview the house — once Alex returned from his so-called trip and I knew he was back at the Westlake's. After all, it wasn't a far cry from the truth.

I did need a place to live.

And if Alex was just a visitor, I could start a background check on the homeowner.

But for now, I needed to backtrack to Airport Freeway and get over to Bruckman's house — still five miles away.

CHAPTER TWENTY

Having dinner with Bruckman before the concert at Bass Hall turned out to be a blast. And the concert itself was spectacular. Our first real date deserved a high watermark. Even though I wasn't ready for the evening to end, the last thing I expected from Bruckman was to be invited into his home to continue the rendezvous. After all, we both needed to get up early the next morning for work.

His sprawling ranch-style house had an open concept with a fieldstone fireplace, terrazzo tile floors and warm colors in predominantly earth tones. He needed a serious visit from Venice. She could start by ripping down the drapes and updating colors. I didn't have long to commit the room to memory though. He hit the light switch and we were enveloped in a darkness that seemed as black as pitch and as unending as the galaxy. I realized then that he'd covered his windows with aluminum foil to blot out the light — like a day sleeper.

The sofa appeared as a reverse image in my eyes like a negative. He sat down hard and pulled me down with him. I snuggled up beside him with my ear pillowed against his chest, listening to the cadence of his heartbeat. After a few minutes a thin snore reached my ears. Bruckman had fallen asleep.

I may be blonde but I'm not boring. I decided to give it five minutes and then off I'd go. I hadn't had a wink of sleep in almost twenty-four hours and I was starting to get slaphappy.

Lying quietly, my eyes adjusted to the darkness, turning objects that were formerly the color of charcoal briquettes into identifiable shapes the shade of ash. I shifted into a more comfortable position, surprised when my careful movements jolted him. I looked over and saw his blue eyes wide awake and watching me. And for a second, I even thought I'd caught him sniffing my hair.

Instead of drifting back into slumber he gently kissed me. While his tongue grazed the undersides of my lips, strong fingers traced the curve of my breasts.

Other than the rush of cool air blowing through the ceiling vents and heavy breaths hot with anticipation, the lack of light and sound made our encounter more surreal. Like the absence of a gravitational pull, I sensed myself floating when he pulled me on top of him and tugged at my blouse.

For no good reason I thought of the way alligators work, snapping their jaws around prey and then rolling over and over to weaken the struggle before finally sinking to the bottom of the water to drown it.

And that was it.

I'd succumbed to Bruckman's magnetism and charm. So when he folded my blouse back over my shoulders enough to constrict my arm movements and unhooked the front clasp of my silky lace bra, I didn't care. Cool air whispered across my skin. Skilled fingers thrilled me.

This was crazy. The guy had close to an eight-year jump on me. Other than a grudging willingness to show me the ropes on detective stuff that would help me start up my business, the only thing I really knew about him was that every time we were together, I took leave of my senses. That, and the fact that I knew he'd somehow managed to ease my skirt past my hips and down to my knees before I realized it.

An alarm went off in my head.

I should go.

Should go before I end up doing something scandalous.

I should go before I can't take back what I'm about to do.

And yet I'd fallen under his spell as completely as if he'd waved a magic wand over me and told me to call him Merlin.

"Is this what you want, Dainty Prescott?"

I turned at the sound of his voice and there went my panties. Distracted, my mouth said, "No," but the gooseflesh on my arms begged to differ.

His disembodied voice continued to taunt me as his tongue applied itself to places I shouldn't have let him go near.

"Don't tell me you don't like that."

A primal groan escaped my lips.

His ability to read minds was starting to scare me.

"Bruckman . . ." My throat closed around his name. He lifted my hips enough to let me hover above his alter ego poised at the juncture of my thighs.

"What do you want?" He leaned in and nipped my shoulder. "Want to go home?" Long silence "Maybe you already are home. Ever think of that?"

Part of me did . . . the nude part wanted me to ease myself down on him and take the bucking bronco ride. But the other part,

264

the sane part of me, was back at the sushi bar listening to Venice relay that warning.

"Don't have anything to do with him, Dainty. He's a loose cannon."

And, *"Your superhero's a scary dude."*

Glowing in the feel of Bruckman's embrace, I shut my eyes, assaulted by an unbidden vision of Drex having stand-up sex with Paislee.

That's all it took for me to give in.

As I eased myself onto him, he asked one last time if this was how I wanted it.

"Yeah, Bruckman," I said, world-weary and needing my fragile underpinnings shored up. "This is exactly what I want."

His whole body seemed to sigh as he sank himself deep inside me. The last thing I remember him saying before I became fully caught up in my own selfish pleasure was, "Call me Jim."

CHAPTER
TWENTY-ONE

Goals for the day:

1. Pull surveillance on Alex Garrett w/o getting caught
2. Rent inconspicuous car
3. Avoid disturbing Gran — tiptoe!

After leaving Bruckman's, I decided to pull a reconnaissance mission. I swung back by the house in Hurst where I'd seen Alex Garrett park his car. It didn't occur to me that I might actually be able to take photographs in the middle of the night but when I got within three or four houses, his was the only one with lights on inside.

I parked the Porsche in front of a neighbor's home, pulled out my digital camera and changed the setting for night photos. Making my way up the sidewalk, I wasn't sure what I'd be able to observe from my place near the brick column housing the mailbox. But when I got within several feet of a large shade tree, I noticed the blinds in a downward slant that partially enabled me to see inside. The place had a creepy feel with the TV blaring. As I crept closer to the window to get the shot, I heard the shrill laugh track of a sitcom through the walls.

If I'd wondered before, I was certain now. Unless the man I knew as Alex Garrett had an identical twin, I was crouched less than ten feet away from Alex Garrett. Or rather . . . the man I'd been introduced to as Alex Garrett.

With the camera to my eye and the lens sharply focused, I snapped the first of several photos.

I got one of him kicked back in the easy chair watching baseball on a big-screen TV. The place had Spartan furnishings, with nothing else I could see inside the living room other than a trash can beside the chair for the empties. Garrett was a beer-drinking man.

I snapped a picture.

Headlights from an oncoming car illuminated the area behind me before I actually realized a vehicle was rolling slowly down the street. I stepped back into the shrubbery and huddled behind an over-grown wax ligustrum as a patrol car spot-lighted the yard across the street. The patrolman had already overshot Alex Garrett's house but that didn't mean Tandy's soon-to-be-stepfather didn't see the beacon flash outside. The chair thudded to an upright position and the inside lights went out. Seconds later, the front door cracked open.

I almost blacked out from shock and froze with the camera half raised. With my heart drumming in my chest, I stood close enough to photograph a close-up of his face and yet couldn't. In the stillness of the night, one click from the camera would echo like a gunshot.

It seemed like he took forever to pull his head back inside. The lock snicked shut behind him. I didn't realize I'd been holding my breath until it hissed out like a punctured tire. Scared beyond belief, I hurried back to the Porsche on an adrenaline high proud that I'd gathered evidence to document the job Tandy hired me to do.

The next day, the warm sun slanting through my bedroom window awakened me. Before I even started my morning routine or went downstairs to get something to eat, I booted up my laptop computer and searched the Internet for the county's appraisal district. I ran the Hurst address through their website and found that the taxes were paid by Molly Jo Clayton. I copied her address off the website and ran her name through the online telephone directory. Now that I had a phone number for Ms. Clayton, I jotted it in the file I'd begun on Mrs. Westlake's fiancé. I'd make the call to her as soon as I knew Alex Garrett was back from his fake trip to Florida.

I didn't have to wait long. Tandy called later that evening to say her mother heard from Alex and that he'd caught a flight back to Fort Worth a day earlier than he'd planned. Without tipping my hand, I told her I was on top of the investigation and to let me know when she got a visual on him — that's cop-speak I picked up from Jim.

Once I knew for certain that Alex was back at the Westlake's, I called Molly Jo Clayton pretending to be a renter. After giving a fake name, and explaining that the townhouse I'd planned to move into burned to the ground, I asked if there was any way I could see the property.

She wanted to know how I got this information. I winged it. Now she thinks one of the neighbors blabbed. I told her I wanted to get my foot in the door before she advertised the listing in the paper. She bought it.

We made arrangements for me to see the house the following morning.

The Porsche is a memorable automobile and I didn't want to chance her mentioning it to Alex Garrett, assuming they ever talked. I tucked my hair under the brown wig and put on blue jeans and an oversized white shirt that Venice had loaned me, and that I hadn't yet returned. This wasn't the time to be a fashion plate. Only the shoes could be thought of as memorable: Christian Louboutin ankle boots with heels.

With my Versace sunglasses pushed back on top of my head and an Italian, circus print handbag swinging from my arm, I called the closest rental car place and asked them to deliver a mid-sized car to Gran's house. When the guy scheduling the delivery wanted a credit card number to secure the reservation, I told him I planned to pay cash.

"We still need a credit card," he insisted.

Once it became painfully clear the rental car company planned to hold their car hostage until I provided them with a credit card number, I told the guy I'd call back.

About the time I hung up the telephone, Gran arrived from her weekly bridge game at the country club. She entered the kitchen through the back door in a cloud of perfume with a double strand of pearls gracing her neck. Then, she removed her Jackie O sunglasses, set them on the credenza and slid me a sideways glance. The half-smile she'd worn in flatlined.

"Hello, Dainty." She did an eye scan, looking me over from head to toe. "I'm surprised to see you home."

"How was bridge?" This was merely a formality, and under no circumstances meant to fuel a dialog about it. Like asking people in a fender-bender if anyone got hurt.

"They were all thrilled to see me, of course." She struck a pose. "I looked gorgeous in my new outfit. Everyone else just looked old."

Spoken by the woman with a face like a dried up riverbed.

I launched right in. "I need a ride to the rental car place."

"What's wrong with your car?"

"Nothing." I thought fast. "But I need a car to run errands for work and the job will reimburse me for it. I didn't want to put miles on mine or get stuck paying for gas."

271

This took her aback. She arched a carefully plucked eyebrow. "That may be the smartest thing you've said since you moved in."

I ignored the jab. It wasn't exactly a lie. I really would be reimbursed for my expenses but it would be Tandy doing the reimbursing, not WBFD.

I said, "Thank you." As if she'd just paid me a compliment instead of getting in a little dig. "So I was wondering, before you get too comfortable, if you could run me over to the rental agency and drop me off." I looked over expectantly.

She must've figured she'd get the house to herself if I had wheels to leave in because she didn't seem the least bit put out by the request. She simply picked up the sun-shades, slipped them back on and said, "Let's go now. I have things to do."

On my list of things not to do, riding in the car with Gran is among the top five on the hit parade. She's a terrible driver. To hear her tell it, she's never had a wreck. But you can sure as heck bet she's caused plenty. It drives me to the cliffs of insanity the way she pokes around in the fast lane, oblivious to the traffic stacking up behind her. It's like she's the official pace car. And when she decides to change lanes, she just does it. Never even checks the rearview or side mirrors to see if anyone's there, just whips across three lanes of traffic — *Damned the torpedoes, full speed ahead.* You'd think my screams would bother her but they don't. For all I know she turns off her hearing aids as soon as I climb in.

And that antique car — it was sitting inside the garage, gloating.

I heaved a sigh just thinking about it.

She drives a shiny turquoise, low-slung Cadillac with quilted interior in aqua brocade. Six months ago it had a little over forty-five thousand miles on the odometer. Amazing for a car that's almost forty years old. It used to embarrass me riding around in that car but I finally worked through the humiliation like a twelve-step program. Now Gran no longer has to make snide remarks about how I'll get curvature of the spine to get me to sit up straight in the passenger seat. Or rant for the thousandth time that the reason she's filthy rich is because she doesn't fritter her hard-earned money away on a vehicle that's going to depreciate as soon as she drives it out of the dealership.

Now that the Cadillac has surpassed the "old" stage and moved into the "classic" stage, the same young boys who used to point their fingers and laugh when Gran drove past now leave notes under the windshield wipers offering to buy it when they see it parked at the grocery store or the country club. Now Gran's car is almost cool.

Almost.

She fired up the engine and we slumped heavily down the driveway. Thirty feet from the road, the electric gate yawned open and disgorged us like a mouthful of undigested food. The gate rolled shut behind us.

I promised myself I wouldn't say anything to my grandmother about her driving habits. No need to load her quiver. After all, she was doing me a favor. And when we got to the rental car place, I was going to need her credit card — a tiny detail I hadn't yet sprung on her. So I decided to zip it and accept my role as the long-suffering passenger as long as the accident didn't occur on my side of the car. My promise to myself waned in inverse proportion to the length of the drive time.

What should've taken no more than ten minutes had stretched into twenty. We'd been following a flatbed truck with copper pipe sticking well past the back end, and without a red flag tied to the load. Each time the truck hit a bump, the copper tubing shifted. At the moment, the load had just sprung back after the flatbed bounced over a pothole. Reminded me of someone tapping out a couple of cigarettes from a pack. Then we hit the same huge rut hard enough to body-slam me into the car door — holy smoke, that grating undercarriage sounded expensive.

We're going to die.

Finally, I couldn't help myself.

I cleared my throat and tried to remain calm. "Do you remember how Alan J. Pakula died?"

She had her parchment hands wrapped around the big steering wheel at the ten and two o'clock positions and was looking dead ahead like a mule wearing blinders.

"Well, I don't suppose I do since I don't even know who you're talking about." She slid me a sideways glance. "Who's Alan J. Pakula?"

"Famous movie director?" When this didn't jog her memory I said, "Directed *The Parallax View . . . Klute . . . All the President's Men . . .*" Still no reaction. "He was killed while driving on the Long Island Expressway. He lost control of his car when a pipe crashed through his windshield. It was kicked up by the car in front of him."

That should've been enough of a hint.

Her jaw tightened. "I see." But instead of

switching lanes and passing the truck, Gran continued tailgating the driver. Suddenly pensive, she pursed her lips. Then she spoke in an ethereal, warbly little bird voice. "Dainty, do you remember how 'Spade' Cooley's wife died?"

I actually felt my eyebrows contort into question marks, *Huh?*

Who the heck is Spade Cooley?

Really — think about it: If I didn't know who Spade Cooley was, how could I be expected to know how his wife died?

The copper pipes bounced again. The load shifted. My skin crawled. "Who's Spade Cooley?"

Without looking my way, she took her hand off the two o'clock position and nonchalantly flip-flopped it through the air between us. "Actor . . . big band leader. Starred in a bunch of westerns. Did stand-in work for Roy Rogers."

I blinked and said nothing but I was thinking *What the hell?*

Okay, I'll bite.

"No, Gran, I don't know how Spade Cooley's wife died. How'd Spade Cooley's wife die?"

"He beat her to death for criticizing his driving."

We arrived at the rental car place in relative silence.

I said, "Would you mind letting me use your credit card to secure the rental?" I could see the frown deepening on her face. "It's just to secure the rental. I intend to pay cash to settle the bill."

"No."

I must've misheard. "What?"

"I said no."

"Gran, it's just to secure the rental. I'm not charging anything."

"No. You're not putting this on my credit card. You know, Dainty, one of these days you're going to learn that —"

I didn't stick around to hear the rest of the lecture. I alighted from the Cadillac and stomped to the glass doors of the rental car agency. When I turned, Gran was churning up dust leaving the parking lot.

I walked inside and took stock of the room. A salesman was talking on the phone while a girl about my age pounded out keystrokes on a computer keyboard. She looked up and said, "May I help you?"

"I called about a half hour ago. I'm supposed to pick up a champagne Nissan Altima."

"Name?" Her eyes slewed to the computer screen as she poised her fingertips to type.

"Dainty Prescott."

She typed in my name and hit the Enter key. We waited.

"Here it is. Now I need a credit card, your driver's license and proof of insurance."

I dug into my wallet and fished out a VISA that hadn't been cut up. I handed it over with my driver's license and insurance and watched her turn and walk to a nearby copy machine. She photocopied my items and returned them. Then she slid my credit card through the scanner.

A series of tones came from the little machine. The girl's facial features abruptly hardened.

My confidence tanked.

She slid open a drawer and pulled out a pair of scissors.

I said, "Don't," loud enough to cause the man on the telephone to turn our way and stare as if a lunatic had wandered in.

She snipped my card in half and let the pieces fall to the floor. "This card's been cancelled."

"I have cash." I pulled out a wad to prove it.

That brought a smile to her face. "Unless you have what the car's valued at, we're going to need a credit card. A *valid* credit card."

"Look," I said in desperation, "my daddy

has an account with your company. We can charge it to him."

"Are you on the account?"

"Of course," I said hopefully. I recited the corporate account number and she manually punched it into the system. The credit card gadget chimed another series of tones. She strained to read the resulting information. Then her jaw flexed. She flashed me one of those "sheep killing dog" looks and snatched up the nearest telephone receiver. After stabbing in a phone number she stared at me through the flat, unreadable eyes of a doper.

"Yes," she said by way of introduction, "I'm with U-Lease-It in Dallas." Short pause. She rattled off a number that I assumed was unique to the rental car agency. "Dainty Prescott." Another pause. She held me in her fathomless brown gaze and spelled my name. "Thanks so much." She banged down the receiver and smirked. "You're not on the account."

"I need to make a call."

"Dial nine to get out," she said and handed the receiver across the countertop separating us.

Desperate, I telephoned Gordon.

After running down the problem, he gave them his credit card number to secure the rental and in another half hour, I was on my way.

Molly Jo Clayton sounded young over the telephone. In person, she turned out to be in her early sixties. And she'd had work done. Not hard to tell since her face couldn't make full expressions. The skin had that kind of iridescent shimmer from being pulled too tight, almost like a pearlized leather purse without a visible scar on it. Bouffant blonde hair in the shape of a biker helmet seemed to start even higher than her actual forehead, and eyebrows framing crystal gray eyes had that look of permanent surprise going for them.

But boy could she dress.

I hadn't seen a woman her age in Manolos that high in years. She practically needed stilts to slide into them. And they were a gorgeous shade of teal that perfectly matched her Chanel-cut suit. She'd even managed to find a teal silk scarf with tiny white polka dots that she'd tied jauntily around her neck.

With my hand outstretched, I stepped up onto the curb in front of the house.

"I'm so glad to meet you," I gushed as we shook. "And I'd like to apologize again for getting you out on such short notice, but you see my plane leaves day after tomorrow and I won't be back in time to see the house again before the first of the month." Words poured out in a hyperventilating rush. "Anyway, like I said on the telephone, the winter couture collection has to be itemized before it's sent to Harkman Beemis and I have to be there to sign off on them."

I'd kept this speech within the comfort zone of my fashion expertise. It didn't hurt that Ms. Clayton understood high-end clothing.

"So I'd like to see the layout of the place —" sweeping hand flourish toward the house "— and take a few measurements —" whip out the retractable measuring device for show "— and that way I'll know for certain what pieces of furniture I can bring down from New York."

Ms. Clayton's face went suddenly hard. "You don't sound like a New Yorker."

I playfully swatted her hand. "Aren't you just the cutest thing? Me? From New York? Why heavens no. I've only been living up there the past several years as a buyer for Harkman's. But I'm home grown. A Texas girl from start to finish."

She instantly warmed, pulling out a ring of keys and sifting through them. "Let's get on with it, then, shall we?"

"Let's." I did one of those touchy-feely

arm contacts with my fingertips and followed her to the door with pep in my step.

Cobwebs floated in the thin light.

After a quick walk-through with Mrs. Clayton shadowing my every move, I snapped the end of the retractable measuring tape for effect. "Don't let me bore you with getting the room dimensions. I'm sure you have calls to make and I wouldn't want to interfere so feel free to leave me to my work and I'll be quick about it."

I'm not sure if it was the fact that there were only three pieces of furniture in the entire house, counting the big-screen TV — all too big for me to carry off by myself, or the spiral notebook I whipped out of my handbag to record the results of my labor, or the new Harkman Beemis catalog that had come to Gran's that morning, the one I'd peeled the label off of and jammed into my purse to shore up my fake identity as a clothing buyer for Harkmans, or if it was the finality in my tone as I handed over the catalog and said, "I brought this for you," that made Mrs. Clayton acquiesce to my request to be allowed to work alone.

But she did say, "Well, dear, I do have calls to make," and that was enough for me to lay down the metal tape and fake-measure the kitchen.

As I piddled around in the living room, Mrs. Clayton sat in the easy chair with the catalogue opened to the dresses.

"You should look at the bed linens," I said with encouragement. "They're fabulous." I recorded a few numbers and then whipped out my cell phone. Tandy's wireless rang and she answered on a chipper hello. "Donatella — darling. Can you please tell me the width of the French commode?"

Tandy said, "What?"

"Thank you so much. And I'll need the exact width of the Italian console for the entryway."

Tandy said, "I think you've got the wrong number."

"And the abbatant? No, not that one. The one with the *trompe l'oiel* finish. I need height and width on that one."

"Dainty, is that you?"

"Yes, thank you so much. And I want the bed. The four-poster, not the Lincoln bed. It won't match. And I'm counting on you to send the Versace pillows from your collection."

Tandy said, "Dainty, are you in trouble?"

"Not yet. Look, I have to go. This nice lady has business to take care of so I need to finish. Are those designs ready? Call you back."

I finished in the living room.

Mrs. Clayton lifted her gaze from the magazine to me. "Is that . . . Donatella Versace?"

Not my fault she jumped to conclusions.

"You mustn't tell anyone about the phone call," I shushed her, patting the air in a downward motion. "I'm under a non-disclosure agreement." Giving her arm a confidential squeeze, I shored up my fantasy background hob-knobbing with the rich and famous. "There may be a few high-profile visitors here from time to time so I can't afford for word to get out. You understand, don't you?"

Finger to lips, mum's the word.

From my place in the bedroom with the cheap futon bed, I saw Mrs. Clayton reflected in the closet mirror thumbing through the Harkman's catalog. Then she opened her wireless phone and dialed.

Listening intently, I carefully opened the closet. A box the size of a tackle box, the kind important papers are routinely stored in, had been pushed into the back corner. The catch had been locked and I needed to get inside.

The echo of Mrs. Clayton's laughter filtered in from the other room. She had a friend on the line and was describing a particular dress. I knew which one it was because I'd marked the page by dog-earing the corner.

I went inside my bag for a screwdriver, dropped to my knees and set my wireless down next to me. Then I pretended to call my invisible friend Donatella.

"Donatella," I yelled, "I think we have a bad connection. No, wait. What about the suede sofa?" The box came open with a pop. I backed out of the closet and rose to my feet, standing partially in the doorway so Mrs. Clayton could see me. For extra effect, and to shore up my reputation as a noisemaker, I reeled out about ten feet of metal and pressed the retractable button. The tape snapped back into place. "I'm sure it'll fit against the window. This is a nice, spacious bedroom and I'd like to bring it. Perf."

When I turned around, Mrs. Clayton was still kicked back in the easy chair. I gave her a little finger wave and disappeared long enough to grab the paperwork out of the lock box and stuff it into my handbag without looking at it. Then I turned the side of the lid with the broken catch to the wall and pushed it inside as far as it could go.

"See you soon," I said in my fake phone call, "and give Paolo my love." I have no idea where that added burst of inspiration came from. I stepped into the living room and said, "I'll take it."

"It's not that easy," said Mrs. Clayton as she folded the catalogue closed and wrangled out of the chair. "I'll need you to fill out an application and there's a credit check."

"Of course. You're a busy lady and I actually have a meeting in . . ." For effect, I checked my watch. "Oh, no. I'm going to be late. If you have the paperwork here I'll take it with me." Palm up, I stuck out my hand and waited.

"It's out in the car."

"Fab. I'll fill it out and pop it in the mail this afternoon."

With that, I waited for Mrs. Clayton to lock the front door and we walked to her car for the rental agreement and credit check application.

CHAPTER
TWENTY-TWO

Jackpot. If I were in Vegas, bells would be ringing and coins would be clattering down the slot machine's chute.

Seated at a booth in the back of a twenty-four-hour diner, I removed the rubber band from the documents and sifted through them.

It's not like I stole the papers.

I had every intention to take them back.

I even came up with a plausible excuse for needing to get back inside. My good friend "Donatella" has offered to fit the house with luxurious window treatments for free. So while I'm inside fake-measuring again, I'll put the paperwork back where I found it.

Meantime, I was like a kid with a cookie jar. No, even better. The cookie aisle at the grocery store. No, no. The entire cookie factory.

Without taking the items in order, I

looked at the passports first. There were three.

The first, not surprisingly, had been issued to Henry Alexander Garrett with a DOB or date of birth that would make him fifty-five. His hair looked darker in the photo but taking into account he probably colored it, I didn't plan to lose sleep over the matter.

The waitress brought my cheeseburger, dry, and I assembled the lettuce, tomatoes, pickles and mustard on my own. After taking a bite, I wiped my fingers with a napkin and looked at the next passport while I chewed.

I almost choked.

The second passport came back to Robert John Taylor. But the face staring back at the camera lens belonged to Henry Alexander Garrett. I flipped to page five and found the U.S. address for Robert John Taylor. It was Broken Bow, Oklahoma.

Dabbing my mouth with the napkin, I pushed aside my plate, too excited to finish, and compared the first passport to the second. The man we knew as Henry Alexander Garrett listed a Pensacola, Florida, address.

I turned the passport photos facedown and picked up the third. This one came back to Jerry Don Grayson — with a picture of the same man. This passport carried the earliest issue date. It also showed a U.S. address in Broken Bow, Oklahoma, but the street address for Jerry Don Grayson was different than the one on the passport issued to Robert John Taylor.

I sifted through the remaining documents, too keyed up to thoroughly read them. After rubber-banding my treasures together, I tucked them back into my purse, wolfed down another bite of cheeseburger and washed it down with diet soda. Once I left a tip and paid my tab, I headed straight for the copy company.

It took forty-five minutes to duplicate all the documents, counting the waiting time for the self-service machine. When I finished, I drove to the hardware store to find a lock box like the one I'd broken into. I struck out. At the sporting goods stores, I struck out again in the fishing gear section. When all seemed lost, I checked the discount stores.

Bingo.

Hard to imagine a supposedly wealthy man like Alex Garrett would keep his personal papers in a cheap lock box rather than a heavy-duty fire safe. Then it hit me. Alex Garrett required portability.

Super energized, I rang up Bruckman.

"You'll never believe this."

"You're in love with me," he said with a roguish inflection.

"Not yet." Wait — I can't believe I just said that. One time. An isolated incident. A few beats passed. "I got the goods on the con man. Now will you help me?"

Bruckman wanted me to define "got the goods on."

"I can prove he's not who he wants us to think he is."

"Enlighten me."

"Wait — do we have confidentiality?"

"Whatever you did, it sounds illegal. Maybe you'd better run this by your attorney."

"Okay, what would you say if I told you I can prove he's not Alex Garrett?"

Instead of being proud of me, he made fun of the Debutante Detective Agency.

Heat blazed in my cheeks.

"Call it whatever you want. The point is I'm good at this. And speaking as somebody who's never been good at anything but shopping, you should be proud of me."

He chuckled without humor. "It takes years to become a good detective. You didn't even realize I'd tailed you to your friend's house. You haven't learned how to follow somebody without getting caught. And those are just the basics."

"Go ahead, make fun of me. You'll see."

But in my head, I was getting ready to pull surveillance.

On Bruckman.

Of course I was ideally suited to pulling surveillance; after all, I trained as a debutante and Bruckman learned police pursuit driving in the police academy.

Let's just see who's good at their job, shall we?

CHAPTER
TWENTY-THREE

> Revised goals for the day:
>
> 1. Update Tandy
> 2. Update Gordon
> 3. Pull reconnaissance on Bruckman

Since the rental car didn't have to be returned before tomorrow, noon, I seized the opportunity to follow Bruckman after he got off work. I couldn't wait to see the expression on his face once I told him I'd tailed him without him noticing.

I waited outside the police station on a side street. My binoculars rested on the front seat within my grasp. The champagne sedan provided perfect cover. Bruckman knew I owned a snazzy little performance vehicle. He also knew my boss had rented me a junker to spy on his wife. He had no idea about this latest acquisition — my Japanese-engineered surveillance car.

A pickup like Bruckman's appeared in my rearview mirror. I slumped over into the seat, still wearing my brown wig, and popped back up a few seconds after the vehicle passed. Now that I knew how to get to Bruckman's house, I didn't feel rushed or pressured to fall in behind him before he reached the traffic signal and made his turn.

But when he went straight through the intersection instead of turning, I panicked.

I whipped out of my parking space and gunned the engine to catch up, flying across the street in plenty of time to look hot while the red light camera snapped my picture.

The signals in downtown Fort Worth are synchronized, so once you hit a green light you can travel ten blocks and catch every light as long as you're willing to exceed the speed limit.

In this case, I am.

Bruckman sailed through the amber light and I got caught behind a car at the red. Keeping an eye on him was hard. He turned left on a one-way several blocks up. When my light turned green I rode the guy's bumper ahead of me until I could whip into the next lane and zoom around him.

I knew what Bruckman was doing. Confidence returned as I took the same left on the one-way and floored the accelerator. Sure enough, he hit the freeway with me not far behind. For the next ten minutes, I relaxed. Bruckman was headed home.

Then he overshot the exit to his house.

Maybe he'd planned to stop for a six-pack?

But he didn't make any detours. He kept going through Hurst and crossed into Bedford.

So . . . maybe he was heading to Dallas to surprise me?

My heart soared, then abruptly dive-bombed.

He took an exit between Bedford and Euless and turned off into a residential area. In order to fly under his radar, I had to lag behind at the end of the block to see which way he turned. Lucky for me Bruckman uses his turn indicators. He made a right and I roared past a block's worth of houses to catch up. Once I reached the stop sign, I glimpsed him pulling into a driveway. As I waited at the intersection, a dark-haired woman bounded past the front door of a seventies-style tract home and flung herself at him.

When they embraced and she kissed him, my stomach lurched.

Tears welled as they went inside the house. The only thing I could do was make a note of the address, turn around and head for Venice's house for my second fitting. While there, I could borrow her computer to look up the homeowner.

Venice said something unintelligible. She had a mouthful of pins and was securing the hem of my gown in place but the look on her face telegraphed rapture. It was hard not to share her enthusiasm. After all, the dress was practically perfect. But seeing Bruckman embracing another woman had upset me. I couldn't wait for Venice to finish so I could log onto her computer.

It didn't take long to un-layer the onion.

When I ran the property owner's name through a search engine, a dozen newspaper articles and television reports from the past week popped up.

My gut sank.

The kissing bandit was also the widow — the woman who used to be Bruckman's girlfriend before his best friend and cop partner stole her heart. Now that the partner was dead, were they plotting to get back together?

The last thing I needed was to end up in the crossfire of somebody else's love life.

I made up my mind then and there to cut my losses and bow out. I had no intention, whatsoever, to trade one cheater for another.

Before I headed back to Gran's, Venice insisted I stay and eat supper with her. While we were in the Hanovers' kitchen making a chef salad, my cell phone rang.

It was Gordon. He'd returned from his trip and wanted me to come down to the station to give him a report. I agreed to meet him in an hour and a half, long enough for me to scarf down salad, head back to Gran's to pick up the photographs and drive to WBFD.

CHAPTER
TWENTY-FOUR

The on-air talent at WBFD — Rochelle refers to the anchors as "blow-dries" — were getting ready to do the ten o'clock news when I arrived at the TV station. I found Gordon framed in the doorway to the studio as I made my way through the foyer.

His hard stare almost bored a hole in me. I realized that he hadn't recognized me in this long brown wig and must be wondering how a stranger got into the building. I flashed my key card. He did a quick double-take. His eyebrows shot up. Then he did a little chin jerk and pointed a sausage finger toward his office. I assumed he wanted me to wait inside so I took a seat on the furry spotted cowhide sofa and telephoned Tandy with a cryptic update.

"I have news. Can't really talk now but we need to meet."

"Good news or bad news?"

"Depends on who's asking."

I started to give her a quick rundown but Gordon walked in unexpectedly, closed the door behind him and locked it. As he rolled up his shirtsleeves and took his place behind the big desk, I hung up my wireless with a promise to fill Tandy in later. After pocketing the phone, I turned the photographs over to my boss.

Gordon studied each shot without comment. When he got to the end of the stack he looked up. "They're grainy."

What'd he expect — scratch-and-sniff pictures to fully appreciate the way his wife reeked of my boyfriend?

Despite the fact that I've taken plenty of photography classes, I found them to be seriously lacking when events distilled down to shooting photos while dangling off a tree limb upside down.

"Yeah, well, I was impaled on a pecan branch when I took most of these, so grainy's good considering I could've broken my neck."

He pulled one out of the stack and tapped his finger against it.

"This guy looks familiar." His words carried a bit of lag time. He looked up and made serious eye contact. "Did you figure out who he is?"

I might've let out a lobster scream — that ultrasonic sound I imagine it makes as it hits the vat of scalding water.

Jig's up.

Here I sat skewered on the middle tine of a diabolical trident — torn between loyalty to the man I'd planned to spend the rest of my life with, or to my boss, a crazy old coot who'd dangled a job prospect within my grasp — when I felt an unexpected tug of affection for Gordon.

Why protect Drex any longer?

Haven't heard from him. Didn't get a birthday present.

Certainly didn't care about my feelings, now, did he?

"You've met him before. He was my date to the office Labor Day picnic."

Gordon let that soak in a minute. "Tell me about him again."

I blew out a long sigh.

He'd heard all this before. But when you're dressed in a Hawaiian shirt, khaki shorts and flip-flops, standing over a flaming barbeque grill flipping burgers with a spatula while your guests interrupt the conversation like you're the host in a receiving line, you tend to forget. I started at the beginning, going into detail about how long I'd known Drex, when we became a couple and the fact that he was getting his law degree at Washington and Lee.

He eyed me with suspicion. "You seem pretty calm. You're not angry?"

Hmmm . . . let's see now . . . how do I put this delicately?

"Are you kidding? I wanted to attach his testicles to a car battery."

Well, what do you know? Made the boss smile.

The truth: If this was the harbinger of things to come, I didn't want any part of Drex and I told Gordon so. The last thing I needed was to work my way up the ladder to the national market, end up with an anchor position on CNN, only to learn that Drex was either sleeping with one of my co-workers or my boss's wife or — God forbid — the wives of the guys on the law firm letterhead he aspired to eventually become a partner in.

"Can you imagine me at age forty with two or three kids, trying to piece my life back together?" I fanned away the image with a dismissive hand wave. "No, thanks."

"You have no plans to take him back? Give him a second chance? Write this off as a youthful indiscretion?"

I could tell by the intensity in his voice that he was weighing this very option.

"Cheating's a character flaw."

"You don't mind being alone the rest of your life?"

I assumed he was thinking out loud and that the remark applied more to him than to me. I let it pass. He pushed his back into the chair and eyed the second set of photos in my hand.

"Are we done now?"

"There's more," I said dully.

"What else do you have?" he asked without a hint of judgment or recrimination swimming in his eyes.

I recounted listening in on the other phone call, the one that led me to believe Paislee might be meeting someone else after her rendezvous with Drex.

Gordon threaded his fingers and lifted an eyebrow.

"I tailed her in the rental car." I'd taken to using Bruckman's detective lingo like a cow to a salt lick. "These are pictures of your wife walking into the homeowner's residence. I cross-checked the address using the county tax rolls."

Until now, the poor man had no hard evidence other than this fling that Paislee was devious or even remotely capable of such cruelty. I handed over the photos and held my breath on the scant hope he wouldn't ask any more questions, knowing that he would. He'd been hurt enough and he didn't deserve to hear this next part.

Gordon prolonged the agony by scrutinizing each picture. I could almost see the cogs in his brain getting a fresh squirt of lubricant.

I envy people who instinctively know how many questions to ask and when to stop. There's no point in being ostrich-headed when it comes to bad news but I had to ask myself if this thing with Paislee and Drex wouldn't have eventually blown over if it hadn't come to a head like a big ugly zit when Rochelle blabbed.

If I hadn't known about their tryst, would I have eventually married him?

Certainly.

If he threw himself at my feet, filled with remorse, could I forgive him? That I can't answer. Losing trust in a person you believed in is gut wrenching. This thing with Drex has been like a death in the family.

As for Paislee, she either hadn't heard the saying *If he'll do it with you, he'll do it to you,* or she didn't figure the warning applied to her.

Gordon tapped a finger to one of the pictures. "Whose place is this?"

The tears I wanted to cry instantly turned

into a headache. "The house belongs to Mr. Welder."

Tig Welder is one of WBFD's investigative reporters. To hear him tell it, he's the crown jewel in the WBFD kingdom. To me, Tig's a forty-ish rake with porcelain veneers, a George Hamilton suntan and the attention span of a gnat. Thinks he's God's gift to women. He's all the time juggling girlfriends and seldom keeps any of them around longer than a few weeks. Either that or they find out about one another and cause a big stink.

When polled in a recent study by WBFD, most women between the ages of eighteen and sixty-five found him dashing.

I found him dashing, too — dashing to the window to close the curtains so I couldn't get a good picture of the boss's wife stripping off her clothes like a skanky pole dancer as soon as she stepped across the threshold.

Gordon opened his desk drawer, pulled out a pair of readers and put them over his wire-rims to get a better look at his wife being pulled into the house by a bare-chested man. He saw whatever it was that he needed to convince him this was Tig and ripped off the cheater lenses and threw them on the blotter.

I'd moved near the corner of his desk in case he needed to ask me about one of the shots, but soon eased away without him noticing. This time I sat in one of the cowhide chairs he was so proud of. He'd gotten Rochelle to furnish his office in modern Texana when WBFD rocketed to the third-ranked station in the metroplex after sweeps month last November.

I half expected him to yell at me or cast blame because I'd brought Drex to the office picnic. To tell the truth, I'd been thinking the same thing — that I was responsible — and beating myself up over it. But Drex was a big part of my life and so was WBFD. I had illusions of becoming an anchor one day.

Now, that lofty goal was probably circling the drain in the toilet bowl of my life.

"Nice job, Dainty."

"Thanks, Mr. Pfeiffer."

"Gordon. You should call me Gordon. After all, we're each holding an oar to the same leaky rowboat."

I gave him an almost imperceptible head nod. "What're you going to do?"

"What're *you* going to do?" he parried.

I gave a lame shoulder shrug. "Part of me's thanking Drex for doing me an unintended favor. Can you imagine if I'd married the cheater?" I wanted to take back my words the instant they tumbled out. "The other part keeps expecting a logical explanation."

"Such as?"

"Like he asked Paislee for help picking out a nice necklace for me at Harkman Beemis so he could surprise me on my birthday. But catching him in the act with your wife the day I got treed by the dog pretty much rules out a happy ending for me."

I empathized with poor Gordon. He had it worse than I did. Because now, not only had his wife cheated with Drex, she was doing it with an integral member of this TV station.

I rose to leave. "Well, Mr. . . . Gordon . . . if you don't need me anymore I'll be heading for my grandmother's house. But I'll be back tomorrow to resume the internship . . ."

. . . *if you can stand to look me in the eye after this.*

"I guess I'll find someplace to stay tonight and hire myself a tit-wrenching lesbian attorney to represent me in a divorce." He gave me a wary headshake. "I'm not even supposed to be in this state."

I wasn't supposed to be in this state either but Drex and Paislee had FUBAR'd things so badly that our collective states of mind now hung somewhere between relief and revenge.

He pulled out his wallet and gave me two hundred dollars, a bonus for taking the initiative and following up on the suspicious phone call. Now that Daddy's no longer financially subsidizing me, a two-hundred-dollar windfall ranks pretty high up there on the *"Aw"* scale. I folded the currency in half several times and pushed the bills deep into the pocket of my jeans.

"I'll pay cash for the car rental so it doesn't go on your credit card," I said, referring to the sedan I was still driving.

"Forget it." He gave me the brush-off hand wave. "It's on me. It's the least I can do."

I thought he might do the gentleman thing and walk me out to my car, but he stopped near the double doors to the studio.

"I put one of the SMU interns on-air tonight," he said, looking as rumpled and unkempt as the shirt he was wearing. "Guess I ought to pop in and see how she's doing."

I couldn't help it. Morbid curiosity got the better of me. I followed him inside and hung back in the shadows. It didn't take long to see what Gordon thought of her presentation. In the time I was there, she'd mangled three proper names, lost her place on the TelePrompTer, got so flustered that she stammered, and then clammed up completely. For the next thirty seconds, she fixed the camera with a bovine stare.

Even though I found this particular SMU intern irritating, I tensed with embarrassment for her. Gordon had fired people for less egregious mistakes than dead air.

The producer signaled the cut to commercial. A truck advertisement popped up on the monitor as Gordon swooped out from behind the curtain and made his presence known.

Like Oz.

Oz the psychotic and glowering.

Gordon let loose with a few colorful expletives. "Well, wasn't that a real testicle thumper?" he yelled to the room at large. "What have I told you? *Keep going. Always keep going. No matter how bad you fuck up, keep going.*"

Screaming louder did precious little to prevent the intern from slipping further into her coma.

He seemed to be on the cusp of a coronary and for a few seconds, the rest of his tirade got lodged in his throat. Then the Gordon Pfeiffer dam broke. "What the hell? Somebody get Helen Keller off the set."

As they led her off, still stricken, she cast him a backward glance and mouthed, "I'm sorry."

Whereupon Gordon mouthed, "You fucking better be."

I'd never seen him so angry. For a moment, it occurred to me he might spontaneously combust. Then I remembered something important: stop, drop, and roll doesn't work in Hell.

In the short time we'd been standing by, observing, he'd started to sweat. With the armpits of his shirtsleeves ringed in crescents of perspiration, he pointed to the regular evening anchor. "Take over."

Unleashing a fresh string of profanity, he pushed past me and headed for the exit. Dumbfounded, I trailed him out of the studio. As Gordon headed for his office popping antacid tablets, I angled out the front door and into the parking lot to find my car.

My mind slipped back to mid-August, to my first day at the station. While Rochelle conducted orientation for the interns, one of the SMU girls remarked that Mr. Pfeiffer seemed a bit high-strung.

"He's not bad," Rochelle said. "You just have to learn how to get along with him. Really, he's just a big old cuddly bear."

That's when the SMU intern from to-night's on-air fiasco muttered, "Grizzly bear, more like."

But I was thinking something totally different.

I was thinking: bipolar bear.

One thing I knew without a doubt — if my shot at anchoring the news turned out like the SMU intern's performance, I'd end up giving swine flu reports from Mexico City.

Instead of taking Interstate 30 to get back to Gran's, I drove Airport Freeway. When I reached Bedford, I took an exit and hung a right from the frontage road. With my heart pounding, I headed into the residential area, to the tract house where I'd last seen Bruckman.

I checked the time on my cell phone — eleven-fifteen — mumbled, "I'll take *Bad Boyfriends* for a thousand, Alex," and waited for my allotted number of *Jeopardy!* seconds to expire.

Bruckman's pickup was still in the driveway, and except for a dim yellow bug light next to the front door, the house was dark.

Made me sick.

I wanted to go somewhere private and have a good cry.

But what I really wanted was to see scissors sticking out of his head.

CHAPTER
TWENTY-FIVE

Goals for the day:

1. Avoid Gran like the plague
2. Avoid Bruckman like the plague
3. Sneak evidence back into rent
   house w/o getting caught

The early morning sun slanted through my window. I slitted my eyes open to witness a tangerine sunrise climbing above the tree-tops.

A light knuckle-rap sounded at my door.

I pulled the covers up to my chin. "Yes?"

The maid announced that my grand-mother wanted me to join her outside on the terrace. I snagged my robe off the chair and hurried down to the second floor for a pit stop before heading the rest of the way downstairs.

I barely had enough time to notice my hair in the bathroom mirror. It didn't look teased; it looked Tasered. And dark circles were starting to form beneath my eyes. There wasn't time to brush my teeth so I popped in a breath mint, padded down to the first floor and made my way out to the terrace.

One of the household staff had lit the *chimenea* on the back terrace. The fire hissed and popped inside the portable clay fireplace as the *piñon* wood burned. Physically, we were sitting at the bistro table having a continental breakfast, Gran yawning into the sleeve of her blue satin kimono, and me fussing with my shorty pajamas and bathrobe. But my head was definitely processing images of Bruckman with the brunette.

The cook had laid out pastries from a Czech specialty bakery and prepared coffee and fresh-squeezed orange juice. I checked out the platter of kolaches, sausage rolls and strudel and would've taken one of each if it didn't matter whether my thighs looked like bridge supports. Instead, I selected a piece of blueberry strudel to start the day. As Gran poured me a cup of coffee from a china pot, I reached for the creamer and turned it into *café au lait.*

Without preamble, Gran said, "You've been traipsing in late, Dainty."

"I'm sorry. I didn't realize I'd disturbed your sleep."

Crystal blue irises hardened behind pleated lids. "What's all this about?"

Fidgeting in my chair, I picked at my cuticles and tried to avoid eye contact.

"Are you hanging out at honky-tonks? Because that's not something we do, Dainty." Disapproval resonated in her tone. She selected a kolache with a cream cheese center. I would've bet money on the sausage roll.

"I'm not hanging out at honky-tonks. I . . ." I took a deep inhale and wondered how much to tell her. "I have a job."

Coffee cup to lips, Gran paused. "What kind of job?"

"A paying job."

Gran sipped, then returned the delicate china cup to its saucer. "You don't need a job, Dainty. You're supposed to be in school finishing your degree."

"I have expenses. I need to buy stuff. I want things," I said, but the voice inside my head was screaming *I wouldn't even need to be worried about money if Daddy hadn't cut me off.*

"That's absurd." Her hand cut through

313

the air as though she was about to perform a re-enactment of her own debutante bow. "Look around you. You have everything you need right here. You have a roof over your head —"

"I'm sleeping in the attic," I challenged.

"There's food in the refrigerator and in the pantry."

"I don't know the first thing about cooking."

"And whose fault is that?" She leveled her piercing gaze at me. "I blame your mother. She should've taught you when you were young."

My lip quivered. I clenched my teeth to steady my chin, unable and not daring speak. I knew better than to open *this* Pandora's steamer trunk and couldn't tell her it wasn't my mother's fault for not getting around to teaching me how to cook before she died. No point in delving into such an oversight on my dead mother's part just because she was too busy caring for me and Teensy, running herself ragged getting us to dance lessons, voice lessons, music lessons, gymnastics lessons, swimming lessons and the like, teaching us about the finer things in life — and being a great mom as long as she lasted.

A visual of Nerissa popped into mind and

I saw red.

"Tell me about this job you have. It's not illegal, is it?"

"You don't have any faith in me," I said dully.

"No, Dainty, *you* don't have faith in you. You're an underachiever because your parents spoiled you. Now you're finding out the hard way."

"I started my own business."

There came the laugh, a high-pitched, squeaky-hinge tone that put me in my place. I looked down at my cuticles and saw they'd started to bleed.

She collected herself, touched the napkin to the corners of her mouth, then refolded and placed it on the table next to the unused sterling. "What kind of business?"

I stiffened. "If you must know, I've started a private investigations firm —"

"A firm?" She made it sound like a nasty word. Then she emitted one of those bird-like laughs, the kind that sounds like the high tinkling notes on a xylophone — or like the crystal flute of orange juice I wanted to shatter against the concrete.

"A small firm." I clung to my pride but my confidence had started to sag. "Actually, it's just me right now but I've already got-ten two paying jobs and eventually, I'll be

315

able to buy more equipment for the business —"

"The business?" Despite the superficial calm, her thin, lip-lined smile faded. The contours of her face hardened. She looked at me, laser-eyed, and her tone turned corrosive. "Dainty, we all agreed on this a long time ago — you're supposed to become a news anchor." Her gaze swept over the emerald expanse of a perfectly manicured St. Augustine lawn. "You're not supposed to think. You're just supposed to sit there, read off a cue card and look pretty."

Wounded, I sucked air. My throat tightened and my eyes started to burn.

Harsh truths should be sugarcoated.

"What?" Blood whooshed between my ears as I sorted through my tangled thoughts. "You don't think I'm smart enough to run my own business?"

"Your father isn't sending you to school to become some . . ." she fumbled for the proper word "some . . . gumshoe. You're supposed to enjoy a pleasant career as a TV journalist until you can find a nice husband who will let you stay home and play bridge while he goes to work."

Gran was being mean. But until this moment, I'd had no reason to believe she was capable of such callous indifference to my feelings. It took all of my reserves to keep from lashing out at her.

"Your father wouldn't want you working at some seedy part-time job as a hack shamus snooping around in other people's business. Now run along," she said dismissively. "Surely you must have homework to finish."

Her work here was done.

Brava! on making me feel like a very bad child.

Slicing me a smile, she pushed her chair back from the table. As she left me to stew in my own juices, and wandered toward the house to find the housekeeper to clear off the dishes, I gave her a parting shot.

"Just so you know, they don't use cue cards. It's called a TelePrompTer."

So, ha.

Weebils wobble but they don't fall down.

A short while later, she returned with what appeared, at first glance, to be a tube of lipstick. She placed it on the edge of the freshly cleared table and gave me a pointed look.

"What's this?" I said dully.

"Under-eye concealer. For the dark spots. Really, Dainty, they're not going to let you get on-camera with half-moons beneath your eyes."

I grudgingly took it, turning it over in my hand for closer examination.

"That-a-girl. Now go freshen up and come back, dear. Then we'll have a nice little talk about what you're going to wear to the debutante ball."

But I wasn't thinking about the debutante ball or eye concealer or looking pretty in front of a camera. I was thinking how I could turn this simple retractable tube into a pin camera. I wasn't aware that I'd left the table but when I reached the kitchen, my grandmother was still standing out on the terrace talking to the maid.

While I was upstairs in my little attic sanctuary, I dismantled the eye concealer. If I had a way to bore a clean hole in it, the tiny pin camera could be recessed inside.

My cell phone rang. As I started to thumb the talk button, I saw "Drex" pop up on the digital display. I let the call automatically route itself to voice mail.

A while later, after I'd found an ice pick in the kitchen and brought it upstairs to punch a hole in the concealer tube, the cell phone rang again.

This time, it was Bruckman.

Part of me wanted to answer.

The other part wanted to stab the ice pick through his name on the digital display. All

I can say is . . . it's a good thing I'm well bred.

I decided to pick up. I'd done a lot of thinking on the way home from the grieving widow's last night and figured it'd be better to nip this disaster in the bud. No need to have him escort me to the debutante ball and introduce him to more of my friends, because where I come from, you didn't do that with a one-night stand.

Horrible as it sounds, that's what I was to Bruckman.

I answered before the call cycled to voice mail.

"How's my favorite girl?"

"Gee, Bruckman," I said, unable to avoid the raging sarcasm in my tone, "I don't know — how is she?"

Chilly silence stretched between us.

"Are you upset about something?"

"Wow. You're an ace detective. How'd you know? Was it something I said?"

"Okay, I get it. You're mad. Did we have a date? Because I don't remember us having any plans before your friend's Halloween party."

"Well, don't worry about going in costume, Bruckman, because you don't have to go at all." Said snootily. "Consider yourself off the hook."

"I told you I'd go." He changed his tune. "Wait. Is this about the costume? Because if it is, I decided to wear one."

"Really?" I said, not caring. "What were you going as . . . a jackass? Because I'd like to see how to put a costume together for that — no, wait — I know," I said cheerily, "you could just go as yourself."

Super-long pause.

"Look, Bruckman, I have to go. I have stuff to do, okay? Forget the Halloween party, forget the debutante ball, forget my number."

"Is this because I wouldn't run your friend's stepfather through the TCIC-NCIC database?"

"Forget that, too. I have everything I need to know and I got it all without your help, thank you very much." Said haughtily.

"Fine," Bruckman said on a sigh. "What's the guy's name? I'll do it right now."

"You're such a schmuck."

"Look, I didn't know it was that important to you. I figured you were just trying this investigator stuff on a lark —"

"Do what?"

"The Debutante Detective Agency."

A scary, low-rumbling, high-pitched tremor came from my throat. I could no longer contain myself. "Stop calling it that.

How dare you make fun of me?"

"All right, all right. Let's call it the Dainty Prescott Agency. That has a nice ring to it."

And then it happened.

A lethal calm so frightening it was almost palpable enveloped me like an invisible shield. I spoke with composure and eloquence, as if I were reporting tragic breaking news: *"This just in — a seven-forty-seven crashed into an oil refinery northeast of Houston, incinerating five-hundred acres of a wildlife preservation habitat where the last whooping cranes known to man . . ."*

I told him about testing my ability to pull surveillance without the mark knowing he was being followed. About how I'd seen Alex Garrett out on Airport Freeway when he was supposed to be in Florida and about how, for fun, I'd decided if I could tail ace detective Jim Bruckman without him knowing, that I could follow anybody anywhere without fear of discovery.

Dead silence spread across our connection.

He spoke with caution. "When did this take place?"

"After work yesterday. So, you see, I know what's going on. I was willing to give you the benefit of the doubt at first, but I know you spent the night with her because I drove by again and your truck was still parked in her driveway. If you like, I can supply you with the evidence — a picture I took with my camera phone."

He said, "*That's* what you're mad about?"

"*Ha* — ever since we first met, you thought I was a dumb blonde. Well who's dumb now, Bruckman? Tell me — who's dumb now?"

Instead of perpetuating the conversation, he invited me to lunch at John-Q's. But I'm not into consolation prizes, so . . . *double ha!*

"If I can see you, I can explain what happened and you'll realize you're mistaken."

If he left right this second, he'd still have a good half hour to plot and scheme up a plausible story before I got there. So no thanks.

"Fine. You don't want an explanation? Then bring the goods on this Alex Garrett guy and we'll have a professional consultation."

"I don't need you, Bruckman," I said nastily. After all, I'd been able to take the unguided tour of Garrett's bedroom. And since borrowing the man's stuff was probably illegal, I certainly wasn't going to brag about it.

"You may not need me, Dainty, but I need you."

And that's how it happened, me having lunch with Bruckman, sitting in the back booth across from him at high noon, with the vapors of a greasy cheeseburger and home fries in one of those plastic mesh baskets snaking up my nostrils, while he kept checking the baseball score on the ceiling-mounted TV.

He carved into a chicken fried steak and forked it, letting the excess white gravy drop onto the thick china plate before lifting it to his mouth. "You want to go first or should I?"

"You." The cheeseburger was delicious and I planned to eat it while it still had steam coiling out from between the buns.

Besides, I was still furious. Not as angry as I'd been on the telephone when I didn't have to see pain in those penetrating blue eyes. Or when memories of our late-night tryst rose like a vision and I felt an unexpected pang of sadness knowing I'd have to give that up.

Not *that* mad.

"You did see me go to her house."

So this was how he wanted to handle it, with our roles reversed — with him giving *me* a full confession while I nodded encouragement and tried to swallow the lump in my throat.

"Got a picture of it so I could remind myself if you lied about it."

"That's one thing you can count on, Dainty. If we're in a relationship, I won't ever lie to you." His eyes flickered back to the television. "Damn. They let them get ahead." To me, he said, "They need a left-handed pitcher."

Then John-Q came out from the kitchen with sweat beading on his forehead and his shaved head gleaming like a black star sapphire. The interruption lasted all of two minutes, whereupon he endeared himself to me by saying, "Same girl as before? This is a first for you, Jimmy."

When John-Q went back to play fry cook, Bruckman said, "I didn't sleep with her if that's what you're mad about."

"I don't care if you did or not."

"Yeah, you do."

"I don't."

"Do, too."

Trouble is, I did care.

"Remember what I told you last week?"

"I'm the guy who's going to teach you what it's really like to be in love."

"Oh, you'll want it all right. I'll give it a week, tops."

"Seven days."

And after being told he was pretty sure of himself, *"No, babe. I'm sure of you."*

I denied recalling any previous conversations. Instead of recounting it for me, he pulled out a sheet of paper that had been folded into quarters and handed it across the table.

I unfolded it. An invoice. From Johnny's Wrecker Service with this morning's date on it. I gave it back to him.

"So?"

"So my truck had to be towed. That's why you saw it there overnight."

"The lights were out."

"I dozed on the sofa until the guy showed up."

"Sure you did." I didn't like the way I sounded. I didn't like the mistrust oozing out of my voice. In short, I didn't like turning into Evangeline Briscoe. "Look, you can see whomever you want. You had a thing with her and now your friend's dead so you're free to have another thing with her. I don't care."

I'd wounded him with the dead friend dig. His eyes told me so.

He settled back into the bench seat and stared at me several long, uncomfortable beats. Neither of us had finished our lunch.

In fact, John-Q probably wondered if he'd served us a bad meal.

I said, "Say whatever you want but you kissed her. I saw it." And then my eyes welled.

He pulled a napkin out of the metal canister and shoved it across the table.

"I didn't kiss her. She kissed me. Big difference. Look, Dainty, I probably shouldn't have gone over there, but when she called . . ."

I wiped my eyes not anxious to hear the rest of it.

"I just thought I should, you know, because I worked the street instead of going to the funeral. I thought she wanted to talk about Mike but when I got there, she had something else in mind. I told her no. That it was too late. That after all this time I'd found someone." He reached across the table and took my hand.

My chin corrugated. "You spent the night with her."

"When I tried to leave, there was fluid all over the driveway. The water pump broke. I called the tow truck to come get it and fell asleep on her sofa waiting. The guy gave me a ride home and that's the end of it."

Please. I'm not that gullible.

"You didn't have sex with her?"

"I'm not saying I couldn't have if I'd wanted to. She came into the living room twice to check on me. The second time she didn't have any clothes on."

"Sounds like a medication issue." I marginally relented. "Hey, I'd have probably had sex with her if she did that."

He chuckled without humor. "Don't you get it? I didn't want to ruin things with you. She had her chance and she married the guy of her dreams without giving me a second thought. All I could think of was, don't I have the right to do the same?"

Wait — what's he saying?

"If I'd slept with her, Dainty, you'd have known. I don't know how you'd have known, but you'd have known. I've said it before: you've got good instincts. Why take a chance?" He cupped my hands in his. "Besides, I don't love her anymore."

"No?" It came out as a pitiful squeak.

He shook his head. "I'm pretty sure I've fallen in love with you."

Whoa.

Wait — did he just say . . . ?

Didn't see that coming.

Tears teetered along the rims of my eyes. My face cracked into a smile.

"Imagine that, Bruckman. And it only took a week."

We spent the next hour discussing Alex Garrett, with me showing Bruckman the paperwork and him threatening my life if I blurted out how I'd gotten it. After he paid the tab and we walked out of the restaurant toward our cars, he brought up the subject about Salem's Halloween bash.

"So are we still on for your friend's party?"

Seized by suspicion, I said, "Depends on what you're going as. I wouldn't want you embarrassing me. Besides, Salem's parents always give a hundred-dollar prize for the best costume, and I have to win so yours can't be better than mine."

He popped open the trunk and pulled out a blanket. As I waited for an explanation, he shook it out and threw it over his head. He waited a few beats, looking at me hard, waiting for the subtlety of the message to penetrate.

"That's your outfit?"

"Yeah. You like it?"

Whatever he was doing went over my head. Then it struck me full force.

I yelled, "Undercover cop," and we both laughed like hyenas.

"See Dainty Prescott? Told you you were smart."

CHAPTER
TWENTY-SIX

From John-Q's restaurant, we went our separate ways, Bruckman, to the PD with DOBs on Harold Alexander Garrett, Robert John Taylor and Jerry Don Grayson, and me, headed back toward Gran's place.

I reached for the cell phone and dialed Mrs. Clayton. When she answered, I told her about my fake colleague Donatella's fake offer to put in window treatments and asked if I could meet her at Alex's rent house. She told me to have the rental agreement and credit application ready, along with a personal check made out to her to cover the fee for the credit check.

Several things went wrong. First, I didn't have the brown wig with me. Second, I didn't have the paperwork with me. I made up a story about looking for fabric all morning but explained that I had cash to give her for the credit check. After me promising to fax the information to her later in the afternoon, she agreed to meet me at the rent house.

I asked for an hour's lead-time and used the opportunity to stop at one of the department stores in a nearby mall. There must've been a big sale going on because I had to circle the lot several times looking for a place to park. Finally, I gave up searching for a shade tree and drove into an area where the angled paint lines resembled fish bones against the asphalt. There, I slotted the Nissan into the only empty space on that row and killed the motor.

Lost in thought, I jumped out of the car like a thoroughbred out of the paddock — Secretariat, with blinders on — in a race for the Triple Crown. For no good reason, I sensed a vehicle bearing down on me. Glancing over my shoulder, I simultaneously heard the roar of an engine and moved aside for the passing auto.

Tires screamed against the pavement.

It's like the driver never even saw me.

If I hadn't leapt between two trucks at the last second, he would've creamed me. For a fleeting instant, a terrifying thought flashed into mind: that the maniac deliberately swerved to hit me. What kind of jerk speeds through a parking lot crawling with pedestrians? The guy behind the wheel of a dark blue sedan with tinted windows didn't even slow down to apologize for almost running me over.

Once my heart fell back into its natural rhythm, I went inside the mall and purchased another hairpiece. This one was almost the same length as the brown one but it came in a beautiful auburn shade that looked wonderful with my skin tone. Before leaving the store, I plunked down a small fortune for an Hermes scarf, then wrapped it around my new hair and cinched it at the nape of my neck like a headband.

Before driving the few miles to the rental property, I ran into a bargain bookstore and found a bestseller on window treatments. I paid for the paperback and a copy of *D Magazine* and sat behind the wheel with the air-conditioning on and the engine idling, tearing out pictures to further shore up my credibility. After putting Alex Garrett's original documents in the new tackle box, I covered them with pictures of pelmets, cornice boxes, pinch-pleat drapes, valances and window toppers, threw in the metal measuring tape and cash for the credit check, and closed the box.

The *D Magazine* was purchased to entertain Mrs. Clayton while I took fake window measurements and swapped out lock boxes undetected. Kind of like giving a kid a coloring book and other distractions to keep them entertained on the long ride to Disneyland.

Did I care that Alex Garrett wouldn't be able to open the box with his key?

Not hardly.

After all of this scheming, with my confidence buoyed from listening to Bruckman telling me how smart I am, you'd think I'd just breeze through this, right?

No.

I keep forgetting that I'm Dainty Prescott, underachiever, and that I was only engineered to look good in front of a camera, not to be fearless and think on my feet.

I pulled up in front of the rental house a few minutes before Mrs. Clayton rolled up behind me. Everything went according to plan, with me standing in the living room, handing her the cash and the *D Magazine,* and making a big to-do over the pictures inside the tackle box. She even lounged in the recliner and let me go about my business, which went off without a hitch until her chipper greeting pricked up my ears.

"Well, hello there, Mr. Taylor. I wasn't expecting you home."

Oh, dear God.

Alex Garrett had somehow entered the

house without me hearing. Oh. One other thing — coming back to this rent house made about as much sense as taking diet pills and blood pressure medication at the same time.

I'd just switched lock boxes and returned the borrowed documents. Had even closed the closet door and was about to step into the living room when I caught a glimpse of his reflection in the mirror, filling the entrance to the house and taking stock of the room. His angry expression curdled my blood. I needed a paper sack to keep from hyperventilating. Dainty Prescott, plus prison, equals the death penalty when it comes to membership in The Rubanbleu.

Where to now?

Frantic, my eyes darted around in search of an escape. I'd never experienced such paralyzing fear in my life. The fact that he'd returned while I'd invaded his digs gave me a dizzying head rush. My heart thudded. Carnal panic seized me in its grip.

Snap decision: go out into the hall and risk being recognized, or flee through the window?

A no-brainer.

My acute sense of hearing had been suddenly eclipsed by the whooshing sound of blood drumming against the veins in my head — absolute terror. Mrs. Clayton's animated explanation of my phony plan to take window measurements faded to an indistinguishable din, like the roar of a crowd. Or white noise. My hands trembled as I thumbed open the cheap aluminum locks, raised the glass, pushed out the screen and threw one leg over the sill.

Clearing the window frame, I plunged to the ground — a much farther drop than I'd gauged it to be. The sharp jolt that punished the soles of my feet zipped through my legs and settled in my knotted stomach. With my chin tucked into my chest and my auburn hairpiece swaying like a pendulum, enough to conceal my face, I crept along the side of the house and then picked up speed.

An eight-foot privacy fence constructed of rough-hewn wooden planks was all that stood between the street and me. But that was enough. There had to be a gate but it wasn't here, and I didn't have time to find it. Short of breath and out of time, I had no choice but to scale the enclosure. Anything less and I'd be cornered like prey. My heart pumped. Massive doses of adrenaline coursed through my veins. Flinging the broken lock box over the fence, I climbed like a rabid monkey until I reached the top and went over it as though my life depended on it. Like Cinderella, I lost one of my Choos, but I could always get another pair.

What I couldn't do is buy a new life.

While I crawled through the shrubs and loped like a hunchback along the neighbor's side of the property line, voices in the house corkscrewed up in anger.

I pulled the keys from my pocket and remote-opened my car door. As I sprinted across the sidewalk that ran the length of the block, and stepped off the curb near the Nissan's trunk, I knew they'd sighted me through the front window.

Then my heart skidded to a stop.

Alex Garrett had parked his car in front of mine, effectively blocking me in.

Popping open the driver's side, I slid behind the wheel and fired up the engine.

The front door flew open and Garrett charged out.

"Hey — come back here. I'm talking to you."

Getting out of this snafu required more dexterity than I had time for. I backed into Mrs. Clayton's car with a hard thump, wrenched the wheel all the way to the left, and drove forward until the front bumper smacked Alex Garrett's car. He ran down the sidewalk, hands waving frantically, as I slammed into Mrs. Clayton's car again. He'd almost reached the passenger door when I pulled forward enough to clear bumpers.

I blew the four-way stop sign and sped away with Tandy's con man receding in the rearview mirror, his flustered face hardening into a look of abject fury.

A mile or so later, with my heart still racing, I pulled off the freeway and into a fast-food drive-through. I ordered a cherry slush and then backed into an empty space at the rear of the parking lot. Sipping my drink, I reflected on this fork in my career path until I got a brain freeze.

I'm pretty sure I just had the most dangerous and exciting experience of my whole life.

And, ohmygod, it felt unbelievably amazing.

I'm talking one heart-palpitating, amped-up, sensational adventure.

Better than the greatest sex I ever had.

I never want to do this again.

CHAPTER
TWENTY-SEVEN

Once I fled the Hurst neighborhood and hit the road to Dallas, I pulled over and inspected the rental car for damage. All things considered, it wasn't bad. I passed a Nissan dealership on the highway to Gran's and whipped in to pick up a nail polish–sized container of touch-up paint.

After I'd pulled around to the back of Gran's house, I sat in the shade of the pavilion and dotted paint onto the scars on both bumpers. I'd been outside for all of thirty minutes when Gran sent the housekeeper to fetch me. The woman clucked sympathy as I tossed the rest of the touch-up paint in the garbage, dusted my hands together, and re-fluffed my hairpiece.

I admit it. The sudden dump of battery acid in my stomach made me queasy. I'm pretty sure my grandmother's giving me an ulcer.

I found Gran in the library sitting at a

leather-topped table in an atmosphere heavy with memories. This was my late grand-father's favorite room. The sweet scent of pipe tobacco, although faded, still lingers in the air. Sometimes, on rainy days, this room is so full of body you can almost feel his presence.

Paused in the doorway, I took a moment to consider my grandmother. Her face was a mask of concentration as she moved a magnifying glass over an old photograph while studying it against an open book.

I cleared my throat. "You wanted to see me?"

Exhaustion from keeping vampire hours for a week had set in, and I wasn't in the mood to be trifled with.

She looked up from behind a stub of gray eyelashes and drew a bracing breath. "What have you done to your hair?"

"It's a wig. Do you like it?"

"It looks cheap."

Of course she didn't like it. This polite exchange on my part was merely a formal-ity before we segued into whatever she'd really summoned me for. It was enough to make me grind my molars.

"It's human hair," I gamely informed her.

"It may as well be rat hair. I hope you didn't spend a lot of money. Why're you

338

wearing that?"

"I'm *in cognito.* Means I don't want to be recognized."

"I know what it means," she snapped. "Doesn't one of your little friends have red hair?" She motioned me into a Victorian channel-back claw-foot chair. "Sit down."

"I don't mean to be short with you, Gran, but I have a lot of stuff to do and not much time to get it done."

"Are you familiar with the story of Moses?"

God save the queen.

I looked at her slitty-eyed.

Here we go again.

"He was never actually allowed to go into the Promised Land." With her gaze downcast to her coffee, she gave a sad, trancelike headshake to the cup. Then her eyes slewed back over to me. "The Lord let him see it but he couldn't actually cross the Jordan."

I glanced around for a letter opener to open a vein.

"Moses took on so much responsibility leading his people. The lost children of Israel wandered around for years looking for the Promised Land. At the end of his life, as Moses lay in his tent, he could barely even raise up." An ethereal look spread over her face, softening the delicate pleats of skin

339

around her eyes, and un-puckering the tiny lines pinching her lips.

Physically, we were sitting in shafts of sunlight slanting through the plantation shutters, Gran in her cream-colored slacks and silk blouse with a peach-colored scarf knotted at the neck and a pair of low-heeled Ferragamos pushed off to one side; and me in my brown suede slacks balancing on one Jimmy Choo, with a dingy tailored tan shirt and buttery-soft brown leather Eisenhower battle jacket with fresh scuff marks from having scaled Mrs. Clayton's fence. But mentally I had my hands clamped tightly over my ears and was making up my own lyrics to the "Camptown Races" melody.

I'm not listening any more, doo-dah, doo-dah . . .

Her voice droned. "There were twelve tribes, you know, with elders and tribal leaders who shared the responsibility of running the individual tribes."

I'm not listening any more, oh, doo-dah day.

"Remember, Moses was an Egyptian. For some reason, the tribe Moses affiliated himself with didn't spread the work around. Moses was doing it all by himself and they let him because he was the guy with a direct pipeline to God Almighty.

"Several of the tribal elders led by Joshua

came to Moses and said, 'Moses, you're going to wear yourself out.' They sent for Moses' father-in-law who was from a different land — what we'd refer to as a foreigner, or in polite society, 'not from here' — and brought him in to assess the situation. The father-in-law was probably the first consultant in the Bible and this was likely the first documented early-day efficiency study ever done. He observed long lines of people waiting to see Moses."

Affecting a look of practiced innocence, I did a mind-flip. "So — and this is just an idle curiosity on my part — was the first documented episode of constipation when Moses took the tablets and went up on top of the mountain?"

"Don't be cheeky."

I gave her a dedicated eye blink, which she obviously mistook for interest. As I was looking around for a spike to drive through my head, Gran kept on talking as she unfurled her cloth napkin and placed it in her lap. She'd said everything up to this point while looking over a platter of pastries, eyeballing them before making her selection.

"Moses was like a judge and people were always getting his input. The father-in-law determined that Moses should learn to delegate authority." She stared into the distance. "I guess Moses was a lot like the first District Judge. After that, he only heard felonies. Others presided over the misdemeanors."

She paused, picking up a cheese cracker from a small china dish. I noticed the cup of tea next to it and realized I was thirsty.

"What's your point, Gran?"

Glittery blue eyes sized me up. "Moses was replaced by many men."

"Oh, for God's sake, just say what you mean."

"Don't be thick, Dainty, you need help."

"Who's going to help me?"

"What about your friends?"

CHAPTER
TWENTY-EIGHT

The branding-iron sun sapped the last of my energy and I fell asleep tanning beside Gran's pool.

In my dream, I walked into The Ruban-bleu wearing my Venice creation. A sea of people parted to let me pass. The din of voices fell to a hush as everyone looked on, admiring my gown and my escort, the gallant —

For no good reason I woke up with a lightbulb idea.

Okay, so maybe my friends don't know any more about how to get the goods on somebody than I do. And maybe I don't know all the law enforcement tricks on how to get information — but Daddy has friends who do.

Daddy knows the president of a nationwide postmasters association and that's got to count for something. Billy Wood is a postmaster in one of those one-horse towns you never think twice about unless you run out of gas there. My daddy's an old school chum. They stayed friends even after he moved from north Texas, when Mr. Wood's wife's parents left her a big farm out in the middle of nowhere.

In this case, the middle of nowhere is Broken Bow, Oklahoma.

I figured if Mr. Wood couldn't tell me about Tandy's soon-to-be stepfather, then nobody could, so I Googled him on the Internet and got his telephone number. When a gravelly voiced man answered, I identified myself and asked for Billy Wood. Turns out I had him on the line.

"I need help." The truth.

"Are you in some kind of trouble?"

Let's see: broke, cheating boyfriend, crazy relatives . . . no, no trouble.

"It isn't me. My friend's mother's about to marry a man named Henry Alexander Garrett. I have a detective agency, but I've run into one dead end after another. I figure if you can't help then it's all over. The wedding takes place in two days."

Billy said, "Where are you living, Dainty?"

I'd grown weary of telling people I was homeless. I told him I was staying with Gran until repairs were made to my townhouse.

"I know where Eugenia lives," Billy said, calling my grandmother by name. "I practically grew up in that house."

I wanted to offer my condolences. It probably wasn't any more kid-friendly when he used to visit.

Then he said, "I don't know a Henry Alexander Garrett. Is he from Broken Bow?"

"He's supposed to be from Florida."

"Well if you ever want to know anything about anybody here in Broken Bow, feel free to call. I know everybody. And if you need to know about anybody else in the good ol' USA, I can find that out, too. You wouldn't believe the number of people I'm acquainted with. And you wouldn't believe the number of contacts I have."

"Do you know a man named Robert John Taylor?"

"Bob Taylor. Good man." I could almost see Billy Wood nodding at the other end of the line.

"Describe him."

"Before or after he died?"

"He's dead?"

"Died of a heart attack a few years ago. Went to the funeral. Sad situation. When the kids went to probate the will, they found out somebody'd closed out all of his bank accounts. Even emptied out his retirement account."

"What was his occupation?"

"He worked for one of the car dealerships here."

I asked Billy Wood if he'd ever heard of a man named Jerry Don Grayson. For a few seconds, I thought my cell phone had dropped the call.

"J. D. Grayson owned the dealership where Bob worked."

It took a moment to digest this information.

"Does Mr. Grayson still live in Broken Bow?"

"Not for several years. Dainty, how'd you get mixed up with him?"

"I'm not sure we're talking about the same person so can you describe this Grayson guy?"

A female yelling in the background sheared his attention. Mr. Wood covered the mouthpiece and yelled in a muffled voice, "I'm on the phone, Wanda." Then he came back. "Dainty, I'm sorry. You called at a really bad time. My wife's in the backyard with our Rhodesian ridgeback. She's having puppies — the dog, not my wife — and we've had to send for the vet."

"I understand. Maybe if you could find

346

somebody who knows Henry Alexander Garrett from Pensacola, Florida — a friend of a friend — you could call me back with the information?"

"If you need to hunt somebody down, all I have to do is call up the local postmaster and ask him to give me the lowdown on that person."

Thanking him didn't seem to be enough. But I was thrilled when he agreed to call me back after the dog crisis passed. By the time I climbed the stairs three hours later and settled into my little room in the attic, I'd pretty much given up hope I'd hear back from him right away.

According to the alarm clock, I'd been asleep all of an hour when the security lights outside flashed on and the grounds lit up like the mothership had just landed. I threw back the covers, crept to the window and peered out. A spotlight recessed in a magnolia tree near the gate hit a lean, spectral figure with a hollow-eyed stare and ashen gray countenance. From my place at the window, the man pressing the intercom at the gate appeared to be elderly. Still, I considered the appearance of a midnight caller jarring.

I knew Gran wouldn't hear the gentleman at the other end. She takes out her hearing aids when she sleeps. So I ran down the steps to the second story and pressed the talk button to the intercom.

"Who's calling, please?

"Billy Wood."

Do what?

"Billy Wood from Broken Bow, Oklahoma?"

"Is that you, Dainty?"

"I'll buzz you in."

I scrambled to throw on clothes, grabbing a pair of freshly washed blue jeans from the drawer and tugging an oversized Stars hockey jersey over my head. After pulling a hairbrush through my tangles, I padded out the door in my bare feet and hurried downstairs.

Nothing stood out when I took a quick look inside the fridge, but I figured if Mr. Wood had driven all the way from Broken Bow to talk to me he'd probably want coffee before making the trip back.

While a pot of Kona grind brewed in the kitchen, I seated my guest across the table from me in the breakfast room. He was tall like my father but his hair had turned almost completely gray, well on its way to white. And his palms showed deep wrinkles, the by-product of handling paper for many years. Haunted blue-green eyes locked me in their gaze. He clasped my hand and pulled me close for a quick, avuncular embrace.

We made idle chitchat for several minutes about the drive down, comparing the price of gasoline in Oklahoma to the price of gas in the metroplex, and other benign topics such as Rhodesian ridgeback puppies and life on the farm.

"Dainty, when somebody travels four hours to tell you something you need to listen."

"You've got my attention."

The coffee sputtered. After pointing Mr. Wood to the closest bathroom, I excused myself to the kitchen. By the time he returned, I'd poured half-and-half into the Herend creamer and replenished the matching sugar bowl with packets of raw sugar. I even found a stash of butter crisp wafers hidden in the pantry, concealed behind a box of shredded wheat cereal, and put them on a cake plate as a snack.

When he returned to the table, he lightened his coffee and thanked me for my trouble. Once he polished off the cookies he said, "Your mother used to fix nachos for us on poker night. They were great."

I sensed he was still hungry and excused myself to the kitchen. "I can make Mom's nachos. I'll see if we have any avocados."

Gran had everything I needed to put a quick and tasty spread together. I turned the burner on low and browned a sauté pan full of ground round seasoned with cumin, onion powder, salt and pepper while I mashed avocados for guacamole dip and blended tomatoes and jalapeño peppers for salsa.

After twenty minutes of preparation, I donned oven mitts. Then I waltzed a platter of nachos into the breakfast room on a burst of air heavily scented with the savory smell of corn chips spread with bean dip, ground taco meat, melted cheddar and Monterrey jack cheese and jalapeño peppers on top. I'd spooned guacamole dip into its own bowl and dollops of sour cream and fresh-made salsa into separate dishes to use as condiments.

Coils of steam were rising off the melted cheese, snaking up my nostrils as I discovered Mr. Wood with his head tilted forward and his chin on his chest, snoring up a blue streak.

I backed up a few steps and cleared my throat, then sashayed in as if I hadn't caught him catnapping.

"Here we go."

"I didn't mean for you to go to all this

trouble, Dainty, but I loved your mother's nachos. Almost as much as I loved her King Ranch casserole." He winked to show he didn't expect me to start boiling chicken and tearing tortillas into quarters to submerge in melted cheese.

Between bites, he told me about Jerry Don Grayson.

"This guy, Grayson, owned a car dealership. The place operated in the red for years. He stood to lose millions and then all of a sudden" — he popped a nacho into his mouth and snapped his fingers — "his wife got sick."

As he picked up another nacho, spooned a dollop of guacamole dip on top, lifted it to his mouth, and let it hover near his lips, he said, "Doctors couldn't figure out what was wrong with her. Eventually, she died."

My mind leapt ahead and I felt a sudden pang of sorrow for his loss.

Mr. Wood crunched the nacho, holding up a finger in the universal request for patience. He wiped his mouth with the cloth napkin I'd provided, tossed it next to his empty plate and rested his forearms on the edge of the table.

"He'd taken out a huge insurance policy on her."

My eyes bulged.

"Enough to pay off his debts and move the dealership into the black."

"You're saying . . ."

"I'm saying he had her cremated against her parents' wishes. Against her wishes, too. She was a good, Southern Baptist lady and she wanted to be buried in the church cemetery beside her other family members. By the time the cops figured it out, she'd already been turned into ashes."

My eyeballs telescoped back into their sockets. "You think he killed her?" My heart quickened.

"I think your friend's mother shouldn't have anything to do with him."

"I'm not sure that's enough to go on to convince her not to marry the creep."

"That's why I drove down here. He sold the dealership a few years later and made a small profit. Word around town was he moved to Pensacola. A buddy of mine in Alabama, also a former postmaster, knows the postmaster in Pensacola. They're not that far away," he explained. "He and I worked on a committee a few years ago and got to be good friends — the guy from Alabama and I. I told him what I wanted and he called the guy in Pensacola and woke him up. Then the Pensacola postmaster called me. He didn't know Jerry Don Grayson but he gave me the lowdown on Harold Alexander Garrett. That's what took so long to get back to you.

"You sounded pretty high strung when we spoke. I don't have caller-ID so I couldn't phone you back. You'd said you were staying with your grandmother. Eugenia's number's unlisted but I knew the house so I decided to get in the car and drive. Driving helps me sort things out. So is your friend's mother well-to-do?"

"She made out okay in the divorce settlement. She was married to an oil baron and got to keep the house and a chalet in the Swiss Alps. And the judge awarded her the horse farm in Colorado along with three-quarters of their portfolio because she proved her husband was cheating on her. The judge knew he couldn't compensate her for a broken heart, but he came pretty close with a seriously inequitable division of their property."

Mr. Wood stared at an invisible point on the wall. "He came here trolling for a rich wife. How'd they meet?"

I drew a blank. Their introduction could've taken place at the country club as easily as it could've occurred at the opera, the ballet, the Van Cliburn competition or the symphony. Mrs. Westlake had her diamond-studded fingers in all of those pies.

Or it could've happened online. These days, who knew? I wilted at the thought I might have to hack into her computer. I'm good, but I'm not that good.

I asked what the Pensacola postmaster had to say about Harold Alexander Garrett and was stunned to find out Garrett was dead. While Daddy's friend waited in the breakfast room, I trundled upstairs to get the copies of the documents I borrowed from Alex Garrett's lock box.

Back at the table, I spread the three passport photos out across the table like a photo lineup.

Mr. Wood tapped the picture of Robert John Taylor. "That's Jerry Don Grayson." Then he pointed to the image of Harold Alexander Garrett. "And that's Jerry Don Grayson."

He took a deep breath and sipped coffee from the china cup. "If I had to guess, I'd say Jerry Don Grayson reinvented himself as Robert John Taylor. Bob died shortly before Grayson left town. It makes perfect sense because, as Bob's employer, Grayson would've had access to all kinds of personal information — his Social Security number, DOB, and other biographical data, do you follow me?"

Big head nod.

"Dainty, I don't know what you've gotten yourself into, but I don't think your father would like this one bit. You should drop it."

"I can't. The guy's about to marry my friend's mother."

CHAPTER
TWENTY-NINE

After Daddy's friend left, I stayed up a couple of hours hovering over my laptop with the keyboard clacking. Starting with the man I knew to be Harold Alexander Garrett, I backtracked.

Harold Alexander Garrett — Harry to his society friends — lived with his wife, Renata, in a Pensacola mansion until his untimely death as a result of a boating accident. His friend, Robert John Taylor, told the police that, from his place behind the wheel of a passing boat, he'd witnessed Harry clutch his chest and fall overboard. Taylor claimed he dove in to save his pal but Harry sank below the surface so fast that it couldn't be done without scuba gear — which Taylor didn't have on board. He further claimed he dropped a life ring into the water and sped back to the Yacht Club for help. But by the time marina patrons got back to the location where Taylor said he saw Garrett disappear, the body was long gone. Law enforcement and TV helicopters flew overhead while rescue divers from the Escambia County Sheriff's Department and the Pensacola Police Department searched until nightfall. No such luck.

Three days after Harry Garrett disappeared, a bloated corpse drifted to shore four miles from where Harry'd last been seen. It was the Pensacola millionaire.

Ten months later, Robert John Taylor married Renata Garrett.

Three months after the wedding, she was pronounced dead after her new husband found her floating at the bottom of their swimming pool and called the police. The Escambia County Medical Examiner's office determined her blood alcohol content to be .02 — an amount hardly worth commenting on, yet enough for a DUI conviction using the "zero-tolerance" statute crafted for drivers under the legal drinking age in the state of Florida.

Then up popped a red flag.

According to close friends of Renata Garrett Taylor, there were two things wrong with this investigation: One, Renata wasn't a big drinker — just an almost-teetotaler who left a hefty portion of her estate to Taylor, along with a whopping insurance policy for five million dollars that'd been taken out two months before her death; and two, Renata, who'd once been an Olympic swimming hopeful in her teens, had spent her whole life around water.

The drowning death was still pending. Something about weird bruises on her ankles.

Yeah — from being held underwater.

Apparently, Renata and Harry's kids suspected Taylor of killing their mother and were making a big stink about the money, the life estate in the house she'd given Taylor, and the other accounts and assets that hadn't been completely liquidated during the short marriage.

I may be a university student without any law enforcement experience but it didn't take but about .02 seconds for me to suspect Renata's death was no accident.

Flopping back in my chair, bathed in the blue glow of the screen, I digested this information.

Jerry Don Grayson probably killed his wife, collected the insurance and paid off the business. Moved to Pensacola and reinvented himself as Robert John Taylor. Probably held himself out to be a millionaire and started hanging out at the Yacht Club, met the Garretts and started hob-knobbing with the rich folks. Almost certainly, he'd murdered Harry Alexander Garrett and misled authorities on where to find the body until it'd decomposed to the point that any trauma findings would be inconclusive.

Or until sharks ate it.

Taylor married the widow Garrett and then drowned her in the family swimming pool. Collected the insurance and whatever else he could get his hands on. And when her kids stepped in and made his life a living hell, he headed for Texas.

Now he planned to marry my friend's mother.

For no good reason, I Google-searched Mrs. Westlake. I had to scroll through three pages of local articles before I stumbled onto a newspaper story in the Pensacola society section.

It appeared two weeks after the death of Renata Garrett Taylor.

Apparently the head of the Pensacola Museum of Art learned through an art broker that Mrs. Westlake owned an original oil on canvas by the French Symbolist painter Gustave Moreau. The museum curator wanted to acquire it for the collection and sent a man to Fort Worth to authenticate it. Once they sealed the deal, museum officials paid for Mrs. Westlake to preview the collection as a way to say thank you for parting with the painting.

That must've been where Alex Garrett saw her. Sweet-talked her. Got his hooks into her. Way to schmooze.

All total, I printed out at least a hundred pages of documentation to shore up my suspicions. At four thirty in the morning, I called it a night. Venice expected me over, mid-day, for the final fitting of my gown for the debutante ball. And she'd finished the bridesmaids' dresses for Mrs. Westlake's wedding.

Now that it looked like there might not even be a wedding, I wasn't the least bit worried about what my bridesmaid dress looked like. After all, if I didn't have to wear it, how bad could it be?

CHAPTER
THIRTY

Goals for the day:

1. Figure a way out of this suck-dog wedding
2. Pick up the most debu-licious rainbow mermaid ball gown <u>ever</u>!!!
3. Break news to Tandy

The only reason Venice, Salem and I went along with this charade to be attendants in this horrible wedding was because we thought we should be there for Tandy, if for no other reason than to do a quick frisk to ensure she didn't sneak a gun into the church and cap the groom.

The idea that Mrs. Westlake would create such falderal over a second marriage was ludicrous, especially one we all expected to end in disaster. Unlike "old money," the *nouveau riche* often skirt the rules of etiquette if they can get away with it. To her credit, Mrs. Westlake planned the event to take place at three in the afternoon so it wouldn't interfere with The Rubanbleu ball. To her detriment, she planned the event.

I called Venice to let her know I was on the way over. Apparently Salem had already arrived and they were waiting on Tandy and me for the unveiling of the bridesmaid dresses.

Even as Venice spoke I was slipping into clean clothes: turquoise capri pants, matching geometric silk shirt in turquoise, aqua and yellow and my yellow and aqua closed-toe sandals. I looked for a matching handbag and had to settle for a buttery soft Italian purse with a big leather flower stitched slightly off-center that was a shade or two between turquoise and aqua. Listening to Venice with the wireless phone scrunched between my ear and shoulder, I hooked a two-strand pearl choker around my neck and hurried downstairs to the guest bathroom that opened out onto the long hallway.

"So you need to get here as soon as you can, Dainty, because I want everybody to see my 'Venice Creations' at the same time. And you know how impatient Tandy gets."

"I'm on the way."

"And, Dainty . . ."

The pause carried way too much hang time. I knew, on instinct, I wouldn't like this next part.

"Drex called last night. He asked what color your dress was so he could order a corsage."

My heart lurched. "What'd you say?"

"I didn't tell him anything. I said he should call you. Then he said law school had been so busy that he'd lost all track of time. It was all I could do to keep from calling him a douche. You should text-message him."

Maybe I would.

Maybe I wouldn't.

I routinely check my emails for spelling and grammar, and have often relied on Salem and Venice to proofread them for general creepiness. Until the training wheels are off and I can do them on my own, this seemed like the way to go with text messages, too.

It's possible that I'm the only person my age who's not good at text messaging. No matter how many times I watch my friends speed-write with their thumbs on their wireless phone touch pads, I'm just not that good at it. Sometimes it takes me twenty minutes to construct a simple message if I don't use the pre-printed option button where you can send a reply message that's already been written: Call me when you get this; I am here; I am in a meeting . . . stuff like that.

When it comes to text messaging, I'm all thumbs.

Not to mention, I couldn't be trusted to string together two sentences to Strayer Drexel Truett III that wouldn't be construed as a terroristic threat.

By the time I finished the conversation with Venice, I was so angry at Drex that I brushed my hair and lacquered it with enough hairspray to keep it from moving in a thirty-mile-per-hour wind. While scampering down to the first floor, I formulated a plan to grab a piece of fruit from the refrigerator, check the leftovers to see if anything could be converted into a sandwich, and grab a cold bottled Vitamin Water on my way out.

That was the plan anyway. Then I ran into my grandmother having her coffee in the breakfast room.

" 'Morning, Gran." I kept on walking, pausing only long enough to sniff the air for signs of food for the taking. "Later, Gran."

"Dainty, I want to speak to you."

Her tone hauled me up short. I backed

into the room and slowly turned to face her. "What's up?" I infused cheer into my voice that I didn't feel.

"About these erratic hours you're keeping . . ."

Here we go again: "You're a mess, Dainty." . . . "Where've you been, Dainty?" . . . "You're not up to mischief are you, Dainty?" . . . "Who's your friend, Dainty?" . . . "Stop gallivanting around, Dainty."

A deflated tire sigh slipped out before I could restrain it. "Did I disturb you coming in?"

"That's not the point. I need to know where you are for safety reasons."

"Gran, I'm twenty-three."

"And that'd be fine if you had a lick of sense."

I started to pull up a chair but she said, "Not that one," and directed me to the one directly across from her.

Gran's the closest thing to a human lie detector I've ever seen. Those glittery blue eyes have always been able to bore their way into my head and poke around in places that are better left unexplored. She's next to impossible to fib to and if you do, by chance, put one over on her, she takes all the fun out of it by guilting you into submission.

I hate these talks. Besides, time wasn't on my side if I wanted to get to Venice's house before Tandy arrived. And yet . . .

I took a walk on the wild side. "What's on your mind?"

"Have you spoken to Nancy McGilroy about your date to The Rubanbleu?"

Nancy McGilroy's the lady in charge of the guest list. When I filled out the information on the "Requested Seating" card a few weeks ago, "B.P." — Before Paislee — I wrote Drex's name as my escort. Since a late-night meal is served after the debutantes make their bows, I asked to be seated at a table with Salem and two other girls who were presented as debutantes last year — and their dates.

"I haven't spoken to her since I mailed in my seating preference."

"Well apparently she didn't receive your information because she called here asking if I knew where to find you." She sighed. "You'll have to call her today, Dainty. It's not right leaving these women hanging. They have to know where to seat people. Nobody wants a repeat of the infamous debacle of 1973."

Even I'd heard of the infamous debacle of 1973. I was raised on it. That was the year Avery Marshall, one of Fort Worth's most talented financial advisors, divorced his wife, Bitsy. When The Rubanbleu ball rolled around, Bitsy invited Avery's friend Harlon; and Avery, who wouldn't even have had standing to attend the ball since The Rubanbleu is a *très* exclusive ladies group, got an invitation from Françesca Edmondson, Bitsy's best friend. Everyone knew Avery'd been having an affair — they just didn't know with whom. And everybody in town knew about Avery's history of reckless behavior at these events. His sketchy conduct generally started with slamming back too many highballs before the presentation of the debutantes. So when Mrs. McGilroy's predecessor seated Bitsy and Françesca at the same table, the ladies went all *Attack of the 60-Foot Centerfolds* on each other.

"I'll call Mrs. McGilroy." I hurried off before Gran could trot out one of her parables and regale me with it. When I made it out the door without her calling me back, I passed a dramatic hand across my brow and flung away invisible sweat.

All the way to the Hanovers', I thought about the bridesmaids' dresses.

Our "Venice Creations" were supposed to look like the "Jump Dress" in *Titanic.* The only thing good about this shindig was that we'd each have our own elegant copy of the movie gown.

Secretly, I'd been relieved when Venice told us she was making them as a gift to Tandy's mother. Not only did I not have the cash to buy a bridesmaid dress, at least we'd be spared the indignity of having to wear ugly butt-bow, off-the-rack garments that we, collectively, wouldn't be caught dead in. And I looked forward to having a piece of fashion art like the one Kate Winslet wore while playing the part of Rose.

Now came the unveiling.

Since Tandy hadn't arrived at the Hanovers' yet, Salem and I sat cross-legged on the floor as Venice laid out the four dresses across her bed. Each one was zipped into an opaque vinyl "body bag" that had a little "toe tag" looped over the hanger with our names on it. She lifted a hanger and removed the garment cover shrouding the first "Jump" dress.

Salem and I moved like synchronized swimmers, reaching out to pluck our dresses off the bed until Venice stopped us with a chopping, "Don't touch." Then she held up her gown for us to see.

We sucked air.

Our jaws dropped.

We exchanged awkward looks.

"Aren't they gorgeous?" Venice, bless her heart, fishing for compliments.

Suck-dog bridesmaid dresses always add insult to injury. But this hideous thing needed scaffolding around it and *Danger — Do Not Cross* tape in a nice Day-Glow yellow slapped diagonally across the front like a "Miss Texas" pageant sash.

This was no "Jump" dress. Instead of flesh-colored lining beneath a red-beaded and sequined dress, and a black tulle overlay with tiny dots and tons of beading all the way down to its rectangular train, the saucy wench bodice looked more like the costume for the St. Pauli girl on the beer bottle.

The shock wore off. A snuffle of laughter built up inside me. I didn't dare make eye contact with Salem. I pinched my lips together, hard, but my shoulders wracked with spasms. The devil on my shoulder goaded me.

Just a peek over at her. See whether she's looking at you.

The angel on the other shoulder tried to stop me.

Dainty, noooooooooo. Don't do it. Don't look.

Devil: *Why not, she's probably looking at you?*

Angel: *Don't listen to her.*

"Can you believe how pretty they turned

369

out?" Venice said proudly.

Pressure from the silence broke us.

We exchanged eyebrow-encrypted messages, and then cracked up in stereo. Like a couple of hyenas, giddy from the rush of adrenaline speeding through our systems, we were convulsed with laughter. Any concerns I had about sparing Venice's feelings evaporated. We doubled over, guffawing like lunatics.

Immature, I know, but I just couldn't help it.

Salem collapsed onto the floor. She rolled onto her back and assumed the dead roach position as I piled on top of her.

Good news, though. I could wear this hideous shroud to her Halloween party tomorrow night. What the heck — add a little seaweed, mime-loud makeup, maybe slip on a life vest with *R.M.S. Titanic* stenciled across it, hang blocks of Styrofoam around my neck for the iceberg, get Bruckman to hose me down before ringing the Quincys' doorbell . . .

That hundred-dollar prize was in the bag.

Venice had the look of an innocent bystander who'd realized, too late, that she'd been caught in the crosshairs of a sniper's scope.

Her enthusiasm faded. "You don't like them?"

Salem unleashed a fresh burst of hysteria.

"You really don't like them?" Venice again, slow on the uptake.

Bingo.

"Don't be silly. That's just not true," I said.

Salem almost choked on her words. "I see you're still on the spine donor transplant list, Dainty." To Venice, she said, "They're . . . interesting."

"Interesting?" I echoed an octave higher. "Why, no, darlin', they're just perfect."

Perfect for a National Lampoon *level wedding disaster.*

Venice's voice quivered. "I put a lot of hard work in on these."

Tears of mirth streamed down our cheeks. Then it hit me.

Oh, dear God. This isn't funny.

We were actually expected to wear these. I wiped away teardrops with the back of my hand. If the "Jump" dresses turned out this bad, what'd my dress for the debutante ball look like?

Swallowing the lump back down my throat, I made a demand. "Show me my gown for The Rubanbleu."

"Now, don't get mad, Dainty . . ."

The words "don't get mad," and "Dainty," when used in the same sentence, are virtually guaranteed to upset me.

Venice pressed her hands against the air in a downward motion. Apparently, I'd forgotten to use my "inside" voice.

"I want to see my mermaid gown."

"It's not here. Mrs. Westlake liked it so much she decided to get married in it."

Her words hit me full force. I pretty much sat, gobsmacked, grudgingly letting the news soak in.

From the moment I first tried on the creation Venice whipped up using my previously worn ball gowns, I'd been fighting the impulse to brag about my designer dress now that I'm more or less poor and no longer financially subsidized by my father.

There went months of planning around the perfect dress with the perfect date all shot to hell in a split second.

"What am I supposed to do?" I moaned, halfway to hyperventilating.

"Don't worry, Dainty, the festivities will be over by five or six o'clock and the ball doesn't start until eight-thirty."

"You don't understand — the people who go to Mrs. Westlake's wedding will have already seen the dress." Sickened, I flopped over onto my side and pillowed my head against my outstretched arm. "They'll know it's not original."

"It *is* an original."

"Not to me — or to them because they'll have already seen it. They'll think I got it off the rack. Or, God forbid, they'll think I borrowed it."

"It won't be that bad."

"It *is* that bad." My eyes jumped her like a starving wolf. "Tandy's mom stole my dress. How could you let this happen?"

Salem intervened. "Calm down. She didn't mean for Mrs. Westlake to make off with your dress. It's just that it was so gorgeous she couldn't resist showing it off. Isn't that right, Venice? You were proud of it and wanted Mrs. Westlake to see?"

This Oscar-worthy sucking-up served as a catalyst to propel me to the top of the spine donor transplant list.

"Nice going, you two. Tell me, Salem," I said with unmistakable sarcasm, "do you see any hemorrhoids while your head's up there?"

"That's not helping, now, is it?"

I flashed her an equally cutting look.

Then realization dawned.

Once I got hold of Tandy and gave her the scoop on Alex Garrett, she'd make sure the wedding didn't take place. Without a wedding, I could get my rainbow mermaid dress back.

CHAPTER
THIRTY-ONE

Goals for the day:

1. Find Tandy
2. Apologize to Venice
3. Win prize for best costume at Salem's party

I spent much of Friday morning trying to contact Tandy, but each time I called the phone cycled to voicemail. When I still didn't reach her by mid-afternoon, I considered reporting my findings directly to Mrs. Westlake. But the results of the Alex Garrett investigation would have the impact of a death message, and my friend should be the one to deliver it — or the police — not me.

Worst-case scenario, I'd see Tandy tonight at Salem's Halloween party.

I drove over to Bruckman's house around

four o'clock that afternoon with the "Jump" dress draped over the passenger seat of the Porsche and waited for him to come home from work. The American GI camouflage fatigues I'd originally planned to wear were in Gran's dryer, their place of honor having been usurped by the bridesmaid dress. After shopping at the one-stop electronics store for a micro-cassette recorder, a packet of tiny tapes and the soundtrack from the motion picture *Titanic,* I planned to record the theme song and enter the party to background music.

Once those purchases had been made, I bought one of those little Styrofoam coolers at the dollar store. Then I picked up a spool of fishing line and pieces of plastic floral greenery that could pass for seaweed, before stopping off at the sporting goods store to buy a spongy white life ring that came with a length of nylon nautical rope. The props for my costume cost all of seven bucks, giving me a ninety-three-dollar profit when Salem's parents judged the winner and gave me the prize for "Best Costume."

Bruckman pulled into the driveway behind me, effectively blocking me in. He looked tired but he kissed me hello and carried the props for my dress into the house. Then he set up his stereo so I could record my tape while he showered.

The plan was to have dinner at the Chinese buffet down the street from his house, go to Salem's party and win the prize. I'd already made a mess of Bruckman's breakfast room by dismantling the cooler and stringing the broken Styrofoam chunks together with fishing line and "seaweed" to make the iceberg boa I planned to drape around my neck. Once I located a black laundry marker to print *R.M.S. Titanic* on the life ring, I finished in less than fifteen minutes.

My cell phone trilled.

Not being able to give my report to Tandy in time to get the wedding called off made me edgy. By now, the police had compiled all the information they needed to pick up Alex Garrett, AKA Jerry Don Grayson, and Bruckman and I were awaiting word of his capture as soon as the arrest went down. As far as I knew, they'd posted officers near the rental house and at the guard kiosk at the Westlakes' gated community. Unless the groom had gotten cold feet and skipped town, I couldn't think of any reason he wouldn't be cooling his hocks in jail before midnight tonight.

Then I could reclaim my rainbow mermaid dress.

For no good reason, I checked the digital display before answering.

Drex.

It was enough to stall my heart. I didn't dare answer with Bruckman in the next room so the call cycled to voice mail. Seconds later, telltale tones signaled that he'd left a message.

I dialed into voice mail and listened.

"Dainty? Babe, where've you been? Something must be wrong with your phone because I've been calling you ever since I flew in last night."

Big fat fib.

Involuntary heavy eye roll on my part.

"Let me know if you want a corsage for the debutante ball because if you do, I'll have to pick it up tomorrow. And I need to know where to pick you up. Did you move into your townhouse?"

Long pause while I gritted my teeth. What a smooth liar he'd become. Probably learned that in law school.

"Sorry we haven't been able to talk lately. Had finals, you know? But we can catch up tomorrow night. Or you can call me tonight. Whatever. Love you. 'Bye."

I saved the message to replay it later so my friends could think he was a jerk, too.

In a way, though, it was good that he'd

called. It helped me remember to telephone Mrs. McGilroy so she could replace Drex's name with a calligraphy place card for Jim Bruckman.

When Bruckman didn't return to the living room by the time I'd cleaned up my mess, I went looking for him. As I walked into his bedroom, smelled the scented candle burning and saw the lump under the bed linens I had no choice but to turn off the lights and join him between the sheets.

At first, I only planned to catnap. But when he slitted his eyes open, threw back the covers and fixed me with a smoldering, sexy look, seeing his naked body melted my clothes off.

Such scandalous behavior was definitely not on The Rubanbleu "approved" list.

He welcomed me with open arms beneath the cool, silky sheets. My lips felt as if they were disintegrating as they touched the hard curve of his shoulder. I traced the shape of his mouth with a manicured finger, melting at his intimate touch.

His tongue caressed its way into my mouth. He kissed me deeply, then whispered in my ear using a soft, hypnotic voice that drove me into a frenzy. We made love by the sweet-scented light of a candle until he called out my name in a rasping cry against my neck. Then I felt the physical tension leave his body. He rolled off and held me tightly to him, with me glorying in the feel of his protective embrace.

Then he growled something low and unintelligible against my ear in that deep, roughly textured voice and I realized we weren't through. What can I tell you? It would've been rude to say no. By the time he was done with me, one thought orbited my brain: *This must be how it feels to survive electrocution.*

For a long time, we held each other, with him stroking my hair back from my face and me grazing the soft skin along his back. He seemed in no hurry to hop out of bed, and I no longer doubted what he meant when he said, *"I'm the guy who's going to teach you what it's like to really be in love."*

We'd used up the time we planned to spend eating Chinese but neither of us minded going to Salem's on an empty stomach.

After a quick shower, I finished preening and dressed in my "Jump" dress. Since I was supposed to spend the night at Tandy's house with Venice and Salem, Bruckman agreed to follow me over to the Quincys' house for the party. After that, he was on his own.

From the drive along Airport Freeway, we doglegged onto Interstate 30 to the west side of Fort Worth. Traffic slowed to a crawl near downtown, giving me time to fumble through the glove compartment for my address book and come up with a telephone number for Mrs. McGilroy. In no time, I had her on the line.

She apologized for misplacing my date card and asked for the name of my escort.

It didn't take much imagination to picture her dressed to the nines, perched on the edge of one of her French needlepoint parlor chairs with her legs crossed at the ankles, plucking a chocolate from the box with her free hand, and then reaching for a pen as I spelled Bruckman's name for the guest card. As always, her white hair would be coiffed to perfection. She'd have on a tailored outfit made from luscious fabric in a bright gemstone color like emerald green or cobalt blue, and her ruby red lipstick would be close by, tucked away in a delicate purse with a tiny powder compact, keys and plenty of cash. Mrs. McGilroy was always on the go.

"Oh, my." A sniff of unsuitability traveled down the line. "Is your young man related to the Connecticut Bruckmans?"

Because of the hope I'd detected in her

voice, and the fact that I like to be agree-able to women Gran's age, I told her I thought so.

Big mistake.

"Oh, dear, Dainty, I'm afraid we have a problem. Those people were notorious bootleggers and horse thieves." She spoke with authority. "I do have a short list of young men who're home from college — any of them would be thrilled to take you . . ."

Are you kidding me?

". . . Bitsy Marshall's grandson is in town . . ."

What — he's not in prison? Shocking. Bitsy Marshall's grandson has a major drug prob-lem.

"Perhaps one of your friends wouldn't mind setting you up with a more appropri-ate date?" she singsonged.

Uh . . . hella rude!

Ladies Gran's age keep their thoughts hot-wired to their tongues.

Stay tough. Think alligator skin without the bumps.

"You're friends with Salem Quincy, aren't you? She always invites such lovely young men to The Rubanbleu. Maybe her young gentleman has a friend?"

I thought on my feet. "Wait — did you

382

say the Bruckmans of Kennebunkport?"

"No, dear . . . the Connecticut Bruck-mans." Spoken with an edge.

"Heavens no," I said with mock surprise. "Jim's from the Bruckman family of Ken-nebunkport."

She let out a sigh of relief. "Oh, I'm so glad."

"Yes, well, I'll tell him what you said. We'll have a good laugh over it. He warned me about those Connecticut people. Told me not to get him confused with the likes of them." I treated her to a fake laugh.

With a heavy eye roll, I thumbed off the telephone.

Should've just told her I wasn't attending the ball. I'd almost rather go stag — heaven help me — than go with somebody Salem's date offered to fix me up with.

Salem's date, Rick, had set me up once, a long time ago, when Drex went abroad the summer of his sophomore year, and I didn't have anyone to accompany me to the Quin-cys' Aspen house for their famous annual family-and-friends weekend. The hitch came about when Mr. Quincy said Salem couldn't bring Rick unless Venice and I brought dates so Venice brought her boy-friend, Brad — who's now her ex-boyfriend Brad — and Rick fixed me up with his friend, Mark or Mick or Mack — believe me, I've tried to forget.

I mistrust blind dates — *quelle surprise!* — so I insisted on meeting Rick's friend before we boarded our flight. But this guy kept putting me off with excuses. When the departure date rolled around and we still hadn't formally met, he said he'd introduce himself to me at the terminal, in the bar near our gate.

From a distance, he seemed okay.

We'd described what we were wearing so we'd be able to find each other: me, in a muted tailored suit belted at the waist, and him wearing blue jeans and a drab green twill shirt.

As I closed the gap between us, I noticed the violent twitch. For an instant, I thought he'd been shot; it was that kind of jolt. Only I didn't hear gunfire so I suspected the shooter must've used a silencer. This unexpected thrashing carried a bit of lag time. The second time he flung himself forward — kind of like Tourette's syndrome only without the barking and curses — I scanned the terminal for a place to take cover.

I wanted to run for my life — rudeness be damned — but an inward, malfunctioning radar that my sister Teensy refers to as "weirdar" overrode my compulsion to bolt.

Perhaps it was that we had assigned seating and the two-hour flight might seem awkward if I ran screaming down the corridor.

As we shared a drink at the bar, me sipping a virgin piña colada and him swilling down beer, there was something scary about the way his face would contort each time he lunged toward me, mid-sentence. I found it increasingly awkward trying not to notice each time he convulsed. I finally couldn't take it anymore and excused myself to the women's restroom, where I telephoned Salem as commodes flushed and water flowed into the sinks.

I recounted the past half hour to Salem, explaining that I intended to beg off sick, ticket be damned. She mentioned this to Rick, who fell into a laughing fit in the background while Salem's voice went ultrasonic down my ear canal.

Turns out it was all an act — the seizure thing — but I decided then and there that I'd never let anyone set me up on a blind date again. What kind of idiot does that? I mean, if you have to fake a personality, why not fake being normal?

After boarding the flight, infuriated, I changed seats. I sat next to a fat guy with halitosis whose belly overhung my armrest. He kept wanting to show me vacation pictures of his family standing in front of national landmarks, saying, "I'm thinking of having a couple of these blown up. What do you think?"

I told him they should all be blown up.

He suggested I find another seat.

That was the longest two-hour flight of my life and the weekend hadn't even really started.

Now, after disconnecting from Mrs. McGilroy, I centered my gaze on the keypad to stab out Bruckman's number. The phone rang in my hand.

Jim.

I did a happy little car dance behind the wheel before answering with a sultry, "Hey, you."

"Will they have food at this place?"

"Tons of it. By the way, you're a descendant of the Bruckmans of Kennebunkport if anybody at the debutante ball asks."

"You didn't tell them I'm from the cattle rustler Bruckmans of west Texas?"

"Don't give me a hard time."

He started to make a wisecrack, and then stopped mid-sentence. "Are you aware there's a car following you?"

My eyes darted to the rearview mirror and beyond. We were on a four-lane highway with so many vehicles it looked like an automobile convention. "Which one?"

"The metallic blue sedan riding my bumper," he said. "Is that the guy you've been investigating?"

"I don't think so."

"I'll change lanes. Then you punch the gas. When he catches up, I'll pull in behind him and get the license plate."

I did as I was told, watching as the car accelerated. Bruckman whipped over and boxed him in.

He said, "Got a pen? Write this down." He called out the tag number as I rummaged, blindly, through my purse.

"Got it." Not a moment too soon, I jotted down the number in my hasty scrawl.

The driver of the blue sedan unexpectedly switched lanes, sped off, and took the next exit.

"You're paranoid," I said.

"Better safe than sorry. Want me to run it?"

"Don't be silly."

Just the same, the offer gave me a warm, secure feeling. Bruckman cared about me and wanted me to be safe.

We stayed on the phone as our two-vehicle caravan made its way to Salem's house.

I was right to have written Drex off as a lost cause.

Now I just wanted to be happy.

And I had a sneaky suspicion that I'd found the guy who did that for me.

CHAPTER
THIRTY-TWO

We arrived at Salem's parents' house fashionably late — enough for me to make a spectacular entrance. After I pulled my string of plastic kelp and fake iceberg slabs from the passenger seat of the Porsche, and flung it around my neck like a feather boa, I looped the *R.M.S. Titanic* life ring through one arm and used it to conceal the tape recorder. As Mrs. Quincy opened the door to greet Bruckman and me, I activated the theme song from *Titanic* and entered the party with the hem of my dress whispering along the floor.

I was a huge success with everyone clapping and cheering — everyone but Venice, that is. I left Bruckman with Salem's parents to see if they could figure out what he was supposed to be beneath the sheet and went off to console her.

I suspected my arrival would touch off fireworks, but I didn't expect the diva-esque kind of attention that I got as I moved through the rooms looking for my friend.

I caught up to her on the back deck, dressed as Cat Woman in a one-piece black leotard, with pointy velvet ears above impressively long lashes that had been made more luxurious with mascara. And that was how I found her, pawing through an ice chest full of soft drinks like a feral feline in a dumpster.

Without glancing up, she handed me a Dr Pepper.

I felt terrible. "I'm sorry, I couldn't help it. I need that prize money."

She reached for a Diet Dr Pepper and looked up at me, wounded, through yellow contact lenses that gave her a jungle predator look. Pouty lips were glossed and berry stained.

"Come on, Venice. I'd never deliberately hurt your feelings."

"Already did." Her cheeks flushed bright red. The canned drink opened with a *pfft* and she lifted it to her mouth without making eye contact.

"Look at me," I demanded, seizing her wrist and tightening my hand around it. "I'm having a great time fighting the impulse to brag about my designer dress when I'm supposed to be poor. And look at you.

You're sensational. Could I win the prize money without this dress?"

She blinked.

We both knew why I wore it.

"Come on, Venice. You can tell everyone you made this. Maybe they'll want one."

I looked down at the black tulle overlay to my "Jump" dress and saw that it served a dual purpose. In the creamy glow of the outdoor sconces, with scores of insects pounding themselves into husks against the protective glass covers, it had become a bug catcher.

"That's just disgusting, Dainty." She burped against the back of her hand and strutted off.

I laughed so hard Dr Pepper spewed out of my nose.

Later, I found her hanging around the dining table, talking to Bruckman over a chafing dish of hot *hor d'oeuvres.* I joined them at the buffet and tried to strike up another conversation with her, but a conga line of caterers unexpectedly *cha-cha*ed in carrying platters of sizzling sausages and other barbequed meats from the outdoor grill. Then they proceeded to uncover several crockpots of *queso* and plates of steaming tamales that surrounded an autumn-inspired centerpiece of chrysanthemums and tiny pumpkins. At once, the strong aroma of meat filled the air. Delicious smells wafted into the living room, turning party guests into a ravenous wolf pack. As they descended on the table and devoured the fare, caterers replenished the empty dishes. Once everyone loaded their plates with pyramids of food and strolled off to enjoy it, the three of us were alone again.

I glanced over at Venice and saw her making sour faces at the condiments.

"Where's Tandy?" I said. "I have to talk to her."

She skewered me with a look. "Since she can't attend her father's wedding tomorrow, she wanted to be at his rehearsal dinner. The sisters went to Mrs. Westlake's rehearsal dinner since they're not attending her wedding."

I caught Bruckman's attention. I looked at him hard but he didn't get the message. Then I did a little face-scrunch-head-jerk-eye-shift combination so he'd realize I wanted to speak to Venice alone.

He got the picture.

In private, I appealed to my friend. "Please don't be miffed."

"You're supposed to wear that dress tomorrow, Dainty. Now the front of it looks like a butterfly net."

"Moths." Palms up, coupled with a *Sorry* shrug.

With an angry hair toss, Venice whipped around and flounced to the other side of the table with her tail sweeping from side to side. She lifted a lid on a huge pot and dampened her nose with the steam coming off of the chili.

"Can you keep a secret?" I looked across the table and made serious eye contact with her. "If I tell you something, do you promise not to tell?"

"Maybe. This better be good. I'm still mad at you." Cat eyes fiercely narrowed.

"It's good."

"Okay." With a sinewy gait, she slinked up next to me, stabbing little treats along the way with one of those frilly party toothpicks. Towering over me in a pair of hideously high black leather boots, she pinky-swore not to tell.

"There's not going to be any wedding tomorrow."

"What?" Salem said this on a whoosh of air. She'd moved into the room without me knowing it, and was standing at my side dressed as Cinderella in the formal white ball gown she'd made her debut in. With a glitzy tiara cocked jauntily on top of her head, she reeked of wine and perfume.

The buffet had suddenly become the main attraction, so I pulled them outside where I turned into the eternal flame for every moth within a three-block radius. After swearing Salem to secrecy, I delivered the basics. It was still enough to start a flash fire of gossip.

"But you can't tell anybody," I warned. Venice gave an enthusiastic head nod, one with the potential for whiplash. Salem, I wasn't so sure about. "And, while I'm sorry for Tandy's mother, this works out perfectly for me because now I can get my mermaid dress back and wear it to the debutante ball. And you know what that means."

Venice brightened. I could tell we shared a simultaneous thought — the dawn of "Venice Creations" ball gowns for the rich and famous. Clothing to the stars.

Salem said, "I haven't been able to reach her by phone."

"Me neither." Venice.

I grabbed Salem's hand and squeezed. "Would you keep trying? I'd rather spring it on her while her mom's not around."

"Don't you think we should all be there — for moral support?"

Excellent point.

Then she cast a sidelong glance into the

house. "Look, I've got to get back to the party. My parents are about to judge the costumes so finish up out here and come on inside."

Pressing my fingertips against closed eyes, I rubbed until white sunbursts exploded behind my lids. When I opened them again, I saw the last swatch of fabric from the hem of Salem's debutante dress disappear into the house.

I turned toward the black sweep of a man-made lake at the back of the Quincys' property, feeling the cool, fresh breeze coming off of the water. An opalescent moon had risen overhead, giving the night a magical quality that I didn't want to end.

Venice did a quick lean-in. "I like him, Dainty. He'll be good for you."

"I like him, too." I sniffed the air and smelled rain. A peal of laughter came from inside the house, but outside, leaves and blown flags from the golf course were the only movements.

Something moved at the limits of my vision.

I sucked air. Where the moon silvered the lake, a silhouette loomed. "Is that a guy out there?"

Venice raised a hand to shield her eyes from the glare of the deck lights. "Where?"

Long pause. "I don't see anything."

"A man. Out there." I darted a look at my friend. "Near the trees. Look."

She waved her hand dismissively. "Probably one of the guests out 'draining the radiator.' " She made air quotes with her fingers. "Did you see the bathrooms? They're like those long lines in Soviet Russia. That's what happens when you give people all the liquor they can swill down."

Before the three of us left for Tandy's house, I pulled Bruckman away from the rest of the group, delighted with the hundred-dollar prize money I'd tucked into my bra.

"Wish you didn't have to go," I whispered. Partygoers faded to the back of the room. My world narrowed to a single focal point. The man made my heart race. "I had a great time with you this afternoon."

He brushed a strand of my auburn hairpiece aside. "I like your friends."

"Sorry I had to mingle. I needed to make peace with Venice over the dress."

He pulled me outside onto the front porch and gave me one of his bodice-ripper, Rhett Butler-sweeps-Scarlett-upstairs kisses. The guy should've come to this party dressed as Dracula. I swear he just drained all of the tension out of my body.

"Call you tomorrow," he said, then left me, limp, on the front porch, using the wall for support, with my mouth disintegrating, my heart fluttering and a head full of static.

I didn't even have time to bask in the glory and the taste of that kiss before Salem yanked open the front door and stuck her head out. She looked the length of the porch. Seeing me propped up against the wall with a dazzled expression on my face, she held the cell phone aloft.

"Where have you been?" she snapped. "I've been looking everywhere for you." Then she shook the wireless at me and mouthed without sound, *It's her.*

I assumed she meant Tandy. I walked over on shaky legs with a heady realization: If Bruckman's kiss could make me reel like a drunken sailor I had to keep him around.

With the phone pressed against one ear and my finger jammed in the other ear to cut the revelry, I waved Salem back inside.

"Tandy?"

"Talk louder."

Music blared at the other end of the line.

"Are you having fun at your dad's?"

"Sucks. The bride's an idiot. And I hate her kids. But, hey, good news. She has a really big dog and I think she feeds him little dogs."

For some unknown reason, the shiver going up my spine had a creepy feel to it that had nothing to do with the brisk night air. Maybe Bruckman's kiss had left such a hypersensitive effect on me that I could hear my skin crawl. Or maybe this had to do with the information I had to tell my friend. For no good reason, I felt the night's eyes on me and moved out from beneath the flickering glow of the gas sconce.

"Tandy, I have news on Alex."

"Good or bad?"

"Depends on who's getting the news."

Long pause. "Are we going to have a wedding tomorrow?" Her voice dissolved into a whisper.

"I'm thinking maybe . . . no."

Her excited voice pealed down the line with a triumphant "Yes." Music intervened in our conversation. "What'd you find out?"

"Listen, I don't mean to be a drama queen but you need to be sitting down for this. I have supporting documentation to show you and I think — we think — you should be surrounded by your friends."

"You told Salem and Venice before you told me?" Said with a touch of defensiveness.

"Not exactly. You're the one who hired me so I figured you should hear this directly

398

from me. But they're the ones who think we should be together for moral support."

Tandy didn't see it that way.

"You get right over to my house and bring whatever you've got. If I decide they should know I'll tell them myself."

"Tandy," I said with finality in my tone, "let them come. This is the kind of thing you need to hear surrounded by people who love you. Not sitting alone in front of the evening news."

It took a few beats for my words to soak in.

"On the way. Meet you at the house."

Then she left me listening to dead air.

CHAPTER
THIRTY-THREE

After rounding up Salem and Venice, we decided to pile into Mr. Quincy's Suburban and drive to Tandy's as a team. Salem, half plastered, handed over the keys to me.

She and Venice wanted a blow-by-blow account of my conversation with Tandy. I just wanted to sort out my thoughts.

Salem pointed to the brown envelope. "Are those the goods you got on Alex?"

Big nod.

"What'd he do? Rob a bank?" Venice.

Big head shake.

"Worse?" Salem.

Big dizzying head bob.

They sucked air. Venice said, "Did he kill somebody?"

Salem chimed in, "That's it, isn't it? He killed somebody. He's a serial killer." She paused. "Mass murderer?"

When I didn't answer, they both flopped against their seat backs, Salem next to me on the passenger side and Venice behind me mumbling a choppy, "Oh. My. God."

We scanned the perimeter for Alex's Lexus and didn't see it as we wheeled up in front of Tandy's house. The porch light was out or turned off, and the only ambient light came when the cloud cover broke away from the opalescent moon.

We stayed in Mr. Quincy's truck listening to each other breathe. Up ahead, headlight beacons swept across the road.

"That's her." Salem bailed out with Venice close behind her.

I wasn't so eager to leave Mr. Quincy's truck.

Did I mention how much I hate this house?

The car wasn't Tandy's but the driver of the dark-colored sedan made a mid-block U-turn and disappeared down a side street. Salem and Venice were already standing on the front porch doing a little jig to keep warm in the brisk night air.

She should've been here by now.

I saw an advancing blur out of the corner of my eye. My stomach gave a nasty flip. A guy dressed in dark clothing had slipped up beside the driver's door without me noticing and tapped on the window.

I came up two inches off the seat and

grabbed my throat. "Jeez — you scared the heck out of me."

He flashed an "Aw, shucks," grin that was a little on the creepy side and held up his hands indicating he was harmless.

I took my eyes off him a second to press a button, the glass rolled halfway down.

"Hi. I wonder if you can tell me where Oakmont Road is." He had a whisky voice and smelled of cigarettes. The fading grin turned feral.

I stared into eyes that were fathomless and flat.

"Sorry, I don't live in this neighborhood," I said, cordial but detached. "Neither do they. We're just here visiting our friend."

"Is your friend home? Maybe she can tell me."

"She's not here."

The headlights on Tandy's Beetle closed in on us. I got out of Mr. Quincy's truck and walked ahead a few steps to flag her down mid-street. The driver's window hummed open.

"This guy wants to know where Oakmont Road is."

She focused on something behind me and her expression changed. Her eyes went wide. She spoke in a low, scary voice, "Dainty, don't move."

"What?" I jumped at the touch of a gun barrel pressed between my shoulder blades. My blood turned to ice. I felt my heart go dead in my chest.

"Nice and easy, step out of the car," he said. "Call your friends over. We're going for a ride or I'll kill her where she stands."

I said, "Don't call them."

He ratcheted back the hammer. Every cell in my body screamed. A chill scurried up my spine. Pure terror snared me in its grip.

"This thing's got a hair trigger."

He got me in a headlock and moved the gun to my ear.

"Don't do it, Tandy," I croaked.

Tandy moved with the sluggishness of a zombie. With a determined expression on her pale marble face, she called out to our friends to come down to the street, carefully modulating her voice to conceal her fear.

The words of Bruckman's colleague came back to haunt me.

"Never . . . never . . . never let yourself be tied up."

"Fight for your life right there."

"The way God points the finger is through DNA."

I screamed, "Run," and got the butt of his gun upside the head for being the town

403

crier. My surroundings blurred. The pavement rose up to meet me.

We're in big trouble.

Then the lights went out.

My first attempt to break through was a primitive one — profound nausea.

When I cracked my eyes open, Venice was sitting behind the wheel of the Suburban, wordlessly staring off into space as she drove; Tandy was in the front passenger seat and I was sprawled across Salem's lap in the back seat letting the chaos wash over me.

Our kidnapper rode in the back with us and controlled the other door.

Salem and I made eye contact. Abduction had sufficiently sobered her. That and the fact that I'd bled all over last year's white silk debutante dress.

I cut my gaze to the man's pale, grave face. With the gun pointed at Venice, he directed Tandy to cut lengths of rope with a penknife. My heart stalled. Light from the mercury vapor lamps shone through the windows, bluing his skin as tires droned along the asphalt. When he looked back over at me I saw hatred so strong it whipped my breath away.

Think, Dainty, think.

I considered my options. Continue pretending to be knocked out, buying time to size up the situation? Come fully awake and try to bail out at the next stoplight, leaving my friends with a psycho while I call for help? Go along with my friends to keep him from punishing them for my perceived misconduct? I mentally rejected each choice. They'd find us in landfill Hell in the enema section of Fort Worth.

I needed a phone. If I had a phone I'd call nine-one-one. Wouldn't even have to talk other than to say, *Why're we driving down University? Why're we going toward the zoo?* Dispatchers are smart. Bruckman said so. They pick up on things.

And I still had the tape recorder on me.

The one with the theme from *Titanic.*

It was fastened to the backside of my dress beneath the black tulle overlay. I knew the value of recording devices. I'd watched, with rapt attention, a case on the forensics channel where the ex-wife and her bully boyfriend threw her ex-husband into the trunk and drove him into the woods. They'd been having problems with their child custody lawsuit, so he'd taken to carrying a microcassette recorder with him to capture incidents of her bad behavior to use in court. Lying in that cold, dark trunk, trussed up like the Thanksgiving turkey, he knew he was about to die. Because when the trunk finally popped open, and he had one last chance to plead for his life, he'd activated that recorder and started that tape whirring.

I could record this ordeal. Only nobody was speaking. He'd frightened my friends into submission.

I'd read stories about Richard Speck. About how he led each nurse off one by one and killed them away from their friends — except for the last girl who rolled under the bed and kept quiet.

Whoever this guy was, he wasn't going to do that to me.

Maybe I didn't have the right to jeopardize my friends' lives but there was only one decision that was right for me and that was to get out of this truck as quickly as possible and take whoever I could with me.

That would be Salem, on the brink of tears. I didn't say it; I'm ashamed I even thought it.

Crash the truck, I telepathically suggested to Venice. She kept driving as if she knew exactly where we were going and how to get there.

My head vibrated.

My lids popped open. I stared up at

Salem, who pleaded through frantic eyes for me to stay quiet.

My head vibrated again. I was lying on her phone.

When you've fallen overboard from the *R.M.S. Titanic* and somebody throws you a lifeline, you grab it. Instinct took over. I pretended to have a seizure, rolling over enough to grab her phone and fall into the floorboard. I bucked and thrashed like that horrible blind date who'd made such an impression on me, and I made guttural noises in my throat like I was gearing up for an exorcism.

I tapped the wireless on and screamed, "Help me."

Not daring to touch the phone, I maneuvered it between Salem's shoes.

"What the hell's wrong with her?"

I'd startled him with my fake seizure. Caught him completely off guard.

Salem said, "She's dyslexic. Don't worry, it'll pass."

"Epileptic," Tandy corrected her from the front seat. "She's having an epileptic seizure."

I wanted my friends to keep talking. If he was preoccupied with them, he wouldn't be paying attention to me.

I whispered into the floorboard. "Call

nine-one-one. We've been abducted."

"If you just leave her alone the convulsions will play out," Tandy went on.

A thin voice reached my ears. "Dainty? Is that you? Where's Salem?"

It was Mr. Quincy, probably upset because we hadn't returned his truck.

"Help us. He's got a gun," I hissed.

"Good lord — call the police," he shouted to someone on his end of the line.

Salem let out a murder-in-progress scream. I didn't want to see what was happening behind me.

"Don't hurt her," she cried. "Just give her some room."

"Make her stop," he growled.

Mr. Quincy asked where we were. And whether I could give him a landmark. All I could see was the carpet mats in the floorboard.

I continued to thrash, knowing I had to get out of the floorboard before this guy figured out I was faking it and shot me in the back.

I started to slip the phone to Venice but she was sobbing so hard in the front seat it's a wonder she could drive. I hoped wherever we were, that the place was crawling with police. I hoped she'd run every stop sign and red light. I hoped she'd think independently of us since she didn't know Salem and I had a live connection with a live body who was now our umbilical cord to a world beyond this prison on wheels.

Tandy said, "Let me help her. I'm a doctor."

Do what?

"Stay put." The guy was going berserk trying to keep everyone quiet. The extra chaos gave me valuable seconds to figure out a way to conceal the phone.

I pulled off my auburn wig. Fanned myself with it a few seconds and pretended to hyperventilate. Then I pushed up on all fours, secreting the phone in the hairpiece. Salem scooted closer to the madman and helped me into the seat by the door.

"Water," I croaked for effect. "Need . . . water." My eyelids fluttered as I darted furtive glances out the window trying to vector our location. Neon-colored scenery flew by like a patchwork quilt unfurling. Then I got my bearings. "There's TCU. Why're we going to TCU?"

"Shut up."

"Hey, that's the journalism school." I held the hairpiece in my grip and rested my hands in my lap. Then I slid Salem a sideways glance.

Her chest hitched. She was about to lose it.

Pay attention, I tried to warn her telepathically.

"If you hurt us, my daddy will kill you," she said. "You'll never be safe. You might get the townhouse back but my daddy will hunt you down like a —"

"Shut up."

My heart died in my chest. Now I knew who'd abducted us. This was the crazy guy who'd destroyed our new place and made me homeless.

Images came rushing back: the car that almost hit me and my friends at the sushi restaurant; the man who nearly ran me down at the mall; the car that followed me on Airport Freeway — the one Bruckman got the license plate to; the silhouette lurking by the lake behind Salem's house. This was the same man. I blinked back my incredulity.

Here sat the reason I had to move in with my grandmother.

It was all I could do to keep from going "mad cow" on him.

Sizing him up from my spot next to the door had all the earmarks of being introduced to the devil. I could almost whiff the sulphur coming off him.

I remembered the open phone line and did my part. "Is that where we're going? To the townhouse? Why are we going to the townhouse?"

Tandy didn't have a clue what was going on in the back seat. She said, "Dainty, please be quiet. You're just making things worse."

The cheese stands alone. Just like the song.

I yelled, "I want to know why we're going to the townhouse. It isn't even ready for us to move into. What are you planning to do to us? Stop the truck, Venice, I want out."

"You stop this truck before we reach the townhouse and I'll kill her," he snarled, carrying on a conversation with Venice's eyes through the rearview mirror.

Okay, when this was all over and we were safe, we needed to take a self-defense class on what not to do. Starting with cutting up lengths of rope to tie up our friends.

I flung my arms around Salem's neck and screamed, "We're all going to die."

Salem held me tight. "I love you, Dainty."

"I love you, too." I buried my head in her neck and whispered, "Your dad's on the phone. Your mom's calling the cops."

Then Venice cried, "I love you girls," followed by Tandy, who went on a crying jag, not loving any of us but distracting the man holding us hostage.

"What're you bitches pulling?"

I said, "I'm sorry, Salem."

"I'm sorry, too, Dainty. And, Venice and Tandy — I'm so sorry."

While *sorrys* were confessed all around, Salem whispered the most wonderful word my ears could've heard.

"Lojack."

And then Tandy bound Salem's hands together.

CHAPTER
THIRTY-FOUR

There went my plan — shot to hell. I'd made up my mind when Venice pulled the truck up to the garage door that I'd make a run for it. If we all bailed out and scattered like quail, he couldn't control all four of us. But now that Tandy had tied Salem's hands and was being directed to tie mine, I felt an unpleasant lurch in my stomach.

I tried to keep the thickening dismay out of my voice. "Why are you doing this to us? We didn't make you homeless. You made us homeless."

"Shut up."

I made serious, soul-searing eye contact with Tandy before delivering my bottom line. "I won't be tied up."

"Tie her," he said. Hostility crackled all around him.

He had piercing eyes like prongs on a stun gun, and I knew I was staring at the malignant side of human nature.

Tandy thought quickly. "If I tie her and she has another seizure, she could die."

His eyes looked as dead as a shark's, his face as unreadable as a blank page.

I don't know exactly what went wrong with my plan. Perhaps it was because none of the others were on board. Maybe it's because we couldn't read minds. I just knew we were running out of time and that Salem's phone was low on battery.

Then it hit me.

I drew in a sharp intake of air.

I made a last-ditch effort to help Mr. Quincy find us.

"You're the one who's been following me," I challenged. "I've got news for you, buddy, you're as good as caught. My boyfriend got your license number and it's in my purse in my car. When her dad finds it —" I pointed to Salem, who had a determined expression on her face "— the cops'll find you."

Salem said, "Drex got his license number?"

"No, silly. Bruckman." The announcement startled me. Had I really just claimed the detective as my boyfriend?

"Run," I mouthed without sound.

The garage door yawned open. As Venice inched forward, I grappled for the truck's handle and forced my shoulder against the door.

Might've worked if the child locks hadn't been engaged.

Venice put on the brake and the door closed behind us. My heart sank.

We would've never been safe if we'd moved in. He'd kept the garage door opener. We could've been asleep one night while he sneaked in *à la* Richard Speck and slaughtered us in our sleep. Now, he'd probably kill us anyway but we'd be wide awake. And as long as we were awake, we'd have a fighting chance.

Despite my best efforts, he herded us out of the garage and into the townhouse at gunpoint.

The back door opened to a prolonged squeak, the kind used in horror flicks just before the leading man takes a hatchet to the back of the head. Nerve-damaging music throbbed from jumbo speakers. The walls pulsed with heavy metal vibrations. We entered through the laundry room, passed through the kitchen and into the living area.

Venice said, "Welcome to Hell's waiting room."

The place looked like a Beirut bombsite. The townhouse had been made uninhabitable again. But even if we'd found it in pristine condition, there was no way we could live here. We'd never feel safe here. Hell, I might never feel safe again.

According to our captor, he'd picked the new lock the landlord installed, and then changed-out the deadbolts and re-keyed them. He'd probably been living here for several days.

Turning to face him, I struggled to keep my voice calm. "You love this place. You should have it."

My friends chimed in unison.

"You betcha." Tandy.

"Have at it." Venice.

"By all means." Salem.

"It's not that simple." He slipped downward against the wall with his back to the front door. As long as he kept us together in a group, he could pick us off if we tried to escape.

Throughout my fear, I memorized details. He was a sharp-featured man with beady, predatory brown eyes and oily skin. The dark, straight hair had the texture of rabbit fur and looked like the matted mess from the shower trap at a cheap motel. My mind scattered and I thought of Richard Speck again and knew, without a doubt, this man would kill us in a heartbeat.

With the gun still trained on Venice, he dug into his pocket, pulled out a pack of cigarettes and shook one out.

"You can't smoke," she said. "I have asthma. I won't be able to breathe."

A crock, of course, the way my epileptic fit had been a ruse, but she got head bobs all around to shore up her imaginary disease.

I said, "She doesn't have her inhaler."

He lit up anyway, inhaling deeply.

Smoke snaked out of his nose. We all stood, wide-eyed, waiting for Venice to hyperventilate. As the smoke floated our way, she grabbed her throat and vied for an Oscar with an onset of fake wheezing. The dramatic hand-to-throat clutch was particularly convincing.

He dropped his cigarette onto the carpet and ground it out with the tip of his steel-toed boot. He was on Venice in three strides, knocking her to the floor. She made a hard landing onto a dingy sleeping bag. Dust shimmered up from the filthy bedding.

"Someone open a window so she can breathe," I screamed.

He grabbed her by the hair and pressed the gun to her temple. "You do that and you'll have her brains all over you."

If we acted in concert we could foil his

plan. The trick was to be able to converse.

I took the rational approach. "You don't really want to hurt us . . ."

He pulled the trigger. The gun exploded. Fire flashed from the muzzle.

The bullet passed so close to my head that I felt its heat. For several stunned seconds, I stood rooted in place. Heavy metal music drowned out our screams. The smell of burned gunpowder hung heavy in the air.

"Do that again . . ." he said, and sliced a finger across his throat to indicate a violent ending. He moved back to his place near the door.

For no good reason, he fired off a second shot. The ricocheting bullet jarred me out of my paralysis and made a believer out of me.

I collapsed onto the bedroll next to Venice, who was sucking in huge gulps of air. I hugged her close, seizing the opportunity to get a message to her.

"We can take him. There are four of us." The words popped out before I realized we had no plan.

Across the room, the man fingered another cigarette from the pack. Venice rolled away from me and curled up on the floor like a tortellini.

I heard a muted click as my tape recorder

shut off. Only Salem was close enough to detect it over the music. She arched an eyebrow. I needed to flip the tape over but didn't dare make a move.

Time passed, I'm not sure how much.

The tension was so thick you could knead it like bread dough.

We had no utilities. They weren't supposed to be turned on until we moved in. Outside, it sprinkled; inside, it was stuffy and hot. Perspiration beaded above our lips. Sweat dotted our foreheads. I made a big production wiping Salem's face with my tulle bug catcher overlay. It gave her enough time to open the micro-cassette recorder and flip the tape over.

She pressed the record button and said, "Thanks, Dainty."

Venice, still pretending to suffer, pulled off her cat ears and flung them aside. Then she tried to unzip her boots. Having her hands tied in front made it difficult. Salem's hands were still tied. But with the huge white fabric of her dress marshmallowing out to conceal their movements, each time Salem moved forward, Venice pulled at the rope binding Salem's hands.

The exchange between Salem and Venice was impossible to make out but the unmistakable intensity on Venice's face assured me they were plotting.

While Salem pulled off the boots and set them near the wall, Tandy fanned her face with the skirt of her cocktail dress.

Our kidnapper removed his shirt. A holey knit undershirt showed off his full complement of tattoos.

Then nature called. I'd noticed how he'd been fidgeting; now realization dawned. This floor plan featured a guest bathroom off the hall. If you moved just so, you could see into the living room from your place on the throne.

He said something.

I turned at the sound of his voice but couldn't make out his comment over the music.

He wagged the gun, ordering us to move against the wall where he could keep track of us. Then he announced he was stepping into the bathroom, if any of us tried anything funny, he'd kill us. He'd know because he'd be watching from the open door.

"No talking or I'll waste the pip squeak," he said, pointing to me as he disappeared from the room. A sigh shimmered through the group. I'd like to think it had nothing to do with relief from not being singled out as the first to die.

Venice and Salem's bindings came loose.

Tandy's hands were still tied. Mine had never been bound. I'd caused too much trouble on the ride over and wasn't worth the effort. I also posed the biggest threat.

The music was so loud I wanted to drive an awl through my head. So why hadn't the neighbors called the cops on a noise complaint?

The commode lid clattered against the tank.

At the same time, the ghost ring of a flashlight passed across the window. For a second I thought I'd imagined it.

Since our arrival, I'd attached myself to my friends like a two-year-old special needs child. Now I said, "We need a distraction. I'm going out the window."

Venice unclasped her hand. My eyes bulged. She had the keys to the Suburban.

Salem said, "Panic button."

"Go." Tandy jutted her chin. "We're right behind you."

I held Venice in my gaze. "Hit it."

The truck's alarm went off. The toilet seat crashed down with a reverberating slam.

We bolted for the living room windows. Venice and I each grabbed a lock and twisted. Tandy fumbled with the door's deadbolt. As I hoisted up the sliding glass frame and threw out a leg my stomach lurched. Salem didn't follow. I watched in dismay as the last of her debutante gown disappeared into the kitchen.

Gun raised, our captor rushed in. Now it was his turn to look flustered. I was already outside, staring at cop cars lined up like crows on a clothesline. While I pulled Venice through the opening, Tandy slammed the door to shield herself and hit the deck. The tail of Venice's Cat Woman suit ripped off, exposing a gaping hole in the seat of her costume as she fell on top of me.

Flashing emergency lights came from four different directions.

Guns drawn, the cops surrounded the place.

I saw Mr. Quincy out of the corner of my eye and screamed, "Inside."

Heading for the entrance, he broke into a dead run. Cops tried to intercept him.

Then Salem appeared, framed in the doorway with a fire extinguisher in one hand and a gun in the other.

We stared, slack-jawed, as cops stormed our townhouse.

They hauled our abductor out in handcuffs, bleating like a tethered sheep. He swung around to face us, infuriated and resentful.

"She tried to kill me," he announced to

the officer stuffing him into the cage of the patrol car.

I wasn't at all certain we'd seen the last of him, but the ordeal was over for now and that was enough.

The rain shower that had started earlier abruptly dried up. A shaft of light from the butterscotch sunrise broke through the low-hanging clouds.

Salem's father shrugged out of his jacket and whirled it around his daughter's shoulders. He held her in his protective embrace as a uniformed police officer questioned her.

Venice was digging at the seat of her Cat Woman unitard, probably wishing she'd worn panties since a couple of patrolmen were discreetly eyeing her up.

We were a scruffy-looking foursome by the time the news media showed up to film the calamity.

The TV crew wanted interviews.

The cops wanted statements.

And I wanted to talk to Tandy.

We still needed to discuss Alex Garrett.

CHAPTER
THIRTY-FIVE

Goals for the day:

1. Help Tandy stop the circus wedding
2. Find acceptable dress for deb ball
3. Start the detective agency

A lot had happened while we were kidnapped. I ran into Bruckman down at the police station when officers took us in to give written statements. He was talking to a couple of grim-faced guys in suits — probably FBI — about Alex Garrett. The detective who transported Venice, Tandy and me halted long enough to give him a thumbnail explanation. When the shock wore off and Bruckman closed his mouth, he pulled me away from my friends and held my hands tightly in his.

"Are you all right?"

424

I nodded. "You were right about the guy in the blue car. He was following me."

"What happened?"

Surprisingly, he had no idea about what'd transpired since we kissed good night, and I saw no need to worry him. "It's your standard boy-meets-girls story."

He cocked an eyebrow.

"Boy meets girls, boy kidnaps girls, girl clobbers boy with fire extinguisher, boy goes to jail." I'd lost him. "So what's the scoop on Alex Garrett?"

"We're working on it. Dainty. You have no idea what kind of guy you're dealing with. You could've been killed."

"Yeah, well." My voice trailed. "Just make sure I get credit for unraveling this mess."

"Who're you kidding? The FBI's involved. By the time Grayson's in custody those grandstanders will be hogging all the credit."

We finished giving our statements around eleven o'clock that morning. Mr. Quincy stuck to Salem like Velcro. Dr. Hanover had been called to pick up Venice so Mr. Quincy gave Tandy and me a ride back to my car.

When we arrived at Salem's house, she urged us to stay together. I knew the feeling but that old adage about safety in numbers no longer applied.

Still, I needed a quiet place to tell Tandy about what I'd learned about Alex Garrett, AKA Jerry Don Grayson, and Salem could supply a room for that. Tandy'd paid a lot of money for this information and I owed it to her to deliver my report. Although the sun was almost directly overhead, I got the documents out of my car while my friends stood by under the protective gaze of Mr. Quincy.

I broke the news to her about Jerry Don Grayson in Salem's bedroom. When I finished, she took a moment to reexamine the evidence.

After checking the passport copies, she looked up expectantly. "Are you sure?"

"The FBI's involved now. I think the best thing to do to spare your mother any embarrassment is to find her before she goes to the church."

I'd been objective about this. My position had nothing to do with getting my rainbow mermaid dress back before Mrs. Westlake actually wore it down the aisle.

No, not hardly.

"I have no idea where she is," Tandy said.

"When's the last time you saw her?"

"Yesterday."

"You think she's with Alex?"

"I don't know." Tandy grabbed my hand.

426

"Dainty, I'm torn. Are you absolutely certain about this? I mean —" she sniffled "— my mom will be heartbroken."

I squeezed back. "Listen to me. You love her. You're probably saving her life. Even if the police don't find him by three o'clock, you can't let her go through with this. You have to tell her, Tandy. He made the FBI's Most Wanted list."

We said good-bye to Salem and I gave Tandy a lift back to her house in the Porsche. Both her mother's and Alex's cars were gone. Next, we drove to the Hurst rental house but didn't see the Lexus. Even though I didn't want to go back to Tandy's house to wait for Mrs. Westlake, I didn't want to leave my friend alone.

Two o'clock came and went. The bride and groom still hadn't returned.

I called Bruckman. "If you want credit for the arrest, then lose the FBI and meet us at the church. Tandy and I are leaving now to look for her mom there."

He left me with a final warning. "Whatever you do, Dainty, do not confront him."

But I was thinking, *Not me.* I'd had my fill of that.

Who would've thought there'd be so many cars at the chapel? I'd been led to believe this would be a small, tasteful family affair with a reception in an anteroom at the church right afterward. I didn't really expect Grayson-Garrett to actually show up for this wedding now that the jig was up and he knew his paperwork had fallen into the wrong hands. He had to figure whoever'd borrowed it had gone to the cops with the information. Either that, or he was expecting to deal with an extortionist. But when we headed into the church parking lot from a side street, there was his car, parked directly behind Mrs. Westlake's.

I spotted Bruckman's unmarked vehicle, stuck my head out the window and waved frantically. He parked near a fire hydrant at the back of the church and three marked patrol cars pulled in behind him. I'd been inside this chapel before and gave them a quick description of the layout as best as I could recall.

Church bells clanged three o'clock.

Tandy jumped out of the car and ran inside to find her mother.

Then Bruckman pulled me aside.

"You know what he looks like. We're going in through the front door. Once we're in, I want you to look inside the chapel and tell me if you see him." I nodded. "If he's there —"

I was trying to listen but my eyes kept dip-ping to the stains on my "Jump" dress. When I first saw it on the hanger I didn't think it could be made to look more horrible.

Silly me.

Bruckman grabbed me by the shoulders. He shook me hard enough to snap my teeth together.

"— listen to me, Dainty, I don't want anything to happen to you. As soon as you point him out, hit the deck. I mean it. Understand?"

I nodded.

Hey, I didn't want to be a dead hero but I didn't want Bruckman to be one either.

As I crept to the door inside the vestibule, there was Salem, freshly showered with her red hair blowing back behind her shoulders, dressed in a knee-length black dress like she had a funeral to attend. Then Venice burst in from an alcove, also wearing black.

"What're you doing here?" I said.

"Are you kidding? I wouldn't have missed this for the world."

Tandy came in on Venice's heels sporting a flaming pink handprint on one side of her face. Her lids were rimmed red. Tears jeweled her eyes. She wore a ghastly expression on her face.

She bypassed me and went straight to

Bruckman.

Clutching his sleeves, she said, "I tried to tell her but she wouldn't believe me." Tears streamed down her face in rivulets. "She called me a bad daughter and accused me of disrespecting her."

Inside, two bagpipers launched into "Scotland the Brave."

We peered through the windows of the massive wooden doors in time to see Mrs. Westlake proceed down the aisle in my rainbow mermaid dress on the arm of some random guy I didn't recognize. From where I stood, my gown fit so tight it's a wonder she wasn't coughing blood. Seriously, she was one Tic Tac away from popping out of the dress. Even if I did manage to get it back, it'd be too stretched out for a proper fit.

Tandy sniffled. Distress puckered her lips. "She said if I didn't support her in this union, she'd find somebody who would. And she ordered me out of the house." Her chest hitched with the onset of sobs. "She said . . . if I . . . she said if I couldn't support her, I could find out what it's like to support myself from here on out. Then she slapped me."

Guests on both sides of the aisle were standing as Tandy's mother pulled Kiki, snapping and snarling, on a leash beside her. Mrs. Westlake's snaggletooth hell hound had been outfitted in a hideous little canine creation that looked suspiciously like the "Deck Dress" that Rose wore on the promenade in *Titanic.*

I was so caught up in the horror of it all that I forgot my role.

Bruckman hissed, "Is he in there?"

The man who'd held himself out to be Alex Garrett of Pensacola, Florida, was standing next to the female officiate looking proud as a peacock and wearing a kilt. The officiate wore a black cape with a collar like Cruella DeVil.

"He's in there." I pointed him out. "The one in the kilt."

Bruckman nodded.

I noticed the side door and figured the groom would bolt if he charged in and held his badge aloft. The glass was fogging up from my hot breath when Bruckman grabbed me by the arm and pulled me aside.

He paused to consider Tandy. "We can take him down before, during, or after the wedding. You make the call."

I didn't envy her position. No matter what, it'd still be embarrassing.

Tandy grabbed my hand. "What do you think?"

Even though I was furious with her mom for taking my mermaid dress, I couldn't imagine anything more embarrassing than having the wedding interrupted. And yet the only thing worse, to me, would be to actually have to admit you'd been married to a murderer.

"Before. At least you'll spare her the legal fees for an annulment."

Then a horrible idea occurred to me. What if Mrs. Westlake was one of these stand-by-your-man types and didn't care if Grayson-Garrett faced murder charges in two states? Legal fees alone would deplete her wealth.

I restated my position. "Do it now."

Tandy nodded.

Bruckman lifted the hand-held police radio to his lips and keyed the microphone. "All units take your positions. Cover the exits."

The bagpipers finished but the echo of "Scotland the Brave" still hung in the air.

The dispatcher acknowledged Bruckman's transmission.

He handed me the police radio. "If a fight breaks out, press this button and tell dispatch what's going on. But if you hear shots fired, hit the red panic button."

Then he gave me a quick peck on the forehead.

"Back in a flash."

CHAPTER
THIRTY-SIX

With badge in hand and his gun still concealed, Bruckman opened one of the double doors and stepped inside the chapel. Instead of shouting, "Police, freeze," like a character in an action movie, he stealthily moved to the far aisle on the side closest to the groom. From there, he walked slowly toward the front.

I saw no way to ward off a spectacle; I also saw no reason not to slip inside the door and feed my voyeuristic side.

The ceremony was well under way with me alternating between boring a hole in the back of Mrs. Westlake's head, willing her to telepathically look at the four of us at the back of the church, and keeping Bruckman in the trajectory of my gaze.

I could no longer see him and assumed he'd taken a seat near the front row. But when I slipped Tandy a sideways glance, her face had gone white and her eyes wide.

Bruckman had nudged the best man aside and had assumed a place at the front of the church with the rest of the wedding party — which, without us girls, looked hopelessly lopsided. The expression on Grayson-Garrett's face was priceless.

I whispered in a ventriloquist's voice, "Who's that woman standing next to your mother?"

"Aunt Suzie."

"You have an aunt named Suzie?"

"We don't discuss her. She's the family embarrassment. You know the type . . . in and out of mental institutions . . . you get the picture."

The groom, who'd been standing at ease, suddenly went rigid. Bruckman stuck his gun in Grayson-Garrett's ribs. The bride appeared to be waiting for him to step off the dais and come to her side.

The officiate appeared dazed and confused. As Bruckman did a subtle lean-in and whispered in Grayson-Garrett's ear, she launched into the love-isn't-boastful story.

The color drained out of the groom's face.

Lacking patience, the officiate turned to the groom. "Will you be joining the bride?" she asked tartly.

The doors behind us flew open with a bang.

A woman in a slutty dress burst through the entrance like the point man on a DEA no-knock warrant. Three stair-step children with dirty faces and filthy clothes joined her.

Framed in the doorway at the back of the church, the wedding crasher pointed to Tandy's mother. "Look kids — there's your little doggie. And there's your new mommy. Daddy's new wife's gonna take care of you from now on so hurry on down and give her a big wet kiss. And don't forget your Christmas lists."

Guests collectively sucked air.

Then they pulled out their camera phones and recorded the catastrophe.

I inwardly predicted this would be on YouTube within the hour.

But hey — Mrs. Westlake would have a long run as a celebrity, like the girl whose fiancé left her at the altar. Only, unlike that poor, jilted bride, Mrs. Westlake's groom would leave kicking and screaming, and in handcuffs.

Tandy's mother had that thunderstruck *What?* look on her face, as if she'd gone to the bank to deposit the winning lottery check and stumbled in on an armed robbery. She unleashed Kiki and pitched her onto the red carpet. The dog bounced once, let out a low, throaty growl, and took off.

Three dirty kids closed in.

They screamed, *"Chica, Chica."*

A predictable name, come to think of it. The dog was, after all, Mexican.

As Bruckman snapped a handcuff onto the conman's wrist, my friends let out a collective sigh.

Tandy's mother saw stars — and not the good kind. She crumpled to the floor in a shock of color. I swear I heard fabric rip.

Bruckman spoke to the officiate. Her mouth opened and closed like a bigmouth bass.

She turned to the guests. "We're going to take a moment here . . . if you'd be so kind as to step out of the chapel, we'll call you back inside in a few minutes."

People exchanged wary glances. An usher lifted his upraised palms in the "All rise" gesture.

Nobody moved. Stupid people with their cell phone cameras.

Salem shouted, "Oh for God's sake, are y'all deaf? Clear out — this asshole's on the FBI's Ten Most Wanted list."

She realized her mistake as soon as her thoughts slipped out unchecked. Profanity was simply not Rubanbleu appropriate. But if anyone else noticed, they didn't let on. The guests were too busy staring at Mrs.

Westlake, who'd gone white in the face.

I keyed Bruckman's police radio. "This is Dainty Prescott calling for Jim Bruckman. We need officers to come into the church now."

As Bruckman's backups burst in through the side exits and helped him lead Jerry Don Grayson away, I wended my way to the front of the chapel and gave the officiate a thirty-second wrap-up.

"He's wanted in Oklahoma and Florida for murdering two of his wives." I slid the crumpled bride a downward glance. Tandy's mother was still proned out on the floor like a . . . well . . . iridescent mermaid. "There's no reason to think she wouldn't have been next."

Short on patience, the officiate doused Mrs. Westlake with holy water. The bride's eyes fluttered open in astonishment.

At the conclusion of the melee, the "almost" wedding was about as trailer-trash-tastic as anyone could've imagined.

Except for my beautiful mermaid gown. The gown was even more beautiful than I thought it'd be.

And I must admit I've never seen Tandy so gracious under pressure. After inviting the wedding guests to adjourn to the hospitality room for food, my friend glided outside with the posture and poise of a runway model. Those who hadn't gotten their fill of drama went next door to gawk at the wedding cake: devil's food covered in flesh-colored fondant, made in the shape of a hand with an engagement ring on it. The only thing missing from this severed limb was the ransom note. But instead of joining the spectators, Tandy strutted to the patrol car and flagged down the officer transporting Grayson-Garrett as he was rolling out of the parking lot.

As for me, I was hot on her heels.

The driver's window slid halfway down. Tandy asked for a word with her almost-stepfather.

She said, "It won't take but a second. Please — he was going to marry my mother."

The officer cracked open the back window enough to allow his prisoner to carry on a conversation, and then pointed us around to the caged area.

"Hey, Alex . . . or whatever your real name is . . . quick question," she said. "Were you aware that the deadliest volcanic eruption of the last century occurred in St. Pierre, Martinique?"

He stared, slack-jawed and flustered.

"Approximately twenty-nine thousand inhabitants were killed by an incandescent high-velocity ash flow called a *nuees ardente* — glowing clouds — in 1902. It was the same kind of eruption that buried Pompeii in 79 A.D."

Grayson-Garrett said, "Go away."

Tandy ignored him. "Only one person survived. Can you believe it? One person out of all those thousands of fatalities."

"Go away."

"Ever wonder about stuff like that?"

Garrett snorted in disgust. "No, I don't."

"Aren't you the least bit curious about where the only survivor was found?"

"If I say yes will you go away?"

Tandy nodded.

"Fine." He oozed sarcasm. "Where was this lone survivor? In church? In a brothel?" He laughed a cruel laugh. "Scuba diving? Please — I'm begging you. Tell me where the lucky son-of-a-bitch was when the volcano erupted."

"In jail. Who says good things don't happen to bad people?"

The back window hummed shut, effectively sealing Garrett off from view.

"Mighty spooky." I gave Tandy a slow head bob. "For a second I thought you were channeling Gran."

She chucked my arm good-naturedly.

"Where do you think I heard it?"

Then she turned on her heel and walked off.

We went our separate ways; Tandy, to the reception to offer her mother a ride home, and me, to find Venice and Salem.

And that's how Tandy found the three of us — sitting on the porch steps leading up to the chapel, watching the camera crew from WBFD set up.

People might think the news crew heard about the wedding debacle from monitoring the police scanner, but the truth is I called Rochelle.

It was the least I could do for Gordon, considering all the information I'd gathered on his cheating wife had pretty much ruined his marriage. WBFD still ranked third in the ratings and we were fast moving into sweeps month again. I knew my boss would appreciate the opportunity to scoop the other stations with breaking news, and it didn't hurt that the university student and anchor wannabe who caught the guy on the FBI's Ten Most Wanted worked for him.

Tandy took a seat next to me and watched the reporter do the lead-in.

"Upset with me?" I waited, doe-eyed.

"Nah. You probably saved my mom's life." She grimaced. "Of course now I have to move out and get a job." She looked up expectantly. "You don't suppose I could move into your grandmother's house with you?"

Enchanting idea but it wouldn't work.

"You're so naive." I gave her a wary head-shake. "So your mom's staying for the reception?"

Tandy nodded. "Had to. My aunt's supposed to take psychotropic drugs and we're pretty sure she's off her meds. Decompensating leaves her with no filters in social situations. My mom was afraid of what Aunt Suzie might say."

"And?" we chimed in unison.

She took a deep breath and let it out slowly. "When I left, Aunt Suzie'd taken off her top and was making a toast to my mom. She said the first time she met Alex she thought he was a gay male awaiting gender-reassignment surgery. Believe me, my feet churned up dust getting out of there."

Venice said, "Other than what happened here, wasn't this just the prettiest wedding?"

Our heads twisted like Linda Blair in a three-way-mirror.

"Are you effing kidding me?" This, from Salem, a former debutante. "Dainty looks like she's been hit with a flamethrower; Aunt Suzie decided the cake looked too plain so she added cherry pie filling until it looked like an amputation oozing blood clots; and there are three caterwauling kids being hauled away by Child Protective Services because it turns out their mother has warrants and their father's facing two life terms, minimum."

"Maybe you should go back," I suggested. "Your mom could use a little moral support."

Tandy shook her head. "No damned way."

Venice stroked Tandy's hair. "I can't remember when I've had a better time."

Tandy said, "What about the time Bindy Johansson got pregnant the night of her bachelorette party? That was pretty wild."

I didn't know Bindy and hadn't heard the story and I told them this.

Venice said, "We hired a male stripper and the company sent this buff African-American guy over."

Tandy chimed in. "Nine months later — you guessed it — biracial newborn with dancer boy's malted-milk complexion and Bindy's green eyes."

Salem said, "Guess we can assume that marriage came to a screeching halt." She slung an arm around Tandy and gave her a little shoulder squeeze. "Hey, we all have bad wedding stories to tell. My sister got a non-denominational preacher to officiate at her wedding. My mother was so upset that she told people my sister joined a cult."

She gave us one of those *Top that* smirks.

"Maybe you can sell your story to *National Enquirer*," I suggested. "They love stuff like this. They'd probably pay you enough to fund med school . . . Dr. Westlake."

Venice turned my way. "Fast-forward, Dainty. Can you imagine what it might've been like if Drex had asked you to marry him? Do you suppose we'd be sitting here like this if it were your wedding?"

"I'm so over Drex. I came to grips with the fact that Drex isn't even somebody I'd get along with as a disembodied brain sitting in the jar next to mine, much less being married to the guy. Face it — some men just aren't marriage material."

I got three simultaneous head bobs for my hard-earned wisdom.

"So when did you figure that out?" she said.

I wasn't about to tell them about my first tryst with Bruckman. But I did drop a big hint. "The thought might've occurred to me as soon as Bruckman pulled me over for running the red light."

Venice said, "Aren't you glad you found out before you made a mistake?"

I remembered what she'd said that night at the sushi bar.

"Maybe Drex is just the guy you're with before you're with the guy you're supposed to be with."

Now the unhappy remembrance brought a smile to my face. Given the choice, we'd all rather find out sooner rather than later, wouldn't we? No need to be ostrich-headed.

Having the spotlight on me made me uncomfortable. I looked around and noticed an integral part of the ceremony missing. "What happened to Kiki?"

"You mean *Chica?*" Tandy shrugged. "I might've given her to those kids to shut them up. It's a cinch my mom doesn't want her."

"Your mom loves that dog."

She gave me a dismissive wave. "She only pretended to like it because of him."

The reporter covering the wedding debacle motioned me over. She was dressed in a riot of colors, wearing clothes I recognized from the wardrobe and makeup department. It was obvious to me she'd scrambled to get here and had grabbed the first thing off the hanger — red blazer — and threw it over a multicolored blouse. Not that it mattered; the photographer would only shoot her from the bust up so nobody would see the ugly shoes and blue jean skirt. Perky in personality, she positioned me, just so, before launching into her intro.

"I'm standing at the front of this little chapel in west Fort Worth with the TCU coed who took down Jerry Don Grayson, a man on the FBI's Ten Most Wanted list who allegedly killed his previous two wives."

With the breeze blowing in my hair, I seduced the camera lens with my eyes.

The reporter said, "This is Dainty Prescott, owner-operator of a private investigations firm called —" she paused and lifted an eyebrow "— tell us the name of your private investigation firm." She tilted the microphone toward my face.

My head was chanting "Dainty Prescott Agency" but my tongue seemed to be hotwired to a different part of my brain.

"The Debutante Detective Agency." My eyes slewed over to my friends. The photographer panned the camera in time to capture their collective "thumbs-up."

"And if people want to hire you, how do they find you?"

I rattled off the number to my cell phone. That was the best I could do on short notice. The reporter hadn't even wrapped up the story before my wireless phone started ringing.

She turned to the camera. "And there you have it. . . . Dainty Prescott, owner and lead investigator of the Debutante Detective Agency, brings down one of the FBI's Ten Most Wanted. Back to you, Steve."

CHAPTER
THIRTY-SEVEN

From the moment breaking news aired, my cell phone didn't stop ringing. My friends and I were out of the church by four o'clock and, with Venice and Salem following, I drove Tandy home. I had to press her into service as my secretary, taking down phone messages until we arrived at Hell House. If I never see the interior of that place again it won't be a minute too soon. Naturally, I declined when she invited me inside.

"Bruckman's picking me up in a couple of hours and I still don't have a formal for the debutante ball. I have to get back to Gran's house to see if I have anything left in the closet that might be appropriate to wear."

"That's what I wanted to show you." Tandy invited me inside again and for the second time, I begged off. Then Venice and Salem converged at my door and tugged me out of the car.

My protests lost effect as Tandy took me by the hand and led me down the hall to the first staircase. I had no idea where we were going until we ended up in Mrs. Westlake's bedroom.

She pulled a garment bag out of her mother's closet and thrust it at me. "My mom said you should have this. She said it's the least she can do after taking your mermaid dress."

"What is it?"

"It's her going-away dress," Venice said. "I worked on it for a month. That's why I didn't have a lot of time to spend on the bridesmaids' dresses." She took my hand and squeezed. "I'm a good designer, Dainty. You'll see."

I drew in a deep breath as Tandy held the bag aloft. The zipper made a prolonged ripping sound as Salem tugged it down enough to remove the gown. A rush of air left my mouth.

It was Rose's "Dinner Dress" from *Titanic*. Only instead of having the underdress made of coral fabric, Venice had chosen a heavy-weight silk in cherry red. The overdress was made of black tulle so fine that it looked almost like chiffon from my place on Mrs. Westlake's bed. Encrusted with beadwork and seed pearls designed with all the characteristics of Sanskrit writing, it must've weighed twenty pounds and taken Venice hundreds of hours to put together.

I couldn't believe my eyes.

My gown for the debutante ball!

I was already shedding the "Jump" dress. It fell to the floor in folds as my friends unfastened this masterpiece and helped me slip into it. Once zipped, it needed to be taken in about an inch on each side, but Venice assured me she could complete the alterations within the hour. She removed a few straight pins from a little sewing kit and pinned in the darts at the back of the dress.

"Call Bruckman. Have him pick you up here. Go to your grandmother's, put on your makeup and get your shoes. Come straight back and the dress will be ready — promise."

I was already dashing out to the car when my phone rang again.

Gordon Pfeiffer, foaming at the mouth.

"Prescott, where the hell are you? You go on-air in less than an hour."

Now I ask you — would it be too much trouble for someone to explain why in the world Gordon Pfeiffer would insist on me doing the news today of all days? Call me suspicious, but maybe he's trying to set me up to fail so he can weasel out of giving me that paid internship. I explained about tonight being Teensy's debutante ball, but this cheating wife thing had set him off on a rampage and he was in no mood to be trifled with. If he didn't come to terms with this divorce pretty soon, there'd be a doctor down at the county hospital waiting to interview him behind the glass.

He put it to me in a way that left me no choice: If I wanted a passing grade, I had to anchor the "Live at Five" broadcast today.

No telling how many traffic cameras shot photos of me during the race to the TV station. I stumbled in looking like a character out of a Dickens novel, and practically threw myself into a salon chair in the wardrobe and makeup area. The frazzled stylist re-fluffed my limp tresses, fumigating me with cheap hairspray while someone shoved news copy into my hand. I was doing a so-so job reading until I came to a foreign name that might've contained the entire alphabet. Because of the lacquer cloud spewing from the can, I couldn't even focus long enough to sound it out.

Two words: I'm screwed.

"Prescott, you're on in five minutes . . . what the hell?" Gordon popped in to check on my progress. I assumed he'd gotten a look at me, half-naked in the salon chair, with nothing covering my perfect breasts except two silk charmeuse-and-lace triangles of fabric from my designer bra. I hadn't even had a chance to inspect the wardrobe for a classy ensemble, assuming such a thing existed in my size, and I'd been dreading what someone might try to foist off on me.

At that moment, the makeup girl whisked in and shoved a cobalt blue jacket at me. The stylist pronounced my hair "perfect" — and let's face it, we all knew that wasn't true. I shrugged into the blazer, which would've looked absolutely stunning if I'd had orangutan arms and linebacker shoulders.

It didn't just swallow me; it ate me whole.

"No way. I'm not wearing this. Nobody wears shoulder pads. I'm a news anchor, not a tight end."

In walked Chopper Deke with a face that looked like a relief map of the Andes, and tufts of eyebrow hairs that broke rank with the others. He'd just passed the door but took a backward step. Framed in the opening, he leered at me with those spooky light eyes.

"Tight end?" he repeated. "Why don't you let me be the judge of that?"

I glanced at his hands to see if he had opposable thumbs as the makeup girl lobbed the empty hairspray can at him. For an old guy, he had good reflexes. Or maybe being a sex pervert helped him hone his bobs and weaves. I only knew that if he ever laid a hand on me, I'd knee him in the stones with my eunuch maker.

Then Gordon darted back in. "Three minutes." His face turned beet red, and for good reason. I'd shaken off the jacket and stood in my bra and panties, frantically scanning the room for anything to cover myself. "There's an empty chair out there, Prescott, and I don't care how you fill it — with or without clothes — but you're, by God, going to be sitting in that chair for the countdown —" he checked his watch "— in two minutes."

"Mr. Pfeiffer, do you mind?" I said, practically slipping into shock. "I'm half naked." I wasn't embarrassed and my cheeks weren't on fire. These people just needed to dial down the thermostat about fifteen degrees.

He stared at me, Dainty Prescott — or rather my perfect body — unfazed by my beauty.

News flash: I may have a lead on that pesky wife-straying problem.

A red wool pashmina looped over the coat rack in the corner caught my eye, and without thinking, I snatched it off the hook.

The makeup girl yelled, "Wait," but I was already out the door, wrapping it around my torso twice and throwing each of two fringed ends over my shoulders like sleeves. This would never work. I got a visual of my makeshift dress falling off before millions of viewers.

Ladies of The Rubanbleu do not show excess skin in public. It's *très* gauche and simply not done.

That's when Gordon gave me my pep talk. "Always keep going. No matter how bad you fuck up, just keep going."

I thought of the weird alphabet name in the second story, and as the crew miked me up — translation: clipped on my microphone — I borrowed a pen. While I wrote English words down that might sound similar to the actual name, I darted furtive looks around the studio for something to hold the pashmina in place.

"One minute." Gordon again, his forehead beaded in sweat.

On the way to the anchor desk, I spied an extension cord, made a quick curtsey and yanked it out of the wall socket. Coiling it around my waist until it came just below my perfect breasts, I tied off the ends behind my back.

The musical lead-in for the "Live at Five"

broadcast crescendoed. I slotted in my ear-piece and slid into my seat. I settled into a comfortable position and looked up in time to see the producer's splayed finger-count disappearing into a fist: four, three . . .

Head high, posture erect.

Two . . .

Cotton Bowl Queen smile.

With a sweeping flourish, he finger-pointed at me.

I'm on the air.

"Good afternoon, I'm Dainty Prescott, filling in for Aspen Wicklow live at five. This just in —"

I read off the TelePrompter, occasionally glancing down at my copy for effect, delivering breaking news of a family overcome by carbon monoxide fumes traced to a new, but faulty, water heater. I couldn't believe how poised I was. I took to the spotlight like a swan to a lake, smiling at all the right moments, sobering at the somber ones.

Next came the report of a non-profit group made up of Fort Worth ladies who'd raised money for an all-purpose psychiatric unit for children. A Thai native who'd donated to the project was being honored at a luncheon during her trip to preview the facility.

The Thai name scrolling down the Tele-

Prompter read: Ployphilay Wongpitiptan-arong.

I glanced down at the news copy unable to find the English words I'd written to help me pronounce the honored guest's name.

I took a stab at it. "Prophylactic Wrong Pity-Pat Wrong responded to the group's plea for support and made the largest donation in the group's history."

Oh dear Lord.

The footage on the monitor didn't match the story. A farm scene of pigs wallowing in mud popped up on the screen. A black pig did a sideways slide, careening into a group of pink pigs. Then a humongous white pig with pink eyes lumbered into the frame.

"Meanwhile, you may remember a story we brought you awhile back, where local farmer Hubert Forrister found his way into the *Guinness Book of World Records* for growing the largest pumpkin. Now he's trying to make it into the record book with the largest albino pig . . ."

The footage on the monitor switched to a close-up of a large woman at the luncheon with the Thai lady.

I admit it. I didn't think it could get any worse.

And then it did.

The knotted extension cord tied around

my waist worked its way loose. The instant I felt my bindings go slack, the fabric on my right shoulder slipped.

Gordon's words echoed in my ears.

"Always keep going . . . just keep going."

It was flubbed up, all right. One might even say FUBAR. The story on the Tele-Prompter took on surreal proportions as the sleeve slid further past my shoulder. I inclined my body to the right, sinking gradually down into the chair.

Even so, I delivered the news.

Then the copy rat ran over and handed off breaking news.

"This just in — the Fort Worth Police Department's Special Weapons and Tactics team, known as S.W.A.T., has converged on the area just north of Harrigan's Jewelers after the store was robbed a few minutes ago —"

Footage of a bizarre foot chase popped up on the monitor. Wait — *what?* — the background buildings were part of a strip center where I bought coffee before coming to work at the TV station each morning.

"We go live now to our eye in the sky, Chopper Deke."

Our resident perv popped up on the screen. I could've sworn I heard the *whuppa-whuppa-whuppa* of rotor blades overhead.

I'm pretty sure that's when things graduated from worse to complete fiasco on the Suck-o-meter.

A close-up of *moi,* Dainty Prescott, popped up on the monitor as the side door to the studio burst open. The foot chase that had begun ten blocks away went right past me while I rattled off the story as it appeared on the TelePrompter. Another door banged open and the robber and three uniformed patrolmen disappeared through it.

I blinked.

"And that's the news. I'm Dainty Prescott, reporting to you live at five. We hope you'll join us again for the recap at six."

Just shoot me now and put me out of my misery.

As the closing music grew louder, I stopped breathing. It was the only way I could be sure my top wouldn't fall off. Mercifully, the final ten seconds of my catastrophic broadcast debut ticked away before my face turned blue.

An explosion sounded behind me. Overhead lights instantly dimmed.

Did I care? Not unless I'd been shot.

Frankly, I was too exhausted and disgusted to even turn around. After we went to commercial, I saw the effects of gravity at work.

One of the overhead lights had plummeted to the floor, smashing the bulb and denting the metal housing.

While I covered my bare shoulders as best I could, wondering if I should just ask the photographers to turn their backs while I made my escape, the click-clack of sensible, low-heeled pumps drummed the floor.

Rochelle entered with a murderous bent. "The phones are jammed."

Since she fixed me with a lethal stare, I assumed the accusation in her voice was directed at me.

"I don't understand what that means."

"It means stop making work for me." Rochelle, who resented being called upon to do anything for the interns, said, "People saw the news."

My heart lurched. "Did my grandmother call in about too much skin?"

"No, but everybody else and their dog did. They want to know who created your ensemble. And where you purchased your belt."

Which just goes to show there's no accounting for taste.

Then Gordon burst in beaming. "Damned, Prescott, you're unflappable. We'll get you a copy of the broadcast." To the station's meteorologist, Misty Knight, who'd trailed him into the studio carrying a lampshade, he said, "Damn it, Misty, I don't care what Dainty did, you're not here to be a trendsetter, and you're, by God, not wearing that lampshade as a hat on the air."

All the way to Dallas, I considered what shoes I'd wear to the ball, while simultaneously praying that Gran hadn't seen *Live at Five.* When I arrived at my grandmother's, I found her in the formal living room reading by the light from one of the Staffordshire dog lamps. I tried to tiptoe past without her noticing but she sensed my presence and called out my name.

It was as if she had eyes in the back of her head.

"Hi, Gran." I stood, marooned, waiting to see if she'd call me over or let me go on about my business.

"Let me look at you."

No thanks, I've had my fill of that.

And yet I slunk in and presented myself like a ghetto commoner before the queen.

Gran marked her place in the book with a leather strip and set the book aside. She was reading a romance and that surprised me. She hadn't had a date since last year's debutante ball. Even then, she'd taken Old Man Spencer, the curmudgeon down at the end of the road, so it was hard to imagine her being able to appreciate a steamy bodice-ripper.

Glittery eyes that matched her fading blue hair fixed me in a stare. She had accusation written all over her face. I exuded every amount of poise I could muster, but inside, my heart was doing the rapid beat thing.

"I don't mean to be disrespectful, Gran, but if you want to talk, you'll have to follow me. I can't be late." I started for the staircase.

"Drex was here."

That stopped me in my tracks. Hearing his name was like getting a poisoned dart to the chest.

"What'd he want?"

"What do you think he wanted? He's supposed to take you to the debutante ball. He dropped off a wrist corsage for you. You'll find it in a box inside the refrigerator. I believe it's in the crisper." She practically slapped me with every word she spoke.

"Thanks. That was thoughtful of you."

No need to explain why I wouldn't be wearing it.

I needed a quick shower, and to tame this wild hair and finish it off with enough lacquer to withstand a category three hurricane. But first I needed to look through my shoes. Rose's "Dinner dress" deserved nothing but the best, and I had the perfect heels to go with it.

"Dainty, are you familiar with the story of the Sabbath?"

My shoulders instantly sagged. How was it that I, Dainty Prescott, an intelligent woman, continually wandered into these verbal mine fields?

Sabbath day? Sabbath school? Sabbath bloody Sabbath?

Too tired to play games, I shook my head.

This was the part where I could either take off running or stay put. I dropped to the floor into the lotus position, closed my eyes for several seconds and tried to take the Zen approach.

Ohm, Ohm, Ohm.

"Jesus met with the people and reminded them that they weren't supposed to work on the Sabbath. He said the Sabbath day was holy and that it should be set aside for the Lord."

I gave her a sacred cow smile but my head was screaming, *What the hell?*

"But some of the men wanted to argue about it. You're familiar with the phrase *Remember the Sabbath day, to keep it holy?*"

Lame head bob.

Ohm, Ohm, Ohm . . . Ohm going to be late.

462

"Well the men started asking Jesus questions. 'What if thus-and-such happens, can we work?' Jesus said no. Finally, one of them said, 'But what if a man's ox is in the ditch. Can we help him get it out?' And finally Jesus said, 'Yes, if a man's ox is in the ditch, you can help him get it out.'"

Long pause.

Ohm, Ohm, Ohm . . . Ohm going upstairs to hunt for my Choos.

Sometimes I just crack myself up.

I was waiting for the punch line when she reached behind the decorative pillow and withdrew three envelopes. Two were brown. One was white. I couldn't make out the return addresses from my place on the Oriental rug but I saw that they'd been opened and I assumed we were about to have a little *Come to Jesus* meeting about the contents.

Lacking patience, I said, "What's your point?"

She fanned the envelopes at me. "Dainty, the ox is in the ditch."

Call me rude, but when Gran asked if I was familiar with the Bible story of how Jehu drove his chariot furiously to the house of Jezreel to slay the house of Ahab, I didn't stick around to hear about the first recorded incident of a hot-rodder.

CHAPTER
THIRTY-EIGHT

Revised goals for the day:

1. Avoid Drex like the plague
2. Make a big splash at The Ruban-bleu
3. Fall head over heels for Bruckman

Looks like I've accumulated two more traffic camera citations to add to the pile. And — *oh, hey, whaddaya know?* — my flirtation with law enforcement continues. The third letter came from Dallas Municipal Court letting me know that if I didn't pay the parking tickets I'd amassed, that my car would be booted.

Later, baby.

I slunk to my room and picked out my Choos. They were black *peau de soie* Choos with a swirly crusting of tiny rhinestones on them. After laying them out on my lumpy mattress, I went down to the second-floor guest bathroom for my shower. Once my hair was blown dry and I finished primping in front of the mirror, I threw on a tastefully subdued gray jersey knit pullover dress and grabbed my things for the trip back to Tandy's.

My original plan for this evening had been to arrive at the country club early enough to help Teensy dress for the ball. But Gran informed me that my sister had opted to stay with friends in Fort Worth and would meet me before the ball in the back room. The events coordinator always sets up a designated dressing area. And they always have wine and prepare little finger sandwiches for the debs to snack on. Since dinner's rarely served before midnight the debs need food in their stomachs.

I suspected Gran might be hiding the truth.

Since Daddy and Nerissa were supposed to return from Europe today, I suspected Teensy'd gone to Daddy's house first since he was supposed to present her when she took her bow before The Rubanbleu.

As for Gran, I didn't know who was escorting her to the ball. Until now, it hadn't occurred to me to ask.

When I got back down to the first floor, she was waiting for me in the foyer.

A mechanism tripped the hammers on the grandfather clock so that the Westminster chimes played the first permutation of four pitches. It was six-fifteen and the six o'clock news had partially aired.

She stared at me, baffled. "I just saw you on television. What in the world's going on, Dainty? They said you captured a man on the FBI's Ten Most Wanted list."

I pretended to search my memory. "Oh, right — that guy." Affecting a look of practiced boredom, I said, "So who's taking you to The Rubanbleu tonight?"

"Mr. Spencer. And I see what you're doing here." Irritation pinched the corners of her mouth. "Dainty, they said that man was wanted for two murders."

"Oh, that," I said airily. "Look, I don't mean to be rude, Gran, but I have to go. I want to catch Teensy before the party, and the ox is in the ditch."

I skirted her with cutting horse precision.

She called me back. "I have something for you. It's your birthday present. I was saving it for a surprise."

Oh, goody!

Disturbing flashback: The best gift I ever got from Gran was the bubble wrap that covered last year's birthday present.

I fidgeted like a kid in need of a restroom. "Can I see it later? I really need to leave."

"You have time for this," she said matter-of-factly. Then she led me to the informal living room. "You were right, Dainty. Blood *is* thicker than water."

My breath caught in my throat.

My cherry silk mermaid dress.

"But you said . . ."

"Oh, shush, Dainty. That was your father talking. What *I* do is *my* business. And after giving it a great deal of thought, I decided to get you what you wanted."

My eyes misted. How could I tell her? But if I didn't wear the Venice Creation, I'd hurt my best friend.

"I can't wear it." Her eyebrows shot up in surprise. I rushed ahead before I lost my nerve. "It's not that I don't appreciate it — I do — more than you'll ever know. But when I didn't get to keep the dress, Venice made one for me. I can't let her down, Gran, I just can't."

She stood, stricken, in the gaping silence.

I traced a fingertip across the fabric. "I think we should take this back and exchange it for whatever you wanted me to have before."

"Are you sure?"

"I'm sure." I looked at her standing there, so pale and withered and small — and infuriating. And I knew that the only thing thicker than blood, in Texas, is oil. "I do love you, Gran. Very much."

Without warning, she threw her arms around me and sobbed into my neck.

Then she gently pushed back, and stared at me in wonderment. "I don't know what I'd do if something bad happened to you."

"Same here."

I decided not to tell her about being kidnapped.

CHAPTER
THIRTY-NINE

Bruckman and I arrived at the country club only minutes ahead of Drex.

We were already inside and had picked up the calligraphy cards for our table assignment when the orchestra struck up a peppy little jazz number. We'd almost made it to the bar when I heard Drex's voice coming from somewhere behind me.

"What do you mean you don't have a card for me? Look again."

"I'm sorry, Mr. Truett. We don't have a card for you."

"I'm her date."

Someone called Nancy McGilroy over to handle him. As we receded further into the crowd, Drex let loose with a unique tapestry of curses.

"I'm sorry, Mr. Truett, but Dainty Prescott has already picked up her card."

"And I'm here to pick up mine."

"Miss Prescott's escort was with her.

You're not on the list. So I'm sorry but you'll need to leave now or we'll be forced to have you escorted out."

Instant celebrity had its price. I didn't stick around to see the rest — too busy. In the last twenty-four hours I'd gone from debutante to celebutante.

Avery Marshall of the seating debacle of 1973 got a few highballs under his belt and "borrowed" me from Bruckman. Which was okay by Bruckman, since he'd found a handful of cops who'd been hired to work off-duty security at this event and practically stampeded toward the uniforms so I could talk business. Really, I think he just wanted his buddies to see how dashing he looked in his tux.

As for Avery, apparently things weren't going so well. He wanted to hire the Debutante Detective Agency but he wouldn't say what for. But he promised to call tomorrow so I could quote him a retainer.

A retainer.

I nearly squealed out my delight. As he sauntered off and I glanced around for Bruckman, Avery's ex-wife, Bitsy, herded me over to a group of doyennes.

"I know it's rude to talk business but we want to hire you, dear," Bitsy said in a hushed voice. "Can we have your card?"

Again, no card on me, but I promised to call her.

Bruckman found me and "borrowed" me back. I was almost mauled by women wanting to know which couture designer made my "Dinner Dress." One woman even told me she'd tried to buy several dresses from the roving exhibit of *Titanic* costumes, but her husband thought they were too expensive. I just smiled and basked in the attention.

When I mentioned "Venice Creations" she assumed I'd picked it up in Italy.

Bruckman and I found our table. Salem and her date were already seated, sipping well drinks and scanning the crowd for people they knew. When the tuxedoed waiter came over to take our order, Bruckman requested a glass of wine, and I asked for a Dr Pepper with a couple of maraschino cherries thrown in. The other people assigned to our table were either hanging out at the bar or blending in with the crowd.

Salem said, "Please don't be mad, Dainty, but my parents insisted on sitting with us. Since our ordeal, my dad refuses to let me out of his sight."

Bruckman, looking handsome in his tux, slipped his hand over mine and made serious eye contact. "I know just how he feels."

I didn't bother Teensy before she took her bow.

There'd be plenty of time to hang out with her tomorrow.

She'd selected a beautiful white dress with simple lines and a hand-beaded bodice that looked like the breastplate on a gladiator, and white kid gloves that rose past the elbows.

I knew she'd be radiant with her long, straw-colored hair. As the orchestra finished the music chosen by the previous deb, my chest swelled with excitement. I felt the electricity in the air as they struck up the song Teensy had chosen to make her bow to — "How Lucky Can You Get." Then my sister appeared on stage. I swear I got teary-eyed.

By the time all of the debutantes had taken their bows, and the wait staff removed the partitions separating the dining area, I'd lined up fifteen jobs for the Debutante Detective Agency and was given six retainers on the spot. Tomorrow, I'd design business cards. I'd have them lettered in pink ink since pink's kind of my signature color, with a little tiara logo on them. And I'd spend the morning returning all the phone messages that had come in since the news broadcast aired earlier.

Bruckman and I stood outside the country club in the crisp clean air, beneath the glow of a blue moon and waited for the valet to bring the car around. I felt the magic of the night and knew I wanted to spend the rest of it alone with him. He deserved to be lavished with attention.

Much later, after he'd swept me into the full depths of his lovemaking, I fell back into my pillow, sated. As I drifted into slumber, I felt like the happiest girl in the world.

In the early morning hours, my cell phone rang. I didn't recognize the information on the digital display so I figured it was probably another call for the Debutante Detective Agency.

"Wait. What? I can barely hear you." I pressed the phone tightly against my ear and plugged the other ear with a fingertip to mute the *whoosh* of acclimatized air whispering over my body. "Who's calling? No, who are you?"

The light on Bruckman's nightstand came on. A sideways glance told me he was wide awake.

"International operator?" I nodded along, hanging on every word. She had a thick accent and I hadn't come fully awake — until now. "Phoning from where? Mexico? Is this some kind of joke? Sure, I'll accept the charges. Put her through."

As I listened to the tiny voice at the other end of the line, chills swarmed over my skin. I knew, in an instant, this call would change my life.

But not in a good way.

Covering the mouthpiece, I said, "Get my clothes. I have to leave. Emergency."

Then I sat up rigid and listened while the world, as I knew it, tilted on its axis.

A thin, high-pitched voice pealed down my ear canal, tinny and distant.

"They want money."

It sounded like Teensy — on the other side of the planet.

"Who wants money?" I realized I was yelling. Just because I could barely make out what she was saying didn't mean that *she* couldn't hear *me*.

"The kidnappers who took her."

"Took who?"

"Tiffer."

My blood curdled. "Somebody took Tiffer?" I shrieked, downshifting into full panic mode. Tiffany — we call her Tiffer — is my sister's best friend. They joined forces in the eighth grade and have spent the last seven years defying the odds by pulling dumb stunts and getting away scot free.

474

Seriously, I don't get how I'm the one who tried so hard to be the perfect daughter, yet I'm considered the black sheep and Teensy's the one with the Miss Goody Two Shoes reputation. I blame Tiffer. "I don't understand." I checked Bruckman's bedside clock. "That's impossible. I just saw y'all . . ."

. . . five hours ago.

"We hailed a cab. They just took her."

"Somebody took her from the cab?" I shot a look at Bruckman, who'd already snagged a pair of clean blue jeans off a hanger and started hopping around on one foot while he stuffed a toe into one of the legs. "Where'd you get a cab?"

"Ciudad Juárez. They drove us to the ATM and forced us to get the money out. They took it and they took her."

My skin crawled. "Where are you?" I looked around for a pen and didn't see one. I caught the word "hospital" but not the facility's name.

"This is bad. I'm hurt. We were together until they beat the hell out of me, dumped me out of the car and left me for dead. I didn't have any debit or credit cards with me."

"Ohmygod, did you call the police?"

"That's what I've been trying to tell you,

Dainty. The police are the ones who kidnapped her."

ABOUT THE AUTHOR

Laurie Moore was born and reared in the Great State of Texas where she developed a flair for foreign languages. She's traveled to forty-nine U.S. states, most of the Canadian provinces, Mexico, and Spain.

She majored in Spanish at the University of Texas at Austin where she received her Bachelor of Arts degree in Spanish, English, and Secondary and Elementary Education. She entered a career in law enforcement in 1979. After six years on police patrol and a year of criminal investigation she made sergeant and worked over the next seven years as a District Attorney investigator for several DAs in the central Texas area.

In 1992, this sixth-generation Texan moved to Fort Worth and received her Juris Doctor from Texas Wesleyan University School of Law in 1995. She is currently in private practice in "Cowtown" and lives with a jealous Siamese cat and a rude Welsh corgi. She is still a licensed, commissioned peace officer and recently celebrated her thirty-first year in law enforcement.

Laurie became a member of DFW Writers Workshop in 1992 and is the author of *Constable's Run, Constable's Apprehension, Constable's Wedding, The Lady Godiva Murder, The Wild Orchid Society, Jury Rigged,* and *Woman Strangled — News at Ten.* Writing is her passion. Contact Laurie through her Web site at www.LaurieMooreMysteries .com.